D1167356

DEFYING GRAVITY

The adventures of a corporate entrepreneur

DEFYING GRAVITY

The adventures of a corporate entrepreneur

Polly Courtney

with

Peter Sayburn and Gideon Hyde

A Paperback Original 2010

First published in Great Britain by
Matador 2010

Matador
5 Weir Road
Kibworth Beauchamp
Leicester LE8 0LQ, UK
Tel: (+44) 116 279 2299
Fax: (+44) 116 279 2277
Email: books@troubador.co.uk
Web: www.troubador.co.uk/matador

ISBN 978 1848765 610

British Library Cataloguing in Publication Data.
A catalogue record for this book is available from the British Library.

Cover design:
Polly Courtney /
Vinney White, Ottawa Graphic Design

Wisdom design:
Emily Tu / Alan Smith, The Movement

Johnny Venture cartoons:
Simon Riviere

Typeset in 11pt Book Antiqua by Troubador Publishing Ltd, Leicester, UK
Printed in the UK by TJ International Ltd, Padstow, Cornwall

Matador is an imprint of Troubador Publishing Ltd

Foreword

"Entrepreneurship is about passion - and the willingness to risk capital - be it tangible or intangible.

We've all heard the stories about people who believe so powerfully in their ideas that they would mortgage their homes, put their - and their family's - money on the table (as I did) to see their idea through. As entrepreneurs, however, we also risk our reputation - our social capital - often trying to break preconceived, societal norms: the blind entrepreneur who was told that blind people couldn't travel independently, the Turkish-Cypriot who was told that he couldn't do business with the Greek-Cypriots, the Greek entrepreneur who was told that consumers wouldn't want to forego travel frills to explore Europe.

It takes an enormous amount of discipline, hard work, creativity and self-confidence - not to mention fortuitous timing and loads of luck - to see an entrepreneurial idea through; but once you've done it - either within the corporate structure or well outside of it - there's no looking back!"

Sir Stelios Haji-Ioannou

With special thanks to following corporate entrepreneurs, who provided invaluable insights, quotations and anecdotes:

Kevin Bell, BT
Lee Clarke, E.ON, npower
José Davila, E.ON, British Gas
Felix Geyr, BE Broadband (O2), BBC
Peter Haigh, E.ON, ELEXON
Sir Stelios Haji-Ioannou, easyGroup
Veera Johnson, ProcServe
Michael Johnson, Orange, BT, Thomas Cook
Douglas Johnson-Poensgen, BT Global Services
Gearoid Lane, Centrica
Julia Lynch-Williams, RWE npower
Jason Murray, Lloyds Banking Group
Ian Price, BT
Payman Saebi, Unilever, RBS, Royal Mail
Rachel Sheridan, Cocosa (Bauer)
Dan Taylor, Tesco
Chris Thewlis, npower
Tim Thorne, RBS
Georges Tijbosch, BP Trading
David Wilson, British Gas, City Link, npower
Danny Wootton, Logica
Andrew Wordsworth, Carbon Trust
Jeremy Wright, Enpocket, Nokia

Thanks also to the following for their patience, resilience and input to Defying Gravity:

Michael Hall, Philip Kohler, David Harrison, Ruth Whitten, Tim Thorne, Philip McCarthy-Clarke, Richard Budd and Robin Scarborough at Market Gravity, Diane Banks at Diane Banks Associates, Antje Schroeder, Blue Martin, Christopher Downs, Kirsten Wrigley and Bryony Sayburn.

They are a rare and distinctive breed.
They exist in large companies in a diverse range of roles.
They thrive on uncertainty when others crave order.
They remain optimistic when most despair.
They don't do it for money but to leave a legacy.
Maybe you know one? Maybe you are one? Maybe you aspire to be one?

This book is a tribute to those who defy the odds and create ambitious new ventures within large organisations.

This is a tribute to the corporate entrepreneur.

1

The wood for the trees: diagnosing the problem

'Doing things better isn't enough;
it's about doing better things.'

Tony in trouble with the CEO

THE CEO let out a long sigh, removed his glasses and squeezed the bridge of his bulbous nose.

'It's not looking good, is it?' he asked eventually, lowering the financial summary onto the desk.

Tony swallowed nervously and let out a quiet noise of concurrence. He had been dreading today's meeting for weeks. It had been a black, looming cloud hanging over him ever since he'd caught sight of the Q2 sales report – the four-page document that lay between them, illustrating just how small an impact he'd made on the business since he'd taken over.

'I brought you in as a trouble-shooter, Tony.' Charles Gable looked at him, one eyebrow raised. 'That's what you do, isn't it?'

Tony nodded warily. Four months previously, he'd been sitting in exactly the same seat, confidently assuring the CEO of his expertise in turning around ailing business units and explaining why he was the right man for the job. He'd meant what he'd said, too. He had nursed two key TransTel departments back to health over the course of the last five years. He *was* a trouble-shooter. On landing the role, he had relished the opportunity to put Synapse – the division that had once pushed TransTel to the cutting edge of the broadband market but now languished somewhere in the number five or six spot behind its younger, nimbler competitors – back on the map. But he couldn't work miracles.

'The situation within Synapse is… different,' he explained, cautiously. Much as Tony would have loved to tell the truth about Rupert Beasley, the old dinosaur who had stood by as the department steadily lost its edge to other players, doing nothing to stem the tide of defecting subscribers, he couldn't. It was a well-known fact within TransTel that Rupert Beasley, who had retired the previous year with a hefty pay-off following thirty years' service – in the loosest sense of the word – was a golf buddy of Charles Gable's.

'What do you mean, 'different'?' demanded the CEO.

'Well… for most of my turnaround projects, I've had a small, relatively new team to work with. But Synapse has more inertia. It's been going in a certain direction for a while now,' Tony explained diplomatically. *Backwards,* he wanted to add. *The department has been losing ground for years, thanks to the over-paid buffoon that you allowed to remain in charge.* 'I'd like to push it onto a new track, but it's going to take time.'

The CEO narrowed his eyes, his gaze dropping once more to the piece of paper that lay between them – the page that spelled out in no uncertain terms the new director's lack of achievement.

'Four percent,' he said, with a sigh.

Tony didn't need to ask what he meant. The figure had been hanging over his head ever since he'd taken the job. In its wisdom, the board had decided that this would be the year of recovery for TransTel. No more declining revenues, no more eroded profit margins… This year, as Charles Gable had proudly announced to the City in his annual presentation, the company's top line would grow by four percent. And that, according to the hare-brained scheme that had been devised to allocate targets to each department, meant that Synapse was expected to increase its turnover by fourteen million pounds.

'I…' Tony considered sharing his doubts with the CEO, then decided against it. 'Perhaps we should go through the changes I'm putting in place?'

Finally, the ruddy face lifted and there was an almost imperceptible nod.

Tony glanced down at his notes, more to avoid the man's glassy stare than for guidance. Having lived, breathed and dreamed Synapse for the past twelve weeks, he knew the business almost better than he did his own wife and child.

4

'As you know, my initial audit identified a number of key inefficiencies, so I've focussed on removing these and streamlining operations...'

Tony rattled off his summary, glancing up every so often to check Charles' expression: plump, pursed lips, furrowed brow. It was impossible to gauge his reaction.

'...and the new call-out schedules have pushed the engineers' productivity up from four jobs per day on average to five point three.'

'The effect being?' Gable asked suddenly.

Tony frowned. Perhaps the CEO hadn't been listening. 'Well, the average productivity has risen from–'

'I'm not deaf,' Gable snapped irritably. 'I heard the numbers; I mean, what has the *effect* been. Overall. On the engineers. Have you made the workforce stronger, do you think?'

There was a pause. Tony knew what the chief executive was getting at. Gable may have been slow and old-fashioned, but he wasn't stupid. Having spent most of his working life at TransTel, he was no stranger to its business practices. Whether or not the CEO had heard rumours about the unrest amongst Synapse engineers Tony couldn't tell, but it didn't seem wise to lie.

'We had a bit of a backlash,' Tony admitted. 'As you'd expect.'

The CEO looked at him questioningly.

'Twelve,' he confessed. 'Twelve engineers defected. They went to Netcomm I believe. But the replacements have been sorted.'

There was a silence which seemed to last for several minutes. Gable's point – which he made without even speaking – was obvious: that the cost of recruiting and training replacement engineers probably outweighed any benefits gained through the efficiency of the new call-out schedule.

'The call centres have shown a marked improvement,' Tony went on, re-ordering his list so that the next piece of news was more positive. 'We implemented new scripts and routing, which means that operators are handling an average of twenty-two calls per hour – up from fifteen.'

'Uh-huh.'

Tony faltered, wondering whether the CEO could have caught wind of the resentment that had swept the call centres in reaction to his changes.

'Subscriber levels are up,' he went on, 'thanks to new sales targets, and...' he glanced down at his notes to guide him swiftly away from the subject of the disgruntled sales team. 'We re-vamped the web support service.'

The CEO grunted. 'You certainly did.'

Tony looked at his lap and then around the room, wishing he'd saved up one of the good-news stories for the end. The online overhaul had been a disaster. On the advice of some expensive media consultants, Tony had set up a community forum on the Synapse website where subscribers could post their questions for trained technicians to answer online. In the words of the young consultants with their black, rectangular framed glasses and floppy hair, it represented 'a new dawn of transparency in telecoms'.

Transparency, it turned out, was something that the TransTel PR department did not relish. Within hours of its launch, the forum, bombarded with derogatory postings about Synapse and TransTel in general, was swiftly taken offline. The clean-up operation was still underway.

'There's always an element of trial and error in these things,' said Tony, regretting his words as soon as they slipped out. He felt like an estate agent describing a cramped bedsit as 'cosy'.

The problem was, Tony Sharp wasn't accustomed to rationalising failure. He was familiar with the process of explaining his actions, but usually because others wanted to learn from his achievements. Most of his twelve-year career had been spent inside the big machine that was TransTel, and whilst his efforts hadn't always paid off, by and large he got the results. Battering his way over hurdles, dodging obstacles and ducking under red tape, he'd become an expert in making things happen from inside. Today's meeting was an unpleasant new experience.

'Are you satisfied with the way things are going?' asked Charles Gable, looking him in the eye.

Tony held his gaze. There was no correct answer to this question. Saying yes would imply that this dire situation was the best he could do; saying no would prove that he hadn't used the past three months wisely.

Several seconds passed before he replied.

'I think I can still turn things around,' he said, his voice resolutely steady.

This was it, thought Tony. This was decision time. In the eyes of certain board members, Synapse had been given enough chances already. Only a year before, under the questionable leadership of Rupert Beasley, the department had undergone an expensive re-brand that involved changing the name from TransTel Connect to Synapse and kitting out the engineers in bright blue boiler suits with the flashy new logo splashed across their backs – to no obvious effect. Tony knew, as did all the directors, that resentment for this drain on resources was running high. The plug could be pulled at any point. Other departments – arguably less flawed departments – had already seen their work outsourced to other companies, other continents; it was quite possible that Synapse could go the same way.

Tony stared at the man's watery eyes, willing him to feel the strength of his conviction. He was determined to transform Synapse back into the cash-cow it once was. He was desperate to give it another chance. It was going to be tough, but Tony had always felt that the harder the challenge, the greater the reward. He knew he could resuscitate it, given time. The question was: did he have time?

After a lengthy silence, the CEO started to nod.

Tony watched as the man's eyes gently rocked in their sockets. Was this his answer, or was it just a pensive nod?

Finally, the large man spoke. 'I'll want regular progress updates, going forwards.'

Tony felt a wave of relief wash over him. He realised he'd been holding his breath and shakily exhaled. 'Of course.'

'And no more trial and error, please.'

Tony pushed back his chair and gathered his notes, cringing at the echo of his own words.

He reached the door and looked over his shoulder, feeling a sudden urge to assure Charles Gable that he wouldn't regret his decision. Then he took in the flared nostrils, pursed lips and angry stare and hurried out, head down.

It was gone eight o'clock by the time he pressed the door shut behind him, peeping into the lounge where his wife's laptop was usually stationed in front of the TV.

The laptop wasn't there.

'Suze?' Tony called gently, not wanting to wake Poppy.

She emerged from the kitchen, shaking off an oven glove and grinning. 'Evening.'

Tony pulled away from their embrace and ran a hand through her short blonde hair. She was still wearing her suit and makeup, but the high heels had been replaced with a pair of large, red, furry slippers – presumably at the request of their three-year old daughter. For a moment, just briefly, Tony was able to forget all about his problems as his hand worked its way down to the small of her back.

'Not on your laptop?' he remarked, guiding her into the kitchen, where something was simmering on the stove. It was almost unprecedented for the ambitious City lawyer to come home without switching on the machine and at least firing off a few emails.

'Nope.'

'What? Why are you smiling like that?' Tony held his wife at arm's length, admiring her freckly complexion and trying to decipher her bright-eyed smirk.

She leaned forwards and kissed him again, running a hand through his dark hair and letting it fall to rest on her stomach.

'We're having another baby.'

Day out with family and in-laws

'NO, NO, I *INSIST!*'

Suze's father slammed down his credit card and waved at a passing waitress. 'It's not every day you learn you're going to be a grandfather again!'

Tony quietly conceded. His in-laws were making a statement, of course. It was the same statement they made every time: *You don't earn enough.* Tony had lost track of the number of times Peter and Rose had paid for lunch over the course of his four-year marriage to Suze.

A certain type of man might have fought back, brushing away his father-in-law's gold card. Tony Sharp wasn't that type. Quietly assertive, he usually brought people around by gentle persuasion and reasoning. But this technique had no effect on Peter Proctor, and besides, Tony had a feeling that the semi-retired actuary rather enjoyed flaunting his wealth in Cambridge's most exclusive riverside restaurant.

'Mummy, can I have another chocolate?'

All eyes swivelled to Poppy, whose hair, although dark, was unmistakeably coated in chocolate. It seemed that the three-year old had devoured an entire plateful of after-dinner mints.

Rose looked up from her lecture on the merits of breast-feeding and shrieked.

'That's what I mean! Susannah, Look!'

Suze suppressed a grin and dipped her napkin in her water glass, reaching for Poppy's face.

'But Mummy, I'm hungry!' Poppy wriggled out of her mother's grasp.

Tony noticed his father-in-law's mouth twitch slightly as Poppy's squeal pierced the background hubbub. He considered side-tracking the man with a new conversation, but then thought, *fuck it*. It was his fault they'd come to the least child-friendly restaurant in Cambridge, where the closest thing to a kids' menu was roasted ox tongue and horseradish ice cream.

'Shall we go?' Suze suggested.

Tony gave her a conspiratorial wink, wondering when his mother-in-law would notice that Poppy had been using her grandmother's white skirt as a napkin.

The cool autumn breeze was a welcome relief on Tony's cheeks, which were flushed with a combination of over-eating and pent-up frustration. *Two minutes,* he told himself. It was just a case of surviving the walk back to the car and fending off suggestions of cups of tea and then they were free.

'Mummy look! Gypsies!'

Tony turned just in time to see his daughter pointing at a woman in a headscarf who was tending her flowers on the deck of a boathouse.

Suze hurried them on, quietly explaining to Poppy that the lady in the headscarf was not in fact a gypsy and that it was unkind to call people names.

'You know where she got *that* from,' Rose said loudly.

Tony closed his eyes briefly, not wanting to hear his mother-in-law's latest theory on Poppy's upbringing.

'Mum…' Suze whined quietly.

'It's your nanny,' Mrs Proctor declared, regardless. 'That's what happens. She's picking things up from her. Once children have learned things, it's very difficult to change their habits.'

Tony dropped back a few paces and held out a hand to his daughter, planning to whisk her away so she didn't hear the inevitable argument. Anja, their Serbian nanny, had proved controversial with the in-laws ever since she'd joined the family three years ago.

Poppy yelped as her mother's hand was withdrawn, snatching wildly at the air above her head.

'D'you want a ride on Daddy's shoulders?' offered Tony.

'No.'

10

Suze laughed and held out her hand once again. Poppy was a daddy's girl, but when she felt threatened, it was mummy she turned to.

'You have no idea what that nanny's saying to her all day'

Suze turned and glared at her mother. 'She's got a name, mum. And it's not all day; it's just mornings and a couple of hours after nursery.'

'Sounds like all day to me, dear.'

Suze didn't reply.

'I suppose you'll be doing the same again, going back to work straight after the birth?'

'I'll be going back after six months again. But only four days a week, and it's not really full time. I'm home every day by seven.'

To work on your laptop, thought Tony, keeping his concerns to himself. Boosting his mother-in-law's case was the last thing he wanted to do. He did worry about his wife though. She was up at six every morning, on the laptop for an hour before getting Poppy ready for the handover to Anja, working nine hours in the office, getting back for bath time, putting Poppy to bed, doing another hour on the laptop whilst making dinner, then finishing any outstanding domestic chores and downing a quick glass of wine before going to bed to start all over again. It made his directorship at TransTel look easy.

'I read a statistic the other day,' Rose went on, like a dog with a bone. 'Apparently working mothers are four times more likely to have post-natal depression than stay-at-home mums.'

'Really?' Suze turned to her mother and smiled. 'I read a stat that said stay-at-home mums were ten times more likely than working mothers to stick their nose in other people's business.'

Tony managed to disguise his snort of laughter in a coughing fit.

'Susannah, please,' her father admonished. 'At least listen to what your mother has to say.'

'You're so opinionated,' Rose muttered, shaking her head.

'Mummy? What does o-pinny-nated mean?'

Tony glanced back at his wife. She smiled wryly.

'It means that you're very sure of what you're saying.'

11

They walked on, to the sound of Poppy's stuttering repetition of the word and the rustle of dry leaves underfoot. It wasn't a new issue, their child-care arrangement. It was incredible, Mrs Proctor's knack for attributing everyday problems in life to faults in her granddaughter's upbringing.

Anja – who, incidentally, was fluent in English, highly qualified and devoted to Poppy – was not the Proctors' only bugbear. The fact that Suze was putting her career ahead of her child also riled them, and the idea that Tony was not the sole breadwinner was clearly bringing them into disrepute. But most horrifying of all, as far as the in-laws were concerned, was the fact the *Suze earned more than her husband.*

'How's the job?' asked Peter, picking up the pace and distancing them from the women.

Tony forced a smile. 'All good, thanks.'

There were people with whom Tony discussed his issues at the floundering TransTel business unit, but Peter Proctor was not one of them.

'Any promotions on the horizon?'

'I'm only three months into my new role,' Tony reminded him. *Not that there was the slightest chance of a promotion, whichever horizon you look at,* he thought.

'Of course you are. And it's all going well?'

'Very well,' he lied.

'Good.' Peter nodded sagely. 'You'll be flying through the ranks in no time, I'm sure.'

Tony switched on a mechanical smile and said nothing. He couldn't tell his father-in-law that he didn't want to fly through the ranks. Peter Proctor wouldn't understand. If Tony tried to explain that he cared more about turning the Synapse business around than brown-nosing his way up the corporate career ladder, or that he got more of a kick out of fixing the problems in the call centre than holding the title 'VP' – whatever that meant, anyway – he'd probably be forced to divorce his wife on the spot. For Tony, it was about making things happen. He wanted to leave a legacy. He wanted to be able to look back and say, *I did that.* Peter Proctor was all about status and wealth. He had no idea.

They turned off the path and climbed the steps that led to the main road. The car was tantalisingly close.

'Are you sure you don't want to stop off at ours for a cup of tea?' offered Rose as they converged at the top, ready to go their separate ways.

'We'd better be going,' Tony and Suze said quickly in unison. 'Long drive,' Tony added unnecessarily.

'Well, it was lovely to see you. Do come again soon.' Rose turned to her daughter. 'And remember what I said, won't you? If you ever need another pair of hands…'

Suze mustered a smile and politely thanked her mother.

After some air-kissing and a bone-crushing handshake, they were finally free. Tony slipped between his wife and daughter and let out a whoop of delight.

Suze looked at him, wide-eyed. 'At least wait until they're out of earshot!'

Tony laughed. 'They don't listen anyway. So, Granny Rose is coming to stay, is she?'

Suze rolled her eyes. 'Come on, she was only trying to help. She means well. What else could I say?'

They stopped at the car while Tony rummaged in his pocket for the keys.

'I don't want Granny Rose to stay,' Poppy declared. 'She's mean!'

Tony and Suze exchanged a look across the roof of the car.

'She's not mean,' replied Suze, opening the back door and strapping Poppy in. 'She's just…'

'O-pinny-nated,' finished their three-year old daughter.

'Er, yes. Yes, I suppose she is.'

Meeting with the team

'MARIANNE, DO WE HAVE a room booked? Have you got a pen? How long do we have – an hour?'

'Room four. Here you go. You had ninety minutes, but you've lost fifteen.' The petite brunette smiled and held out a biro.

Tony flashed her a look of gratitude and grabbed the pen, scooping up his papers and spilling tea all down his hand.

'Shit. D'you have a paper towel? Roy, you should be in this meeting. And you, Matt. Come on guys! Management meeting in room four!'

It was a familiar sight that greeted Tony as he reversed into the room, nursing his scalded hand and shaking the drips off the agendas. Louise, Head of Marketing, was perched at the end of the table, composing a text message. Norm, the Technology Manager, was picking away at a dubious brown splodge on his knitted tie. The other seats were unoccupied. In the middle of the table, next to the ancient overhead projector, was a small bowl of sweets – an incentive from the lovely Marianne.

'After you…' He held open the door as Roy, the Operations Manager, ambled in and made his way slowly towards the furthest seat. Just as the door clicked shut, it burst open again and the burly Sales Manager swaggered through.

'Hi Matt. Right! That's everyone then.' Tony set his papers down and wiped off the worst of the tea. He didn't feel nervous, exactly, but he wasn't looking forward to today's meeting. In truth, he'd been putting it off for a while, waiting until the next sales update, the next board meeting, the three-month mark… He'd run out of excuses now. He had to tell them how it was.

'You'll see from the agenda,' he said, handing out the tea-soaked sheets, 'that we've got three things to cover...'

The cloud was right overhead now, dark and menacing, eclipsing everything else. Tony's stomach felt a little unsettled, but it wasn't anxiety, exactly. It felt more like... guilt. Guilt for letting things come to this. Guilt for having underestimated the scale of the task when he'd taken on Synapse – for being so naïve.

'First, we'll do a quick update on where we are. Then we'll get a bit of feedback on what we think we could be doing better, where we could improve... Then we'll work on next steps. That's the plan. Okay?'

The faces stared blankly back at him. Louise, as ever, was the only one making eye contact, blinking keenly at her boss through her glasses, her ringlets framing her mousy smile. Tony didn't expect any more of a response. He had learned from experience that this was the best he would get.

'Let's go round the room.' Again, no response. 'Matt... D'you want to kick off?'

The Sales Manager looked up from his Blackberry, lifted his muscular shoulders and then let them fall, reaching for a sweet. 'Well,' he said, popping the toffee into his mouth and rolling it around a few times. 'Sales is sales. My team's workin' hard but it ain't easy at the present time, as I'm sure you're aware. We're all doin' our best.'

Tony nodded slowly. 'I think, if I'm correct, the figure is twenty-two percent. We're twenty-two percent down on last year. Is that right?'

Matt shrugged again and turned back to his Blackberry. Tony began to wonder why he'd asked Matt to speak first. He knew what the cocky young salesman was like. Too many hours had been wasted trying to penetrate Matt's thick, hard shell, trying to coax him into speaking out, taking some responsibility... It had failed in the past and it clearly wasn't going to succeed with an audience.

'Okay. So, Marketing?'

Tony felt himself relaxing a little as Louise's bubbly Lancashire accent filled the room, picking up pace as her thoughts began to overtake her tongue.

15

'…and then with the re-brand we saw a bit of an uplift and the direct marketing drove a bit of a spike too, but of course that was run in parallel with the outdoor campaign so it's difficult to tell which had the greater effect–'

She paused for breath and Tony seized the opportunity.

'Great – thanks.' He smiled at Louise, wishing all of his employees were as easy-going and eager to please as the young Marketing Manager – although perhaps with a dash more commercial nous. Whilst it was impossible to fault her enthusiasm, it was an unfortunate fact that Louise Brayshaw was blessed with a scatty, somewhat illogical mind.

'Norm?'

The Technology Manager looked up with a jolt.

'Oh. Um… Well. Obviously we're working on lots of, um… things. So… I suppose the main one is the routing algorithm re-vamp…'

Tony nodded encouragingly as Norm described, in painful detail, the progress made on the various technology projects. His stuttering monotone was soporific and it was only when Tony spotted Matt's pencil flying across the table towards him that he realised he'd completely switched off and was thinking about bedroom arrangements for Poppy and his unborn child.

'Thanks!' He slid the pencil back to Matt. 'Great. So… Roy?'

The Operations Manager grunted and with one hand still doodling on his pad, started stroking his balding head.

'Well,' he said eventually. 'I 'ave to say, I'm not sure why we're going over all this.'

Tony maintained his placid expression, waiting for Roy's explanation. This was always going to be the hardest nut to crack.

'Why d'you say that?' he prompted when it became apparent that Roy had nothing more to offer.

'Well, we're sitting around the table, waffling on about how we've done this and that, and how the business has gone to shit – pardon me language –' He looked at Louise, who dipped her head gracefully. 'When it'd be far better to be back at our desks or whatever, trying to sort out a way of gettin' us *out* of the

16

shitter – sorry.' He glanced again in Louise's direction. 'That's how it seems to me, anyway.'

Tony sighed quietly, trying to ignore Matt's nod of agreement. 'I'm sorry you feel like that,' he replied, trying to catch the eye of the obstinate fifty-year old. 'I know you like to be out there in the field, so to speak,' he opened his hands in a peace-offering gesture, 'but sometimes it's good to step back, assess what we've done, what we should be doing... so we can decide where to go next.'

Roy pulled a face across the table at the young Sales Manager, as though the two men were fellow sufferers. 'I know where I wanna go,' he muttered.

Tony cleared his throat and decided to ignore this comment. Roy, despite his attitude, was actually very good at his job. He was thorough and diligent and he knew the business inside out. He just didn't *want* to be good – not for Tony Sharp. He didn't want to work for a man nearly twenty years his junior. He resented taking direction from a man who had never soldered a wire in his life, never fixed a telephone line and didn't know his transistor from his transformer.

Roy Smith had started his working life as a sixteen-year-old apprentice at TransTel. From apprentice he'd graduated to engineer, then made it to junior manager, then eventually he'd earned his place in the management team of TransTel Connect, as it was then known. It was a progression he was clearly proud of – as any of his colleagues would testify. Tony could understand why he felt a little resentful, reporting to someone who barely remembered the days before mobile phones. Tony's predecessor had been a fool, but at least he had been a *senior* fool. Roy's problems, apparently, had only started when Rupert Beasley stepped down and Tony took over.

'Shall we move onto the next point on the agenda?' Tony asked rhetorically. 'What we think we could be doing better, where we could improve...' he trailed off, distracted by a sizeable yellow fleck that was skittering across the table towards the sweets, presumably from Norm's tie. 'Louise. Tell us your thoughts.'

Louise nodded keenly, her messy curls bouncing about on her head. 'Well! I guess we can work harder at building up the new brand and getting the word out there about our services –'

'It's bollocks.' Matt interrupted, shaking his head accusingly at Louise. 'The fucking re-brand is bollocks. We're still offering the same old service, just dressed in stupid blue jumpsuits instead of the old brown ones. How's that gonna sell more subscriptions?'

Tony nodded calmly. He didn't like to admit it, but he agreed with Matt's stance on the re-brand. 'Okay, so I think we've agreed that Marketing and Sales need to work together if we're going to achieve our goals. Matt, what do you think we could be doing to improve sales?'

Matt shrugged and pulled the bowl of sweets towards him. 'Lower our prices,' he said, fishing about in the bowl. 'That's the only way we'll do it.'

Unfortunately, Matt had suggested the one change that just wasn't going to happen – and he knew it. Margins were already squeezed to a minimum and there was no way the Synapse package could be sold any cheaper.

'Any other ideas…?' Tony asked hopefully.

Predictably, Louise piped up. 'We could do some more direct marketing,' she said, 'but using the new brand as a hook. I think if we –'

'Jesus!' cried Matt, slamming his Blackberry down on the table and whirling round to confront his colleague. 'You're not listening, are you? We can't sell any more. Can't. Sell. Any. More. That's the problem. Customers are going to Netcomm because they offer a better deal, and however many times we shout about our shiny blue costumes and wanky fucking name, they won't switch back to us!'

There was silence. Even Louise didn't have anything to say.

Tony tried to catch her eye to check she was okay, but she was staring at the table as though in shock. Poor Louise; she'd only been with the firm for six months. Rupert Beasley had hired her, as one of his parting shots, to take on the extravagant re-brand. It hadn't won her any popularity points at the time and her presence clearly continued to rile certain members of the team.

'Okay…' Tony glanced down at the redundant agenda. The objective of the meeting – to expose the seriousness of the situation within Synapse – had been met, although not quite in the manner he had intended. 'Norm? You've been very quiet. Do you want to add anything about how we could improve?'

The awkward Technology Manager shook his head quickly.

'Roy?' Tony ventured apprehensively.

'Well, you know what I think. This business is about getting engineers out to people's homes, and that's what I make happen. And I'd do a much better job of that if I didn't have to sit in these pow-wows talking about bum fluff.'

Tony breathed a small sigh of relief. It was one of Roy Smith's more measured responses.

'Right. Thanks. So, what I suggest is that we call it a day for now, but we all spend some time thinking about how we can ramp up our efforts even further. I'll get Marianne to set up some one-on-one meetings with each of you over the next few weeks and we'll go from there.'

The room emptied quickly and Tony soon found himself sitting alone, head in hands, staring at the stained agenda in front of him.

We can't sell any more. Can't. Sell. Any. More. The words were still ringing in his ears. He knew it was true. Matt was an annoying git, but he had a point. The sales team were doing their best. There had to be a way of bringing the department back to life, boosting its subscriber base, making more money… He just couldn't think what it was.

'Tony?'

He looked up. Marianne's pretty face was poking round the door.

'Bit of a problem. The call centre operators have gone on strike.'

Tony scrunched his eyes shut for a second then let out a long, loud sigh. Things really couldn't get much worse.

Dinner with Emmie and Luke

'ALL HOME-MADE, of course,' said Suze, carving a generous slab of cheesecake and coaxing it onto Luke's plate. 'According to the packaging.'

Emmie laughed and passed the enormous helping down to her husband. 'Secret's safe with us.'

'And what about Poppy and Bradley?' asked Suze, tilting the remaining dessert towards the kids, who were perched at the end of the table on matching highchairs.

'Chocolate!' screamed Poppy, banging her hands on the table and inadvertently hitting her plate, which tipped, rolling dangerously close to the edge of the table.

'Chocolate!' echoed Bradley, copying her actions and splashing playfully in the puddle of gravy he'd made on the table. Being three months younger than Poppy, he saw her as something of an inspiration.

'I'll take that as a yes.' Suze smiled and cut another two healthy portions, glancing briefly at the gravy dripping onto the floor.

Emmie was Suze's best friend. They had met at university, where they'd both set out to read Law. It turned out, only Suze had graduated. Shortly after freshers' week, Emmie had discovered the university radio station and established herself as an amateur talk show host. Talking was something she and Suze were both very good at. Falling further and further behind with her studies, eventually Emmie had dropped out altogether and got a job as a DJ on a local station. Ten years later, she had a late-night slot on Jack FM and ran her own media consultancy in the daytime, whilst bringing up Bradley.

20

It was a convenient coincidence that the children had been born just a few months apart. Emmie and Luke lived less than an hour's drive away, which meant that the kids had play mates on tap.

'How did she take the news?' asked Emmie, nodding at Suze's bump, which was just beginning to show.

'She seems excited.' Suze looked over to where her daughter was enthusiastically demolishing the crumbly dessert. 'Poppy, what do you think about your new brother or sister?'

Poppy paused for several seconds to consider the question. 'Is he still in your tummy?' she asked suspiciously.

'Yes!' cried Suze, patting it gently. 'Just waiting to come out.'

Luke pushed his plate away and rubbed his own belly. 'Feels like *I'm* expecting after all that delicious food. Thanks.'

'Mummy,' Poppy went on, using the contemplative tone that implied she'd been thinking about something for a while. It was in this respect that she took after her dad. She was a problem-solver. 'Mummy, does the baby want some food?' She held up her plate, which contained some cheesecake, a carrot and a crisp. 'He can have this.'

'Oh, how kind!' cried Suze. 'That's very sweet of you. I think he's asleep right now but I'll keep it for later. Mmm. Thank you.'

Suze grabbed the plate, along with a couple of others and the jug of cream that was dangerously close to Bradley's elbow, and before long the clear-up operation was underway.

On Suze's suggestion, Luke and Tony took the children into the lounge whereupon Poppy started laying down very strict rules on the use of her den (a cloth strewn over the arms of two chairs).

'…and you can't come in with your shoes on,' she finished.

Luke raised his eyebrows and nodded at Tony. 'Her mother's daughter.'

Tony laughed. It was good to see Luke. Emmie and Suze met up all the time, but it was quite rare for them all to get together like this – probably because the men never got round to organising anything themselves.

Like his wife, Luke worked in radio – that was how they'd

21

met – but he preferred to stay very much off-air, on the 'commercial side', whatever that meant. Tony had never been entirely clear on what Luke did at Box 100, but he did very well out of it, whatever it was.

'How's the job?' asked Luke, sinking into an armchair. 'Or daren't I ask?'

Tony closed his eyes, shaking his head and sighing.

'Not good?' Luke twisted round as someone called out from the kitchen. 'YES PLEASE!'

Tony heard the word 'nightcap' and added his vote before turning back to Luke.

'Well… Revenues are down by a quarter on last year and my Sales Manager won't accept that he can do anything about it. The marketing team are obsessed with their flashy new re-brand which is having no effect on our top line, and my Operations Manager won't speak to me because I'm young enough to be his son. Oh and our call centre operators went on strike last week so we had to give them all a pay rise. Which means that our profit margin is now approximately zero.'

Luke grimaced. 'Sounds dire. Have you got an escape plan?'

Tony's head danced from side to side. An *escape plan*. It wasn't something he'd considered. Luke was clearly talking about a way out for him, as an individual: a way of salvaging his career, but ironically, that was the last thing on Tony's mind. He was more intent on getting the business back on its feet – doing what he'd been brought in to do. He'd only been at Synapse for three months; he wasn't looking for an exit route yet. *Although…* Tony smiled gratefully as Emmie set down two glasses of whisky. Maybe Luke was right. Maybe he should start laying out a few options.

'Bradley! No!'

The men jumped as Emmie launched herself across the room and caught her son in mid-air as he leaped off the back of the sofa towards the curtains. He was an acrobatic child, but quite how he had climbed up so quickly without them noticing was a mystery.

'Naughty boy!' gasped Emmie, depositing Bradley roughly

on the floor. She looked at Luke, then Tony, then Luke again and shook her head.

'Sorry,' Luke grovelled.

'Sorry,' added Tony. 'Didn't see him there.'

Emmie rolled her eyes and returned cautiously to the kitchen. Meanwhile Bradley, shoes off and looking angelic, appeared outside Poppy's den and started begging to be let back in.

'An escape plan,' Luke prompted.

Tony hesitated. If he told the truth, he'd come across as naïve for not having protected his own interests. In fact, it wasn't like that. He knew, deep down, that he could jump from Synapse, or even from TransTel, any day he liked. He just didn't want to.

'You have to sing a song!' Poppy squeaked bossily from inside her fabric empire.

Tony stirred his coffee, thinking about how to explain his rationale while a strange, whining noise started emanating from Bradley's direction.

'I want to see it through.'

Luke laughed quietly. 'Typical Tony. No Plan B, because you'll never need one.'

'Not loud enough!' Poppy declared.

'Maybe,' said Tony, doubtfully. He often heard people talk like this about him. As if things came naturally to him, as if it all just slotted into place without him having to try. In fact, the opposite was true. Tony worked harder than anyone to make sure things came together.

The whining increased in volume until it sounded like a high-pitched version of bagpipes.

'Poppy!' yelled Tony. 'Can you please let Bradley into your den!' He turned back to Luke. 'Sorry. No offence, but your boy can't sing.'

Luke smiled. 'He takes after me. No, seriously, you're gonna pull this off, mate. I know what you're like once you've got your teeth into something.'

Tony gave a hollow laugh, wishing it was as easy as Luke implied. It was true that he'd achieved great things in the past. He had taken business units from near-collapse to profitability, but this time, the challenge seemed tougher.

Perhaps he always went through a period of self-doubt, he mused. Maybe Luke was right. Maybe he would get there in the end. They sipped their drinks, keeping a vague eye on Poppy's den, which had fallen suspiciously quiet.

'What about you?' asked Tony, trying to clear all thoughts of angry call centre operators from his mind. 'How's Box?'

Luke swallowed a large slug of whisky and grimaced as it burned his throat. 'Good and bad.'

'Go on,' said Tony, peering sideways as a small pair of feet emerged from Poppy's den.

'Well, we're launching a cool new application that lets you stream the music you want, when you want, with no ad breaks. It's a fully-sponsored, user-generated, online radio station.'

'Wow.' Tony nodded, impressed. 'Sounds great. A bit like...' He tried to remember the name.

'Yeah, that's the bad news: everyone's doing it.'

'Oh.' Tony grimaced. 'Sorry.' He knew very little about the media world.

'The problem is...' Luke trailed off, frowning as the feet started wriggling and an irritable growl came from inside the den. 'Bradley, what's going on in there?'

Tony leaned over and gently lifted the corner of the fabric entrance. There was an immediate screech from inside and the cloth was yanked back down. The men looked at one another blankly.

'Sorry. The problem...?'

'The problem is that the whole radio industry –' Luke lowered his voice to a hoarse whisper – '*is fucked.*'

Tony waited for an explanation, which eventually came, after a dramatic pause.

'The listeners won't pay, because they know they can get their music for free. And advertisers won't pay, because they know that the listeners flick channels to avoid the ads. There's no way of making money.'

'Shit.' Tony nodded. He was already drawing parallels with his own business dilemma. 'So you're doing this new thing instead?'

Luke nodded enthusiastically. 'Yeah. I've got high hopes. It's completely new and different – well, for us it is. We'll be the first traditional radio station to try anything like this.'

Tony voiced his admiration, feeling just a little envious that Luke had been able to push through something so seemingly radical.

'Just like that, eh?' he asked. 'No regulatory issues? No stuffy old farts on the board saying no?'

Luke smiled. 'Oh, jeez. This wasn't *easy*, mate. I first had this idea *twelve months* ago. If we'd moved then, we would've beaten all the competition to it. You wouldn't believe the opposition I've had from inside.'

I probably would, thought Tony, picturing the TransTel boardroom full of frowning men in starched suits.

'But they came round in the end. I think they just realised, you know… Sometimes you've just got to do things differently. Try something new.'

Suddenly, the air became filled with the ear-splitting sound of a child's scream.

Tony whipped back the fabric of Poppy's den just as Emmie and Suze rushed into the room.

The four adults crouched down, peering into the space between the armchairs.

'What's going on?' demanded Suze.

The children were sitting cross-legged, facing one another, Poppy scowling menacingly at her playmate. As far as it was possible to see, they were both completely unharmed.

'Baddy won't play soldiers,' she spat, glaring at Bradley.

'Want to play ducks!' the boy wailed.

Emmie gave Suze a long-suffering look. 'I think someone's a little bit tired, don't you?' She reached forward and lifted Bradley into her arms. 'Shall we get you into your pyjamas and take you home?'

Poppy was still sulking ten minutes later, when Tony tucked her into her bed.

'Night, Pops.'

She glowered back at him.

He held her sleepy gaze. 'Poppy, listen to me. You can't always have things your way. Bradley wanted to play something

25

different, and maybe… Maybe you would have liked it.'

He hesitated, feeling a sense of deja-vu as he kissed her goodnight.

'Sometimes, it's better to try something new.'

Team reports back

'OKAY, WELL I guess it might work. I'll take a look at the budget and we'll go from there.' Tony managed a faint smile. 'Thanks.'

Louise beamed back at him and collected together her coloured charts. 'No worries!'

'Leave the door open,' he called out. 'Roy's due any minute.'

Tony slumped back in his chair and rolled his head to one side, then the other. He caught his reflection in the shiny metal surround of the ceiling strip light. His eyes looked sunken and small, his dark hair lank and in need of a cut. He wasn't tired in the sense that he'd been running around using up energy; this was a draining, deep-rooted mental exhaustion that threatened to sap his will to go on. But unfortunately, he had to go on, because it was only four o'clock and he still had the worst to come.

The one-on-one meetings were not going well. On reflection, Tony wasn't sure why he'd expected differently. He'd been heading up the division for three months now and he had a pretty good idea of his direct reports' capabilities. He knew that Norm stood less chance of coming up with a sensible, commercial idea than his three-year old daughter. He was aware of Matt's attitude problem and the rift that seemed to exist between him and Louise – who, in all honesty, spent far too much time colouring in and dreaming up whacky ideas that would lose the business more money. And then there was Roy.

Tony leaned forward and squinted at the clock in the corner of his monitor. Eleven minutes past. Clearly his Operations

Manager felt no obligation to turn up on time. A string of emails had appeared in his inbox, all with the same subject. Tony started at the bottom of the most recent message and worked up.

From: Brian O'Keefe - TransTel Network Direct
To: Tony Sharp - Synapse; Amit Chaudhuri – TransTel CBN
Subject: YOGHURT POTS, ANYONE?
Help!
Urgently require yoghurt pots. With string if poss.
Network in so-called 'networks' department has been down all morning. Running out of excuses to give clients...

From: Amit Chaudhuri – TransTel CBN
To: Tony Sharp - Synapse; Brian O'Keefe - TransTel Network Direct
Subject: Re: YOGHURT POTS, ANYONE?
Think we have some pigeons in our stationery cupboard from the last time that happened to us. Will send them down if you like.
PS Tell clients you've been flooded – natural disasters v.g. as tend to be unpredictable.

From: Brian O'Keefe - TransTel Network Direct
To: Tony Sharp - Synapse; Amit Chaudhuri – TransTel CBN
Subject: Re: YOGHURT POTS, ANYONE?
That would be great, thanks.
Flood line not going down so well – think clients know we are on 5th floor.

From: Amit Chaudhuri – TransTel CBN
To: Tony Sharp - Synapse; Brian O'Keefe - TransTel Network Direct
Subject: Re: YOGHURT POTS, ANYONE?
Tsunami? Localised earthquake?

Tony smiled, wishing for a moment he'd stayed in the comfort of a middle-management job within Network Direct, the department where he'd first met Brian and Amit. They had joined at about the same time – Tony and Brian as ambitious twenty-somethings, Amit a few years their senior. Their paths had crossed whilst working together on a project that went on to become the foundations of a whole new business unit, TransTel CBN, which was now headed up by Amit.

Volcanic eruption? typed Tony, feeling slightly rejuvenated by the distraction. *Trust pigeons have arrived safely?*

'Afternoon.'

Tony's newfound cheer quickly melted away.

'Hi Roy.'

The clock said quarter past; Tony couldn't be bothered to point this out. He waited as the Operations Manager shuffled into the room and planted himself in the seat opposite – without so much as a notebook or pen, noted Tony. At least Louise had tried, even though her multi-coloured creations were largely pointless.

'How are things?'

'Well, you know…' Roy shrugged.

Tony let out a sigh. He briefly considered his options and then made a decision.

'Roy, I'll be honest. You were in the meeting the other day. You've seen the sales reports; you know where we stand.'

The man started rubbing what little hair was left on his head.

'We need to buck up our ideas. I know you're not keen on my management practices –' Tony raised a hand to silence any protests from Roy, which, as it happened, never came – 'but the fact is, I'm in charge and I'm putting everything I've got into turning this division around.'

Roy nodded vaguely.

'The efficiency measures I've put in place have been…' he faltered, knowing exactly what Roy thought of his operational changes. The call-centre walk-out spoke for itself. 'Variable, in terms of success. But we still need to try.'

Tony looked pleadingly at the man, hoping – even though he knew it was optimistic – for a sign of solidarity between them. Roy continued to stare out of the window.

'Roy, I need your help.'

Tony was surprised by his own words. He was clearly getting desperate. There was still no response from the manager. 'I don't mean that you have to agree with me the whole time; I'm happy to take input and feedback, but I need to you come up with some ideas. Ideas about how the hell we can claw back some of the thousands of subscribers we've lost in the last year, and how we can win over new ones. How can we do that, Roy?'

Roy's gaze wandered over to Tony's face. As their eyes met, he started shaking his head.

'Bloody hell,' he said scathingly.

Tony's hopes faltered. Nothing more seemed to be forthcoming.

'You got no idea, have you?' Roy said eventually. 'You don't get it. There ain't nothing more we can do. It's the same as with Sales. The guys are doing their best. I can tell you they are, 'cause I see them out there, operators taking their calls, engineers doing their installations… it's all happening as well as it can do, but the problem is, the customers ain't wanting our service no more. Or if they *are,* then they're going to Netcomm and the rest, where they get a bundled service for less money. Simple as that.'

Tony swallowed. He wasn't enjoying Roy's sermon at all. It wasn't just his bullying tone; he was used to that now. He had dealt with enough old-timers to know how to handle them. What worried him, deep down, was that he knew Roy was right.

'With all due respect mate,' Roy concluded, 'we're fucked.'

Tony stared at the floor for a few seconds. Something was distracting him: a bell, ringing somewhere. *We're fucked. It's fucked. The whole industry is fucked…*

That was it. Luke had said it. Synapse was in exactly the same position as traditional radio. It was doing its best, but the revenue streams just weren't there any more. The market had changed. Customers wanted different things now and TransTel was no longer providing them. New competitive threats had emerged and they had just carried on doing what they always did.

The answer wasn't in trimming fat, oiling cogs or fine-tuning. It was futile to go on making incremental changes. He needed to do as Luke had done: something completely new and different. Instead of doing things better, it was a case of *doing better things.*

A surge of adrenaline ran through Tony's bloodstream. It was the first time he'd felt truly excited in weeks.

'Roy?'

The Operations Manager tilted his head, eyes narrowed sceptically.

Tony opened his mouth to share his revelation. Then he closed it again, realising that it might be too soon. He didn't want to come across as a lunatic.

'Thanks for your time.'

This was a breakthrough, for sure, but he needed more time to work out what exactly the breakthrough meant.

Tony watched as Roy lolloped out of the office, feeling more and more certain that he was right about this. If he was to succeed in turning Synapse around, he'd have to do something radical. Just like Box. It was just the small matter of working out what the radical thing was.

THE SUCCESS TRAP AND THE NEED FOR CHANGE

THE SUCCESS TRAP AND
THE NEED FOR CHANGE

 MarketGravity

In this opening chapter Tony realises through a series of timely conversations that no amount of restructuring, cost cutting, marketing campaigns or fist-pumping can significantly lift Synapse's sales to the level of growth being demanded. It's no longer about doing things better, but rather, doing better things.

Here are some of the warning signs to look for in your business:

- Your sales teams are getting even more vocal and critical about the product set and pricing
- Margins are falling in your most important segments
- New competitor names keep cropping up in conversation
- There are new regulatory or structural changes being implemented or proposed in your industry
- You have no confidence that you can hit your targets
- The changes you are making are having a diminishing effect

In the end, price competition will become so fierce that the market will be dominated by a small handful of established players. Margins will be squeezed ever tighter whilst companies will still be expected to deliver double digit growth selling commoditised products and services (think credit cards, mobile phone minutes or electricity tariffs). The bottom line is that you risk becoming a prisoner of the economics of the industry you helped to create.

"BECAUSE THE MAIN BUSINESS WASN'T SINKING THERE WAS A FEELING OF 'WHY PUSH THE BOUNDARIES TOO FAR IN OUR THINKING?'

–

THERE'S NO BURNING PLATFORM, SO WHY JUMP TOO FAR?"

Felix Geyr, O2, BBC Worldwide

There are a number of simple things that you can do today to spot the warning signs and prepare your own growth plan before it's too late.

1. Take a market view, not a product view. Monitor how well you and your competitors are satisfying target customer groups rather than focussing on your share of a particular product category.

2. Talk to customers. Seeing the sales figures is not enough. To get the real picture you need to experience how your customers are reacting to sales conversations first hand. Are sales being lost because the product isn't competitive, or because it's no longer needed?

3. Update your scorecard. Introduce metrics that are tuned to changing markets and areas of future growth.

4. Look for the discontinuities. These are the things that can completely derail markets from their current course. Often several trends can combine to create new customer behaviours. Changes in external factors like regulation can produce new threats and opportunities.

5. Get curious about other markets, companies and geographies. Don't just keep tabs on your usual competitors. Look outside your industry. Consider adjacent markets that also service your customers, or other geographies, where new innovations may have changed the landscape.

6. Ask your employees. Routinely gather a cross-functional team of colleagues. Identify current challenge areas and issues and derive the main themes. Are growth bottlenecks due to a lack of internal coordination, product/service deficiencies or changing customer needs?

Market Gravity has developed a range of tools and techniques to help uncover business issues. Two examples that you can try are outlined below:

1. On the Front Line
Getting insight from people on the front line

Approach:

Objectives:
- To gain insight from colleagues at the front line who deal with customers daily
- To apply the insight and generate new ideas

Conversations with employees on the front line

↓

Share conversations and specific insignts

Tips:
- Keep the conversation informal and try to uncover what people really think – not what they think you want to hear
- Dig deeper into what is said to try to uncover what the real insight is

↓

Generate ideas to address them

↓

How could your company realise the opportunity?

2. Global Leaders
Learning from other industries and geographies

Approach:

Objectives:
- To learn from successful ideas elsewhere
- To find ways of applying that success in our own company

Identify a range of successful businesses

↓

Identify specific opportunities to "learn from"

Tips:
- Remember that examples can be small as well as large; success doesn't necessarily mean global
- Look beyond your own sector and apply the principles as well as a specific idea

↓

Apply the idea onto your business and modify

↓

Define how the specific opportunity works for you

2

The spark of creation:
where do good ideas come from?

'Innovation can come from a variety of sources; the
challenge is to extract it on demand.'

Brian and Amit advise

TONY HANDED his TransTel cash card to the checkout girl and waited as she slowly counted the items on his tray. The lunchtime chatter was almost loud enough to mask the soundtrack on the TransTel Initiatives Centre show reel that was blaring, in melodramatic tones, from the widescreen TV at the end of the canteen.

A hand shot up from nearby. Tony changed his course and drew up at Brian's table, which appeared to be covered in plates full of meat.

'You bulking up?' he asked, sliding the trays around in an attempt to make everything tessellate.

Brian shrugged casually and patted his gut. 'Never too late to start, mate. How's things?'

Tony picked up the fluorescent yellow box that was preventing everything from fitting on the table. 'Not bad,' he lied. 'What's this?'

Screwing up his nose, Brian reached for the cardboard cube. '*TransTel Bright Sparks,*' he read, turning it over in his hand. There was a small slit in the middle of one of the faces. '*Pitch your ideas and you might win a prize.* Wow. That's new.' He rattled the box near his ear. 'Nope. No ideas in there.'

Tony snorted and started spinning his fork around in the over-cooked spaghetti. 'One of our esteemed COO's *innovation* schemes, you reckon?'

Brain nodded. 'I'd say so. Has Wanker-Jones' initials stamped all over it.'

Tony laughed, watching the slippery strands unwrap

themselves from his fork. Graham Walker-Jones had become Chief Operating Officer last year, having previously headed up BusinessReach, the B2B equivalent of Synapse – to questionable effect. It was generally accepted that the newly created position of COO had been devised purely to make room for Charles Gable's old buddy at the boardroom table.

The TransTel Innovation Scheme, one of Walker-Jones' first and most extravagant initiatives, had been set up six months ago to great fanfare and acclaim. Its mission statement was to *instil original thought and entrepreneurial spirit throughout the TransTel business,* the initiative having taken the form of a small team of managers whose jobs were to dictate to other managers how they went about their business, imposing frameworks and protocols and imposing penalties if said frameworks and protocols were not duly enforced. Tony could see the reasoning behind the scheme. There certainly was a lack of original thought and entrepreneurial spirit in TransTel, but there was something a little odd about the idea of introducing it by means of regulation.

'Waste of money,' Brian muttered, getting started on his third sausage.

The sound of a man's polite cough made them look up.

Tony's panic faded quickly as he realised that it was Amit standing over them.

'May I?' He removed some of Brian's empty plates and set his lunch down on the table. It was salad, as usual. Amit was a few years older than them and determined not to let it show.

'Let me guess... Wanker-Jones?'

They nodded.

'Hey, Tony.' Brian waggled his knife in the air. 'Maybe you could go round stealing the suggestions from the *Bright Sparks* boxes to make up your fourteen million pound shortfall!'

Tony looked at him. 'Not funny.'

'How is it all going, anyway?' asked Amit, poking around in his plate of limp lettuce. 'Making headway?'

A strangled sound came from Tony's throat, almost involuntarily. A week ago, he had felt quite elated after his apparent breakthrough. The revelation that Synapse needed to do *something different* had seemed like a partial solution. But, having spent seven days and most of seven nights thinking about it, he was now experiencing a sort of anti-climax. The revelation was in fact a question: a massive, daunting question to which he didn't know the answer.

'Oh dear.' Amit shook his head. 'You look like I felt last week when I got told that my development budget was being cut in half.'

Tony grimaced. *In half?* Sometimes he wondered whether the boardroom decisions were being made by throwing sticks on the ground, voodoo warrior-style. They were slashing resources from departments like TransTel CBN – ones that actually made money for the firm – and spending millions on projects like Walker-Jones' 'innovation scheme'.

'What's the latest?'

Tony realised Amit was looking at him. He thought for a few seconds, in two minds about whether to tell them about his half-brainwave. Eventually, he pushed away his plate and looked up.

'Last week, I realised something.'

They continued to munch in silence, eyebrows raised. Tony braced himself to go on. This was the first time he'd shared his thoughts with anyone in TransTel.

'I realised that it was no good trying to make Synapse more lean. I've spent the last three months scraping away at inefficiencies and fine-tuning… but it's no good. You can't polish a turd.'

'Nice.' Brian nodded approvingly – more, Tony suspected, at the metaphor than the implication.

'So,' Amit looked at him. 'What are you going to do?'

Tony drew a breath. 'Well, I need to turn Synapse into a new business. With a new product. Completely change its remit.'

Brian was looking at him, head cocked as though he suspected Tony might have had a minor breakdown.

'What will its new remit be?' asked Amit.

Tony thought for a moment. They were both watching him, waiting for enlightenment.

'I don't know,' he said eventually.

'Organic produce?' Brian suggested unhelpfully. 'It's doing very well at the moment.'

Amit shot him a look and returned his gaze to Tony's troubled face. 'You don't know, or you don't know whether the board will like it?'

Tony shrugged sheepishly. In a way, he wished he hadn't opened up to the guys. He wasn't sure where he was going with the non-idea, or indeed whether he was going anywhere at all – except perhaps to HR to collect his P45.

'I don't know. I can't think what it is.'

'Have you brainstormed?' asked Amit.

'Well…' Tony wasn't sure whether his thinking time in the shower counted, or the commute to work, or the period between sleep and waking when his mind would spring into life, desperately snatching at ideas that made no sense when lucid. 'Sort of.'

'How do you sort-of brainstorm?' asked Brian.

'With your team, I mean.' Amit clearly understood. He had been here before.

'No.'

Tony watched as Amit's head started nodding, his eyes narrowed in thought.

'You remember the early days of TransTel CBN?' he prompted. 'Before it became TransTel CBN?'

Tony nodded. Of course he remembered. If it hadn't been for Amit and Brian, Tony's first two years at TransTel might have cost him his sanity.

'You recall how it all came about?'

'Um…' It was a long time ago now. Tony only really remembered the highs and the lows – their first round of funding, their victory in the battle with Finance to bypass their preposterous targets, the ongoing feud with HR to enable them to work more than the statutory thirty-five hour week. 'Not really.'

'I wasn't heading up the department at the time,' Amit explained. 'Piers was in charge. But we all sat in a room together and thrashed ideas about. That was where the idea originally came from.'

Tony frowned. He wasn't averse to the idea of brainstorming; he was just highly sceptical about the idea of brainstorming *with his team*. The TransTel CBN lot, from what he remembered, had been enthusiastic and dynamic, relatively speaking. Thinking about his direct reports, and their direct reports beneath them… Tony shuddered. 'I'm not sure it would produce the same results.'

'That doesn't matter much, really.'

'What?'

Tony's frown deepened. He wasn't an expert in idea generation, but he was fairly sure that the results were the critical part.

'The key thing is to get everyone together, to make sure the ideas *start* with them. That's one thing I've learned. If you want to lead people in a new direction, it's much easier to get them to walk there of their own accord than pull them kicking and screaming.'

Brian popped the last piece of bacon into his mouth and looked at Amit. 'That's a bit deep, isn't it? Have you been taking management classes?'

Tony smiled. He saw what Amit was saying. If he wanted his grumpy old Ops Manager and the obstinate sales force to follow him into this new territory – whatever territory that might be – then he needed to get their buy-in from the start. Which meant, rather worryingly, that the idea would have to originate from the core team. Or at least, it would have to *appear* to originate from the core team.

Tony's mind wandering again to the enormous question that wouldn't go away. What was this new direction? Maybe a brainstorm would be a good idea. He certainly wasn't getting anywhere on his own.

'Not wanting to piss on your parade,' said Brian, picking at a piece of gristle between his teeth, 'but this *changing direction* lark… Is it actually part of your job?'

Tony hesitated. Brian had a point. Officially, his title was Managing Director of Synapse. Synapse played in the broadband installation market. When Gable and co. had handed him the job, they almost certainly hadn't envisaged him changing the core product line. This proposal – whatever it turned out to be – would be radical. He was intending to change the department's whole raison d'être.

'There's no other way,' he replied. 'It's a sinking ship, and they brought me in to turn it around.'

'I don't think they meant literally.'

Amit smiled, shaking his head. 'Tony, you're right. You're the managing director. You've identified the problem and now you're trying to fix it. Go for it.'

Tony nodded appreciatively.

'Whether the board will approve it is another matter, of course.'

Tony's smile faded. It was true; coming up with the idea was the easy part. Getting permission to implement it was the challenge.

'And getting funding from Draper will be the real problem,' added Amit, 'given the circumstances.'

Tony frowned. He was about to enquire about their Finance Director's 'circumstances' when suddenly Amit pushed back his chair with a little screech and reached for his tray. 'Good luck, Tony. Keep us posted.'

Tony returned Brian's blank look, then spotted the reason for their friend's swift departure: Alan Mulchingham, the fossilized bore who headed up the company's Health and Safety department, was lumbering towards them, trying hard to make eye contact.

'Let's go,' muttered Tony, gathering his debris and standing up.

Brian cottoned on quickly and followed suit. 'Hey,' he said as they headed back to their separate offices. 'Those brainstorms. Let me know if you need an extra brain.'

Tony smiled. 'Thanks mate. I will.'

Antagonism leads to ideas

'DADDY, LOOK!'

The jet of warm water shot out through the hole in the duck's backside and met squarely with Tony's left eyeball.

Poppy laughed and plunged the plastic toy back into the bath, pumping frantically with her little pink fists just under the surface. Nursing his eye, Tony half-watched as the water around the duck turned white with bubbles and he realised, with mixed feelings, that his three-year old daughter had discovered Archimedes' principle.

'Look!' she squealed again, pressing her fingers against the duck and sending a spurt of water across the bathroom.

Tony chuckled obligingly and hoped that his wife's bathrobe would be dry by the morning. 'Shall we play Noah's Ark?'

The suggestion was met with another squirt, this one rising up in a giant arc above Poppy's head and landing on her pile of clothes, with another shriek of excitement. Even dropping the purple plastic pony into the bubbles produced no reaction. Tony backed down and decided to sit this one out. His Blackberry buzzed against his backside and carefully, with his dry eye on Poppy's next shot, he slid it out, shielding the screen with his palm just in case.

Hey mate,
Would be happy to help if I can. Must admit that our brainstorms were a bit 'beanbags and pink hats' but they worked for Box. What d'you need?
Luke

41

Tony's spirits lifted a little. He clicked on Reply and started to tap out his response, at which point the duck, leaking through its orifice like a punctured oil drum, was pushed over the edge of the bath, into his lap.

Whisking the device out of harm's way, Tony grabbed the toy, turned it to prevent what was left of the water escaping and held it in front of his daughter, preparing to give it a hearty squeeze.

'Ready...' He held it for a moment longer, then clenched his fist firmly for maximum effect. A lukewarm dribble of water trickled out.

Poppy snatched the duck back, unimpressed.

The squirting continued and, twisting himself so as to protect the screen of his Blackberry, Tony typed his reply.

Great – tjanks Luke.
If u hsve amy frameqorks or slides tjat u used for yr qorkshop
it wd b great to have thwm.
Sorry- bsthtime!
T

The clattering noise from the kitchen abated and the sound of his wife's voice drifted up the stairs. '...which is *fine*, I don't need ... No... What problem?...'

Tony smiled. He could tell who was on the other end of the line.

'Dadda!'

In an instant, Tony realised what was about to happen and lunged for the shampoo bottle, which Poppy was clutching in the same way she'd been clutching the duck.

'Let's...' he cried lamely, tucking the Blackberry away. 'Let's play a new game!'

Tony's game – entitled Scrubbadubdub and designed to be practical as well as entertaining – was a surprise hit. It was especially fortunate that they were mid-scrub just at the moment Suze reversed into the room, phone clamped under her jaw, linen basket on one hip and milk balanced on a pile of Poppy's books.

'I don't need any extra pairs of hands,' she said, as the bottle tipped off the books and all over the linen, prompting Suze to drop the basket on Tony's foot in an attempt to salvage the washing. Tony's yelp was met with a menacing stare.

'No she wasn't... What? She *was* breast-fed!'

'Was bessfed,' echoed Poppy, happily scrubbing her duck as her mother manoeuvred out of the room. 'Was bessfed.'

'Shall we...' Tony gently prised the sponge from her grasp. 'Shall we play Scrubbadubdub on *your* back now?'

There was a vibration in his back pocket as Suze's voice carried across the landing.

'...Well, it's not necessarily *right*, is it? Just because some nineteen-fifties handbook says...'

Tony tickled and scrubbed, eavesdropping on snatches of his wife's conversation. She was always like this with her mother. Both women had very prescribed views on the wrongs and rights of child rearing.

'*Think* about that, mum... No... *Why* should it really be me who...'

Poppy's giggles drowned out the sound of the argument and Tony realised it probably wasn't a good idea to tickle a child that was waist-deep in water.

'Shall we get you dry?' He tugged at her dark, downy hair, which for some reason set off a fresh bout of giggles. Eventually the laughter died down and the enormous mermaid towel was called into action. Tony loved doing bath time, although he always got the impression there were quicker and more efficient ways of achieving the results.

Stealthily, whilst Poppy was bouncing up and down inside the towel, Tony whipped out his Blackberry and glanced at the message from Luke.

No probs. Here you go.
We did actually use pink hats for the first exercise but I suspect that might be more applicable to radio than telecoms(?). Also, ignore the references to the 'silver wall' – we coated one side of the room in foil.
Enjoy bsthtime!

'Why?' barked Suze, appearing again in the bathroom doorway just as Tony was one-handedly locking the keypad. She shot him a look and slid a fresh nappy out from the pile. 'I'm sorry mum, no. It's... No... Listen... Jesus! Why do you...'

'Geezas!' cried Poppy, dancing around inside her towel and tripping herself up, falling flat on her face and letting out a blood-curdling scream.

Suze reappeared in the doorway as Tony tried to soothe their wailing daughter.

'No, she's *fine*...' Suze glowered at her husband. 'No...'

The wailing reverted to a whimper, which became more of a distracted whine, as though Poppy had forgotten what she was supposed to be crying about. Tony laid out the night-nappy and set about fixing it around his daughter's legs. It was one of those tasks that required at least six arms to do properly. Having only the standard complement of limbs, Tony always found it a bit of a struggle.

After a brief battle to fit the pyjamas onto Poppy's hot, wriggling body, Tony allowed himself to be led into his daughter's bedroom. Suze, somewhere downstairs, was drawing her case to a climactic close. It was no wonder she had been tipped to make partner this year.

'I don't care,' came the words, loud and clear despite the doors and walls between them. 'You shouldn't just accept these old wives tales as though they're fact... There's *lots* of evidence to suggest... No... Fine... Just Google it! *No*, Goo- oh, never mind...'

It was not pixies that occupied Tony's mind as he read his daughter *The Poisoned Pixie*. It was his wife, or more specifically, his wife's attitude – her way of thinking.

'The pixies all sat round the table, waiting for Grombo...'

He had never given it much thought before now – only enough to know that he could never win an argument with Suze. But this evening, he realised that what she was doing was what *he* needed to be doing.

'...and Grombo said to the princess, *You can eat some of our cheese...*'

He needed to question the facts. Or rather, he needed to

44

question the wives tales that were so well-engrained in the TransTel business that they seemed like facts. Like his mother-in-law, he had become stuck in his ways. They all had. Synapse had been going for so long, providing the same things to the same customers, using the same people... nobody questioned anything any more.

Why that target market? *Why* that price-point? *Why* direct sales? *Why*, and what else could Synapse deliver?

'Then, while the pixies' backs were turned...' Tony paused for dramatic effect. 'The princess turned and fled, and the cheese was nowhere to be seen!'

Tony looked at his daughter's round, pretty face, her heavy eyelids fighting a losing battle with sleep.

'Good night,' he whispered, kissing her gently on the cheek and creeping across the room.

It was all he could do to prevent himself bounding down the stairs, so energised was he about this new revelation. It was just a question of asking *why*. If he could break down some of those assumptions, challenge the superstitions that plagued the workforce, maybe he could make some headway in this challenge of his.

Suze was stirring the casserole with one hand and highlighting words in a legal document with the other. The cooker light shone off her blonde hair like a halo.

'Asleep?'

Tony nodded, wrapping his arms around his wife's waist and kissing her neck.

Suze turned, pen in hand, frowning at him suspiciously. 'Why are you grinning like that?'

Tony squeezed her slender shoulders. 'Because you've inspired me.'

'Inspired you?'

Tony nodded again.

Suze shook her head, looking heavenwards. 'I don't know, Tony. Sometimes I wonder what's going on in that head of yours.'

Structured group brainstorm

'OKAY... That's great.'

Tony ripped off the page from the flip-chart and stuck it to the far wall, where it flapped gently in the sterile office breeze, drawing attention to its near-blankness. As a warm-up exercise, Tony had taken Luke's advice and asked the group to come up with a list of companies that had changed their core product line in the last fifty years. The combined effort of the twelve brains in the room was a list of four names – five, if you counted Norm's one about the Star Trek perfume. Dyson, Sinclair, Caterpillar and Apple.

It wouldn't have been too disappointing if the ideas had come from all over the enormous conference room he had booked, but the truth was, aside from Norm's contribution, every suggestion had come from Brian.

'Next, we're going to take a look at our assets and capabilities.' He paused and looked around the table. 'Matt, are you with us?'

The Sales Manager looked up from his BlackBerry. 'Assets and capabilities,' he replied, pointedly.

Tony nodded. He had toyed with the option of imposing a BlackBerry amnesty at the door, but decided that on balance, the sales guys would be less cranky if their addiction was fed. 'So, let's get a list up here of everything we have within TransTel – not just Synapse. Everything and anything we have at our disposal.'

A silence settled on the room. After a couple of seconds, a heron could be heard crowing in the lake outside. Tony tried not to panic. He knew that Brian would rescue him if it came to it. The problem was, he didn't want to be rescued. He didn't want this session to consist of a stuttering role-play between two individuals surrounded by a dozen onlookers. Hell, if it was going to be Brian and him coming up with the goods, they could just as well save their energy for a Friday night in the pub with a pen and a couple of beer mats.

'I'll start you off,' he said, yanking the lid off the marker and scrawling *Sales Force* across the flip chart.

'Marketing!' shouted Louise from the other end of the room, quickly catching on. 'Ooh, and research!'

'Good,' Tony nodded, scribbling the words down. 'What else?'

'Customer insight,' the girl whose name Tony could never remember called out. She worked for Louise and was like a younger version of her boss: curly hair, freckly smile, glasses. *Customer insight* was duly noted.

Slowly, the sheet filled up. It was a predictable list, consisting mainly of names of TransTel departments with a couple of curve-balls thrown in by Norm, but it was a start.

'Sales force, marketing, research, customer insight, financing, logistics, partnerships, web tools, network of engineers, Project eFlow… Norm, perhaps you could quickly talk us through Project eFlow…?'

Tony knew, even as the words were leaving his lips, that he was making a mistake. Asking Norm to quickly talk anyone through anything was a contradiction in terms, and in a brainstorm situation, where the swift flow of thoughts was essential, it was a particularly bad idea.

Several minutes later, the Technology Manager finished describing what sounded like a very complicated piece of kit that they were trialling in R&D and that, somehow, he had got his hands on and was trialling in his mother's home.

'So, to summarise,' Tony jumped in, trying desperately to inject some energy back into the session, 'it's a device that allows you to remotely monitor the flow of energy through a device? Wow, okay.' He nodded, intrigued but not convinced that Project eFlow fitted here in the proceedings. 'So, you can see from this list that we have a good set of capabilities to draw on.'

Tony whipped off the page and stuck it up on the wall, glancing briefly at his notes. This was the part where participants were supposed to stand up and put on party hats, each one representing an asset or capability. Looking around at the glum set of faces and the drooping heads, Tony felt glad he had taken the time to tweak the agenda.

'Now, let's think about the Synapse business specifically. I want everyone to come up with a statement about what we do, whether it's relating to the service we offer, the way we deliver it, the market we play in, our business model... anything. Just a simple statement of fact.'

The room fell silent. Even the heron was speechless. Tony looked at his shoes, cursing his own foolish optimism. They didn't know what he was on about. Of course they didn't. This may have worked in a boisterous media firm where everyone wanted to have a say, everyone wanted to be the genius who came up with the winning solution, but TransTel was different. In TransTel, people just wanted to sit at their desks and get paid to do the same thing they did every day. Tony was contemplating the idea of a rejuvenating coffee break when suddenly somebody spoke.

'Synapse provides broadband installation and support for the domestic market.'

Tony couldn't believe it. The voice wasn't Brian's. It was coming from a part of the table that had until now remained silent. The person speaking, he realised, was *Roy*.

'Er, yes,' Tony stuttered and turned to immortalise the statement. Not only was Roy joining in, but he was coming up with exactly the sort of thing Tony had in mind.

'When its members ain't sittin' around starin' into their belly-buttons and talking shit. 'Scuse me language,' he added, with a nod to the Marketing girls.

Tony stopped writing, wondering how to respond. Thankfully, Brian stepped in with a couple of good suggestions before he had time to decide.

Synapse uses own team of engineers, Tony scribbled, relieved to hear Louise and her co-worker joining in from the back. *Operates with subscription model. Markets to household budget-holders.* After a while, even one of the sales guys piped up with a point, much to his boss' disgust. Brian filled the gaps like a hero and before long, they were onto their third page. The team was really getting the hang of the exercise.

'So!' Tony danced away from the row of flip-chart sheets on the wall, feeling buoyed by the rush of activity. 'Now we're going to challenge each of those assumptions. *Why* do we use our own engineers? *Why* do we conform to regulations set out by Ofcom?'

'Because we'd get shut down if we didn't,' murmured Matt, his thumbs still tapping away.

'Okay...' Tony was stumped momentarily. He had chosen a bad example. 'But what if we were to offer a service that didn't sit within Ofcom's jurisdiction?'

Matt looked up. 'What, like we suddenly start selling garden furniture?'

Tony dipped his head as though considering the idea. Garden furniture was probably one step further than he wanted to go today. 'Let's start with the first one on the list, shall we?'

Despite the occasional obtuse interjections from Matt and Roy, the brainstorm was going better than Tony had expected. They weren't 'storming', exactly; perhaps brain-dawdle would have been a more appropriate term, but at least they were moving. The ideas, which weren't *all* feasible or strategically wise, were at least starting to circulate.

'So, to summarise,' Tony looked at the chart and drew a breath. 'It looks as though there are opportunities for us to provide an improved service that caters better to our customers' needs, potentially using some of the new technologies in trial... Oh, and we could change our business model, but we're not sure how.' He paused for a moment. It suddenly seemed as though they hadn't got very far at all. They had succeeded in criticising every element of the current Synapse offering but in terms of concrete solutions, they had nothing.

'Let's talk about *how* we might cater better to our customers' needs,' he said, glancing at the elaborate doodle on Roy's notepad. 'What *are* our customers' needs?'

'To get their broadband installed well and on time,' the marketing girl replied obediently.

Tony nodded. As he turned to write down the point, it dawned on him that *this* was the question they needed to answer. If they were going to offer the market something radically different, they needed to think about what the market was after. It wasn't just about owning the broadband pipe into the home; it was bigger than that. It was about solving a problem in their customers' lives.

'In a *general* sense, what are their needs?' he asked. 'What do they want? What do they lack? What gets them worked up?'

The marketing contingent suddenly burst into life, with Louise and the girl shouting phrases like 'blue collar affluence' and 'municipal dependency segment', all of which Tony felt obliged to write down.

'So... let's take, say, *suburban home-owners*,' he said when they'd finally run out of steam, picking the one with the most comprehensible name. 'What do they need? And don't say broadband.'

It took a while for the others around the table to latch onto what he was asking, but eventually there were some hesitant suggestions.

'To be connected?' muttered one of the sales guys, prompting an evil sideways look from his boss.

'To not spend all their cash on boring things like utilities bills?' said another.

'To live in peace without being psycho-analysed by people like us?' Matt added, unhelpfully.

They were, Tony felt, beginning to make some headway. Roy and Matt aside, everyone seemed to be trying really hard to get inside the minds of their customers, to work out what kept them awake at night, to think up ways in which Synapse could help.

'Great!' cried Tony, frantically scribbling. Someone had even engineered a way of involving Norm's eFlow widget. The session was really kicking off. Suggestions were flying around the room, bouncing, growing, fusing together; there was no stopping them. At least, there *was* no stopping them until

Marianne poked her head round the door and explained, apologetically, that somebody else had the room booked.

'Sorry,' she said, a few seconds later, as she swept the debris from the table into the bin while Tony peeled the pages from the conference room wall. 'Looked as though you were in full swing.'

He nodded, still deep in thought. If they'd just had half an hour longer, he felt sure they would have come up with something.

'Did you get anywhere?' Marianne stamped on the contents of the wastepaper bin.

'Maybe.' Tony rolled up the pages, hoping he'd captured all the trains of thought. He picked up the flip-chart frame and reversed over to where Marianne was waiting, her hand on the door handle.

'Tony,' she said, not opening the door.

Her tone of voice, coupled with the fact that they both knew they had to clear the room quickly, made Tony stop and look up. Marianne's face was deadly serious. For a brief, mad moment, the thought flashed through Tony's mind that she was about to declare her undying love for him, but then he remembered the pictures of the husband and kid that littered her desk.

'This is it, isn't it?'

Tony remained confused as to what this was about. 'I'm sorry?'

She swallowed and looked anxiously about the room. 'I mean… This is it for Synapse, isn't it? If you don't find the answer, they'll shut us down, won't they?'

With a speed that impressed even himself, Tony pulled a face that implied she was way off the mark. 'Don't be silly! Sales are down, but we still have a viable business and one that's an integral part of TransTel.'

Marianne's smile looked as shaky as Tony's convictions felt. 'Right.' She nodded. 'Good.'

Tony beamed back at her, feeling the knot of tension return to his gut. 'No need to worry,' he said. 'Everything's under control.'

Re-deployed, playground with Poppy

'I'M GETTING hassled from all sides. The other day – shit. Where's...?'

The two men rushed over to where the kids had been galloping round an old tree. Suddenly, Poppy was heading off very purposefully towards the playground and Bradley was nowhere to be seen.

'Where's Bradley?'

Poppy giggled. 'Baddy under ground.'

The men looked at one another, then back at the tree where the kids had been playing. The pile of brown leaves at its base started to stir. A tiny pink fist poked out, followed by the rest of the dirty-faced, spluttering three-year-old.

Tony grimaced as Luke brushed off the worst of the debris and picked out a twig from Bradley's hair.

'Sorry mate...' Tony coughed awkwardly.

Luke shrugged, scooping a wad of damp leaves from the back of Bradley's trousers. 'He'll live. Just don't tell the wife, eh.'

'*Wives*,' Tony corrected. It had been Suze's idea for them to take the kids to the park today. She'd been suffering with morning sickness all week – not just in the mornings but all day, every day; the term seemed to be a misnomer – and she needed a break. For her own sake, Tony would spare her the details of their daughter's latest escapade.

'Poppy,' he said, squatting down in front of her and putting on his most serious face. 'You mustn't bury Bradley. It's very unkind.'

She looked earnestly back at him, nodding slowly.

'Will you go and say sorry?'

Poppy looked left, then right, not moving her head. Then she waddled over to Bradley and took his hand. 'Sorry Baddy,' she said, before yanking him in the direction of the swings.

They followed the kids to the play area.

'Sorry,' said Luke. 'You were saying. The pressure.'

Tony watched as his three-year-old spelled out the rules of their next game.

'Well… I've got the chief exec breathing down my neck for his extra fourteen million, the sales guys moaning that the price-points are too high, the whole world on my back about the ridiculous re-brand that happened before I even arrived, and now even my PA's asking what I'm planning to do.'

'Your PA?'

Tony shrugged. 'Everyone's wondering. It's just that Marianne's the only one with guts to ask.'

They arrived at the playground and watched, hands in pockets, as Bradley obligingly pushed Poppy round on the roundabout.

'And what *are* you planning to do?'

Tony looked over and sighed. 'I don't know.'

It was a question he'd been asking himself for the whole of the last week. The brainstorm had helped, but it hadn't provided the answer. It had unlocked a whole load of possibilities, but they were nothing more than that: vague ideas, floating around in his head.

It was like a jigsaw; all the pieces were there but he didn't know how to configure them to create the solution. Or at least, it *felt* as though the pieces were there. Maybe that was the problem; he didn't have enough to work with. He clenched his fists inside his pockets. It was as though his brain would only go so far and then give up.

'It's as though I've got all these assets at my disposal and I can't find a way of using them to make money. It *can't* be that hard.'

'What assets?'

Tony shrugged. Luke was a high-flying radio executive; he

didn't want to know about the tedious inner workings of TransTel.

Luke was looking at him, he realised. Waiting.

'Well,' he said, taking a deep breath. 'We've got a great brand that everybody trusts. We've got marketing and PR capabilities. We can sell, we can work with third parties, we can send engineers into people's homes, provide financing... We have websites and a load of weird and wonderful technology being trialled in R&D–'

'Like what?'

Tony pulled a face, thinking back to Norm's long-winded explanations. 'There's some gadget that lets you remotely track the energy consumption of devices around the home, and then there's–'

'Bradley!' Luke lunged forward. With his full weight, he brought the spinning roundabout to a halt just as his son was about to attempt a kamikaze leap off the edge.

'Poppy said...'

Luke glanced at Tony, planting his son back on firm ground. The little boy stood for a moment, then wobbled and collapsed in a dizzy heap.

'Your daughter has a lot to answer for,' said Luke. 'Smart homes.'

'What?'

'I said, *smart homes*. You're talking about monitoring energy consumption. Controlling what you use, automating how you use it. Isn't that what smart homes are all about? It's a massive growth area.'

Tony stared into space, trying to bridge the gap between Norm's little gadget in R&D and the concept of smart homes. It was true; this was a growth area. Everyone was trying to ride the energy-saving wave – not just the gas and electricity providers but house builders, supermarkets, double glazing firms... it even got mentioned at TransTel from time to time, although nothing ever got beyond the mutterings-in-the-boardroom stage. TransTel was a telecoms company; its only cross-over with energy was when elderly customers got confused and tried to pay them their gas bill.

Smart homes were, as Tony well knew, a long way from TransTel's core line of business – but more than that, they were a long way from *reality*. Every so often, a large corporation would unveil a showcase of their vision for the future – a vision that involved biomass-fuelled households with motion sensor heating and self-cooking food. But invariably they were talking about a world that was forty or fifty years off. Smart homes only existed in showcases and people's heads.

'D'you think…' Tony was trying to blot out the inconvenient details like the fact that the device was still in development and that TransTel had no experience in the energy sector and that his team would probably all walk out on him if he so much as uttered the phrase 'smart home'. 'D'you think that's what people want?'

Luke looked at him, eyes wide. 'Who *wouldn't* want to only pay for the energy they need?'

'But…' He was about to query the way in which such a scheme might be implemented but realised he already knew the answer. They had the network of engineers. The remote monitoring idea was ambitious, but they had the broadband and web capability. They had the call centres. They had the sales force. It was all in place. If anyone could make it work, then TransTel could.

The enormity of Luke's suggestion was only just beginning to sink in. There were flaws in the plan – TransTel's lack of experience in the field, the fact that the product had only so far been trialled in Norm's mother's house, the inevitable reaction of the risk-averse CEO and everyone else – but putting those aside, Tony could see the beginnings of an exciting new proposition. This widget, assuming Norm was right about its potential, could transform the whole concept of energy saving in the home.

'I like it,' he said, vaguely tracking the progress of their children, who were pottering across the playground towards the miniature slide.

'Daddy!' cried Poppy, standing on tip-toes at the top of the plastic structure, her arms stretched towards the sky.

Tony emerged from his thought bubble and realised, too

late, that his daughter was intending to jump from the slide to the rope-swing hanging nearby – although not *that* near. He sprang into life, throwing himself at the ground in the hope of breaking Poppy's fall or perhaps catching her – he didn't have time to form a plan.

A moment later, looking up and blinking into the low winter sun, his daughter blinking down at him, Tony realised what had happened. Poppy had successfully cleared the gap and was hanging haphazardly from the little rope. She looked very pleased with herself.

'Here,' said Luke, standing over him with one hand outstretched. Tony grabbed it. 'I won't laugh.'

Tony allowed himself to be hauled up. 'Thanks.' He shook his head, grinning sheepishly.

Luke nodded at Poppy's writhing body. 'Sometimes the riskiest ideas are the best.'

The idea is born

'SO, THIS JUST CLIPS onto the power cable and monitors the flow of energy?' Tony turned the little grey device around in his hand, suspicious of its apparent simplicity.

'Exactly,' replied Gerry Clark, TransTel's Head of Research and Development.

'Does it run on batteries, or what?'

Gerry shook his head, his hazel eyes crinkling at the edges. 'That would slightly defeat the purpose of an energy saving device, would it not?'

Tony acknowledged the point with a dip of his head. He had very little idea of how these things worked.

'No,' Gerry went on, touching the crop of grey stubble on his chin. He was one of the few men at TransTel who got away with the permanent five o'clock shadow. 'It draws its own power from the magnetic field created by the current passing through the cable.'

'Right.' Tony nodded, none the wiser. 'Good. So, what stage are you at with it? In-house testing? Live trial?'

Gerry looked down and then stared at his feet for a few seconds. 'Ah,' he said eventually.

Tony frowned. 'Norm mentioned he was using a trial version in his – his mother's house,' he prompted.

'Mmm,' Gerry grunted, still talking to his feet. 'You see, that's the problem.'

'What? Norm's mother's–'

'No.' He looked up and shook his head. 'No, the problem is

57

that we can't proceed to the testing or trial stages because we don't have the funding.'

'Oh. Well, have you applied for–'

'No. No, it's not that simple.' Gerry grimaced. Tony was reminded of the time they had worked together – or rather, *tried* to work together in the early days of TransTel CBN. A certain member of the board had been determined to undermine Gerry's work in order to outsource the technology development to a business which, they later realised, was run by some old codger with whom the board member had gone to school. It was the same grimace he was looking at now, only a few years older. 'We don't have the funding *or the authority.*'

Tony waited. He knew how the process worked. He understood that obtaining permission to get things done was often harder than actually getting the job done. But Gerry was an old-timer. He knew the tricks. He could get round the roadblocks, cut through the tape. Why didn't he have the authority?

'We've been, er, developing this product for a few months…' He sucked on his bottom lip. 'Under the radar, if you will.'

Tony nodded, slowly.

'Remember the divisional re-structure back in March? When R&D got split into two?'

Tony nodded again, still uncertain. He remembered the company re-structure; his current position was a product of the fall-out. But as for the effect it had had on R&D, he hadn't a clue.

'Well, officially I now head up 'core' R&D, and all 'non-core' initiatives have to go through the incubator – headed up by Ethan Winterborne. Project eFlow was deemed 'non-core', so that went with him.'

Ethan Winterborne. Of course. Tony remembered it now. The least dynamic member of the executive committee had been put in charge of incubation. It was no wonder TransTel was in trouble.

'Anyway, Ethan didn't think much of it.' Gerry leaned forward and lowered his voice. 'To be honest, I don't think he really understood the concept.'

'Ah.'

'So the project got canned and for a while, that was that. But I happened to keep most of the original team, and we sort of carried on working on it, you know, in our spare time…'

Tony began to smile. Yes, he knew. He had worked 'under the radar' before. He had pinched budgets, borrowed resources and been creative with his reporting to keep side projects afloat. Sometimes it was the only way.

'So…' Tony looked at the director. 'Would you be allowed to resurrect it if there was deemed to be a commercial application for the device?'

'Ah.' Gerry pulled a face. 'Well. See, I tried that. I got the guys in TransTel Tech to work on an in-home energy monitoring system.'

'And?'

Gerry's smile didn't reach his eyes. 'The whole thing backfired. I was talking to the wrong people. TransTel Tech didn't have a clue how to write a business case, so the board turned the idea down and it was dead in the water.'

'Oh.' Tony couldn't hide his disappointment. It was one thing to propose taking a new, risky idea to the TransTel board, but taking an *old,* risky idea was in another league of insanity.

'And then there's the patent.'

Tony looked up, sensing more bad news.

'It was pending until a few months ago, but we had to withdraw the application in the clean-up exercise.'

Tony leaned forward and rubbed his eyes. The whole idea was becoming less and less appealing.

'It's a joke,' said Gerry, shaking his head. 'It's obvious that sooner or later, someone's going to come up with a gadget exactly like this and it'll become the household standard in British homes. But instead of putting everything we've got into it, we're going to let someone else get there first.'

There was a short, contemplative silence.

'D'you really believe that?' asked Tony, holding the grey gadget between them. 'That this is going to become a household standard?'

Gerry narrowed his eyes. 'Yes, I do. If we could get it to trial stage, I'm almost certain we could push it out there.'

'Hmm.' Tony let the device drop onto the table and thought for a while. The situation was far more complex than he had imagined. The idea of pitching his 'smart home' surprise to the board had been daunting enough before he had discovered that they'd already heard it. And to re-kindle a project that had officially been extinguished by the powers that be... well, that was a fool's game. For a start, it would mean Gerry admitting that he'd been stoking the fire for the last few months – spending time and budget allocated to other things on his pet project, keeping the embers aglow. It was a lot to ask of the man. But then...

'What were you hoping would happen?' asked Tony. 'Were you planning to take it to trial, still under the radar?'

Gerry laughed. 'No. It's a bit tricky getting people to test TransTel devices without telling the TransTel exec.'

'Other than Norm's mum.'

'Other than Norm's mum. Actually, he shouldn't have done that – the device hasn't passed Health and Safety yet.'

Tony drew a breath. 'Tut, tut.'

'No, to be honest, I'm not sure where we were going with it. We've hit a brick wall. The product's been refined and refined but we can't trial it until it's been sanctioned.'

They lapsed into silence. It was no longer a straightforward decision; Tony could see that now. The see-saw was loaded more heavily than he had imagined, at both ends. On one side, there was the risk of being turned down by the board, being laughed out of his job, dragging Gerry down with him. But on the other, there was the steady, unrelenting decline of his existing business and, in a way, the same risk of being laughed out of his job – just for different reasons.

The rewards had changed, too. With Gerry's superior insight into the potential for this device, he felt more buoyed than ever about the prospect of rolling it out across the nation. *Household standard.* Of all the phrases Tony would have liked to have associated with his name, that was right up there at the top. The idea of working on a venture that went on to become a household standard made Tony want to jump up and start writing the business plan.

At exactly the same time, the men looked up. Tony couldn't be sure, but he had a feeling, judging by the expression on Gerry's face, that they were thinking the same thing.

'Would you back me, if I tried to get this thing going?'

Gerry looked at him. 'What do you think?'

They returned to the open plan office, both wearing quietly confident smiles.

'Oh, and Tony?' Gerry lightly tapped his shirt sleeve. 'Word of advice. When you're pitching to the board, remember: *it was all their idea.*'

Tony nodded. He knew exactly what Gerry meant.

COMING UP WITH A WINNING IDEA

COMING UP WITH A WINNING IDEA

 MarketGravity

In this chapter Tony recognises the need for transformational change but has no effective way of identifying how. Internal brainstorming sessions are frustrating and fail to deliver much insight. It's only when Tony begins to look outside his industry and begins to challenge existing assumptions that his efforts bear fruit. The following are typical challenges that businesses face when trying to come up with innovative new growth opportunities:

- Struggling to generate new ideas that are also commercially viable
- Failing to produce breakthrough ideas using traditional brainstorming methods
- Not being able to get the most out of the expertise in the organisation
- Not knowing when an idea is good enough to take forward or bad enough to kill
- Trying to do too many things at once

Indicators that your idea generation process may lack commerciality include: an addiction to brain storming but no process for identifying and progressing good ideas; a myriad of small projects that don't go anywhere or have no commercial significance; an inability to elevate ideas beyond single concepts into big commercial initiatives; a culture of scepticism with a feeling of "here we go again". If this sounds familiar, it's time to reconsider your approach.

"THE COMPANY HAD LOTS OF IP, CLEVER WIDGETS AND SYSTEMS THAT COULD ENABLE A FUTURISTIC HOME OWNER TO DO CLEVER THINGS, BUT THEY WEREN'T THINKING ABOUT WHAT PEOPLE ACTUALLY WANTED TO DO. THEY WERE DRIVEN BY THEIR TECHNOLOGY, NOT THEIR USERS' NEEDS."

Michael Johnson, Orange, BT, Thomas Cook

There's a big difference between an idea and a great idea that can genuinely stimulate growth in your business. Here are some things to try:

1. Take stock of your capabilities. Often you have more going for you than you think. A workshop with people from different parts of the business can reveal new opportunities.

2. Break your assumptions. Big business are often myopic about what they can and can't do because of legacy views and sacred cows. Take a major assumption and see what opportunities arise when you break it (think Dell and the PC industry assumptions that home computers had to be manufactured in advance and sold through retailers).

3. Assume the role of a challenger brand. Think like a new market entrant and attack your own company or other market leader. What would you do differently and how would you win?

4. Look at adjacent markets or new geographies. Some of the best ideas are out there already. Trawl the internet to see what you can learn from other industries and territories.

5. Learn the art of clustering and theming. Nine times out of ten you won't find a silver bullet. Much of the art of opportunity identification lies in combining ideas together. Write all your ideas onto post-it notes and get them up on a wall. See how they can be combined to form something bigger and better.

6. Don't get hung up on feasibility, focus instead on size of the prize. This is the time for "what can we do?" Not, "can we do it?" Don't kill ideas too early because you have reservations over how to deliver them. If the prize is big enough, you will find a way.

Market Gravity applies a variety of approaches to focus creative thinking. Two examples that you can try are outlined below:

1. Challenger Brands
Thinking like a new entrant or market challenger

Approach:

Objectives:
- To enable entrepreneurial thinking within the organisation
- To develop ideas that challenge the industry norm

Introduce the concept of the Market Challenger

↓

Apply a Challenger mindset to your industry

↓

Tips:
- Use an example of a well-know challenger to get into the mindset
- Ask "how would this company compete in our situation?"
- Ask "what can we learn from the new entrants? How will we compete against them?"

Select the best Challenger ideas

↓

Define the characteristics of your new offering

2. Clusters and Themes
Clustering related opportunities and common themes

Approach:

Objectives:
- To build several smaller ideas up into a single bigger proposition
- To concentrate activities around a number of common themes
- To help prioritise a wide range of options

Identify a large numbers of ideas or projects

↓

Isolate the main themes and common elements

↓

Group similar ideas together

↓

Tips:
- Try to align the themes to the overall business objectives
- Cluster in a way that the sum is greater that the value of the parts
- Use clusters to create a proposition roadmap, linking ideas in a sequence

Define the combined opportunity

3

Winning hearts and minds: the art of stakeholder management

'You can't build a new business in isolation.'

Explaining the proposition

'NO, NO, STAY THERE. I'm buying.' Tony dumped his coat on the brown, threadbare seat and forced a smile. 'What're you drinking?'

The Sales Manager puffed out his cheeks and squinted in the direction of the taps. 'IPA. Thanks mate.'

Mate. Tony weaved his way through the Thursday night drinkers and planted an elbow on the bar. It wasn't the term he would have used, but then, he was hardly in a position to criticise. Tony was the one who had stopped by Matt's desk and casually dropped into conversation his suggestion for an after-work beer. It had been his idea to pretend they were pals.

The Red Lion was situated exactly half way between the TransTel business park and the M4. Furnished with plastic, foam-filled seats and fake oak beam rafters, it wasn't the most atmospheric establishment, but it served beer and it was within walking distance of the office. As usual, a good proportion of its clientele looked to be TransTel employees: young men in nylon suits, young graduates, one or two overall-clad engineers and more than a few grey heads. Tony ordered the pints and a packet of crisps, trying to work out how to start the conversation.

His meeting with Matt would, he knew, be more demanding than the equivalent exchange he had had with the bubbly Louise over a cappuccino and muffin earlier in the day. Even Roy, whom he was taking for a slap-up lunch later in the week, would probably prove less of a challenge to bring round than the young Sales Manager. Tony pocketed the change and stretched his fingers around the drinks. There was only one way to play it, he decided: be blunt.

Matt glanced up from his BlackBerry for just long enough to ascertain where his pint was on the table, then with impressive dexterity, continued to type with one thumb, drawing his beer towards him with the other hand.

'So,' said Tony, breaking open the bag of crisps and hoping to lure the salesman's attention away from the handset. 'How're things?'

Suddenly, the device was slammed face-down on the table and slid out of arm's reach. Matt sipped the head off his beer and set it down firmly, looking Tony in the eye.

'Look,' he said. 'No disrespect or anything, but I've got a feeling you didn't ask me for a pint to discuss how "things" are.' He etched quotation marks in the air.

'No,' Tony mumbled, wishing he'd stuck to his plan and got straight to the point. 'You're right.'

'I figured you were either gonna sack me for not hitting my targets or tell me that the department's being shut down and I'm no longer needed.' He raised an eyebrow.

'Um... No. No, it's neither of those things.' Tony felt flustered, all of a sudden. 'I, um, I have some news. It's about the direction of the department.'

It was impossible to gauge Matt's reaction as he reached for a handful of crisps. He was a true salesman, rarely letting emotions interfere with his cocky charm.

'As you know, we've been looking at various options following on from the brainstorm.'

Matt supped his beer, nodding slowly.

'And I'm sure you're aware of the idea being floated...' Tony watched for a sign: a curl of the lip, a roll of the eyes. There was none. He could only guess what Matt thought of the smart home plan. 'So I wanted to give you more of an idea about what it entails, what we're aiming for... that sort of thing.'

There was the briefest of nods. Tony knew – in fact, they probably both knew – that he wasn't being entirely honest about the objectives of their meeting today. A lot had happened since their team brainstorm two weeks ago. Without making anything official, Tony had spent much of his time working on the feasibility of the smart home concept. But sharing details of call-out schedules and sell-on potential was not Tony's goal for this evening. What he really wanted to do, what he *needed* to do, was get his Sales Manager on side. This was about persuading Matt to buy into the vision. Without the support of his team, there was no point in pitching the idea to the board.

Reaching for the pen in his pocket, Tony grabbed a napkin from the greasy container on the table and drew a small, square house in the middle. Without daring to look at Matt's face, he added a line for the broadband and, on the other side, one for the gas and electricity. A minute later, with various representations of the Synapse divisions incorporated, the sketch was complete. He spun it round on the table and talked the young manager through the proposition.

'And on that basis, we could be looking at revenues of up to fifty million within three years,' he finished.

Matt picked the last crisp from the packet and said nothing. He stared at the napkin for what seemed like a very long time, his expression remaining unreadable.

'Bloody hell,' he said eventually.

Tony waited. He wasn't sure whether Matt was impressed or annoyed.

'I can't believe we're pinning our hopes on a brainwave of some Trekkie who can't even get dressed properly in the mornings.'

Tony nodded, no longer in any doubt about the camp in which his Sales Manager sat. 'Um, is it the smart home concept that worries you?'

Matt stared back at him as if he had completely missed the point.

'I'll tell you what worries me,' he said, tipping back the remains of his pint and staring straight at his boss. 'It's the fact that we're a broadband business in a telecoms company. For my whole career, I've been selling telco products. I manage a team that sells telco products. And now, suddenly we're talking about *energy reduction. That's* what worries me.'

Tony tried to decide how to tackle the accusation, aware that Matt's glass was empty while his was almost untouched.

67

'You're right,' he said, wondering how quickly he could sink a pint these days. 'We *are* a telecoms company and up until now, we have been selling broadband products.' *But not enough of them,* he nearly added. 'However, we need to move with the market. Smart homes are a natural extension of what we do now, and actually fit better with telcos than they do with energy providers.'

Matt grunted and picked at the salty crisp crumbs in the bottom of the packet.

'Let me get you another drink.'

Matt didn't even pretend to protest.

Watching as the amber liquid slowly filled the pint glass, Tony tried to think of a way to bring the young man around. Of all his direct reports, Matt was always going to be the hardest to persuade. He was sharp, cynical and suspicious of change – like most of the team – but he was also arrogant. He had sufficient nerve to doubt his superiors. Louise had been easy in comparison. Whatever misgivings she'd had about Tony's proposal, she hadn't dared voice them. Even Roy would eventually come round, with enough persuasion. Matt, though, he was a problem. You couldn't brainwash him; he needed to *want* the change.

'I suppose it'll mean more bloody marketing campaigns,' said the salesman, lifting his fresh pint in grudging appreciation.

'Well, that tends to be the case with new products,' Tony replied, risking a smile.

Matt looked up at the ceiling. 'More coloured jump-suits and flowery logos from Louise's lot?'

Tony opened his hands ambiguously. At some point, he needed to address the rift that seemed to exist between his Head of Sales and his Marketing Manager, but now was not the time. 'There will be a marketing push, yes, but not on the scale of the re-brand.'

Matt grunted again, looking uninspired. Tony desperately tried to think of a way to bring him round. He wasn't lazy, just averse to the idea of change – particularly change that involved his job.

And then Tony realised. Suddenly, it was obvious what

turned Matt on and off. Tony couldn't believe he hadn't seen it before. It was all about *him*. His position. His salary. He didn't like the idea of extra work for no extra reward. There was no point in describing the merits of the smart home project in terms of revenue forecasts or strategic rationale. Matt didn't give a shit about the bigger picture; he didn't care whether Synapse entered new markets with a ground-breaking new technology that pushed TransTel ahead of all its competitors. He just cared about the cash.

'Look,' said Tony, watching as Matt tipped back his head and took another large swig of beer. 'Whilst I envisage your role ending up not that dissimilar to the one you perform at the moment – just with a different product – I acknowledge that the transition period will involve quite a bit of extra work.'

'No kidding.'

Tony wasn't sure, but he thought he saw a slight hesitation as Matt lowered his glass to the table – a recognition, perhaps. A faltering of opinion.

'So,' Tony went on, winging it now. 'I'm going to request pay rises for certain members of the team – you being one of them.'

There was a twitch at the corners of Matt's mouth.

'No guarantees at this stage, obviously. Keep this to yourself. I've yet to take the idea to the board. But I just wanted to make you aware that your efforts won't go unnoticed.'

'Right.' Matt nodded into his pint glass. There was an unmistakable smirk on his lips.

'So, any questions? Does that all sound okay?'

'Yeah.' He looked up and caught Tony's eye. 'Yeah, I guess so.'

'Good.'

The salesman shrugged his well-worked shoulders. 'Thanks for the beer, mate.'

HR *doesn't like promotions*

'I KNOW it's not *protocol*,' Tony explained, looking at Natasha's over-plucked eyebrows and willing the girl to see his point. 'But if I don't incentivise my staff, they'll walk out. And the cost of recruiting and training a replacement far outweighs the costs associated with the promotion.'

The HR representative looked down at her notes and started drumming her long, fuchsia finger nails on the desk.

'Hmm.'

'Do you see the problem?'

'Hmm.' The drumming stopped. 'I do, yes. I'm just thinking about how we'd get round this without going outside company protocol.'

Tony sighed. They were going round in circles. All he wanted to do was get provisional approval from HR for the performance-related pay rise he was proposing for his Head of Sales and for Roy's potential promotion.

Two things had come to light during his lunch with Roy the previous week. Firstly, there was the realisation that Tony, however hard he tried, would never earn the respect of the embittered Operations Manager who was twenty years his senior. In Roy's eyes, he was too young, too middle-class and too well educated to be running a business unit within the TransTel institution. Secondly, Tony had discovered the pride Roy felt in achieving his position from such a humble roots. He would stop at nothing to protect his reputation as Apprentice-done-good. It was a long shot, but Tony's hope was that the stubborn Operations Manager might be brought round if it meant enhancing his career prospects further. All Tony needed was the carrot.

'What title are you proposing for...' Natasha looked at her notes.

'Roy,' Tony put in. 'Managing Director of Synapse.'

She frowned. 'But... that's *your* title.'

'I know. But if the new venture takes off then I'll be Managing Director of the new business unit. My current day-to-day role will need filling while I'm working on the pilot. Roy is a very capable individual and I'd like to put him forward for the role.'

Natasha squinted at him as though Tony had suddenly started talking in Cantonese.

'Look,' he said, resisting the urge to reach across and shake the girl. 'It's complicated. Roy won't *literally* be taking my job, but it needs to look as though that's what's happened. On paper, Roy needs to be Managing Director.'

'On the same salary?'

'No. Just a little more than he's on at the moment.'

'Taking effect from... now?'

'No!' Tony took a breath and exhaled, slowly. 'No. This is all hypothetical. He'll only be MD if the project goes ahead. But I need to motivate him in order to get the project moving.'

'Right.' Natasha nodded. 'Okay.'

'So, can I take it as a yes?'

'Take what as a yes?'

'The promotion,' Tony replied, nearly losing it. 'Permission for the promotion. And the pay rise for my Sales Manager.'

'Oh, well I'll have to look into it. It's just that there's–'

'Protocols?' Tony couldn't believe it. This was like talking to one of those self-checkout machines at the supermarket. *Please remove item from bagging area...*

'Yeah. That's the thing. I mean, there's a pay freeze at the moment...'

Tony leaned forward. He wasn't a violent man, but there were moments when he wished he had a more menacing physique. 'Natasha, that's why I'm here. I *know* there are protocols. I know there's a pay freeze. I realise I'm asking for something different here. But I need your help. I need to make sure I've got the authority to offer my team the incentives they require to get the job done and keep making money for our firm.'

Natasha bit her lower lip and started to nod.

'Is that okay?'

She stopped nodding and looked at her notepad. Then she wrote something down that ended with a very deliberate full-stop and smiled at Tony.

'Okay. I'll see what I can do.'

Nicholas Draper calls Tony in

'OKAY, NOW THE OTHER ARM...'

Poppy's limbs were whirling like miniature wind turbines in a gale. Tony glanced at his BlackBerry as he attempted again to insert the sleeve into the slipstream. It was nearly nine o'clock.

'Peppa Pig! Peppa Pig!'

Poppy skipped over to the sofa and started ferreting around for the remote control, her top rumpled up around her ribs.

'Okay, let's wait for–' Tony sighed as the TV sprang into life. 'Right. Peppa Pig it is.' He reached for the device just as Poppy discovered the volume button.

Usually, Suze did the handover. Apparently she managed to get Poppy dressed, fed and settled at the kitchen table doing something constructive like drawing by eight a.m., giving her an hour to clear her inbox and get started on her day's work before Anja arrived. Tony didn't understand how this was possible. On the rare occasions when Suze had an important meeting or a problem at work, like today, their nanny would invariably open the door to a scene of chaos involving either Poppy or Tony in a state of undress and toys all over the floor.

'Duce, daddy!' cried his daughter, slipping off the sofa just as Tony had opened his first email of the day: a note from Marianne to say that she'd managed to secure a half-hour slot with Charles Gable in two weeks' time. Tony slid the device onto the kitchen work surface and poured a small measure of orange squash into Poppy's favourite cup. He had a fortnight to pull together something that would persuade the CEO to sign off on the concept of the new proposition. Or rather, he had small snatches of borrowed time taken from his and his colleagues' day jobs between now and the end of November. It wasn't long.

Poppy breathlessly guzzled the squash and planted it back on the table for a refill. 'Better than Mummy's,' she said, banging the cup a few times to prise her father's attention away from the Blackberry. Tony was absorbed in the reply from Amit's whiz-kid in Finance whom he had asked for covert assistance on the smart home project.

Sounds interesting. I'd be happy to do some back-of-envelope forecasts for you. I actually know some guys in the energy sector, which might help with assumptions? Do call to discuss.
No probs re. keeping quiet. More interesting than my day job!
Chek-Han

Tony smiled, absent-mindedly refilling Poppy's cup. That was something. At least he wouldn't be plucking figures out of thin air to show the CEO in two weeks' time. *Shit.* Tony swooped down and retrieved the freshly-poured squash, suddenly registering what his daughter had said a minute earlier. They were supposed to be trying to remove E numbers from Poppy's diet. Suze's mum was convinced that she was hyperactive and in an effort to prove her wrong, Suze had imposed a strict ban on Smarties, mini muffins, the whole Bob the Builder snack range and orange squash. The idea was to report no overall difference in behaviour, which seemed to Tony to defeat the purpose of conducting the experiment, but rules were rules.

'Sorry Pops,' he said, tipping the orange liquid down the sink. 'You can have a different juice instead.'

'Whyyyyyy?' whinged Poppy, wiping her sticky fingers on his suit trousers.

'It's even nicer,' Tony lied, taking the organic fair trade orange cordial out of the fridge.

'Whyyyyyy?' she screeched, tugging at Tony's trousers just as he was pouring the juice, causing the cup to jerk sideways, over the edge of the counter, onto her head and all over his right shoe. Just as the screaming rose to a pitch beyond human hearing range, the door opened.

Anja stood for a second, surveying the situation. Then she made a heroic lunge for Poppy, who seemed so taken aback by the nanny's appearance she forgot all about her sticky hair and orange squash ban. Tony shot Anja a grateful look and grabbed the dishcloth, wiping the worst of the cordial from his shoe.

'Where is Poppy's bottle?' asked Anja, cleverly engaging in a game of hide-and-seek that meant that Poppy had to be quiet for at least a minute at a time.

'Er... her cup's in the sink.'

'No. Her bottle. Special bottle.'

Tony gathered his jacket and BlackBerry. *Special bottle*? When did his child's drinking arrangements become so complicated?

'You know... Special milk.' Anja started gesturing with her hands. Tony looked at her blankly.

'I have no idea,' he said, putting his jacket down again and poking speculatively in all the obvious places.

Having failed to find any bottles that looked vaguely special in the dishwasher, in the cupboards, on the draining board and in Poppy's bedroom, he did what any competent father would have done.

'*Yes?*' hissed Suze, in a way that indicated she wasn't all that pleased to hear from him.

'Sorry, are you busy?'

'*Yes*,' she said, slightly breathlessly. The background hum suggested a large roomful of people. 'Is something wrong?'

'Oh, well, no. Um...' It was overwhelmingly obvious to Tony, suddenly, that he should not have called his wife to ask the whereabouts of Poppy's special bottle. 'It doesn't matter. Problem solved. Sorry.'

'Tony, what is it?'

'No, don't worry. You're busy.'

'Well I'm here now. You've already interrupted my conversation with the Right Honourable Lord Justice, Chairman of the Law Commission, so you may as well tell me what's up.'

Tony briefly considered inventing some dire emergency to justify the phone call but decided against it. 'Well, Anja was asking for a bottle of some description and we can't find it, and I have to go–'

Suze let out a noise that was somewhere between a growl and a scream. 'Tony, I am speaking at the Annual City Lawyers' Convention in ten minutes. I've been vomiting all morning and you're calling me to ask about Poppy's bottle?'

'Sorry, I'll–'

'Try her den. I've got to go.'

Tony started to wish his wife good luck with the speech but the line was already dead. He darted across the room, stooped down and ran a hand around the inside of Poppy's playpen, bringing out an elephant-shaped bottle filled with what looked like milk. Anja gave him a thumbs-up and tossed him his jacket in exchange for the bottle, virtually pushing him onto the street.

It was nearly half past nine by the time he arrived at the business park entrance, having spent his journey half-tuned in to the weekly team conference call, cursing his own stupidity and trying to decide whether flowers were the right way to apologise to Suze.

'Nicholas Draper called,' said Marianne, as soon as he stepped over the threshold. 'He wants to see you in his office at ten. Roy's been skulking around, complaining about something or other, and the quarterly sales reports are on your desk. I asked Matt to email them to you as well.'

Tony nodded, glancing at the clock above Marianne's head. He had twenty-five minutes to work through his inbox, pacify his disgruntled Operations Manager and come up with some sort of excuse for the latest set of disastrous sales figures to appease the FD. Tony knew they were disastrous; he didn't need to look at the sheets on his desk. He could only imagine that Nicholas Draper, the sour-faced FD, had got wind of the situation and was calling him in for an explanation. Dumping his jacket on the back of his chair, Tony switched on his machine and held the sales report up to the dull grey light that was trickling through the blinds.

'Matt,' he called, hanging out of his office a moment later. 'Can you come and explain something?'

They both sat in silence for a minute, the print-off lying between them on Tony's desk.

'Ah, yeah mate.' Matt nodded, still looking at the graph on the first page. Ever since their little chat in the pub, the Sales Manager had taken to appending the word 'mate' to everything he said to his boss. It would have been touching, had it not been so obvious that Matt's affections were driven purely by his desire for promotion.

'What d'you mean?' asked Tony, eyeing the sharp kink in the revenue chart with disdain. 'How d'you explain it?'

'Huh. That'll be the Netcomm thing.'

'The *Netcomm thing*?'

'Well, yeah. They introduced this bonus scheme thing for their sales guys, so a few of our men went and joined them.'

'Right.' Tony paused for a second, hoping he didn't need to ask the obvious.

Matt looked back at him across the table and it became clear that Tony *did* need to ask.

'Why didn't I know about this?'

Matt shrugged. 'Dunno.'

Tony considered asking *why* Matt didn't know why Tony didn't know, but decided that aggravation would be futile. 'Can you send me a detailed summary of the incentive package they're offering at Netcomm? If our competitors are working on that basis, there's no reason why we can't too. I'm especially keen to review our pay schemes for the new business, if and when it goes live.'

'Right. Yeah. 'Course, mate.' Matt got up and left the room, looking buoyed by the prospect of a pay review.

Tony tried not to let the situation affect his mood as he opened up Outlook and watched the messages pour in. Initiative wasn't something that could be taught. In an ideal world, Tony would have picked his own team of managers: a group of smart, motivated individuals, all working for the same goal, all skilled in their own respective fields. But he didn't live in an ideal world. Tony was stuck with the mixed bag of co-workers he had inherited from Rupert Beasley's reign, and there was no point in lamenting the impossible.

Skimming the back pages of Matt's sales report, Tony grabbed a pen and his BlackBerry and with his spare finger, hooked the mug of tea that had magically appeared on his desk.

'Oh, hi.' Tony reversed back into his office, taking care not to spill his tea as the large figure barged his way through the door. 'Sorry Roy, I'm just...'

'Won't take long,' said the Operations Manager, lumbering over to the visitor's chair and settling heavily into it. 'I just came to tell you my opinion.'

Tony hesitated, the tea starting to burn his knuckles. It was two minutes to ten. There was barely enough time to get over to Nicholas Draper's office, let alone hear Roy's opinions – which, given the look on the bald man's face, Tony suspected might be considerable. Their lunch meeting the previous week had gone better than he had expected, but that wasn't saying much. They had parted on an agreement whereby Roy would come back to his line manager 'in due course' when he'd had time to think about the proposition. Tony didn't believe in miracles; he knew that this would be an iterative process. He just didn't have time to iterate right now.

'I'm just heading off to see–'

'Don't worry,' said Roy, spinning round gently in the swivel chair. 'Won't take a sec. Basically, I've thought about this smart home thing and I've decided what I think of it.'

Tony looked at him, shifting the mug in his hand.

'It's bollocks.' Roy shrugged. 'I've worked for this company for nearly forty years. *Forty years.* I know it inside out. I know what works and what doesn't. And I can spot a duff idea when I see one.'

'Okay.' Tony was torn. He didn't want to leave their conversation like this, but he didn't want to aggravate the FD. 'Can we have a proper chat about this later?'

'No need,' he said. 'I've made my decision.'

Tony hesitated, not wanting to point out the fact that the decision about the future direction of Synapse was not actually Roy's to make.

'I'll get Marianne to put in some time this afternoon,' he

said, slipping through the door before the Operations Manager could object.

Roy was a problem. The quality of his work was never an issue; he worked hard at everything he did. He just had an aversion to working for Tony.

Two minutes later, Tony burst into the Finance Director's office, apologising like a schoolboy summoned to see the headmaster. Lukewarm tea was dribbling slowly down his wrist.

'Anthony.' Nicholas Draper looked up, acknowledging Tony with a slight narrowing of his eyes and a vague nod towards the vacant seat. He was the only person in the company who insisted on using Tony's full name.

'So,' said Tony, finally getting a grip on his breathing. That gym membership was going to waste. 'Doesn't make great reading, does it?' He slid the sales report onto Nicholas' desk between them.

Nicholas glanced at the print-out, then at Tony's face. He wasn't the type to ever look cheerful, exactly, but today he seemed positively morose.

'It never does,' he replied. 'But that's not why I wanted to catch up.'

'Oh?' Tony blinked at the man's bony face, feeling like the schoolboy again.

'No. It's about your plans for turning around the Synapse business.'

Tony held his gaze, wondering what exactly he meant. Of course, the board was disappointed with the small impact he'd made so far. But he already knew that, and besides, that was for Charles Gable to say – not Draper.

'Plans for a… *smart home* business?' Draper clarified.

Tony's heart started pounding. Draper wasn't supposed to know about the smart home proposition. Nobody was, aside from the members of his core team and a few trusted aides, who had all been sworn to secrecy. He hadn't even explained it to HR. It wasn't ready for public scrutiny. At this point, it was little more than a vague idea that he hoped might take them out of the hot water. It certainly wasn't in any state to discuss with Nicholas Draper.

'How...'

'On the grapevine,' Draper cut in. 'But that's beside the point. The point, I suppose, is more along the lines of why you're looking into something that has already been assessed and dismissed.'

'Oh, right. You mean the TransTel Tech team's—'

'Yes, I do.'

'Well, as I understand it,' Tony explained, thinking back to Gerry Clark's advice, 'that was a slightly different concept. This one fits well with our—'

'And how much investment are you looking for?'

'Well...' Tony tried to compose himself. He wasn't ready for these questions. 'We're not at a stage where I can answer that yet.'

The FD's cheeks, which were so gaunt that he appeared to be permanently sucking on his cheeks, hollowed further. 'You mean, you're not at a stage where you *want* to answer it?'

Tony looked him in the eye. Nicholas Draper was known for his caustic questioning technique. 'I mean, we've barely started looking at the business case, so we don't know what we'll be looking for.'

'But you know that your proposition is sufficiently different from the one TransTel Technology put forward?'

'I believe so.' Tony maintained eye contact, determined not to follow up with one of his rambling, apologetic explanations.

'Tell me, Anthony. Are we talking hundreds of thousands? Millions?'

'I don't know.'

'I only ask,' Draper went on, 'because I don't like to see valuable resources wasted on a project that won't come to anything.'

A surge of anger flared up inside him but Tony managed to keep it contained. Who was Draper to say what would or wouldn't come to anything? He controlled the purse strings, but that didn't mean he could play God. Synapse was sinking, fast. The smart home plan was currently their only hope of a turnaround and yet he was trying to kill the venture before it even got off the ground.

'I'm being very economical with resources while I work on the investment case,' he said calmly. 'I see this as a real opportunity for TransTel and I don't want it to slip through our fingers.'

'The problem being,' said Draper, making a pathetic attempt at a smile, 'we can't afford to *keep* it in our fingers.'

'With all due respect, Nicholas, I don't think we can afford to go on as we are, either.'

The FD's lips pulled together like the draw-string on a bag. Tony watched him, trying to work out what was going on. He knew that the FD was tight; everyone in TransTel knew that. But this was worse than tight. This was insane. Draper was effectively writing off a prospective revenue stream without even cursory consideration.

All of a sudden, he was itching to get out. He needed to think this through – to arm himself properly. If he was going into battle, he needed to know who his enemy was.

'I'll pull something together in the next few weeks,' Tony said, grabbing his mug as he rose to his feet. 'That'll give you more of an idea of what we're looking at.'

The FD stared for a moment at the brown ring of tea that had formed on his desk. Then he looked up and shot Tony a withering look.

'Really, Anthony. Don't waste your time.'

12-week scan; Amit explains politics

'THAT TOO COLD?'

The sonographer dabbed a small amount of jelly on the bulbous, exposed flesh.

Suze shook her head from behind the swathe of blue paper towels. Tony looked away. It wasn't that he was squeamish, exactly, he just didn't like hospitals, or most of the procedures that went on inside them. God only knew how he'd get through the birth. He'd probably keep his eyes shut as he had done the last time.

'It won't show anything yet,' said the woman, nodding at the blank screen. 'I haven't started the scan.'

Tony nodded awkwardly and tried to find something else to look at. The hospital room was full of things he didn't want to see: spongy foetus replicas, giant ovaries, cut-away wombs containing cut-away babies. He settled on a vase of plastic flowers by the window.

'Oh!' gasped Suze.

He whirled round to see, in black and white, a grainy image of their unborn child. He or she was lying face up, curled neatly with one partially-formed hand up against his or her mouth. The sonographer pointed out the little beating heart and Tony felt something lurch inside him.

'It looks so peaceful!' cried Suze, wiping a tear from her eye with a corner of one of the enormous blue paper towels.

'It's a good size,' said the woman, pressing buttons on a machine behind the monitor and setting off a chain reaction of bleeps and whirs. 'The head circumference is... nearly seven centimetres.'

82

Tony couldn't take his eyes off the screen. It was incredible to think that this tiny thing, with its jelly-bean body and cricket-like legs, was nestled inside his wife.

'Here you go,' said the sonographer, presenting Suze with a print-off and briskly wiping the gunk off her belly. 'You'll want to keep this with your notes for the midwife. Your due date is June the second.'

Suze broke free of the paper towels and pulled down her top, studying the image as though every pixel was a small miracle – which it was.

'Good luck.'

Stopping briefly for Suze to empty her bladder (which, for reasons Tony didn't want to understand, had had to be full for the duration), they headed into the watery sunshine of the hospital car park.

'It all feels a bit surreal,' Suze remarked, touching her belly instinctively and taking Tony's hand.

Tony looked at her. She seemed to be pulling him away from the direction of their car.

'I don't feel like going back to work,' she explained.

Tony smiled. He couldn't have agreed more. The very thought of going back to his office and his stalling 'turnaround' project made him want to stay on this soggy patch of wasteland forever.

They wandered in silence across the piece of grass that seemed to serve as the local dog-walking spot. Tony felt euphoric, having seen the scan of his unborn child, but also frustrated. Usually, he was good at drawing a line between his job and his personal life. When he left the office on a Friday, he would leave behind his spiralling sales, discontented employees and missed deadlines. When he pulled up outside the house, he would slam the car door on his budget constraints and walk through the porch already thinking about bedtime stories and dinner and Suze. But over the course of the last few days, the line had blurred. Little reminders of his problems at work kept leaking into his private life. Only this morning he had caught himself replaying his conversation with Nicholas Draper as he tried to coax spoonfuls of porridge into Poppy's mouth.

'Maybe that's what I'll be saying in six months' time!' Suze squeezed his hand.

Tony echoed her laughter, trying to remember what they were talking about. Then he realised, with horror, what his wife was implying.

'You don't think you'll want to be a stay-at-home mum, do you?'

He was appalled on two fronts. Firstly, it would mean that he had completely misunderstood the principles on which his wife operated, but secondly, and more importantly, Tony was worried because if she *was* considering taking a break to bring up the kids, it would mean that their household income would drop by more than half, overnight. And with four mouths to feed…

'I don't know yet,' she snapped. 'God, you sound like my mum.'

'I wasn't *hoping* you'd want–'

'Does it matter, anyway?' Suze looked tetchy, all of a sudden.

'No, no.' Tony shook his head firmly. This was a technique he had learned during his wife's first pregnancy. *Agree at all costs.*

'Why did you ask then?'

'I just… wondered.' He didn't dare point out that it had been Suze who'd brought up the subject.

'Well, I don't know yet. Haven't decided. It's nothing to do with what mum says, by the way. She's not rubbing off on me if that's what you think.'

'No, of course not.' Tony carefully led her around a puddle on the path. In fact, that wasn't what he'd been thinking. His mother-in-law's opinion had been a long way from his thoughts, which, he was ashamed to realise, had flitted across to another problem altogether. He'd been trying to work out a way of hauling his stubborn Operations Manager on side for the doomed smart home project. It was all linked, of course. His thoughts of Roy had been triggered by the burning issue of how to turn Synapse around in order to maintain his current position.

'We'd manage, wouldn't we? On your salary, I mean.'

Tony nodded, pushing out a casual laugh. 'Assuming I have a salary!'

Even as the words rolled off his tongue, Tony knew he'd made a mistake. Suze was upon him almost instantly.

'What's that supposed to mean? Are you saying you might not be working in a year's time? Seriously? What d'you mean?'

'Calm down,' Tony reached for her hand, which had been wrenched from his grasp. 'I didn't mean it. I was joking.'

'Tony, you did that 'ha!' thing you do when you're pretending to joke. I know when you're lying. Tell me. What d'you mean? Are you planning to quit your job or something?'

'No!' Finally, Tony caught her flailing hand and brought it down between them. 'No. Of course I'm not.'

It was easy to say, really, because it was true. He wasn't lying when he said that he had no intention of leaving his job. The real worry was his job being *taken* from him, either through the implosion of his department or through being forced from his position by someone with better ideas. Clearly Suze hadn't picked up on this possibility.

'Good,' said Suze, more quietly. 'Sorry. I just freaked out at the idea of me being the breadwinner as well as running the household. I'm not having a great time at work right now.'

Tony made the jump back onto the path and held out his arms to help Suze across.

'I know you're not,' he said, brushing a lock of blonde hair out of her eyes. Her hot-headed anger was at odds with her elfin beauty.

'It's probably just a phase,' she said, resting her head against his chest.

Tony nodded, pulling her close. Suze's outlook was heavily dependent on her workload, her clients and the other lawyers assigned to her case. She was currently working with two of her least favourite colleagues on a libel case that showed no signs of settling.

'You don't need to worry,' he lied, stroking her fine, cropped hair. 'Everything's going to be fine.'

Eventually, they agreed that it was time to head back to their respective offices. As Suze undid her seatbelt to leave, Tony grabbed her arm, bringing her gently towards him and planting a kiss on her cheek. Suze smiled, stroking his jaw as she pulled away.

'You need a shave.'

He grinned. 'I'm growing a beard.'

She shook her head. 'Don't you dare.'

'See you later.'

'Love you.'

An unexpected feeling of relief washed over Tony as Suze left the car. He pulled onto the road, realising, slowly, why he felt this way. He was lying to Suze. He loved her so much and he wanted to be honest with her in every sense, the whole time, but the truth was, he *didn't* feel confident that everything was going to be fine. Suze didn't need to hear truths like that right now, so Tony's only option was to lie.

Waiting for a gap in the traffic, Tony extracted his BlackBerry and trawled through a morning's worth of largely unnecessary correspondence. There was a message from Natasha in HR, demanding to know why he hadn't attended a compulsory wellbeing course, a bunch of emails from colleagues who, for no discernible reason, had felt it necessary to cc most of TransTel in their conversations, a bit of banter from Brian about the new 'wise worker' initiative from their esteemed COO and the usual array of gripes from various members of his department.

The only gem shining out from all the dross was an email from Chek-Han in Finance, who was confirming that his elaborate first-stab forecasting model did include sensitive industry data from his anonymous source and that the pessimistic three-year revenue forecast was in excess of thirty million.

Tony eased out and joined the stream of slow-moving vehicles, for once not feeling the urge to jump out and walk. Driving gave him a rare opportunity to think. Time, space and solitude were rarities in his life these days.

Suze's attack had scared him. It wasn't that Tony hadn't considered the precariousness of his situation before now. He was a natural risk-taker; uncertainties were a part of his everyday life. But taking a risk for yourself was very different to taking one on behalf of someone else – particularly someone who hadn't even been born. In six months' time, they would have two children to support and a few months after that, there was the possibility – although Suze might not admit it to her mother – that he'd be responsible for the entire household income. If she wanted to take a career break to bring up the kids, of course he'd support her in that. *Which meant...* Tony put his foot down as the traffic lights turned amber. *Which meant that he had to turn the Synapse business around.*

Tony knew, deep down, that another job was a possibility. He knew that with his CV he could walk into any number of jobs both in TransTel and elsewhere. But he truly believed he could make the smart home proposition work. It wasn't just a desperation thing; he really had faith in the concept. The problem was, he wouldn't get a chance to make it work if the FD continued to stand in his way.

Tony thought back to their encounter, Nicholas Draper's words reverberating inside his head: *I don't like to see valuable resources wasted on a project that won't come to anything.* It was peculiar. Admittedly, the board was averse to change. Draper didn't write out cheques without a rock-solid business case, but this wasn't even *at* the business case stage. The implication was that Tony should drop the idea before he'd even scoped it out. It was as though the FD had some hidden agenda. As though...

Tony rammed his BlackBerry into the hands-free holster and scrolled to the first section of his address book.

'Hey.'

'Hi Amit, have you got a minute?'

There was a noise that sounded like a long, exasperated breath being released into the handset. 'I've got all the time in the world. I just heard that my business unit's getting swallowed up into the cable division.'

Tony faltered, dumbfounded by Amit's revelation. 'Right. Um... What does that mean for you?'

He sighed again. 'Not sure yet. They've assured me I'll still have a role; just not sure what it will be.'

Tony made the appropriate noises of sympathy. Amit had worked at TransTel for years. He had joined around the same time as Tony. He was loyal, diligent and a good leader who had built up the department from nothing. And this was his thanks. It was yet another blow in the series of punches that TransTel was dealing its employees, as a consequence of the battering it was taking in the market. It was largely due, Tony believed, to TransTel's resistance to move with the times. The company was haemorrhaging customers and employees to younger, nimbler competitors. Its response? Trim fat, cut back. There was no fighting spirit, no effort to leapfrog the opposition. Every month, another announcement hit the newswires about job cuts, re-structuring, departmental closures and mergers.

'I'm sorry, mate.'

'Don't be.' Amit sounded quite sanguine. 'These things happen for a reason. What're you after, anyway?'

Tony felt slightly uncomfortable, asking for help from someone clearly more needy than him, but couldn't think of a way to back out.

'The other day, at lunch, when we were talking about turnaround projects for Synapse... You said something about getting sign-off from Draper being a problem. What did you mean?'

Amit laughed.

'What's funny?'

He barked again. 'You've been to see him, then?'

'He asked to meet,' Tony explained. 'He got wind of our smart home idea.'

'Huh. Let me guess, he advised you to call it off or put it on ice for a couple of years.'

'He basically told me I was wasting my time.' Tony racked his brains, trying to work out what it could be that Amit knew and he didn't.

'Surprise, surprise. That'll be the Wanker-Jones effect.'

'What?'

'Our COO,' replied Amit. 'Have you not noticed how he can lean on Draper to get whatever he wants?'

Tony had indeed noticed this particularly trait from time to time, but he was having trouble working out how it fitted into all of this.

'That's who's behind it, I bet. Walker-Jones won't want you to use up funds that could be better spent on his darling BusinessReach.'

Now Tony was wholly confused. Graham Walker-Jones *had* headed up BusinessReach, the B2B equivalent of Synapse and the division with whom they shared a budget. But last year, when the board had mysteriously agreed that they could do with one more old boy round the table, Walker-Jones had slipped into the previously non-existent role of COO. BusinessReach was now headed up by an officious American ex-consultant called Janine Cook who seemed to have spent much of the last few months mapping out an ambitious, hundred-page 'five-year roadmap' for her division.

'He's not in charge of BusinessReach any more,' said Tony, feeling obliged to point out the obvious.

'Tony, Tony.' Amit chuckled. 'You're forgetting the most important thing.'

'What?'

'Walker-Jones' bonus!'

'What d'you mean?'

'God, I thought everybody knew. Don't you remember when the whole world went mad over the bonus culture? Remember Gable's speech to the City about how remuneration would be based on long-term success alone, yada yada yada?'

'Y-yeah…'

Tony vaguely recalled such a speech. He wished Amit would spit out the punch line.

'Walker-Jones' bonus became dependent on the three-year performance of BusinessReach. When he left, he only got stock options. To get the cash, he has to make sure the unit doesn't sink. That's why Janine What's-her-face is having such a hard time of it with him on her back. That's why you're not gonna get funding for your little enterprise.'

Finally, it made some sense. Tony pulled into the office car park, thinking about all the parts of the puzzle and how they affected him. To get the smart home project off the ground, he needed the FD's backing, and to obtain that, he could either try to sever the tie between Draper and Walker-Jones – a tie that he didn't fully understand – or he could find a way of making things work that wouldn't affect the COO's bonus.

The options spooled through his mind as he sat there, fingers clasped around the soft plastic. He thought about Charles Gable, Nicholas Draper, Graham Walker-Jones, Janine Cook... all the pawns in this elaborate game. Then he realised. It was obvious which was the weakest link.

'Hi,' he said to the Directory Enquiries operator. 'I need the numbers for some golf driving ranges, please.'

Golf with Graham W-J

'YOU LOOK RIDICULOUS.'

'Thanks.'

Tony reached for the door, glancing down at the figure-hugging tank-top he'd found in the back of his wardrobe. He could only imagine it had been purchased for Luke's stag do in Majorca, five years ago. In principle, that had been a golfing weekend, although the image Luke, dressed as a chicken, behind bars in a Magaluf police cell seemed to have eclipsed most of the golf-related memories in his mind.

'How many holes are you playing?' Suze leaned forward and brushed a cobweb from his chinos, eyeing him up and down in mock despair.

'I guess that depends on how I get on.' He caught her as she straightened and kissed her quickly on the lips.

Suze shot him a pitiful look. 'Well, good luck.'

Tony raised a hand and slipped through the door, wondering whether he'd gone a bit far with the golfing attire. The lady in the charity shop had assured him that his choice of footwear would suit the golf course, but in the cold light of day he could see that they looked more like dancing shoes from the nineteen fifties.

Pulling up in front of the Tudor-beamed castle that was Oaklands Golf Club, Tony silenced the engine and sat, contemplating his action plan for day. It wasn't complicated. There were only a few things he needed to say, a couple of seeds to plant. The difficulty would be planting them with sufficient subtlety so that Graham Walker-Jones didn't realise he was being used.

'Over here!' The unmistakeable tufts of greying hair poked up from one of the armchairs in the clubhouse bar. Graham waved him over, grinning moronically.

It was immediately obvious to Tony that the woman in the charity shop had lied. The only shiny shoes in the bar were on his feet, and Pringle tank-tops didn't appear to feature heavily in this season's range either. Tony casually dropped his white visor behind an armchair as he reached for Graham's outstretched hand. He was beginning to wonder whether four hours at the driving range would prove adequate.

'This is Terrence,' said Graham. 'And Charlie, Prattie, Geoffrey…' The list went on. 'Boys, this is Tony.'

Tony joined in with the hand-shaking and pleasantries, suddenly paranoid that Graham might have invited the 'boys' on their golfing jaunt. His plan had been formed very much with just the two of them in mind.

This, thought Tony, looking around the bar in which they were stood, was where it all happened. It wasn't just a club house; it was an establishment. It was a place to do business. As it happened, Tony *was* here to do business, but he wasn't a regular. Even if he hadn't been dressed like Rupert Bear, he would have felt like an outsider. It was as though, by not playing golf on a regular basis, he was missing out on a whole array of career prospects. Much to Tony's relief, Graham bid the men adieu (literally) and led the way out.

'Not got your irons?' He reached for the handle of a well-loaded rocket launcher of a trolley and looked down at Tony's empty hands.

'I, er…'

Tony had thought about this. He knew that he had to be honest about his lack of golfing expertise. The truth would come out as soon as he took his first swing, so there was no point in lying.

'I had a lot of stuff in the car,' he lied.

'Ah. How tiresome. Never mind. Follow me.'

Graham reversed the giant tripod and led them through to the shop, where Tony managed to get through the whole exchange without exposing his ignorance, wheeling his new acquisition down the ramp and promptly over his foot, sending the contents of the bag clattering to the floor outside the clubhouse.

'Duff trolley ,' muttered the COO, bending down to pick up a putter. 'Blasted things.'

Finally, they were standing at the first hole, gazing out at the sweeping expanse of dewy grass. Tony's eyes wandered nervously to the scrubland on either side of the lawn, where sprigs of spiky ferns protruded from the untamed foliage.

By some miracle, Tony's first shot was not all that bad. It soared into the air, slightly off kilter but still within the bounds of the grass, curving as it went and landing only a few metres away from the putting green.

'Gosh!' Graham's watery eyes widened. 'Going for an eagle, eh?'

Tony dipped his head modestly, wondering what an eagle actually was. They followed their shots down the fairway, their pace determined by the speed at which Tony could haul his trolley through the rivulets of mud that Graham seemed to glide over with ease. They hadn't discussed how many holes they would play; Tony assumed they would stop at some multiple of nine, although at this point, even nine seemed like an impossibly ambitious target.

There were, it transpired, a lot of unwritten rules governing the golf course that didn't apply on driving ranges or on stag holidays in Majorca. For example, it was frowned upon to hit a ball into the hole without first removing the flag. Not that Tony's ball made it into the hole on his first attempt. Or the one after that. There were lines in the dew where his ball had rolled: up, down, left, right, tracing a sort of star-shape around the hole.

This was all part of the plan, of course. Tony had done his homework; he knew that Walker-Jones played with a handicap of six. He had never intended to impress the man with his golfing prowess – quite the opposite, in fact. Perhaps he hadn't meant to be *quite* so poor on the putting front, but that couldn't be helped. The intention was simply to build up a relationship with the COO.

Tony had looked at the man's track record and worked a few things out. Graham was not a man who respected ingenuity or original thought. He didn't like renegades. He was averse to change and uncertainty. Status and salary were everything to the COO. He held a set of traditional values, he believed in hierarchy and he liked to command respect from his subordinates. Or, to put it another way, he was a pompous old fool who lived for his fancy title and a fat bonus cheque. Tony's plan played on this fact.

'Tony!'

Tony froze. Graham had stopped dead in his tracks and was staring at him.

'What are you doing?'

Tony tried to ascertain what was wrong. Graham looked like a criminal who'd been caught in the act, his head darting furtively from side to side. When it became clear that nobody was watching, he rushed onto the green and threw himself at Tony's trolley, hauling it onto the fairway and returning to the silvery grass to erase all traces of the trespassing cart.

Graham shook his head, looking shell-shocked. 'Never, on the dance floor!'

It was probably at this point that any ambiguity surrounding Tony's golfing expertise evaporated and the relationship between the two men shifted firmly to one of tutor and pupil.

By the sixth hole, it felt as though some kind of rapport had been established. Tony stepped up to tee off and looked at Graham.

'Great to be outdoors, eh.'

'Quite.' The COO nodded.

'Especially after the week I've had.'

Graham looked slightly wary, perhaps sensing the direction in which Tony was taking the conversation.

'Like a rollercoaster,' said Tony, balancing the ball on the tee and trying not to think about broken wrists. 'The high-point being the revenue forecast for this new venture idea we're looking at – *fifty million by the end of year three* –' he looked at Graham, making sure the figures had sunk in – 'and then the low-point being when Nicholas more-or-less told us we wouldn't get the funding.' He glanced again at the COO.

Before Graham could respond, four men in flat caps and white gloves appeared, clearly eager to overtake.

'Please,' muttered Graham, gesturing for Tony to step aside and clearly welcoming the distraction.

The men took their shots swiftly and easily, sending their balls flying into the distance.

'Carpe diem!' cried one of them, doffing his cap as the group moved on.

Tony stepped up and realigned his body for the shot. 'The frustrating thing is,' he went on, swiping the ball with a decent pace, albeit in the wrong direction. 'It wouldn't require an awful lot of investment – for a *fifty million* pound business.'

Graham grunted, switching places without meeting Tony's eye.

'And what got me really excited about the idea was the fact that it could bolt on to our existing business,' Tony went on, watching as the ball sailed past the patch of thorns in which his own ball languished. 'It's just an on-sell for the customers we already have.'

They started to walk down the fairway. Still, there was no response from the COO. They parted briefly as Tony headed into the brambles. Having spent a good deal of time in the last ninety minutes foraging in bracken looking for balls, he had discovered a trick for minimising embarrassment and nettle stings. He would take a spare ball from the trolley, pop it up his sleeve and then after a nominal period of plant-bashing, drop the spare and shout, 'Found it!'.

They converged again on the green.

'How *much* investment?' Graham asked quietly.

Tony almost smiled. 'Eight hundred thousand, for the pilot. Eight million for the scale-up. Pennies, really.'

Graham potted his ball and grunted, impressed either with his shot or with the response.

'The potential is even larger than the fifty mil, of course.' Tony gently nudged his ball with the putter, the way Graham had taught him. Incredibly, it rolled in.

'Very good. What d'you mean, larger?'

Tony stooped down to pick up the balls. 'Well, in theory this smart home concept could be rolled out not just to homes, but hospitals, workplaces, schools... The fifty million is just for the domestic market. It's a *massive* opportunity.'

He handed over one of the balls and headed for the next hole. Behind him, Graham could be heard drawing a breath.

'I've just thought,' said the COO, picking up pace to draw level with Tony. 'If what you say is correct, we could do something like this with BusinessReach.'

Tony's jaw dropped as though it was the first time he'd heard the idea.

'You're right!' He let out a jubilant cry. 'Of course! Why hadn't I thought of that? Our BusinessReach customers might represent a whole untapped market! If we can test the waters with the domestic offering, we could be up and running within months... not just smart home, but smart business... smart everything!' His voice was rising uncontrollably. 'Great idea, Graham. *Great* idea.'

'Always worth raising something up the flagpole,' the COO muttered smugly. 'See who salutes.'

Tony nodded, not entirely sure about the metaphor but sensing proximity to a small victory. It was true, in a way, that the smart home proposition might work in the B2B marketplace. It was an option to explore – although not an option that Tony planned to explore in the near future. His immediate goal was to get over the next hurdle and convince the FD to buy into the concept. Rolling out a B2B solution was a project for another year, or another person – namely Janine Cook, Head of BusinessReach – but for now, it suited him to bolster Graham's vision.

Tony, feeling pleased with himself but careful not to let it show, spent the next twenty minutes losing balls and replacing them with spares, hoping that the man in the shop wouldn't count them on their return. There remained only one thing left to do: convince Graham to lean on Nicholas Draper.

'Last hole?' Graham suggested, nodding towards the little wooden stump that was inscribed at its base with the number nine.

Tony looked up the fairway. The flag was so far away, it was just a dot somewhere near the horizon, like France from the Dover coastline. With renewed resolve, he lifted the club and took an almighty swing.

'Super!' cried Walker-Jones as the ball flew off into the distance.

Tony stepped back, feeling the full weight of the COO's support and deciding that now was the time. 'So, how d'you think I should play it with Nicholas Draper?'

'Well,' Graham smiled to himself, scratching his head as if debating whether to say something or not.

'Shall I try talking to Janine first, to get the backing of–'

'No!'

Tony feigned surprise. He knew full well the COO didn't get on with Janine Cook and didn't trust her decision-making skills. It irked Walker-Jones that his bonus was now dependent on her actions.

'No, er… No. I'll tell you what.' He stepped closer, looking confidingly at Tony. 'I'll talk to Nicholas. Get him singing from the same hymn sheet, so to speak. We, um… We go back a long way.'

The ball shot off into oblivion.

'Leave it with me,' he said, winking at Tony. 'Leave it with me.'

Presenting the investment case; Roy agrees

'IS THAT in the latest draft? Can you print off a copy?'

Marianne dipped her head toward the printer. 'Already done. Just waiting for Louise's pages.'

Tony rushed over and scooped up the slides, rehearsing his pitch as he shuffled the papers. He had eleven minutes in which to tie up the business case presentation and compose himself before rushing over to the CEO's office. An hour ago, they still hadn't even received the customer insight from the agency.

'Louise?'

The Marketing Manager looked up, beaming. 'All done.'

'And?'

Louise knew what he was asking and smiled. 'Ninety-one percent. That's the proportion of home owners who'd like to be able to monitor their energy usage remotely.'

Tony returned the smile. 'No dodgy filters or cross-tabs?'

Louise's ringlets shook as she denied the accusation.

Tony gave her a quick, congratulatory slap on the back and pulled the final draft from the printer.

Half-sitting, half-hovering at his desk, Tony flicked through the pages for the last time. Louise was right. The customer insight unquestionably backed up the rationale for the smart home proposition – which was just as well, really, because Chek-Han's financial forecasts relied upon the premise that a certain proportion of Synapse subscribers would take up the new offering. It was all coming together.

An email popped into his inbox just as he straightened up.

He would have ignored it, had he not spotted the subject line of the message.

From: Natasha Billingsley– HR
To: Tony Sharp - Synapse
Subject: Incentives

Hi Tony,
Further to our previous correspondence, I can now confirm that for the two individuals concerned, the incentive schemes you suggested will be enforceable should the project come to fruition. Attached is the authorisation documentation.
Please keep HR informed of project progress and any other personnel issues that might arise.
Kind regards,
Natasha

Tony checked the time. It was four minutes to three. He bashed out the most humble yet assertive email he could in the time and sent it to Roy. If the prospect of taking his boss' job didn't bring the miserable sod round, thought Tony as he grabbed the papers and headed out, then nothing would.

'There's three sets there,' yelled his PA. 'Nicholas Draper's joining you, you know that?'

Tony looked back as he reversed through the door. He probably should have known that, but he hadn't had time to study the details of the appointment in his calendar.

'Oh, and your wife called!'

The door had already swung shut. Tony strode down the corridor towards the lifts, trying to extract the BlackBerry from his pocket without dropping the bundle of papers. Suze, it turned out, had left him a message.

Tony dialled his voicemail and stepped into the lift just as the message started to play. Suze's voice turned to white noise as the metal doors slid shut. In other circumstances, he would have stayed in the lobby to hear it out, but the time was nearing three o'clock and the lift was half-full so there was no option to hold it.

He rose to the sixth floor, resolving to call his wife back as soon as he came out of the meeting. Clearly Gable had sanctioned Nicholas Draper's attendance today, or possibly even requested it. The two men were close, as were most members of the TransTel board. Perhaps they had already colluded, already decided what their answer would be today. The big question was whether Graham Walker-Jones had managed to lean on the FD. Tony had had no contact with the COO since their day on the golf course.

Charles Gable was in a bad mood. Even if he hadn't ignored Tony's joke about the window cleaners (who were hanging outside in a little metal cage; Tony had suggested they were from Netcomm), then his disposition would have been evident from the way that his ruddy nose was fixed in a permanent snarl and his lips were drawn tight, like a cat's bottom.

'Go on then,' he barked.

The presentation, for which Tony could take very little credit – he had scribbled his intentions to Marianne, who had translated them into PowerPoint – was a masterpiece. It felt to Tony, as he tore through the slides, as though he was making the most logical argument in the world. It even covered the thorny issue of TransTel Technology's previous pitch for the same idea.

He came to the end and looked up at Charles as if defying him to turn down the opportunity.

'Well.' Gable pinched his nose, closing his small, piggy eyes for a second. 'I have to say, it's a fantastic proposition.'

Tony hesitated, perplexed by the CEO's unexpected words of praise.

'…for an energy provider.'

Tony swallowed and looked at the table, quickly preparing his defence. The criticism was one he'd been expecting.

'I realise this seems like a departure from our core business, and it is, in a way. But at the same time, it's an extension. We already play in the home services market with our broadband and network solutions, so this is just the next thing.'

Charles snorted again. 'Next, according to whom?'

'Well –'

'If I asked ten different people what the next thing was, I'd get ten different answers.' The CEO scowled. 'Why am I to believe you?'

Ten different answers, thought Tony, *not all of them bringing in fifty million pounds.* 'The financial model indicates that this is a huge opportunity,' he explained, 'and one that I don't think we can afford to miss.'

'Huge opportunity, eh. I hear space travel's doing a roaring trade; should we look into that, too?'

Tony cleared his throat, leaving Gable's question hanging in the air. He decided to change tack, to approach the issue from the angle of Synapse's fourteen million-pound shortfall in revenues. But as he opened his mouth to speak, Nicholas leaned forward and cleared his throat.

'If I may, Charles...'

There was a dip of the head that implied permission had been granted.

'I am sceptical of veering too far from our core area of strength – namely, telecommunications. As you know, taking on indefinable risk is something I aim to avoid, and I would advise against endorsing a proposition that engages valuable TransTel resources on a venture that might fail, or damage our credibility.'

'Quite.' Charles nodded. '*Quite.*'

Tony held his breath, hoping desperately that the FD would follow on with another sentence – preferably one starting with 'However'.

'However,' Nicholas said, still holding the CEO's gaze. Tony waited in silence. 'I have given this opportunity some considerable thought, and two things strike me as interesting.'

Tony still couldn't breathe. He wasn't in the clear yet, but it was beginning to sound as though Graham might have had words with his pal.

Charles raised an eyebrow.

'First, the level of investment required.' Nicholas looked at his copy of the presentation and jabbed at one of Marianne's charts. 'Eight hundred thousand to pilot, if approximations are to be believed, and eight million in total.' He turned to Tony. 'These are realistic estimates, are they, Anthony?'

Tony nodded, sucking in a huge breath of air. It seemed

almost too good to be true, but it was looking as though his golfing extravaganza had paid off. 'We'll refine the cost estimates if and when we proceed with the business plan, but yes, it's realistic.'

'And secondly,' Nicholas went on, whipping over a couple of pages. 'There is the scalability. This venture might not just be applicable to the domestic market, but also to industry – to businesses. I can see potential for this not just to be 'smart home' but 'smart business'… 'smart industry'!'

Tony stared determinedly at his notebook, trying not to smile.

It took a while for Charles Gable to respond, but when he did it was obvious that the wind in the room had changed.

'Hmm,' he said, squinting thoughtfully at the FD. 'Good points, both of them.'

Draper bowed his head self-deprecatingly. 'Worth thinking about, anyway.'

The CEO nodded. It wasn't a firm, *decision made* nod, but Tony could see that progress had been made. The cat-bottom mouth had disappeared and the cheeks had returned to a more flesh-like colour.

'It'll still have to go past the board,' he said, his piggy eyes flickering up at Tony.

'I can get a paper written up in the next week or so.'

The chief exec made some more non-committal noises and then dismissed Tony from the room, commanding Nicholas to stay behind.

Padding along the carpeted passageway, Tony let out an audible sigh of relief. As far as grillings went, it hadn't been too bad. If the skeletal smile Nicholas had flashed him as he left the room was anything to go by, there was a decent chance he might get this one pushed through.

His BlackBerry bleeped as he stepped into the lift. A brief scan of the email pushed his spirits yet another notch higher.

From: Roy Smith - Synapse
To: Tony Sharp - Synapse
Subject: Re: New role

Tony,
Appreciate being considered for the role and would have no problems stepping up. Will await further news.
Roy

Tony smiled. It was as close an approximation as he would ever get to reconciliation with his Ops Manager. Everything, it seemed, was starting to slot into place. He pushed on the glass doors and re-entered the Synapse office with a spring in his step.

'Tony!' Marianne turned to him, a phone pressed up against each ear. 'He's back,' she hissed into one of the handsets. 'I'll send him over.'

Even before she had explained about Anja falling sick and Suze being stuck at work and Poppy being left stranded at the nursery, Tony could tell that he'd messed up. All at once, he remembered Marianne's earlier message, the voicemail he'd ignored, the seven missed calls he'd spotted whilst reading Roy's email.

'*Shit*,' he said, dumping his papers on the nearest desk and running to get his jacket. 'I'll be right there.'

EFFECTIVE STAKEHOLDER MANAGEMENT

EFFECTIVE STAKEHOLDER MANAGEMENT

 MarketGravity

In this chapter Tony starts to try and galvanise his team. His enthusiasm is quickly dented by scepticism and internal politics. For the first time Tony must deal with the leadership challenges of starting something new, whilst not letting the current business go to ruin.

Challenges you're likely to experience at this stage of the journey include:

- Team mates and colleagues expressing fears and scepticism about changes and new ideas
- Reluctance to do extra work outside "business as usual" and having to convince others to help you
- Colleagues in other departments being dismissive and critical of what you're trying to do
- Rival initiatives appearing and turf battles ensuing
- External stakeholders (e.g. regulators, industry bodies, lobby groups, journalists and even existing customers) may have a reason to block your progress

The Corporate Entrepreneur has to apply all his or her political savvy and communication skills to build a strong network of advocates. Understanding who you need to win over and how to do it is a critical skill for getting any non-standard investment off the ground and, like any good strategy, should be planned in advance.

"GET THE EVENTUAL OWNER ON BOARD FROM THE START. THAT WAY THEY'RE FULLY BEHIND IT WHEN THEY TAKE OVER."

Gearoid Lane, British Gas

To influence people at different levels Corporate Entrepreneurs must learn to be actors and play different roles. Here are a few things you can do to create a powerful stakeholder network for your own organisation:

1. Don't leave it to chance. Turn sceptical colleagues into advocates by creating a power map of the organisation showing who you need to influence and how to gain their support.

2. Get the eventual owners on board from the start. That way they are fully behind the venture when they take over. Many new ventures need to be incubated away from the core business, but then need to tap into the strength of the parent to grow. Find a likely future owner and get their support from the beginning.

3. Create a vehicle for sponsoring and supporting new initiatives. Assemble a new venture board with clear criteria for success and decision making that are free from short-term targets and constraints.

4. Create your own momentum and don't let others knock you off course. Become your own PR machine and use your success to influence and attract others.

5. Create a bigger role for yourself in the market. Take a lead role in forums, industry bodies and lobbying groups to help shape the market and create the space into which your venture will move.

Two frameworks to help you manage the stakeholders in your venture are shown below. The first table classifies who you're dealing with, the second how to handle them.

TABLE 1		Attitude to the Venture	
		Positive	**Negative**
Power	**High**	**A** Advocate	**B** Terrorist
	Low	**C** Cheerleader	**D** Irritant

Most important in this framework are the Terrorists. Identify them early and try to win them over.

TABLE 2		Attitude to the Venture	
		Positive	**Negative**
Power	**High**	**A** Engage and inform	**B** Manage closely
	Low	**C** Encourage	**D** Monitor (low effort)

4

Beg, borrow and steal:
the art of building a team

'You can choose your friends but you can't always choose
your colleagues.'

In-laws staying; Amit agrees

'YOU REALLY SHOULD CONSIDER herbal remedies, you know. Ginkgo Biloba, that's what she needs. It's very good for treating attention deficit disorders.'

'*Really.*' Tony nodded obligingly, rummaging again in the box of hats and scarves in search of his shoes. The in-laws had arrived two days ago but already it felt as though they'd been here for weeks. In future, he thought, stooping to see if he'd left his shoes under the dining room table, he would happily pay for their nanny's 'flu jabs – in fact, Tetanus, Measles, Chickenpox and any other vaccinations that might prevent her from getting sick.

'Tramp-lene, tramp-lene!' squealed Poppy, jumping about on the sofa, watered-down juice splashing out of the splash-proof beaker and onto the cream fabric.

'You see?' said Rose, shaking her head admonishingly as Tony glanced around, at a loss. His shoes were nowhere to be seen.

'Has anyone–'

'Morning all!' cried Mr Proctor, emerging from the small back yard, his cheeks flushed with cold. 'And what a glorious one it is too. I can feel Christmas in the air. Ah, coffee! Is that for me?' He reached out and grasped Tony's untouched cup.

'Actually–'

'Chris-miss!' yelled Poppy, bounding over with her hands held high, the beaker abandoned, face-down, in the folds of the sofa. 'Grandpa, swing! Swing!'

Mr Proctor grasped his granddaughter's little wrists and

swung her in a giant arc across the kitchen, singing a tuneless rendition of Jingle Bells.

'Peter!' cried Rose, as Poppy's feet flew dangerously close to the hood of the cooker. 'Not straight after breakfast!'

Tony looked at his watch. It was nearly half-past eight. He was meeting Nicholas Draper at nine.

'Feel sick,' moaned Poppy.

'What did I say?' Rose glared at her husband. 'Now, Tony. Shouldn't you be going to work?'

'I can't find my–'

'Feel sick! Need sweeties!' Poppy looked up expectantly.

Tony shook his head firmly. 'That only works on car journeys.'

Poppy pouted.

'*Sweets?*' Rose gasped. 'No wonder she struggles to focus!'

'She doesn't–' Tony cut his argument short, realising that he had better things to do with his time. 'Has anyone seen my shoes?'

'Have you looked in the cupboard under the stairs?' asked Rose.

Tony frowned. *No,* he thought, *I haven't looked in the cupboard under the stairs because that is where we keep the vacuum cleaner and the broom and the tins of food that Suze likes to stockpile in case we get trapped inside our house for a month; not where we keep our shoes.* He pulled open the cupboard door and saw, neatly wedged in the gap between the dustpan and the clothes horse, his office shoes.

'I had a little tidy-up,' Rose explained pleasantly. 'There was so much clutter around the place, I don't know how you get in and out!'

Tony thought about coming back with a sarcastic rejoinder about his mother-in-law getting out, but decided against it.

'Have a good day,' he said, tousling Poppy's hair and slamming the door shut behind him.

It wasn't the best way to prepare for what might end up being one of the most important meetings of his career, thought Tony as he slipped the car into gear and joined the queue of crawling vehicles, trying to block out the homicidal thoughts.

The Finance Director had set no agenda; he'd simply sent

out an invitation entitled 'Smart home project catch-up'. The terminology was mildly reassuring, of course, although Tony wasn't naïve enough to read too much into it. The word 'project' got appended to just about every TransTel initiative, from printer toner refills to multi-million pound venture roll-outs.

The board had nominally approved Tony's proposal to write the smart home business plan, but progress depended on the resources available. The previous week, Tony had submitted a request for an external consultant, a research agency, a marketing expert, a financial analyst and access to certain key personnel around the TransTel business. It was ambitious, but he knew how these things worked; you had to go in high and accept that you might not get everything you asked for.

The FD was sitting, bolt upright, behind his desk when Tony entered. With a brief but pointed glance at the clock on the wall, he turned to Tony with a thin smile.

'Morning, Anthony.'

'Nicholas.' Tony returned the man's nod.

'How's it all going?'

'Well, you know how it is.' Tony dipped his head to one side and then the other. He had to tread carefully. His department's decline worked in his favour in terms of bolstering the case for Synapse's reinvention, but it didn't reflect well on him. 'It's not an easy market to play in right now.'

Draper nodded slowly. 'Which is why we are meeting today, is it not?'

Tony looked him in the eye, risking another nod, despite not actually knowing the purpose of the meeting.

'I've had a look through your proposal,' said Draper, sliding two familiar-looking sheets across his desk and arranging them so that their edges were exactly aligned. Tony could see that the summary bullet-points had been annotated in neat italic handwriting that was too small for him to read upside down. 'I'll cut to the chase. There's no budget for the resources you've requested.'

Tony frowned. 'What, *none*?'

Draper opened his hands apologetically. 'I'm afraid not.'

'But...' Tony tried to think. He knew that the FD would start his bidding low, but not this low. 'How are we to proceed with the business plan?'

Draper shrugged. 'The same way you've proceeded up until now. Using the resources you already have at your disposal.'

'You mean... my existing team?'

'Is there a problem with your existing team?'

'N-no,' Tony stammered, trying to imagine Matt and Louise joining forces on the market sizing exercise or Roy pulling together an implementation plan. 'It's just... They've never worked on a new venture before.'

'But they can learn?'

Tony nodded reluctantly. He could hardly admit that he had doubts about his own management team – not if he wanted to convince the board that they were capable of pulling off this initiative.

'Good.' Nicholas Draper looked down at one of the pages. 'So, we're looking at...'

Tony half-tuned out as the FD started talking about gates and sign-offs and KPIs. He couldn't believe that the board seriously expected him to knock out a business plan with no additional resource. Quite apart from the lack of expertise in the department, there was the small matter of keeping the existing business afloat. He would effectively have to ask his team to work on the plan in their *spare time*. Tony could imagine what his Operations Manager would have to say about that.

'...by the end of the calendar year, do you think?'

Tony looked up, replaying the echo of Draper's last sentence in his mind. With horror, he realised that the suggestion being put forward was for him to work up the business case in the three weeks leading up to Christmas.

'No problem,' he said, when he realised he didn't have another option. It was a blessing that the board was allowing him to work on the idea at all; he was in no position to dictate the terms.

'Oh, and Anthony?' said the FD as Tony reached for the door. 'Fifty million within three years, you think?'

Tony hesitated for a second, wondering what Draper might say if he realised that the estimate had been pulled together using various unattributed sources by a finance whiz-kid he'd never met.

'That's the plan.'

'Well then, I hope you're right.'

Tony returned to his desk feeling apprehensive. *If* his team could fabricate something that approximated a robust business plan in the next three weeks and *if* the early estimates proved correct and *if* he could convince the board to invest, again and again, at each stage of the process, then there was a chance the Synapse business could be turned around. That was a lot of ifs, and every one of them depended on his actions. Suddenly, it felt as though he'd taken charge of a huge oil tanker staffed by chimpanzees and was attempting to override the autopilot that was set on a collision path with an iceberg.

'Morning!' sung Marianne, returning from the kitchen and placing a cup of coffee on his desk. 'Three messages: one from Nicholas Draper at nine o'clock, wondering where you were–'

'I was a few minutes late.'

'One from Amit Chaudhuri; he said he'll call again later. And your mother-in-law phoned just now. She wants to know whether you'd prefer two small Christmas puddings or one large one this year, and...' Marianne consulted her notebook. 'And whether you'd like her to make a suet-free one for Poppy?'

Tony closed his eyes and sighed.

'D'you want me to call her back?'

'Could you?' Tony smiled gratefully.

'I presume you don't care either way about the puddings?'

'You presume correctly.'

Tony logged on and watched as the emails popped into his inbox, all fifty-seven of them.

'Tony?'

He looked up. Louise was hovering sheepishly a few feet from his desk, clutching a piece of paper.

'What's up?'

'Um...' She moved closer and shakily laid the sheet on his desk.

He recognised the photocopied page. It was the contract that bound them to Interactive, the online advertising agency that had been under review since Tony had noticed how little exposure they were getting for their money.

'Why are you showing me this?' he asked.

'It's for next year.'

He looked down. 'But... I thought we agreed that our budget would be better spent elsewhere? Weren't you going to have a look around?'

'Yes.' Louise bit her lip awkwardly.

'So...'

'The thing is, I inadvertently signed us up to Interactive again for next year.'

'Inadvertently?' Tony frowned.

'Well, it's a rolling contract. I meant to cancel it before it rolled over to next year, but... well, I forgot.'

'You've committed our entire annual online advertising budget to Interactive?' he clarified, rubbing his hands over his face and bringing them to rest over his mouth.

Slowly, Louise began to nod. 'I'm sorry. I didn't think.'

Tony didn't know how to react. The problem was, he knew that his Marketing Manager was doing the best she could; he knew that she hadn't done this deliberately. But still... *How was it possible to make such a basic mistake?* How could someone inadvertently blow a hundred thousand pounds? And, more importantly, was the person who made that mistake really capable of pulling together a plan for a business worth fifty million?

'Let's talk about this in the budget meeting later,' he said, eventually.

Louise tiptoed away, leaving Tony alone with his doubts and the incriminating piece of paper.

He had no idea how long he'd been sitting there, mulling over Louise's mistake, when the muted purr of the office phone broke through his melancholy.

'Hello?'

'Hey, it's Amit. How's things?'

'Pretty shit, actually. You?'

'Pretty shit too.'

Tony forced aside his thoughts, remembering that Amit's

plight was probably far worse than his. At least he was still in a job – for now at least. 'Any news on the new role?'

'Yup.' Amit sounded weary.

'Well? Go on then'

'Interim Manager of TransTel Cordless Enterprises.'

'TransTel what?'

'Exactly. It's one of those dying divisions that they're trying to phase out.'

Tony sighed in sympathy. His friend's frustration was understandable. It was absurd. Amit was a pioneer. He was a visionary. He didn't deserve to be shelved in some dead-end position in a dusty corner of TransTel.

'I'm sorry, mate.'

Amit exhaled down the line. 'Oh well. I'm looking around. Reckon there are some opportunities at Netcomm and that.'

'I'm sure there are. I reckon – ooh. Hang on.' Tony hesitated. 'What notice period are you on?'

'Six months,' said Amit, his voice laden with resentment.

Tony's brain was suddenly whirring. 'Excellent,' he said, as the idea began to bed in.

'What's excellent about me having another six months in this shit-hole?'

'Well,' said Tony. 'I've just told Draper I'll write this smart home business plan without any extra resources... and my managers don't have a commercial brain cell between them. My Head of Marketing just accidentally spent our entire year's online marketing budget on something we didn't want.'

'Ahha,' replied Amit. There was a smile in his voice now. 'I see.'

'Fancy helping us out?'

Amit chuckled. 'You know, Tony... I think that sounds just up my street.'

Assigning the work

'THEN YOUR SECTION will slot in here,' Tony explained, drawing an arrow between two headings on the skeletal contents page.

Norm nodded, fiddling with a little device that was clipped onto his belt. It looked like a doctor's pager but Tony suspected it was something more obscure.

'Shall we talk through the sub-sections?'

Norm nodded again, looking up and focusing on the document as if seeing it for the first time.

'Okay...' Tony braced himself. He still wasn't sure that Norm was the most suitable person to write what would ultimately be the most important part of the plan – the section entitled *The Proposition* – but Amit's advice had been clear: assign each section to the appropriate manager. Given that Norm knew more about Project eFlow than anybody else in the department, it was only fair to assign him the task. 'First off, an introduction to the proposition. What exactly is it?'

'Ah, well.' Norm brightened at the question. 'The device itself is a solid-state protective relay for three-phase voltage–'

'No,' said Tony, his worst fears confirmed. 'I mean, what is it, in layman's terms? What is it to the people who are going to be signing up to this service? What *is it*?'

Norm looked at him blankly.

Tony sighed, trying to find a kind way of saying what needed to be said. 'Not everybody thinks in the same way you do. This document is going to be read by a handful of TransTel board members, all of whom have very short attention spans and not a lot of time. We need to hit them with the facts, top level. They need to grasp what we're talking about instantly.'

'So... I'm going into too much detail?'

Tony nodded encouragingly. 'Exactly. You just need a simple paragraph that describes what the proposition will be.'

'Got it.'

'Great. Next, then... the vision. This is where we talk about where we see the business in five or ten years. What we–' Tony stopped, seeing the expression on his Technology Manager's face. It suddenly seemed overwhelmingly obvious that Norm was the wrong man for the job. Network routing algorithms were his forte; strategic visions were not. 'Tell you what. How about I do that bit?'

Tony looked down the list of sub-sections. Pricing structure. Revenue model. Barriers to entry. Future growth path. 'In fact... Shall we skip to the technical section?'

Eventually, after an infuriating conversation about exactly how much detail was required on the specification page, Norm shuffled out of the office. Tony sank back in his chair, letting his head roll back and his eyes fall shut. The task was turning out to be even more challenging than he had envisaged.

There was a knock at the door.

'Tony?' It was Marianne.

'Yeah, come in.'

'Sorry to interrupt. You had a few messages.' She pulled a face. 'From your mother-in-law. She said it was urgent.'

Tony groaned. 'Go on.'

'Right.' Marianne looked down at her notebook. 'Firstly, where do you keep your Tupperware?'

'Haven't a clue.'

'Okay... Has Poppy seen Mr Fox at the cinema?'

'Why can't she ask Poppy?'

'Is that a yes or a no?'

'Haven't a clue.'

'Right... and... are you planning to get a real Christmas tree this year, because there was a nice young man who came round selling them for–'

'And she said it was urgent?'

Marianne shrugged helplessly. 'What shall I tell her?'

'Tell her to stop calling me at work.'

Marianne looked at him uncertainly.

'Sorry. Just tell her I'll get back to her this evening. I'm up to my ears.'

Marianne smiled, nodded and quietly closed the door.

The message alert pinged, drawing Tony reluctantly towards his computer.

From: Chek-Han Liu - TransTel CBN
To: Tony Sharp - Synapse
Subject: Re: Help on Smart home project

Hi Tony,

Thanks for the message. I'm glad you found my financial model helpful and flattered that you'd like me to work on the business plan.

Whilst I'm generally happy to help out, I'm afraid I have recently taken on a lot of extra work (you probably heard that CBN is getting absorbed into the cable division – I'm responsible for merging the accounts) so I'll be unable to help you until after Christmas.

Sorry I can't be of more help.

Chek-Han

Tony stared at the message, drumming his fingers on the desk and trying not to let the despair take hold. Slowly, steadily, his confidence was being eroded. He had started out with such ballsy determination, but now there was this persistent drip, drip, drip of setbacks. Holdups, problems, mistakes... Everything, it seemed, was stacking up against him.

There was another knock at the door. Tony checked the time. Five o'clock. It would be Matt and Louise. It had been Amit's idea to summon his direct reports in this way. Apparently it helped to establish ownership of the different sections of the document. It made sense, in a way, although he had doubts about the idea of co-ownership between his Head of Sales and his Marketing Manager.

Tony switched on a smile as the two colleagues established themselves as far apart as it was possible to do in such a confined space. Louise was brandishing a marked-up copy of the draft document, while Matt carried nothing but his customary blank notepad.

'Here you go.' Tony passed him a clean copy.

'Thanks, mate.'

'Right. Shall we launch straight into the Market Opportunity section?'

Louise nodded keenly. Matt shrugged.

'I was thinking that Louise, you'd be best-placed to populate the first few sub-sections. Consumer trends, competitive landscape, market size and growth...?'

'No problem!' Her curls bobbed manically. 'I've already made a bit of a start, as it happens.'

Matt grunted and rolled his eyes.

Ignoring him, Louise slid her version of the document across the desk, revealing whole paragraphs of text that didn't exist on the master copy. Clearly Louise had been working overtime.

'Well, that's... impressive.' Tony nodded, skim-reading some of the lines. They were laced with the usual marketing bullshit, but stripping that out, it was evident that most of the essentials were in place.

'So I don't need to be here, then?' Matt raised an eyebrow.

Tony dipped his head. 'There are elements of the document I'd like you to work on together. The first being the volume of addressable customers.'

'Oh, I've had a first-stab at the market size,' Louise piped up, leafing through the pages of her document.

Matt shot her a venomous look.

'Excellent,' said Tony. 'But we'll need to drill down into that market to find the volume of *addressable* customers, and that's where Matt comes in.'

Louise looked deflated, then confused.

'We'll need to determine some year one sales objectives, based on the marketing plan that we'll be putting together.'

'Oh, I've already drawn up a marketing plan,' Louise piped up, flipping through more pages.

'See?' muttered Matt.

'Right.' Tony looked down at Louise's document, which was littered with phrases like 'first-mover advantage', 'core target' and 'key message'. 'This is great. It'll serve as a good basis for our sales estimates, won't it Matt?'

He shrugged again, as though he didn't care one way or the other.

'Look, Matt, I'm afraid we're all going to have to work together on this.'

'Looks like she's done it all anyway.'

'No,' said Tony, waiting for the Sales Manager to meet his eye. Eventually, he gave up and addressed the side of Matt's face. 'Louise has completed the *marketing* sections, but the ultimate goal here is to get to some *sales* estimates. That's what we'll use in our financial model to validate the whole proposition.' *If we find someone to work on the financial model,* he nearly added.

'I'm not a psychic,' muttered Matt. 'My job's to sell broadband, not to look into the future.'

'Yes,' Tony replied patiently. 'I see what you're saying, but if you use Louise's marketing plan as a guide then you can at least make an estimate of sales. That's all we're after.'

Matt sighed, glowering at the lengthy document on Louise's lap. 'Fine.'

'Okay. So, can I leave it with you to get something over by the end of next week?'

'Sure!' Louise beamed back at him.

Matt nodded grudgingly, then pushed back his chair and walked out, leaving the door to swing in the Marketing Manager's face.

For several seconds, Tony sat at his desk, head in hands. Two weeks ago, he had been so full of optimism. The board had granted approval for the business plan and he had a solid idea for a proposition that operated in a fast-growing market. There was so much potential. But now, he could only see problems.

His mobile phone buzzed on the desk, reminding him of an unplayed voicemail.

'Hi, it's me.' It was Suze. She sounded stressed. 'I've had a shocker of a day and I need to unwind. I'm going to Emmie's for a drink. Sorry to leave you with my parents, but I'm sure you'll cope. Oh, and I had a few messages from mum about a Christmas tree or something. Can you sort it out? See you later.'

Tony lowered the phone and stared for a second at the calendar on the wall. Suze was into her second trimester now; she was supposed to be blooming, whatever that meant. She looked radient, that was certainly true, but as far as Tony could tell, she seemed as tired and hormonal as she had been during the first term – if not more so. He thought about the prospect of returning home for an evening with his in-laws and then looked down and dialled Brian's number.

'Mate, are you around for a pint or two?'

The in-laws leave; Amit helps

'NOW DON'T FORGET, the one with the blue label is suet-free. Oh and I put the leftovers of that casserole in the–'

'Mum, you'll miss your train.' Suze bent down to pick up her mother's suitcase.

'Susannah!' screeched Rose, batting her away. 'Not in your condition! Honestly...' She glared at Tony as if somehow his wife's attempt to help was his own doing.

With great restraint, Tony stepped forward and walked the last few yards of the concourse, dragging his mother-in-law's giant case behind him. He looked up at the row of grey ticket barriers and smiled. It was like seeing the gates to Heaven. Beyond it lay freedom and peace and the prospect of uninterrupted leisure time.

'Thanks again.' Suze hugged her mother. 'We couldn't have managed without you.'

'Well,' Rose smiled primly. 'You know where we are if she lets you down again.'

Tony nearly said something but managed to stop himself. There was no point in arguing on Anja's behalf; the Proctors were never going to change their views.

'Thanks,' muttered Tony, returning Peter's manly handshake and turning to peck Rose on the cheek.

It took a while for the in-laws to make it onto the platform, due to Rose's insistence that the station attendant let them through the gate marked Exit Only, but eventually, they were off.

It was eight forty-two by the time Tony started the engine.

He was going to be late for his nine o'clock meeting, but he didn't care. Even just chugging along in the rush-hour traffic was a happy prospect this morning. The in-laws were gone. There would be no more compulsory Antiques Roadshow or Songs of Praise. No more barbed comments about the way they were raising their child. No more repulsive trifles.

The office, when he finally arrived, was almost unrecognisable. Swathes of tinsel hung from the ceiling, interspersed with gold bells, snowflakes and giant baubles. In the corner, dwarfing the photocopier, was a plastic tree wrapped in lurid, flashing lights.

'Wow.' Tony looked around, trying to ascertain who was responsible for the display. He was fairly sure they had no budget for decorations.

'Merry Christmas!' sung Louise, solving his conundrum as she tried to attach a sprig of Holly to the top of Roy's monitor, much to the Operations Manager's annoyance.

'Merry Christmas,' he muttered, making his way through the mayhem. Had he been talking to anyone else, he might have pointed out that it was in fact the eleventh of December, a full fortnight away from the holy day, but he couldn't bring himself to burst Louise's bubble. She had been trying so hard ever since he'd pulled her up on the budget balls-up.

Tony entered his office to find Amit sitting in his seat, feet up on the desk, engrossed in the latest version of the smart home business plan. He looked up as Tony walked in.

'Festive greetings to you, my friend.'

'And to you.' Tony jabbed his thumb over his shoulder, indicating for Amit to take the visitor's seat.

'In-laws dispatched?' asked Amit, straining to heave his legs over the keyboard.

'Finally.' Tony smiled. 'I've never been so happy to see Anja's face in the morning.'

'I bet.'

Marianne knocked gently and edged her way in, wielding two cups of hot, steaming coffee.

'Mmm,' said Amit, taking his first sip as the door clicked shut. 'Wish I had one of them.'

Tony smiled. 'She's a saint. I don't think I'd get through a day without her.'

They set down their mugs and pulled up either side of the desk, the document lying flat between them.

'So... What d'you think?'

Amit's eyes narrowed. He looked at the cover page for a long time, slowly stroking his clean-shaven jaw. 'Honestly?'

Tony nodded, the apprehension growing in his gut.

'Honestly...' Amit grimaced. 'I think it needs a lot of work.'

Tony picked up the business plan and flicked through the pages. His heart suddenly felt very heavy. Deep down, he knew that Amit was right. That was why he'd asked him to take a look at the draft. His team was made up of reluctant contributors whose competence varied from mediocre to inept.

'Some parts more than others,' said Amit. 'The proposition section, for example, is fine.'

'I'm glad you said that.' Tony managed a laugh. He had spent most of the previous night writing that part of the plan.

Amit leafed through the pages, lost in thought. 'Except this bit.' He pointed. 'What *is* this?'

Tony followed his finger and let out a quiet groan at the sight of Norm's eight page technical 'summary'.

'I tried to read it,' said Amit, 'but I kept nodding off.'

Tony nodded sceptically. 'It's our Technology Manager; he hasn't quite grasped the phrase 'top level'.'

'And then there was something weird here, too...' Amit skipped back a few pages. 'The opportunity section. It all makes sense until you get to the addressable market bit, which bears no relation to the figures that go before it.'

'Ah.' Tony cringed. 'Yes. We've got some internal issues. My Head of Sales doesn't get on with my Head of Marketing.'

Amit nodded slowly, stroking his chin.

'They just don't seem to see eye to eye,' Tony mused, more for his own benefit than Amit's. 'Matt has no respect for the marketing team after the re-brand, and Louise thinks Matt's an arrogant bully. Which he is, in a way.'

Amit pulled a face. 'Not an ideal dynamic for a new venture team.'

They looked through the mismatching sections for a while, eventually coming to the conclusion that Tony would have to re-write most of it, plugging the gaps and translating it into a language that the board would understand.

'Operations,' said Amit, eventually. He turned the pages and let the document fall open at Roy's section, revealing in all its pure white glory the lack of content.

Tony looked at him sheepishly. 'My Ops Manager doesn't like working overtime,' he explained. 'At least, not for me.'

Seeing the business plan in its entirety, through fresh eyes, it was suddenly obvious how much work there remained to be done. Roy had put in minimal effort – enough, presumably, that he wouldn't jeopardise his chance of promotion should the venture become a success, but it was obvious that his heart wasn't in it. It was also apparent that his writing skills weren't up to the job.

'It just doesn't make sense,' said Amit.

Tony shook his head despondently.

'So I took the liberty of sketching out my own alternative.' Amit slipped a page of biro scribbles onto the desk between them.

Tony watched in respectful silence as his friend talked him through a fully re-written draft of the section.

'Incredible,' he said when Amit had finished. '*Thanks.*'

Amit shrugged modestly. 'That's what I do. I'm not much good for the soft and fluffy stuff, but operations... that's my bag. And besides, it's more interesting than twiddling my thumbs up in Starship Enterprise.'

Tony laughed wryly, although Amit's situation was far from funny. His skills were going to waste in the Cordless division. It would be TransTel's loss when he walked into a job at Netcomm.

'Is that everything?' Amit thumbed through the document, squinting at the annotated pages.

'Well, there is one... small... thing.' Tony grimaced. 'The financial forecasts.'

Amit turned to the end of the document and frowned. 'Ah. I see.'

'That Chek-Han guy was a star. But the model's out of date

now and he says he's too busy to work on it. D'you have any more bright sparks up your sleeve?'

Amit thought for a second, lips pursed. 'That's a bugger,' he said. 'I guess he's been shunted over to the cable division.'

Tony nodded.

There was a knock at the door and Marianne's head poked round. 'Sorry to interrupt,' she said. 'Just need an answer on the Christmas party budget.'

Tony let out a quiet moan. 'I dunno... as little as possible? Say thirty pounds a head?'

Amit rounded on him, eyes wide. 'Are you joking?'

'Well, I'm trying to build a new venture here... We can't piss all our money against the wall before we've even started.'

Amit looked beside himself. 'Wh...' He turned to Marianne. 'Make it eighty.'

'What?' Tony stared.

'Eighty pounds a head,' declared Amit, nodding authoritatively as Marianne jotted something down on her notepad and slipped away, clearly sensing an altercation.

'What are you doing?' asked Tony, jumping to his feet, ready to chase his PA down the corridor.

Amit wheeled out on his chair, blocking Tony's path.

'Tony... Tony...' He was smiling. 'How long have you been running departments?'

Tony frowned, unable to see the relevance of the question. He really needed to get Marianne to change that figure.

'This is your answer,' said Amit, looking him in the eye. 'This is how you build your team. You throw the party of a lifetime – the party that gets talked about for years to come. The party that every TransTel employee wants to be a part of. *That's* how you get lads like Chek-Han on board. You might not have a budget for headcount, but you have a budget for a Christmas party. Use the cap-ex as op-ex! How big is your team?'

'Forty-five... Maybe fifty?' Tony fell back into his chair, trying to see Amit's logic.

'There you go! What's a few thousand in the grand scheme of things?'

'But...' Tony tried to think of a counter-attack.

'Seriously... a well-bonded team of no-hopers is worth more than a dissatisfied bunch of high-flyers.'

Tony thought for a second.

'It's not your money, anyway,' Amit reminded him.

Eventually, Tony allowed himself a reluctant smile.

'Alright,' he said. 'But you'd better make sure your man Chek-Han comes along. I need him to fix my financials.'

Team Christmas Do

TONY LEANED FORWARD and peered at his bearded reflection, trying to secure the moustache to his upper lip. Beads of sweat were appearing as quickly as he could wipe them away – a consequence of the cheap felt outfit that he'd managed to don over the top of his suit.

'You need to take the paper backing off first,' said a voice.

Tony turned, grappling with the over-sized hat that had slipped over his eyes. Matt was standing at the urinals, watching him in the mirror. He seemed to be swaying slightly, or maybe it was the lighting; it was difficult to tell.

He squinted at the stick-on moustache and realised that the Sales Manager was right. He had forgotten to peel off the adhesive paper. Perhaps he was drunk after all.

'Ladies and gentlemen!' Marianne was standing at the head of the table, tapping her glass so hard that it was only a matter of time before it shattered. 'Please welcome... Santa Claus!'

On cue, Tony re-entered the restaurant, to the whoops and cries of his inebriated underlings. He swung the black sack onto the table and made a great show of rummaging around inside it, taking care to avoid sudden movements for fear of the outfit coming apart.

'The first present...' he lisped through the hairy white beard, 'is for Marianne!'

More whoops, more cries. Marianne squealed with delight as she tore off the packaging, then turned it over and over in her hands. It looked like a giant fly swat. 'Oh!' She giggled as she tried it on Roy's bald head. 'It talks!' She hit Louise, then one of

126

the marketing girls, then Roy again. Every time it made contact with somebody's head, it let out a robotic-sounding phrase. Whack. *You're late for your meeting!* Whack. *Timesheets please!* Whack. *This room is already booked!* Marianne seemed delighted.

Next was a small parcel for one of the techies in Norm's department: a booklet on how to break dance. Then Louise opened her crate of RedBull and Matt, nonplussed, extracted his inflatable Barbie doll while somebody else read out the accompanying note: *Because no woman is good enough.* A large proportion of the marketing girls' presents were genitalia-related: soaps, candles, chocolates. Similarly, the sales guys came away with a selection of breast-based tat. Tony opened his own gift and was relieved to find he had got away lightly with a set of office politics Top Trumps cards.

The party was ushered through to the bar, where fifty sickly-looking shots were being prepared on Marianne's command. Tony watched his PA round up the team, her organisational skills having apparently strengthened, rather than diminished, with alcohol. He was coming round to the idea that Amit had been right about the budget. The cocktails and free-flowing wine had got people talking – as well as shouting, laughing and swapping clothes with one another.

'Everybody!' screamed Marianne, holding out a shot glass for Tony. 'One, two, three!'

The drink tasted like a mixture of cough syrup and lighter fuel, but he tipped back his head nonetheless.

'How's the tab doing?' he yelled at the barman.

'Still got nearly a grand left,' he replied through the din.

'Jesus.' Tony looked around. Marianne was riding piggyback on one of the salesmen, Louise was handcuffing two telecom specialists together and Matt was attempting to drink a pint through his sock. 'Get another round of shots in.'

Later, Tony found himself propped up at the bar, talking to a man in an afro wig.

'Cracking night,' he slurred

'Yeah,' grunted the man.

'Never seen anything like it.'

'Not at a Synapse do.'

Tony looked at him. It was hard to see much of the man's face, what with the afro. 'You been to many Synapse dos, then?'

'Half a dozen or so.'

Tony had another look. Despite his muddled state, he knew that he really ought to know the man if he'd been part of the team for six years.

'I gotta say,' said the guy, nodding slowly, 'You ain't done a bad job. I can't say I agree with half of what you're doin' in this place, but you ain't done a bad job of rallyin' the troops.'

Tony watched as the man shuffled off, his chequered shirt coming haphazardly tucked into his old, beige trousers. There was only one person in Synapse who wore trousers like that, thought Tony, and that was his balding Operations Manager. Roy Smith, it seemed, had just paid Tony a compliment.

'Tony?'

Tony looked down. A young Asian man was blinking up at him, flanked on either side by two pretty girls from Sales.

'Hello.'

'I'm Chek-Han,' said the guy, stumbling sideways into one of the girls. He looked about fifteen years old.

Tony smiled as the name hit home. 'So *you're* Chek-Han.'

'Yeah. I just wanted to say thanks for inviting me.' He hiccupped.

'Don't be silly,' said Tony. 'It was the least I could do after all your hard work.'

Chek-Han flushed as the sales girls looked on admiringly.

'If... If you need another pair of hands...' He hiccupped again.

Tony smiled. 'Funny you should say that.'

'I'm sure I can fit it in, somehow.' He flashed a flirtatious look at one of the girls.

'So, if we get anywhere with our new venture, can I assume you might be interested in a full-time role?'

Chek-Han's smile said it all. Which was just as well, really, because his hiccups were becoming incapacitating. Eventually, the girls led him off towards the bar.

'Pleased?' Marianne slipped into the seat next to him. Her cheeks were glowing.

'Very.' He nodded. 'You've done a great job.'

They looked out at the drunken chaos. Roy, still sporting the giant afro, was reluctantly engaging in a group dance routine led by the marketing girls, while in the middle of the room, a space seemed to be clearing for a performance of some sort.

'Oh my God.' Marianne clasped a hand over her mouth.

'Is that...' Tony stared. He couldn't believe what he was seeing.

'I *never* thought I'd see *that.*'

'Me neither. Norm's *breakdancing.*'

Marianne grabbed hold of his arm and squeezed. 'No, not that! Look!'

Tony followed her gaze into the corner of the room, where, beyond the makeshift dance floor, beyond Norm's spasmodic attempt at a power move, two people were standing beneath the sprig of mistletoe, entwined.

'Is that...'

'Yes! It's Matt and Louise!'

Business plan coming on; Marianne quits

TONY RUBBED HIS EYES, shook his head and looked at the numbers one last time. He'd been staring at them for so long now they were blurring together on the page.

'Okay,' he said, feeling as certain as he ever would. 'Louise, are you happy with the market sizing?'

The Marketing Manager looked solemnly through her mousy fringe and nodded.

'Matt? You sure about the sales targets?'

The young man dipped his head.

'Chek-Han? Do the revenues look okay to you?'

'Yes.'

'Roy? Costs?'

'They're as good as they're gonna get, this late in the day.'

Tony managed a reluctant smile. It was half-past three on Christmas Eve. He could hardly blame his Ops Manager for being irritable. Every other TransTel employee had long since clocked off.

'Okay Marianne, we're ready to go!'

Marianne sprang to life, checking paper and toner levels and clearing an area around the binding machine on the desk. The rest of the team stayed put, flaked out in their swivel chairs, watching the whirlwind through tired eyes.

'Haven't you got homes to go to?' Tony looked around, waiting for someone to take the lead. What he was trying to say was *thanks*, for staying late nearly every night this week, for working on something that didn't strictly fall under any job description and for living on a diet of pizza and Coke for the last five days. But Tony wasn't one for opening up.

'We should go for a drink,' said Matt.

For a moment, nobody seemed to know what to say. Tony looked at his Sales Manager, trying to remember the last time something positive had come out of that mouth.

'Good idea!' cried Louise.

Too stunned to think properly, Tony found himself nodding. 'Great! Let's do that. You more than deserve it. Drinks are on me.'

He couldn't believe the change that had come over Matt in the last few days. It wasn't just the uncanny bond that seemed to have developed between him and Louise, following the mistletoe episode at the Christmas do; it was his attitude. He had become more approachable and... well, it seemed almost as though he'd become *enthusiastic* about the new venture.

The Christmas party had been a turning point; he saw that now. It had broken down barriers and brought people closer together, just as Amit had predicted. Chek-Han had slotted straight into the team – a result of some HR negotiations on Tony's part, coupled with Chek-Han's desire to escape the male-dominated cable division – and Norm had earned himself newfound respect after his antics on the dance floor. Even the pig-headed Ops Manager seemed slightly more amicable since his night wearing the 'fro.

There was, of course, another reason for the team's dedication. As a reward for their hard work, Tony had promised them the three days between Christmas and New Year as extra holiday. It was an easy deal to make; he had promised to get the business plan over to Gable and Draper by the end of the year, and he wanted to spend Christmas week with his family. Business was always quiet during the festive period, so this way, everyone was happy. that said, Tony knew that his managers weren't putting the hours in just so they could get their three days off.

This business plan, if it got past the board, would dictate what the members of Synapse would spend the next few years of their lives working on. This would steer the direction of the division – possibly of the whole company. The words and figures inscribed in the plan would determine the path of their careers. They were writing their own future.

A month ago, or even as little as a week ago, Tony might not have felt this way, but today he would openly admit that he felt proud of his team. Maybe he was just tired, but he had a strange urge to reach out and hug them all, to thank them for their efforts.

'One down, four to go,' said Marianne, handing Tony the first bound copy.

Tony flipped through the plan, admiring its crisp, glossy perfection. They *had* to go for it. Gable and Draper were sensible men; they knew where the business was heading. They knew that if they were ever going to turn things around then they'd have to take a risk on something like this. Didn't they?

'Why don't you all go down to the pub? Take my card. Marianne, you can teach me how this thing works, can't you? I'll stay and finish up.'

Matt, quick to grab Tony's Amex card, was already shrugging on his coat. Louise swiftly followed suit.

Marianne was looking at him, cock-eyed. 'Don't take this the wrong way, but...' She looked at Tony, then the machine, then back at Tony. 'I think I'd better stay.'

'I'll help you then. Go on–' Tony shooed the others away. 'We'll catch you up.'

The door eventually slammed behind them, leaving Tony to watch helplessly as Marianne manipulated the machine.

'Shall I...' He made a half-hearted attempt to line up the pages.

'Seriously, Tony. It'll be quicker if I do it.'

'Right. I'll...'

'You want me to get that?'

'What?'

'Your phone's ringing.'

'Oh.' Tony hurried back into his office.

'Hey, it's me.' Suze sounded tired.

'You okay?' Tony checked the time and baulked. It was nearly four. He had promised to be home by two.

'You're still working?'

It was a statement, not a question. Tony knew what it meant. He was letting her down. Again. He'd hardly been around all week. For two nights running, he had crept into bed in the early hours, waking up again four hours later without exchanging a word.

'I'm nearly done,' he said, wondering what to do about the drinks he had promised the team.

'So, are we going up to Cambridge tonight?'

Tony closed his eyes. They were due to drive up to the in-laws' that night and then head north to see his parents on Boxing Day, before spending the rest of the week recuperating in the Lake District. He'd been so preoccupied with brand propositions and implementation plans that he'd blotted out everything else. 'Of course we are. Sorry; I should've called. Let's aim to leave at five.'

'So, that'll be seven o'clock then,' Suze said peevishly. 'Along with everyone else.'

Tony sighed. Suze felt hurt, and rightly so. It *would* probably be seven o'clock by the time he got home and the roads *would* be rammed. He hated himself for letting her down like this. 'I'll make it up to you. I promise. I won't work next week. I won't even take my laptop.'

'I'll believe that when I see it.'

Tony thought for a second, wondering whether he could risk not taking his laptop away with him. There was a chance that Gable or Draper would be working during those interim days; what if they called him with questions about the business plan? Maybe he could bring paper copies, he thought. But then what if they needed something sent over? 'Okay, I might take it, but if I do I won't open it.'

'Look, I don't care. Just get on with your work and come home as soon as you can. Poppy's forgotten what you look like.'

Tony grunted helplessly. He wished more than anything that he could be there with his little girl and his wife, not stuck in an over-heated tower block on the side of the M4.

She sighed. 'I'm sorry. It's been a long day.'

'A long year.'

'Yeah.' There was a smile in her voice again. 'I'll see you later.'

'Love you.'

'Love you too. Now get a move on.'

Tony replaced the receiver and looked over to where Marianne was stacking what looked like the final copy of the business plan, ready for binding and dispatching. It pained him to hear the weariness in Suze's voice. It pained him, yet he couldn't seem to do anything about it. If he came home at six every night, there was no way he'd get his job done, and if he couldn't do his job properly then... well, then he'd be letting her down financially. And he'd be letting himself down. It wasn't just a question of earning the salary – which he knew was important, more than ever now they had a second child on the way. It was a pride thing. Tony didn't do things by halves. He made things happen. He stuck it out when things got tough.

'Tony?'

He jumped. Marianne was standing in the doorway, arms laden with bound copies of the plan.

'D'you want to look through them before I courier them out?'

He hesitated. 'You've checked for upside-down pages?'

Marianne rolled her eyes. 'What d'you take me for?'

'Sorry. In which case, no. It's too late to change anything. Just get them out.'

'Will do.' Marianne turned, then stopped and returned to the exact same spot. She was looking at Tony strangely, her lips slightly parted, eyes narrowed.

'What's up?' he asked.

'Um...' She lowered the bundle of documents, edging her way back into the office. 'Er, there's something I need to tell you.'

Tony swallowed. All sorts of panicky thoughts flashed across his mind.

'I'm leaving TransTel.'

Tony just stared at her, mouth open.

'I'm really sorry, Tony. I know this is a bad time for you. I know you've got loads on and you need a PA, but...' Marianne was wringing her hands, her eyes pleading for forgiveness. 'I need job security and I'm just not sure I've got it here. I've been offered a job in a City firm that pays nearly double my current salary.'

Tony opened his mouth to reply but there was nothing to say.

'I'm sorry,' said Marianne, carrying the documents out, head down.

Slowly, painfully, the implications began to sink in. There was no way round this, no option to barter, no compromise to be made. His PA was walking out. There was a gaping hole in his perfect team.

Gravity Wisdom

THE ART OF
BUILDING THE TEAM

THE ART OF
BUILDING THE TEAM

 MarketGravity

In this chapter Tony gets his plans approved by the board, but discovers there is no budget and no additional resource. In-fighting ensues within the team due to uncertainty, long hours and cultural pressures.

Here are some of the challenges that you may encounter in your business:

- The existing culture is not conducive to building a growth business
- Junior people now have to fulfil senior roles and lack confidence
- General scepticism and negative attitudes from team members
- You are constrained by existing HR policies and timeframes
- Existing incentives are not aligned with the new roles and level of experience required

Unlike Private Entrepreneurs who have carte blanche to build their team from scratch, Corporate Entrepreneurs must utilise what they have, good and bad. Understanding how to get the very best out of people and keep them motivated through the ups an down of a new venture is a big leadership challenge. It requires a balance between towing the company line and bending the rules.

"I DELIBERATELY PICKED PEOPLE WHO WOULD DIE TRYING. THEY ALL HAD PERSONAL INCENTIVES TO MAKE THINGS WORK – NOT FINANCIAL. NOBODY GOT BONUSES. THEY ALL NEEDED IT ON THEIR CVS."

Douglas Johnson-Poensgen, BT Global Services

There are a number of simple things that you can do today to address these challenges and build the ultimate team:

1. Create a can-do culture. Lead by example and demonstrate how you'd like others to act.

2. Set a very clear direction and common objectives. This will be a new direction and a new way of working for many in the team so keep the priorities simple and keep restating a few consistent messages.

3. Let people do what they are good at. Build on their strengths. Your venture will succeed due to the confidence and ability of the team.

4. Create co-dependencies between team members. The team will recognise that they can only succeed individually if they work together and help each other.

5. Over-invest in your people. Even small gestures like buying the first round, or remembering people's birthdays will do a huge amount for team morale. You really don't want to lose the ownership and commitment of a founding team member.

6. Get the expertise and mindsets you need. Build a team for three year's time. From the outside this team will appear over-qualified and over-paid. In reality, unless you get the right skills and experience in place, you won't have a business in three years!

Do you and your team have the right traits to be effective Corporate Entrepreneurs?

	YES	NO
It's more important to lead my own project than receive a job promotion		
I'm happier when mapping out the direction than I am when getting into the detail		
I'm more interested in leaving a legacy than in climbing the corporate ladder		
I try to find ways to get around internal barriers rather than working within the rules		
I persuade others to help me work on problems rather than going it alone		
I get impatient when things don't happen fast enough rather than remaining calm and collected		

You don't need (or want) everyone in the team to exhibit these characteristics, but they should exist between a few key people.

5

Show me the money: getting the FD to back you

'Be careful what you wish for ... The board will always want to see rosier forecasts – but you're the one that has to deliver.'

New demands from the board

CHRISTMAS PASSED in a blur of food, traffic jams and stilted conversations with in-laws, with New Year week coming as a welcome relief. In Suze's own words, the Lake District 'took away the bitter taste' from the previous week. The cottage was primitive, with no television, no internet and a single board game to serve as the week's entertainment. It was perfect.

By day four, Tony was beginning to get used the lack of mobile phone reception and the strangely clean-smelling air – just in time for the six-hour journey back to the emails and bustle and smog. Now, standing in front of the circle of bleary-eyed executives, his veins pumped with caffeine, Tony had almost forgotten how it felt to be relaxed.

'Turning to the financial summary, you'll see we're looking at a payback period of two years and one month. Top-line revenues for the first year of profitability...' Tony stepped backwards and pointed at the figure on the slide. 'Fifty million.'

He looked around. Heads were nodding, glances were exchanged, notes were being scribbled in margins. Tony cleared his throat and prepared his parting words.

'On the basis of revenue, profitability and current market trends, I therefore urge you to consider putting the smart home proposition at the centre of TransTel's medium- to long-term strategy.'

Maintaining the jaw-aching smile, Tony waited for a cue to step down. The presentation had gone well, as far as he could tell. No one had interrupted. No one had shot down his idea or pointed out any glaring omissions. In fact, no one had said very much at all, come to think of it. Some of the board members had looked positively corpse-like as he'd run through the elements of the proposition, but Tony assumed that was just the way they were. Several of the non-execs were nearing retirement; they were probably just here to keep away the January blues.

'Thank you,' said Charles Gable, eventually.

With a respectful dip of the head, Tony returned to his seat, taking some discrete deep breaths in preparation for what lay ahead. He knew, from his limited experience, that the questions would be as taxing as the presentation itself.

'Tony.'

He looked up. Nicholas Draper's angular features bore down on him from across the table.

'You say you're looking at a payback of two years and one month. How does that fit in with the TransTel criteria that clearly state payback must come *within eighteen months?*'

'Ah. Well,' Tony acknowledged the question with a nod. 'Good point. This does sit slightly outside the standard criteria, but you'll see that we're talking about revenues of nearly ten times–'

'So it doesn't fit the criteria?' Draper looked at him in the way that Suze looked at Poppy when she'd done something wrong.

'Not quite, but–'

Charles Gable gave a meaningful cough. 'I'm sure I don't need to remind you that the eighteen month rule is imposed for a *reason*, Tony. It's a matter of risk.'

Tony nodded patiently. *Exactly*, he wanted to say. *And maybe if we took a bit of a risk from time to time, we might actually get somewhere, like our competitors, instead of going round and round in the same old circles.* They were looking at revenues that eclipsed most of their B2C divisions put together, and all they could see was the bloody eighteen month rule.

'You'll have to get the payback down to eighteen months,' declared Nicholas.

'Okay,' Tony acknowledged limply. 'We can do that, but it'll mean ramping up the early subscriber base to very ambitious levels.'

'Even *more* ambitious?' screeched Anita Reynolds. She was one of those dumpy, power-dressers who spent most of her time trying to prove her worth in the boardroom by dropping acidic comments about other people's ideas. She was supposedly an expert in marketing.

'I believe the current targets are attainable,' Tony replied calmly. 'But to raise–'

'Do you?' Anita whipped over several pages in quick succession.

'I do, yes. They've been developed with the Synapse sales team in mind, off the back of rigorous market analysis.'

'For a market that doesn't yet exist?'

'We've used–' Tony hesitated; he didn't want to go into detail about Louise's market sizing techniques now. 'If you want to see our methodology, I'd be happy to take you through it.'

'Oh, please!' Anita waved a hand dismissively in his direction. 'Don't try and teach *me* about methodologies.'

There was an awkward pause, which Tony felt compelled to fill. 'I, er... Maybe we can... I'll have a look at, er... reducing the customer uptake.'

'On what basis,' asked Sir Anthony Knowles, the ancient non-executive whose purpose on the board seemed to be to slow down the decision-making process, 'are we assuming uptake of this... service, if you will?'

'Well, as I said, I can take you through the methodology we–'

'And I ask this,' he went on, ignoring Tony's attempts to explain, 'because I for one wouldn't have any need for a... what are you calling it? A *smart home?* I find, and I have reason to believe that there are others of a similar disposition, that life these days is complicated enough as it is, and I cannot see the need to complicate things further.'

'Actually, the idea is that this would *simplify* energy usage in the home, as well as saving the customer–'

'I feel quite sure that *I* would not be a subscriber of such a scheme,' Sir Anthony concluded, looking around as though waiting for approval from his fellow directors.

Tony was still trying to think of a tactful way of explaining that the old man didn't fall within the target market for the smart home proposition when he realised, with horror, that other board members were nodding their heads.

'No, I must say...'

'I'm not convinced.'

'It's a tough call...'

'Maybe we should be thinking about the *customers,* rather than our own individual preferences,' suggested Tony, forcing his features into a pleasant expression. 'We've done some thorough market testing, which reveals that ninety-one percent of homeowners in the target group would go for such a scheme.'

'Tony!' barked somebody from the other end of the table. Even before he'd turned round, Tony knew who it was. There was only one person who got away with shouting and swearing at the boardroom table. It was Carl Spragg, the bearded Rottweiler. ''Ave you considered the fact that TransTel ain't in the business of energy reduction? And that Breersh Gas or Enpaaah might come along an' eat your lunch?'

Tony smiled cautiously. Clearly Spragg hadn't read the competitive analysis section of the plan that outlined exactly such concerns, but Tony wasn't about to point this out. 'That is a risk, yes. It's quite likely that the leading energy suppliers will make a move in this direction – which is all the more reason for us to get in quickly. We need first-mover advantage.'

'I'm still not convinced by your targets,' declared Anita, letting the document fall shut in front of her and shaking her head. 'They seem exceedingly ambitious.'

'Well, as I said, I'll have a look at–'

'Well, you can hardly lower them!' cried Nicholas Draper. 'As it is, you're not hitting the eighteen month payback!'

'Quite,' muttered Graham Walker-Jones, unhelpfully.

'We can't give the green light for a venture that doesn't pay back within eighteen months,' Charles Gable declared profoundly.

'Okay,' said Tony, forcing himself to remain composed. They were sounding like a broken record. 'I'll take another look at the numbers.'

'Well, I think it's a goer!'

There was a collective turn of heads. The voice, it transpired, was that of Josh Green, the aptly named Head of Sustainability at TransTel. Despite his youth – he was one of the few people in the room who, like Tony, still had a good head of hair – he held a powerful position on the board, increasingly powerful, in fact, with every environmental regulation that came into force.

'It's right on trend,' he said, beaming at the blank faces around the table. 'Energy saving is hot; it's high time we embraced it. Think of the PR potential!' He turned to Tony. 'I'll bet you haven't even factored in the effect of good press on the numbers, have you?'

'Er, well, no.' Tony blinked, taken aback by the sudden display of support.

'Well then!' Josh was getting some very dirty looks from around the table but he didn't seem to care. 'I'd say there's half a million's worth of intangibles in there, if you do things properly. It shouldn't be overlooked.'

'Point taken, Josh,' said the CEO, like a teacher to a hyperactive child. 'I'm sure there's all sorts of additional value locked away in the proposition. That said, I don't see any point in discussing it further until we know we can hit the eighteen month payback target.'

'Quite,' muttered Draper.

'Okay,' said Tony, sensing that his time with the board was up. 'I'll make some changes to the plan.'

'And look into those ambitious take-up figures!' cried Anita as he rose from his seat.

'Will do.' Tony managed a business-like smile. 'Thanks for listening.'

He got as far as the sixth-floor atrium before he stopped, leaned back on the wall and let out a long, shaky sigh. He had never, in all his years at the company, left a meeting feeling so deflated or so unsure about what to do. An hour ago, the business plan had seemed so robust; the targets seemed achievable, the costs affordable... Now it felt as though he needed to tear it up and start all over again. Nicholas Draper wanted higher, quicker revenues, while Anita wanted lower, more realistic sales targets. How could he please them both?

His desk, when he finally dragged himself back to the office, was covered in Post-It notes and scrawled-on pieces of paper. *Call Amit – x3404. No department mtg? Suze phoned – call her back. How was board pres? Need budget figs for online research. Call Chek-Han 3342.* His voicemail light was flashing and his inbox was overflowing.

'I need a PA,' he moaned, to nobody in particular.

Louise popped her head round the door. 'Didn't you get my message?'

'Which one?' he asked, scraping a row of notes off his monitor.

'From HR. Natasha called. She said they were having problems with the temp agency, so it'll probably be a week or so before they find you a PA.'

'A *week*?'

Louise nodded anxiously. 'How was the board meeting?'

'Oh...' Tony smiled falsely. 'Great. Fantastic. Couldn't have been better.'

Arguing with HR

'TONY, IT'S NATASHA. Good news. I think we're a little closer to finding you a PA.'

Tony looked up from the latest revision of the sales forecasts. 'Excellent. What start dates are we looking at?'

'I said we're *closer*; we haven't started interviewing yet. There are three candidates in the picture.'

'Okay... So, how long does it take for them to go from being *in the picture* to being *in my office*?'

Natasha sighed. 'Please, Tony. We're doing our best. We have to follow procedures when we make a new hire.'

'Ah, right. *Procedures*.' Tony grimaced. 'So what do you need from me?'

'I just wanted to get your initial impressions ahead of the interviews. Number one is called Danielle. Thirty-seven, based in Leeds, good ref–'

'Based in *Leeds*?'

'She's a home worker.'

'As in, she wouldn't come into the office?'

'That's right, yes.'

'Wh... But... How would she do the job?'

'She has a phone and email.'

'But...' Tony frowned into the handset. 'Are you serious?'

'Why wouldn't I be? These days, most jobs can be done remotely. All you need is–'

'Not *this* one,' he said. 'I need someone here.'

'Well, I'm afraid that's not a requirement in the job

145

description, so we can't penalise her on those grounds. Number two, Shaianna. Seventeen, recently joined–'

'*Seventeen?*' Tony echoed, momentarily lost for words. 'Can she read? Is she still in school?'

'Age doesn't come into this. In fact, I shouldn't even have mentioned it. She's a perfectly good candidate and she's recently dropped into the reallocation pool. Her last manager–'

'Oh, great. So we're scraping the piss-pool for dregs, are we?'

'Shaianna's role became redundant, through no fault of her own. Please don't make judgements.'

Tony managed to hold his tongue. 'Right. Fine. Look... I just want someone who can do the job. Someone who's organised and smart, who can come into the office and work a computer – that's all. Can't we put an ad in the local paper or something?'

Natasha breathed wearily down the line. 'That's not how it works, I'm afraid.' She cleared her throat noisily, in the manner of a chairman of a very important meeting. 'Finally, Annabel. Previously PA to two directors at National Electric, glowing references, immaculate CV...'

'She sounds perfect. Get her in.'

'Ah. Um, she does have an aversion to stress. Would you say the role was particularly stressful?'

He thought for a second, baffled by the complexity of it all. 'Maybe. A bit.'

'Yes, I thought as much. Better not risk it. So, I'll ask Danielle and Shaianna for an interview.'

'What? Isn't Danielle the one based in Leeds?'

'That's right. We haven't ruled her out.'

'But... *I* have. She can't do the job from there.'

'Tony, I'm afraid we can't be seen to be discriminating against home-workers.'

'*Discriminating?* So it's discriminating to stipulate that someone has to actually *turn up to work,* is it? Is it discriminating to ask that they can use a phone? Or write an email?'

Natasha didn't dignify his question with an answer.

'I'll send over their details so that you can interview them this week.'

'So that *I* can interview them?'

'It's standard procedure. You have to interview all suitable candidates.'

'But...' Tony baulked. This was bureaucracy gone mad. 'I don't have time!'

'Well, I'm sure you'll make time. You'll have to, won't you, if you want a PA.'

'Natasha, I'm sorry.' Tony took a deep breath and levelled his voice. 'I'm trying to run a department here. On top of that, I'm also attempting to build a new venture with no budget and no extra resource. I *need* a PA and I don't have time to go calling people who live in Leeds just to meet some political correctness requirement. Can you please just call me when you've found someone suitable?'

In the three seconds that it took for the Head of HR to respond, several thoughts crossed Tony's mind. He wondered whether he'd blown his chances of ever getting a replacement for Marianne. He considered the possibility that he had just inadvertently put himself forward for one of those Godforsaken diversity awareness training courses. Then he realised that his second line was blinking.

'It's not protocol,' said Natasha, eventually. 'But I'll see what I can do.'

Tony let out a sigh of relief, his finger poised on the phone. 'Thank you.' He kept the handset against his ear as he switched to line two. 'Hello?'

'Hey, it's me.'

Tony smiled at the sound of his wife's voice. 'Thank God. I thought it might be someone else trying to stand in the way of progress.'

'Ah. Er...'

'What's up?'

'Um...' Suze hesitated. 'Well, I think I might be one of those people after all. I need you to do me a favour.'

'Go on.'

'Can you be home for bath time tonight?'

Tony looked down at the to-do list. He still had to re-work the revised marketing budget with Louise, talk to Chek-Han about the financials, take a look at the Christmas sales figures and plough through the action points from the seventy-odd emails in his inbox.

"Course I can.'

'Thanks, love. We've just been told we have to get our appraisals sewn up by tomorrow, ahead of next week's review. Ridiculous timescale, but...'

Suze started talking about the annual review process at Lockharts. Tony tried to listen, but email had just appeared on his screen, flagged as *Urgent*, which was odd, because there was nothing urgent about the December sales report as far as he could tell. He leaned forward and clicked on the attachment.

'...which means that everyone has to get ten people to rate and review their performance, including–'

'Suze, I'm sorry.' Tony stared at the bar charts in horror. 'I'm gonna have to go.'

'Right.' Suze sounded put out.

'I'm sorry. I'll see you later.'

Tony frowned. He couldn't believe that the figures were correct. It was as though someone had missed off a zero somewhere, or mistyped a decimal place. Sales for the week between Christmas and New Year were practically non-existent.

'Matt?' he yelled, leaning out of his office and beckoning the manager over.

Matt swaggered in, looking exceedingly chipper. Ever since Christmas, or more specifically, since the Christmas party, he'd been walking on air. 'What's up, mate?'

Tony didn't reply directly; he just strode over to his desk and pointed at the chart on the screen. '*That* is what's up.'

'Oh, right. Yeah, I saw that. A bit of a dip.'

'A *bit?* Would you call falling off a *cliff* a bit of a dip?'

The Head of Sales shrugged defensively. 'Sales are always down over Christmas.'

Tony exhaled as calmly as he was able. 'I am aware of the sales cycle, Matt. I have seen previous years' accounts. I realise that the holiday period isn't our most profitable time, but usually we're talking about a drop of twenty to thirty percent; not *ninety-five*. What happened?'

'Well, I guess we didn't have the full team.'

'What d'you mean, you *guess*?'

'I wasn't here, was I? You said we could have the days between Christmas and New Year off.'

'I said *you* could. The people who worked on the business plan. Not the entire sales team. What happened?'

'I dunno,' Matt snarled, as though Tony was being highly unreasonable. 'I was kind of busy before Christmas, wasn't I? If you remember?'

Tony closed his eyes, pressing his finger and thumb against his brow. He could feel a headache coming on.

'Look, Matt. I know you worked hard on the business plan. I appreciate that you pulled out all the stops for this smart home proposition. I did say that writing the plan was a priority, but... I didn't mean you could drop the ball on the day-to-day stuff. We still have a business to run.'

Matt glowered at him like an angry child. 'I *know*.'

Tony looked at the floor. This was his least favourite part of running the department. He wasn't a man who enjoyed conflict.

'We're going to have to explain this to Draper,' he said quietly.

Matt shrugged, although it wasn't very convincing. There was no point in trying to pretend that this wasn't his problem. This was every bit his problem. It was *their* problem. And if they were going to convince Nicholas Draper that they were fit to run a fifty million pound business, they had to solve it as soon as possible.

'I'll give you some time to think about it,' said Tony. 'Then let's reconvene at four. Draper will probably want an answer in the next few days.'

Slowly, Matt started to nod. Then, without meeting his boss' eye, he turned, yanked open the door and walked out.

Tony fell into his chair and slumped forwards, head in hands. He stayed like that for a while, thinking about what had just happened, what Draper would say and what it meant for the prospective new business. Would the FD seriously allow him to run a project of such proportions when his team couldn't even carry out their day jobs?

Tony jumped at the sound of his phone.

'Hello?'

'Tony, it's Natasha. Good news.'

'Really?' Tony was sceptical. It was hard to remember what good news actually sounded like.

'Yes. We've found you a PA. Everything's sorted. She's highly experienced, comes from the reallocation pool and she can start on Monday.'

'Not...' He struggled to remember the name of the prepubescent girl Natasha had mentioned earlier.

'No, not Shaianna. This is a lady called Maureen and she's come straight from Network Direct.'

'Wow.' Tony tried to force some enthusiasm into his voice, pulling up a new email and typing the start of Brian's address. 'Thanks for that.'

'No problem. I'll send you her details.'

Tony replaced the receiver, quickly tapping out his question to Brian and pressing Send.

He was staring at his to-do list, wondering which item to tackle next when he heard the soft ping of the message alert.

From: Brian O'Keefe - TransTel Network Direct
To: Tony Sharp - Synapse
Subject: Re: Do you know of a PA called Maureen?

I certainly do. She worked here until enough people complained about her laziness / indiscretion / disorganisation / general uselessness to get her moved on. Sincerely hope she hasn't been sent your way?

Tony shut his eyes, collapsed in his chair and let out a long, loud groan.

Suze livid post-appraisal

TONY SWITCHED ON his desk lamp and squinted at the screen. There was something different about his inbox. It looked emptier. Not just in terms of the number of messages, but... That was it. The folders were missing.

After a couple of minutes spent clicking on various buttons and menus, Tony gave up. He pushed back his chair and headed into the main office, hoping that his new PA might have more success than he usually did in eliciting support from IT Support.

'I know... I know... That's what I said to her. Linda, I said, there's no point in livin' in hope. A leopard doesn't change his spots...'

Tony stepped forward into Maureen's field of vision. She turned, registered his presence and held up a finger as if to say, *one minute.*

He watched, stunned, as his PA continued to loudly impart her relationship advice.

Tony had always considered himself a lenient boss; he deliberately tolerated a degree of workplace cheek. It would be hypocritical of him to condemn every personal call made during office hours or every website he saw being perused. He tolerated it because he knew that when push came to shove, his employees would be lenient with him in return. They'd put in overtime or cancel an evening engagement. But this... This was a level of cheek he had never encountered.

'Mmm. Mmm, I know,' Maureen went on, glancing up and him and making an impatient winding gesture with her hand.

Tony's outrage intensified as the one-sided conversation continued to be broadcast around the office. He was about to confront her when suddenly her voice dropped to a murmur.

'Anyway, listen,' she hissed. 'I've gotta go. I'll call you back, yeah?'

'Maureen,' Tony said sternly. She turned, her plump lips spreading into a lazy smile. 'I...' He lost his nerve. It was only her second day; perhaps this Linda character was having some sort of crisis. He would give her the benefit of the doubt. 'I've done something to make my email folders disappear. Could you get IT onto it?'

Maureen looked at him blankly for a couple of seconds and then finally registered. 'Email folders?'

'That's right.'

'I already sorted your inbox this morning, didn't I?'

'No, I'm talking about –' Tony frowned. 'You what?'

Louise, he noticed, was sitting nearby, fingers stuffed into ears, trying to turn the page of a document using her elbows.

'Well, I was de-cluttering. I got rid of all them folders down the side.'

'You *what*?' Tony stared, trying to decipher what the PA was telling him. Could she really have undone all of Marianne's careful filing?

'I got rid of–'

'No, I heard what you said,' he explained, patiently. 'I just wanted to clarify. What did you *do* with all the emails in the folders you deleted?'

'Oh, I archived them.'

'So...' Tony was about to ask what this meant in terms of accessing the messages that had once been at his fingertips, but he realised that Maureen's phone was ringing. 'D'you want to get that?'

She looked up at him, frowning a little. 'What?'

'The phone,' he said pointedly. 'Are you going to get that?'

Suddenly, from nowhere, Matt was towering over the PA's desk, fists alarmingly close to her face.

'PICK UP THE FUCKIN' PHONE!'

Louise popped her head up and mouthed him a *thank you*,

followed by what looked like a flirtatious wink. Tony sighed. Just as one rift healed over, another opened up.

'It's for you,' said Maureen, blinking moronically at him.

'Who is it?'

'Um... Nicholas...' She narrowed her eyes, clearly dredging her memory for a surname.

'Draper?' he suggested apprehensively. Now was not the time for a conversation with the cantankerous FD.

'That was it!'

Tony sighed, looking over at the back of Matt's head. They still hadn't agreed on a convincing explanation for the disastrous December sales.

'He says, where are you?'

'What?'

Maureen shrugged. 'Guess he's expecting you.'

Tony frowned. Nothing had been arranged as far as he knew. 'Pull up my calendar,' he said quickly, motioning for the PA to close her numerous celebrity websites and open up Outlook.

Together, they peered over the hand creams, herbal teas, photos and tasteless plastic figurines, while the computer whirred into action. Eventually, they concluded that there was nothing in his calendar that resembled a meeting with Draper.

'Can you check he's–'

'Ooh!' cawed Maureen, at eardrum-splitting volume. 'I know! I've just remembered. That name rings a bell. Ha! I should've thought.' She scrolled through the days on the screen. 'Yep, there it is. I've put it in for next week!'

Tony frowned. 'So... I *do* have a meeting with the FD?'

'Yes – look!' She laughed, pointing at the evidence of her incompetence.

Tony took a deep breath, trying not to think about the long-term implications of this new addition to the team. 'Can you please tell him, then, that I'm sorry and I'll be right up?'

Maureen seemed confused. 'Who?'

'Nicholas Draper,' he replied, through gritted teeth.

'Oh!' She looked down, momentarily confused by the phone in her hand, then eventually did as she'd been told.

Draper, when Tony finally made it into his office, did not look amused.

'Trouble-shooting, were you?' he sneered as Tony burst through the door. Using the stairs had been a mistake; four flights was a lot of steps for someone still struggling to work off the Christmas lunch.

'Sorry,' he gasped. 'Bit of a problem with my calendar.'

On the way up, between lungfuls, he had contemplated various possible explanations for his lateness. Ordinarily, he tried to stick to the truth, but he had to think carefully about blaming problems on members of his team – even though the PA had only been a part of the team for five minutes. It was his team, after all, that Tony was promoting as the saviour of TransTel – the group of individuals who would work together to put the company back on the map with their smart home proposition. If he even hinted of dissent in the ranks, or incompetence, he jeopardised the success of the venture. Which was also the reason he intended to lie about the Christmas sales figures.

'Shall we get straight to the point?'

Tony nodded, still trying to control his breathing. In his lap lay two copies of the December sales report, hastily printed off by Matt. Unsurprisingly though, the FD already had his own copy.

'This is diabolical,' said Draper, looking down his nose at the page. 'Would you care to explain?'

Tony nodded slowly, hoping to give the impression of composure. 'It's my fault.'

The FD raised an eyebrow.

'I decided to run a trial of a new sales script during the festive period. I knew that business would be slow, so I thought it would be a good time to experiment.'

'*You* decided to trial a new script?'

Tony nodded. 'Yes.' It was a conscious decision to take the blame away from Matt and to bring it onto himself. It ran the risk of making him look stupid, but that was preferable, he decided, to the implication that his Head of Sales didn't know how to lead a sales team. 'I know what you're thinking; I shouldn't have got involved. I should have let my Sales Manager run the shop. In future, that's what I'll be doing.'

'So your Sales Manager didn't know about this… trial?'

'Well,' Tony dipped his head. 'He was aware of it. But it was my idea. And not a very good one, at that.'

'Did he not advise you against the initiative? Or suggest that you roll out the trial on a smaller scale, perhaps?'

Tony hesitated. He hadn't had time to think this through properly. 'He, um… Actually, well, yes. He did advise me, as you said, but, um… I didn't listen.' This wasn't ideal. Now he was coming across as a micromanaging control freak. 'But I've learned my lesson now.'

'An expensive lesson,' Draper remarked, circling one of the figures on the page in front of him.

'Quite.' Tony nodded shamefully. He still wasn't sure his fabrication was the best approach, but he was in too deep to change his mind now.

The Finance Director sighed and pushed the sales report away. 'So,' he said. 'Any progress on the smart home proposition?'

With a sense of relief, Tony found himself slipping out back onto familiar territory. The FD was clearly more interested in the prospect of fifty million pounds than the loss of a few tens of thousands.

'Excellent,' said Draper, when Tony informed him that they were well on the way to agreeing a payback period of less than eighteen months. It was a slight exaggeration; Chek-Han had massaged the numbers to enable the venture to turn profitable within the stipulated timeframe but the sales targets were now so inflated that Matt was refusing to put his name to the plan. They'd find a way, somehow, but they weren't quite as close to doing so as Tony was implying.

'I'll send you the latest when we've nailed down the details,' he said, rising from his seat and flashing the FD an assertive smile.

Within minutes, Tony was back at his desk, trying again to find the email from Chek-Han that outlined the steps that they still had to take to 'nail down the details' – or rather, to fudge the forecasts by an acceptable level.

One of the marketing girls poked her head round the door.

'You had a call,' she said. 'A woman called Anna? Or Anya, maybe?'

Tony nodded, his heart rate picking up. Anja only called in emergencies.

'What did she say?'

'She said she'd left a message on your mobile.'

Tony reached into his pocket, panicking. 'Thanks.'

The girl slipped away, leaving Tony to study the message in private.

TONY, BETTER COME
HOME QUICK. SUZE
VERY ANGRY! ANJA

He read it twice, the fear in his gut slowly mounting as he dialled Anja's number. It rang and rang with no reply. He tried Suze's phone. The voicemail kicked in immediately. Nobody picked up the landline. Checking the time, he started gathering together his documents. He could postpone the rest of the day's meetings.

'Mari – Maureen?'

There was no reply. Tony had intended to ask his PA to divert all calls to his mobile, but then, on remembering her handling of his calendar earlier that day, he did it himself.

'I'll be working from home this afternoon,' he explained as he passed.

'*Terrible*,' cried Maureen, shaking her head into the phone. 'And a twenty-three year old, too...'

Tony tried Anja and Suze several times on the way home but neither was picking up. A montage of horrific scenarios flashed through his mind as he navigated, on autopilot, through the afternoon traffic. Something had gone wrong with the pregnancy. Something had happened to Poppy at play-school. Suze had been made redundant. Something had happened to her parents.

As it happened, the situation that greeted him as he rushed through the front door was remarkably calm. Suze was hunched over her laptop on the sofa and Anja was doing the washing up.

'Afternoon,' he said, tentatively.

It was only as his wife turned her head that he noticed the tension in the room. Suze had that glint in her eye. He'd seen it before, and he knew what it meant. *Approach with caution.*

'Everything okay?'

Suze didn't reply. She just continued to type, quickly and furiously, staring down at the screen. Anja waved from the kitchen, but it was a timid, wary gesture – more of a warning than a greeting.

Tentatively, Tony edged towards the sofa.

'I'm writing my resignation letter,' growled Suze, continuing to hammer at the keys.

'*What?*'

Suze loved her job. Or rather, she thrived on the stress and the prestige that came with the role. She had her bad days, but she'd never hinted at wanting to leave.

'What brought this on?'

Suze continued to type, either not hearing the question or choosing to ignore it. Tony knew better than to ask again.

Eventually, the rattling stopped and Suze laid the laptop on the coffee table, leaning forward to assess her work.

'Suze...' Tony was torn. He desperately wanted to intervene before she did something she'd later regret, but he knew what she could be like. If he tried to get involved, she'd go to great lengths to act against his advice.

'That should do it,' she said, making a small amendment and moving the mouse across the screen so that it hovered above the Send button.

'Suze, please.' There was no other option. He would have to beg. 'Just save the draft and come back to it later.'

'What's the point? I'm done with Lockharts. I can't stand any more of their chauvinist, Boys' Club practices. Meritocracy, my *arse.*'

'What...' Tony crept closer and tried to read the text on the screen. 'What are you talking about?'

'Promotions!' she cried as though it was obvious. 'They announced the promotions today, didn't they?'

157

'Oh... Yeah...' Tony tried to remember whether Suze had mentioned this before. Maybe it had something to do with the review she'd talked about. He wasn't sure. The smart home plan had taken up way too much of his thinking time recently.

'Three people up for being made partner, two men, one woman. Guess who gets made up.'

Tony nodded slowly, the explanation finally hitting home. Suze had been in line to be made partner this year. She'd been led to believe it was a foregone conclusion.

'I can't *believe* they made Roger Harrison partner ahead of me!'

Tony eased himself onto the sofa, hoping to distract his wife from the laptop. He didn't know Roger Harrison or any details of the situation, but he felt quite sure that the email she was about to send could only damage her career prospects.

'Do they have criteria?' he asked. 'Can you appeal?'

'If only!' Suze threw her eyes heavenward. 'Actually, they do have criteria: Young, Caucasian, male.'

He looked sideways at Suze, trying to think of an adequate response. Her jaw was set forward, her eyes narrowed to slits. On her lap, like an over-stuffed cushion, her belly was pushing out on the fabric of her woollen top. He wanted to reach out and hug her, to reassure her, to tell her it didn't matter that she hadn't been made partner, but he knew that she'd only push him away. Suze was too strong-minded to let someone else dictate what mattered.

'And *definitely* not female with child,' Suze spat. 'After all, part-timers may as well not work at all!'

Tony frowned. 'You work *more* than a full-time employee,' he pointed out. 'You're always on your laptop.'

She laughed wryly. 'As if that counts for anything! No, working on your laptop doesn't count. It's all about the hours you spend at your *desk*...'

Tony shook his head sympathetically but Suze evidently wasn't finished.

'Once you have a kid, you're just a statistic – someone they keep on the payroll to maintain their gender ratio.' She shook her head angrily. 'I feel so useless! Being a mother makes me a bad lawyer, and being a lawyer makes me a bad mother. What am I actually doing well?'

Tony shifted closer, reaching out and laying an arm around his wife's shoulders. To his relief, it wasn't shrugged away.

'You're not a bad mother,' he said, sliding his other hand onto her bump.

Suze shook her head witheringly, but Tony could see that the anger was dissipating. He wasn't always good at detecting these things, but it felt as though the atmosphere in the room had changed.

'I don't know what you're like as a lawyer, though,' he added, grinning a little. 'Being a woman and all that.'

Slowly, reluctantly, Suze started to smile. She leaned in and punched him in the stomach, upon which he grabbed her hand, pulled her closer and pressed his lips against hers. As they kissed, Tony felt the last few droplets of tension drain away and silently, with his arm outstretched, he pressed the laptop shut and pushed it away.

Staged finance plan emerges

TONY SIGHED. 'Can't we shave off some of the marketing budget? Or sales? Is it worth refining the financial model to see if we can tighten things up a bit?'

'Don't bother,' said Amit, leaning in and shaking his head at the blank, tired faces around the room. 'The problem is not with the model. It's with this ridiculous target that the board has set you.'

They sat for a while, staring at the various print-offs that littered the meeting room table. Tony could see people's eyes glazing over. It was gone seven; they'd been holed up in here for nearly three hours and it felt as though they were no closer to solving the problem than they had been when they'd first arrived. It was beginning to look as though Amit was right. Maybe there *was* no way of forcing the business to pay back within eighteen months.

Louise's phone buzzed.

'Pizzas are here,' she said, as brightly as was possible in the circumstances.

When nobody offered to go and fetch them, Tony stood up. He wandered down the harshly-lit corridor, glad of an excuse to escape the stuffy room.

It was ridiculous, as Amit kept pointing out, the directors' obsession with the targets. Other companies didn't impose such inflexible rules – but then, other companies didn't have cretins like Sir Anthony Knowles at their helm. Other companies pushed initiatives out quickly. They took risks. They applied common sense to their decision-making instead of *rules* and *procedures*.

Padding across the TransTel atrium in his socks, Tony scooped up the pizzas, reaching for his phone and dialling home.

'Hey, it's me.'

'Hi,' Suze said flatly.

'Are you alright?'

'I'm just...' She sighed. 'I dunno. Tired.'

Tony flinched. 'Sorry I'm not there.'

'That's okay,' she said, in a tone that implied that it wasn't really okay. Suze was having a rough time. She had decided, following her non-promotion, to stick out the job for as long as she could, taking it one day at a time. There was a chance, she had warned him, that she might consider not going back after the birth of their second child – a chance that appeared to be growing with every encounter she had with her chauvinist male counterparts. Tony was beginning to accept the possibility that he would at some point be responsible for the entire household income.

'Is Poppy there?'

'I just put her to bed. She asked where you were. I told her you'd run off with another woman.'

Tony laughed softly. 'Right.' He reversed through the door of the stairwell, emerging on the second floor. 'Speaking of which...'

'You've got to get back to her.'

'Afraid so.'

'I'll see you later.'

'Not too much later, I hope.'

Plodding back to the meeting room, Tony set down the warm, greasy boxes on the edge of the table and returned to his seat, Mexican Meatfest in hand. It might have been hunger, but it felt as though all the energy had drained away in his absence, leaving his colleagues in a near-vegetative state.

There was no conversation for a few minutes, only the hum of the strip-lights and the occasional bleep of a mobile phone. Tony felt guilty – not just for keeping them here, away from their loved ones, but for *being* here, away from *his* loved ones. His phone call had reminded him, yet again, of the sacrifices his wife had made for the family in the last few years. She had slogged her way through another bad day in the office and come home to feed, bathe and tend to their daughter, and here he was with a mouthful of pepperoni, staring at botched attempts to get a hopeless project off the ground, knowing that maybe – in fact, quite possibly – these late nights in the office would all be for nothing.

'One hour,' he said, resolutely. 'If we don't crack this by eight o'clock, we're all going home. We'll call the whole thing off. We've spent long enough going round in circles in the last two weeks.'

He pushed his pizza aside and leaned back to open a window. A rush of cold air whirled into the room and at last, either as a response to Tony's announcement or as a result of the open window, there was movement. Eyes blinked, shoulders lifted, throats cleared. Matt stood up and started challenging colleagues to slices of his Chilli Supreme.

Tony watched his Head of Sales. It was incredible, the transformation that had come over the man following the Christmas do. The aggressive, cocky charmer had been replaced by a docile equivalent who seemed intent on bestowing all of his cocky charm on the Marketing Manager, his one-time nemesis. Tony could only hope that the relationship lasted the duration of the project.

Looking again at the mass of papers that littered the table, Tony had one last go at trying to think of an avenue they might have overlooked. It was tempting to go for the easy option: inflate the sales targets so that the project paid back in eighteen months. But once they had laid down the targets, they needed to hit them – and it would be his neck on the line when they failed to do so.

Tony polished off one more slice and then folded the lid on the remaining pizza, tossing it onto the floor. He was about to suggest that they take a five minute break before coming back for a final attempt at cracking the code, but he didn't get a chance. Chek-Han was banging his palm against the table like an attention-craving child.

'That's it!' he cried, banging one final time and staring at his pizza crumbs.

Tony glanced sideways to see if anyone else had grasped what 'it' was. There were blank faces all round.

'That's *it*,' said Chek-Han again, looking from the box to the mass of papers and quickly fishing out a blank sheet. 'I don't know why we didn't think of this option earlier.' He grabbed a pen and quickly sketched some axes on the page.

'Um...' Matt peered at him as he scribbled. 'Are you okay, Chek-Han? Are you having a sugar rush?'

'Shh.' Louise scowled at him.

'It's just like that network trial we ran in CBN,' Chek-Han went on, looking excitedly at Amit as he populated the graph with a series of lines. 'Instead of getting all the investment up-front, we need to eek it out. Get it in stages. That way, it'll keep us going longer and Draper won't need to sign off more than a few hundred grand at a time. It'll get us out of this eighteen month payback problem!'

Moments later, the sketch was complete. Chek-Han swivelled it round on the table and talked them through his idea. 'So this is the funding...'

In slow succession, heads began to nod. Tony stared at the illustration, thinking about what it would mean for the various departments. There would have to be some fairly hefty budget re-works, he thought, but none, as far as he could immediately see, that would prevent the business from taking off. In fact, the only burning question he kept coming back to was one that had already been asked: Why hadn't they thought of this before?

'We'll need to work on the payment structure,' said Amit, 'but I don't see why it can't work.'

Tony looked around at the nodding heads. For two weeks, they had argued and haggled, fighting over how the cut-backs would be applied, and now suddenly they were sitting here, *agreeing*.

'And of course,' added Amit, 'there's no guarantee that the board will go for it.'

Tony leaned forward. Amit was right. This was a breakthrough, but until they had Charles Gable's approval in writing, they were no further forward.

'Draper's your man,' said Amit. 'You'll need to convince

him before you present at the next board meeting. If he thinks it's a goer, everyone else will too.'

Tony nodded pensively. Again, he was right. But the prospect of trying to sweet-talk Draper into agreement was not an appealing one. The FD was notoriously risk averse and Tony's relationship with the man was hardly flourishing. Tony considered the idea of leaning on the Walker-Jones again. It was an option. He had a relationship of sorts with the man. The problem was, he needed to *know* that he'd got Draper's backing ahead of the next board meeting. This time, he couldn't just hope that the COO's support would trickle through. He had to tackle the FD head-on.

'D'you think Nicholas Draper's a beers-after-work sort of man?'

Matt snorted. Amit pulled a face.

'No,' Tony conceded. 'I didn't think so.'

'What's wrong with a meeting?' asked Louise.

Amit shook his head. 'You need to show him how much this means to you.'

They lapsed into silence. Tony was about to declare that the hard work was done, that he would think up a plan on his own, when suddenly it came to him. It wasn't free of risk and he sensed that Suze might not like it, but it seemed like as good a plan as any.

'I've got it,' he said, smiling. 'Leave it to me.'

Nicholas Draper comes to dinner

'I SAY,' muttered Tony admiringly as the chocolate torte was eased onto the table. 'This looks *delicious*.'

Suze managed a smile as she carved out the first slice. She'd been on her feet since noon and she looked exhausted.

'Not for me.' Edith Draper held up a hand. 'I don't eat dessert.'

A hurt expression flickered across Suze's face. Several hours, Tony knew, had been spent mixing, stirring and folding in an attempt to create the perfect torte.

'Can I offer you something else?' she asked brightly. Her perseverance was commendable. 'A tea or coffee?'

Edith shook her head, still not cracking a smile. 'I don't drink caffeine after five o'clock.'

'Right.' Suze nodded. 'Um, Nicholas?' She tilted the dish towards him. To Suze's evident relief, the Finance Director accepted her offer.

Tony gave Suze a supportive wink as he received his sizeable portion. It hadn't been the most raucous of evenings. In the humour stakes, as Tony had always known, the FD languished somewhere in the bottom percentile of the UK population – a spurious outlier on the statistical map. But tonight, Tony had realised that Nicholas Draper *wasn't* the dourest person on Earth. His wife, with her permanent knitted brow and drawn lips, took dour to a whole new level.

Suze topped up the wine, stopping over Edith's glass. 'Are you sure...?'

'Quite sure.'

Suze raised an eyebrow, smiling. 'Not because...?'

Edith shook her head quickly. 'Certainly not.' She glanced at her husband. 'We're not able to have children.'

'Oh.' Suze hovered uncertainly at the table, the bottle beginning to shake in her hand.

Snatches of the evening's conversation flashed through Tony's mind: the discussion about Suze's pregnancy, the assessment of schools in the area, the references to kids' TV, their thoughts on popular children's names, the rising cost of childcare...

'Anyone for some... cheese?' Suze staggered back into her seat.

Edith politely declined, which was just as well, thought Tony, because they almost certainly didn't have anything more to offer than the lump of half-grated Cheddar that had been skulking at the back of the fridge for a month.

'So...' He put on his breeziest smile and tried to think of something to say. 'Excellent torte, Suze.'

'Mmm.' Nicholas nodded.

'Thanks.'

Silence reigned once again.

Eventually, Suze spoke.

'So, Nicholas. I hear you're on the board of directors?'

Tony shot her a warning look but she didn't see. TransTel was the one topic he *didn't* want to discuss at the table – that and now babies. If Draper sensed that he'd only been invited to dinner because of his position on the board then the conversation Tony intended to have with him later might never happen.

'I bet that's interesting.'

'Well,' Nicholas dipped his head modestly. 'Sometimes.'

Suze knew that the topic was out of bounds, of course. They had discussed the agenda for this evening at length. She was clearly nervous.

'Plenty of colourful characters on the board, from what Tony tells me!'

Nicholas frowned. Tony stared as hard as he possibly could. He tried to locate Suze's shin under the table, but he didn't want to risk kicking Edith.

'Perhaps *colourful* isn't quite the way to describe them, darling.'

Suze looked put out at being corrected. 'Your words, not mine,' she said.

Tony tried again to meet her eye, but to no avail. 'I probably... Well, I'm sure *some* of the directors are colourful. Metaphorically speaking,' he clarified unnecessarily.

'Like the one you played golf with,' Suze prompted. 'Who was that? He sounded like a–'

'I don't know!' he laughed, cutting her off. 'Ha! I actually can't remember!' This was all going wrong. Suze had to stop. Perhaps her half-glass of wine had gone to her head. 'Anyone for more torte?'

'Graham something-or-other,' Suze went on, clearly oblivious to Tony's discomfort – desperate to fill the silence.

'Graham Walker-Jones?' Edith suggested, raising an eyebrow.

Tony stared at his plate. This conversation was getting out of hand. Now all four of them seemed to be discussing the colourfulness of the COO – even people who had never met him.

'D'you know him, then?' asked Suze.

Tony buried his face in his wine glass.

'Know him?' Edith drew her head back and rolled her eyes. 'Of course I've met him! He's my brother-in-law.'

Tony nearly spat the wine back into his glass.

'Brother-in-law?' he asked, wine safely consumed.

'He's married to my sister,' Edith explained primly.

'Right.' Tony nodded, trying to maintain his composure. 'I suppose... Yes... That would make him...'

Draper was Walker-Jones' brother-in-law. That explained the mysterious bond. It explained why Draper's decisions tended to have a favourable impact on the COO's business interests and why Walker-Jones, whose expertise and intelligence left a lot to be desired, had managed to secure himself a place on the board.

'So... um...'

Suze pushed back her chair, at last sensing his unease. 'Shall we adjourn?'

Tony took a deep breath and led the Drapers through to the lounge. It was safe to say that the evening had not gone according to plan – and yes, there had been a plan. Tony and Suze had run through it at length that afternoon. The objective was to give Tony his best shot at the casual, private conversation he wanted to have with Nicholas after dinner. What with the pregnancy faux-pas and the offensive brother-in-law comments and Edith's refusal to eat or drink most of what Suze had prepared, Tony was beginning to wonder why he'd thought this would be a good idea in the first place. But there was no point in wondering. He had engineered the situation; he had to try and use it.

Suze's array of herbal teas proved a surprise hit with Mrs Draper, leaving Tony to take the FD aside, as planned. He had been in two minds about breaking open the Churchills. It was difficult to tell whether Nicholas was a cigar man or not. Having no other ideas up his sleeve, he took the risk.

'Can I interest you...?'

Nicholas' spindly hand shot into the box, his face lighting up. Tony felt his heart lurch.

They smoked in silence for a minute, wrapped in their coats and sheltering under the eaves from the sleet-like rain. Tony puffed on the toxic cigar, loathing every breath but enduring it for the cause.

'Thank you for a wonderful dinner, Anthony.'

Nicholas blew a perfect smoke-ring into the night air.

'Thank *you*, for coming.'

'Your wife is an excellent cook.'

'I'll pass on the compliment.'

To begin with, Tony assumed they were going through the motions; saying the things people always said at the end of a dinner party. But as they stood there, looking out from under the dripping gutter, something occurred to him. The Drapers were pedantic and tedious. They probably didn't have many friends. Which meant that they probably didn't get invited to many dinners – something borne out by their lack of social skills. So perhaps, thought Tony, incredulously, Nicholas Draper *had* actually enjoyed the dinner.

Tony looked at him. 'Can I ask your opinion?'

Draper turned. 'Ask away.'

He went straight for the jugular. 'It's about the smart home project. We've come up with a way of financing the venture and I'd appreciate your thoughts.

Draper's mouth twitched. 'That sounds intriguing.'

'Yes. It's... Well, we think it'll work. Essentially, it involves a staged financing programme.'

Draper took a long pull on his cigar, turning away to exhale but maintaining eye contact.

'Well,' he said eventually. There was a glimmer of a smile on his lips. 'This sounds like something I might like to hear more about.'

Gravity Wisdom

GETTING INVESTMENT

GETTING INVESTMENT

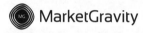 MarketGravity

In this chapter Tony is being pulled in two directions. The Financial Director wants to see higher forecasts whilst the Sales and Marketing Director thinks they are overly optimistic. On top of this he has to deal with team disruptions and the continued pressures of running the existing business.

Here are some of the difficulties that you may encounter when trying to obtain backing for your business:

- Overcoming the inherent risk aversion of a large company
- Applying mature business hurdle rates to an early stage and therefore riskier venture
- Having the financial model take over such that the business rationale gets forgotten – everyone is buried in the numbers
- Dealing with conflict between long-term investment and short-term results
- Not being part of the decision making process – the investment committee takes over and the business owners lack sufficient influence

This chapter illustrates the classic corporate venture conundrum of pitching an investment case that's achievable but not big enough, versus one that's financially significant but too big to deliver.

"THE MUSIC VENTURE DIDN'T PASS THE BOARD'S APPROVAL BECAUSE OF AN UNREALISTIC TARGET THAT SAID IT HAD TO BE A £XXM BUSINESS. IN THE END, THIS TARGET HAD TO BE LOWERED BECAUSE NOTHING WAS GETTING THROUGH."

Felix Geyr, O2, BBC Worldwide

There are a number of approaches that you can take to address the investment case challenges and secure the backing that you need:

1. Create a new venture investment board and a ring-fenced budget. If your company is serious about new growth initiatives, it needs to establish the governance and funding structures needed to drive them forward.

2. Ensure financial assumptions are ratified before seeking investment. Any investment case should have clear assumptions with solid rationale. Use benchmarks, previous launches, or competitor comparisons to validate your forecasts.

3. Propose staging of investments to improve risk/reward balance. Many proposals are denied funding because the overall case is too risky. Break the total investment down into phases, each with clear milestones and targets so that the risk can be managed.

4. Consider how to structure your investment case. Choosing the right mix of capital expenditure (CAPEX) and operating expenditure (OPEX) will also make a case more attractive.

5. Ensure budget holders are part of the solution. Your Operations Director won't back a big change to the IT systems if they've not been involved in scoping and costing the change. However, if your case adds further weight to their existing proposal the chances of it being approved are greatly increased.

6. Look outside. If your own company is unable to see the full value of your proposal, seek backing from partners or strategic investors. However, they are likely to expect your own board to match their external funds.

Use the checklist below to ensure that you have addressed the most common requirements of a corporate investment case.

Clear logic and structure, easy to follow	
Numbers that link directly to the proposition and the action plan	
Key assumptions identified and referenced with real benchmarks or proxies	
Realistic expectations of risk, reward and payback period	
Realistic timeframes for when first revenues are realised and when first costs are incurred	
All assumptions tested and validated by experts in each functional area and Finance	
Main sensitivities identified and modelled	
Single inputs and assumptions sheet	

6

Can you see what it is yet?
Creating the operational plan

'Plans are fantasies, the real work starts here.'

Board sign-off; ball rolling

'OKAY, LISTEN UP!'

Tony clapped his hands, trying to restore order. Usually, the weekly meeting was a low-key affair with attendance figures peaking at around fifty percent. Today, it was standing-room only.

'Let's talk about how this is going to work!' He raised his voice to compete with the din.

It was no bad thing, really, that they were so keyed up. He was still buzzing from the news himself. At last, after what seemed like an endless succession of meetings, presentations and conversations behind closed doors, the board had granted permission for Synapse to start work on the smart home project. The team had cleared its first hurdle.

'I've asked Norm to head up the technology side of the project, with immediate effect,' he announced.

There was a patter of applause and a few exaggerated whoops from the lads in Norm's team. In fact, the manager's new title did not entail any change in rank or pay grade, but that didn't seem to matter. Norm grinned proudly at the tips of his shoes like a nerdy schoolboy on prize day.

'Norm will work closely with Gerry Clark's team to get the product out of the labs and into trial as soon as possible. He'll also deal with the IP and infrastructure.'

Tony glanced down at his notes to see who was next on his list. There were people in the room who, for the last month, had given up most of their spare time to get to this position today; he couldn't afford to leave anyone off.

'Louise,' he said, waiting for the murmurs to die down, 'will be responsible for the marketing strategy, spending three days a week on the smart home project. Some of you have been privy to the numbers we've put in the business plan, so you'll know that we're working to some ambitious targets. It's not going to be easy, but I think we've got the right team to make it happen. Please support Louise in any way you can.'

Tony cleared his throat meaningfully as the marketing team descended into excitable chatter. 'Working closely with Louise,' he went on, 'will be Matt. Now...'

The air became filled with wolf-whistles, cat-calls and smart remarks.

'Working closely! Oi oi!'

'Who's responsible for positioning?'

'Keep an eye on those penetration figures!'

Tony waited for the racket to die down, as Matt calmly showed his colleagues the finger and Louise, cheeks aglow, pretended to discuss some intricate element of the business plan with one of her subordinates.

'And now I'd like to introduce you to a new member of the team.' Tony looked around, finally locating the young man amidst the huddle of marketing girls. 'As some of you know, we had a little help pulling together the business plan. I think I can safely say that without the help of this person, we wouldn't be where we are today. So, if you haven't already done so, please go and introduce yourselves to Chek-Han, our new financial analyst.'

There was another round of applause while everybody turned and stared at the blushing young man. Tony added his voice to the chorus of whoops and cries; he meant what he'd said. If it hadn't been for Chek-Han's tireless re-working of the financial model or his inspirational staged financing programme, they almost certainly wouldn't have got the go-ahead from the board.

Strictly speaking, the young analyst was only on loan to the Synapse team. It had been hard enough persuading the powers that be to release him at all from the newly merged Networks division. In the end, it had been Chek-Han who had clinched the deal, threatening to walk out if they didn't authorise the secondment. Tony smiled fondly at the young man. It was a good sign when team members were willing to put their jobs on the line for the sake of the project.

'And finally,' he went on, 'keeping Synapse afloat while we're all trying to get this new business off the ground will be Roy. So, any departmental questions that you'd usually ask me, Roy's your man.'

Roy raised a hand from the corner of the room, trying to hide his self-satisfaction beneath a nonchalant smile.

'Does that all make sense? Any questions?'

If there were any questions, they couldn't be heard above the ensuing hubbub. Tony looked over and signalled for Louise to open the door. The meeting, evidently, had reached its conclusion.

Matt caught his eye as they filed back into the office, gesturing with his hand as though he wanted a drink. Tony frowned. Then he understood what Matt meant.

'One more thing!' he cried, waving his hands to retrieve people's attention. 'Celebratory drinks, this Friday in the pub. And then every Friday after that. For all of Synapse!'

The noise level rose another notch as the staff took in this new initiative. The drinks had been Matt's idea, or maybe Louise's; they seemed to think as one these days. Perhaps foolishly, Tony had offered to put his own card behind the bar as a way of saying thank you. He had no idea what turnout to expect, but if the Christmas do was anything to go by, he figured, then a few morale-boosting beverages couldn't do them any harm.

Tony returned to his desk, jiggling the mouse and scanning the stack of emails that had appeared in the last half-hour. He glanced down at the hand-scrawled to-do list next to his keyboard, then up at the array of Post-It notes that adorned his monitor. He felt restless. His mind was still buzzing from the excitement of the weekly meeting – or rather, the excitement of seeing everybody else's excitement. It was contagious, this buzz that was sweeping through the office. The news about the smart home project had energised the whole team, injecting a dynamism that Tony hadn't seen since he'd joined the department nearly a year ago.

His phone rang, jerking him out of his jubilant daydream.

'Hello?'

'Hi Tony. It's Maureen. I've got a Natasha on the line.'

'Natasha from HR?'

'Um...'

'Put her through,' he snapped. It was incredible how quickly the euphoria wore off.

There was a beep, then another beep and then silence. Maureen had cut him off.

Tony sighed, looking again at his list and deciding to focus on the item at the top: securing a finance partner for the smart home subscription service. He needed to start making calls.

'Sorry about that.' Maureen lumbered into his office wearing a foolish grin. 'Must've pressed the wrong button.'

Tony looked at her. 'Did you retrieve the call?'

'Well, no.' She leaned heavily against his desk. Tony could feel his blood pressure rising. 'I didn't, because I didn't catch her surname. I was wondering –'

'Billingsley,' said Tony. 'Her surname is Billingsley. And if it's not important, perhaps you could take a message. I'm quite busy.'

'Righto,' she sang, pushing herself off the desk and wandering back into the office.

A couple of minutes later, Tony was wading through the list of Graham Walker-Jones' financial contacts when the phone rang again.

'Hello?'

'Hi,' said an unfamiliar voice. 'Is that Tony Sharp?'

'It is.'

'Good,' said the man. He sounded curt, whoever he was. 'I'm Harvey Grainger, Head of TransTel Technology. I don't believe we've met.'

'Er, no,' replied Tony, trying to remember whether he had encountered anyone from TransTel Technology in his career so far. The company had so many departments with such similar-sounding names, it was impossible to keep up – especially with the endless stream of seemingly random reorganisations, mergers and de-mergers.

'I'll get straight to the point,' said Harvey. 'I understand that you're planning to pilot a smart home project in the next few months?'

'That's correct, yes.' Tony frowned. Controversial news travelled fast within TransTel, evidently.

'I see. Well, in that case, we should meet. I presume you're aware that all technology projects must pass our scrutiny before getting the green light?'

Tony hesitated, suddenly remembering where he'd heard the name TransTel Technology before. Gerry Clark had mentioned it in their early conversation about the energy monitoring device. TransTel Tech was the division that had tried and failed to make a commercial success of the idea two years ago.

'I'm not aware, no,' replied Tony, slowly. He wasn't a naturally suspicious person, but it did seem like a strange coincidence that the department supposedly tasked with approving such projects was the one that had given it a go in the past – and failed. 'I should probably explain,' he said. 'We have the authority to work on this project from the highest level. We've already got the all-clear.'

After the briefest hesitation, Harvey's voice sounded again. 'Be that as it may, all technology propositions must be run past us.'

Tony watched as the light on his phone started flashing. Someone else was trying to get through.

'I'm sorry,' he said, running out of patience. 'If you want to look through our business plan, feel free. We're based on the second floor and I'll happily take you through it. But as for approval, I'm afraid that as far as I'm concerned, we have all the green lights we need to proceed. Charles Gable has given it his endorsement. Look, I have another call waiting. I have to go.'

Tony pressed the transfer button and barked a greeting down the line. He was angrier than he'd realised. Here he was, trying to make something happen, and meanwhile there were people like Harvey Grainger going to great lengths to stand in his way, just to fulfil some personal vendetta. It was absurd.

They worked for the same company; they were supposed to share the same goal. No wonder TransTel struggled to keep up in the marketplace; its departments were expending all their efforts fighting civil wars.

'Er, hi. Is that Tony?'

Tony tried to compose himself. It was Natasha. 'Yes, hi.'

'I've been trying to get hold of you.'

'We're having telephony issues, thanks to your latest hire.' Tony stared furiously at the back of his PA's head.

'I'm sorry?'

'The PA you recruited for us. I want to make an official complaint.'

Natasha sighed. 'On what grounds?'

'On the grounds of her being utterly useless. She can't take messages, she doesn't hear the phone ring and when she does, it's usually a friend of hers who she chats to for six hours at a time, disrupting everybody around her. She's a disaster.'

'Sorry, but if you want to give her an official warning, you need to have grounds to do so.'

'I just –'

'Has she displayed signs of racism or sexism in the workplace?'

'No. But that's–'

'Has she offended anyone?'

'She's offending me right now, by being there.'

'Tony, I think you're over-reacting. If you want to see an improvement, perhaps you could take her aside for a little chat?'

Tony groaned. He had already tried taking Maureen aside for a *little chat*. Several times. Each time, she had nodded and smiled and apologised, and for approximately one day, there had been peace across Synapse. Then she was back to her old ways. People like Maureen knew how to play the system.

'Now,' said Natasha primly. 'About these performance-related pay schemes you've proposed for your sales staff.'

Tony waited, not liking the tone of her voice. He and Matt had worked tirelessly to devise a pay structure that incentivised staff for up-selling, new sales and upgrades without burning too quickly through cash.

'No can do.'

'What?'

'I said, no can do. There's a new policy that restricts the way bonuses can be awarded. I'm afraid your business won't be making enough money for your staff to qualify.'

'But...' Tony closed his eyes, trying to straighten out his argument. 'We're a start-up. Of course we won't make much money in the first few months. But we need to encourage our sales people to sell the new product, otherwise they'll just carry on peddling the broadband. We *have* to offer them bonuses.'

'Hmm. I see what you're saying, but unfortunately we can only allow bonuses in areas of the business that bring in more than–'

'That's ridiculous!'

'Well, I'm afraid–'

'How are we supposed to get started? Are we expecting the sales guys to just start selling the new stuff out of the goodness of their hearts?'

'Sorry, Tony. I don't write the rules.'

'But you can try bending them?'

Even as the words came out of his mouth, Tony could feel his hope fading. The last time Natasha had bent the rules, the result had been the lazy, incompetent PA sitting ten feet away, yakking into the phone to one of her friends.

'I'll see what I can do.'

'Thanks.'

Tony put the phone down and sat, staring into space. He was wondering how these things happened elsewhere: in other telcos, other industries, other countries. Surely workplaces existed where people pulled together to get things done, where they worked around problems instead of creating them, where common sense was applied ahead of the rules? He looked up, sensing a presence in the room.

'Um, hi,' muttered Norm, shuffling into the office.

Tony sighed. 'This had better be good news.'

'Er, well, not exactly.' He looked at the floor. 'It's about the patent. Apparently there's already one pending. Registered by somebody else.

179

20-week scan

TONY STARED at the screen, transfixed. In his lap, Poppy wriggled, trying to reach out and touch the buttons on the machine.

'What's dat?' she asked, pushing herself up on his knee and poking at the black and white image.

Tony glanced at his wife and smiled.

'That,' he said, 'is your baby brother.'

'Baby brother!' squealed Poppy excitedly. 'My baby brother!'

The sonographer looked over apologetically. 'I'm not actually at liberty to disclose the gender of your baby,' she said.

Tony stared again at the image on the screen. There was a distinct patch of grey tissue at the base of his stomach. 'Isn't that–'

'You may draw your own conclusions,' she said with a hint of a smile.

Tony looked over at Suze, who grinned back at him. The sonographer turned the screen away as she set about checking the baby's organs, muttering softly to herself while she worked.

Poppy twisted round in Tony's lap. 'Why is he on television?'

Tony smiled. 'It's a special television,' he explained. 'One that looks inside mummy's tummy. It's to check he's growing properly.'

'Oh.' Poppy frowned thoughtfully.

Tony leaned back and reached for Suze's hand, giving it a quick squeeze. He could sense her anxiety. The next five minutes would reveal the likely chances of their baby being born healthy. They had both confessed their nerves, earlier in the morning. It was natural, he'd told her, to fear the worst, but deep down, Tony knew that his wife's fears were disproportionate to the risks. Suze wasn't used to being in somebody else's hands. In every other element of her life, she took control, but there were occasions, such as now, when there was nothing whatsoever she could do to influence events. It was just fate, or genes, that determined how things would pan out.

Poppy looked up again.

'Daddy?'

'Yes?'

'What happens if he isn't growing properly?'

Tony hesitated. 'Then we see what we can do to correct the problem.'

The sonographer twisted the screen round again. She was smiling. 'No problems, as far as I can see,' she said.

Tony felt Suze's hand relax.

'Thank you.'

The woman talked through various details of the pregnancy, addressing Suze and leaving Poppy and Tony to gawp at the image on the screen. Eventually, Suze swung her legs off the bed and pulled down her top.

A light snow was falling as they left the hospital. A layer of slush coated the car park – enough for tyre marks and footprints but not enough for snowballs. Poppy chased the flakes as they fell, mouth wide open, head tilted up to the sky.

'So,' asked Suze, watching as their daughter nearly collided with the back of their car. 'Are you sticking around for snowman contest, or is it back to the office?'

Tony looked at his watch. It was nearly eleven. He had booked the day off work, having taken almost no leave in the last nine months. It was a Friday, Suze's day off, so the idea had been for Tony to join them at home for a long weekend. Unfortunately, though, in the time that had elapsed between booking the time off and taking it, several problems had unfurled. Norm had discovered that the patent for the device at the heart of their proposition was no longer pending – or rather, it was pending, but registered to somebody else. The financing deal was proving harder to arrange than he had imagined;

Walker-Jones' contacts were all too happy to be taken for slap-up meals but they were less than forthcoming when it came to actual negotiation. Meanwhile, countless individuals had crawled out of the TransTel woodwork with the apparent sole purpose of scuppering Tony's chances of success. 'I don't know.'

'That means you're going into the office,' said Suze, dolefully.

Tony reached for his car keys, trying to decide what to do. 'Not for a while,' he said eventually. 'I'll go in after the snowman contest.'

Suze smiled. 'Ever the competitive one.'

Tony laughed, strapping his restless daughter into her car seat.

By the time they got home, the snow had reverted to sleet, washing away the shallow coating on the ground. Poppy was not impressed and insisted on settling at the kitchen table to draw what she'd seen, in some kind of optimistic attempt to bring it back.

'Sit,' instructed Tony, pressing Suze into one of the chairs while he made the tea. He had read in one of her pregnancy books that stressed mothers were prone to having stressed babies. At this rate, the little mite would be hooked on Valium before his first birthday.

He carried the tea over to where she sat, studying the print-off of the baby scan.

'Gorgeous, isn't he?' she said, grasping the mug without taking her eyes off the image.

Tony nodded, leaning in to take a closer look. The baby was lying on his back, his tiny hands scrunched up into balls near his face, like those of a boxer preparing to throw a punch.

'It's amazing.' Suze sipped her tea, still gazing at the scan. 'It's all so perfect, before the birth. You look at this piece of paper and all you see is this beautiful thing... You don't think about the sleepless nights or the screaming fits or the stinking nappies.' She shook her head, smiling.

Tony sipped his tea. He could feel his BlackBerry buzzing in his pocket but he didn't dare bring it out. Slipping into the seat next to Suze, he laid a hand on her sizeable bump, thinking about what she'd said. It was true. You never thought about the messy realities until you had to deal with them. It was human nature.

The smart home offering had seemed so simple, so perfect, on paper. The business plan had developed into this beautiful thing for which he and everybody else in the team could only feel a burning pride. It was their baby. But now the plan was becoming a reality, and suddenly it felt as though things weren't so perfect after all. There were complications. It wasn't growing properly. They were all permanently exhausted.

Suze laid a hand over his, guiding him down to a different part of her belly. Initially, he could only feel the hard, bloated lining of her stomach. Then something else. Two short, sharp thumps. Tony smiled. Again and again, the baby kicked. Tony turned to say something to Suze, but as he did so, he felt something else. His BlackBerry.

He tried to ignore it, but the buzzing was incessant. Suze could obviously feel the vibrations too. Eventually, she let out an exasperated sigh.

'Are you gonna get that?' she asked wearily.

Tony tried to feign indifference, waving a hand as though it could wait. He felt torn.

Suze rolled her eyes. 'I know you want to.'

Shamefully, Tony delved into his pocket and took the call. 'Hello?'

'Tony, it's Louise. Um, sorry. I know it's your day off, but I thought you should probably know... The focus group research has come back. It looks, well... It looks as though maybe we should have a bit of a re-think.'

'A re-think about what?'

'Well,' Louise hesitated. 'This whole proposition.'

The market's not ready

WITH A SHAKY FINGER, Louise pressed play and returned to her seat, facing the screen that took up most of the end wall. Tony followed her gaze, waiting for the frozen image to burst into life.

'This is the Suburban Families group,' explained Louise, not looking him in the eye. 'They're all bill-payers. The sound quality isn't great but I think you'll get the idea.'

Tony nodded. Eventually, the five women on the couch started fidgeting, nodding, looking at one another. Above the background hum that reverberated from the speakers, the moderator's voice could just be heard in the background.

'...concerned about reducing your energy consumption?'

The woman in the middle, a large, buxom forty-something wearing a low-cut top and hooped earrings, started nodding vehemently.

'Definitely,' she said, prompting the others to nod too. 'We're *well* concerned. Not just to save money, like, but you know – to save the planet. Definitely.' She nodded again in earnest.

The woman on the far left leaned in, catching the first woman's eye. 'Likewise. I'm always tellin' Leanne – that's me youngest – to turn off the lights. Costs us a bloody bomb, the electrics.'

There was a muffled prompt from the moderator and the women started nodding again.

'Computer games,' declared one. She had the haggard look of a young mother who hadn't had a decent night's sleep in years. 'That's what does it for us. Darren comes home with his mates an' they'll stay up all night – never switch the bloody thing off. Same with Mercedes an' her computer. I dunno what they find to do all night but I can't drag her off it some nights…'

The moderator could be heard trying to deflect the conversation back to the subject in hand. After a brief period of mutual appreciation for one another's problems, they were asked whether a device that monitored and controlled energy usage in the home would be of interest.

'Too right!' cried the buxom brunette, leaning forward and giving the camera a good view of her sagging cleavage. 'Anything that'd help save us money.'

'It'd make my life easier,' remarked another.

'Tell me about it! Can you get them with cut-off switches?' The mother of Mercedes and Darren cackled loudly.

Tony glanced at Louise, eyebrows raised. From what he could make out, the focus group seemed to be wholeheartedly approving of the concept they were putting to the test. Louise just looked at him as if to say, *just wait.*

Above the crackly background noise, the moderator could be heard explaining the energy saving device to the women, who were frowning, squinting and occasionally nodding.

'…likely that you would adopt such a device in your home?'

The woman in the middle leaned back, crossing her arms beneath her sizeable rack. Some of the others glanced sideways, waiting for her to speak first.

'Hmm,' she said, narrowing her overly-painted eyes.

Before she could expand, one of the young mothers spoke up.

'I wouldn't,' she said blankly. 'I don't 'ave time to go round lookin' at what sockets are usin' what energy. Sorry, I know I said I cared about savin' money an' that, but I don't 'ave the time for analysin' and whatnot.'

'Same,' said the woman next to her. 'It's a good idea, but it wouldn't work round ours.'

'I might use it,' declared the buxom brunette. 'Depends 'ow much it costs.'

There was a brief explanation from the moderator of the

subscription fees and a further question about whether the women would pay for such a service.

'Not sure,' one said cautiously. 'Probably not at that price.'

'To be honest,' said the haggard-looking mum, 'I doubt it.'

'I wanna *save* money, not spend more.'

The questions and responses went on, but Tony had already tuned out.

'Okay,' he said, rubbing his eyes and turning to his Head of Marketing. 'I get the message.'

'I was going to show you something from the other groups too,' she explained timidly, reaching for the controls and pressing Fast Forward. 'We've got Affluent Singles, Upwardly Mobile Unmarrieds, NEETs, Professional Landlords and Empty Nesters; they all tell roughly the same story. D'you wanna whiz through Affluent Singles?'

Tony sighed, wondering what the hell an *empty nester* was and which category his own family fell into. He didn't really want to see any more evidence that his business case had been built on an unsupportable hunch, but he knew it would be irresponsible not to.

'Go on then. Let's have it.'

The video began in much the same manner as the last one, this time with five young City slickers sitting around a pine dining table agreeing that reducing their energy consumption was a key priority in their lives.

'I'm totally trying to reduce my carbon footprint,' bleated the malnourished-looking girl in the well cut suit.

'Yah,' the pinstriped man nodded. 'Very important to play one's part.'

The moderator guided them through the script as before, quickly bringing out their drive to cut down on the gas-burning patio heaters and four-wheel drive, eventually presenting the prototype device and asking for feedback.

Slowly but unmistakeably, the respondents' expressions began to change. Their perky optimism became tainted with doubt.

'How is it installed?' asked the young man with the quiff.

The skinny girl waggled her finger as if to acknowledge his

point. 'If it's one of those tiresome engineer call-out jobs, count me out. I'm sick to death of having to take the afternoon off work, only to find that the guy couldn't find my flat or didn't have the tools to do the job…' She shook her head despairingly as the moderator started to explain that indeed it was a tiresome engineer call-out job.

'You know,' interrupted the pinstriped man, 'frankly I'm not sure I'd bother to look at some online interface to see where my energy was being used. I mean, maybe to begin with, but…' He cast a haughty glance in the direction of the moderator. 'No offence, but I'm a busy man.'

The third guy nodded. 'It does sound like an awful lot of effort for a somewhat small gain.'

Tony looked over at Louise, who was staring at the screen, biting her lower lip.

'That's enough,' he said brusquely. 'Turn it off.'

She fumbled for the remote control.

'Okay,' he said. 'Thanks for playing me these.'

The Marketing Manager looked away, clearly reluctant to take credit for a piece of work that had such negative implications.

'In your opinion,' he went on, 'is the market ready for a smart home proposition like the one we're considering?'

Slowly, Louise raised her head, only taking her eyes off the spot on the floor when it moved out of her field of vision. She looked at him through her mousy fringe, her eyes filled with shame and regret.

'I don't think so,' she said eventually.

Tony nodded once, closing his eyes and letting out a lungful of air. The premise that underpinned the entire proposition, the idea that bill payers across the country would subscribe to a service that would keep their bills to a manageable level, had just been disproved. There was no demand for such a scheme. Their early research, the questionnaires they had sent out to hundreds of bill payers across the country before putting pen to paper on the business plan, had given a false impression of the demand.

After a short exchange of words, Louise left the room, leaving

Tony to dwell on the depressing new revelation. For nearly six months, they had been plotting and scheming, working overtime to build up a launch plan to save Synapse. Their newfound focus had even been at the expense of the core business – as the Christmas week sales had proved. And now, just when the plans had started to become a reality, it was transpiring that they would have done better to just concentrate on business as usual.

Forlornly, Tony left the meeting room and slunk back to his office.

'Ooh,' squawked Maureen as he passed. 'Somebody called for you. It was…' She scrabbled around in the paraphernalia on her desk. 'Anita from TransTel Technology. Harvey Grainger's PA. She wanted to set up a time for you and Harvey to go through your, um…' She squinted at the note she had scrawled. '*Shark home project?*'

Tony sighed. 'Smart home,' he corrected. He thought about reminding Maureen that the project in question was the undertaking that had occupied nearly every waking hour of most members of the department since her arrival, but decided it might be more trouble than it was worth. 'Can you please tell her that won't be necessary? We've got sign-off from the CEO; there's no need for TransTel Tech to get involved.'

'Ah.' Maureen's face puckered into a grimace. 'Too late, I'm afraid.'

'What?'

'Well,' she tapped her screen. 'I've scheduled the meeting for Thursday morning.'

Tony groaned. He had enough on his plate right now without Harvey Grainger adding more. 'Can you please unschedule it? Thank you.'

He strode through the open-plan office, finally making it back into his own private domain and flinging himself into his chair. Instantly, there was a knock on the door.

'Um, hi.' Norm shuffled in, uninvited.

Tony waited as the Technology Manager laid a hand tentatively on the back of the visitors' chair.

'It's about this patent.'

Tony nodded. It was highly probable, he thought, that whatever Norm was trying to say would turn out to be irrelevant in light of the latest discovery.

'It turns out that TransTel *does* own the patent,' Norm explained. 'But it was registered under the name of the department, which is why it didn't initially come up as TransTel.'

'What, R&D?' asked Tony, barely interested. He was already thinking about what he'd tell the board about his imminent U-turn.

Norm shook his head. 'No. TransTel Technology.'

Tony's head shot up. 'What? TransTel Tech registered the patent under their name?'

'Correct. Apparently it was entered under their name because of some project they were working on. Someone called Harvey Grainger heads it up.'

Tony nodded, his mind whirring. Harvey Grainger had registered the patent for the energy monitoring device. Against company protocol, he had applied for it under his departmental name and now, citing some unheard of corporate procedure, he was demanding a meeting in which Tony would take him through the details of his business plan.

Putting the disastrous customer insight to the back of his mind for a moment, Tony thought about Grainger and TransTel Technology. He had been in this situation before. He had seen his ideas swiped from under him – the credit for his hard work taken by some other department or individual. Whether or not the smart home proposition came to anything, he wouldn't have his thunder stolen by some backstabbing, ladder-climbing executive he'd never even met.

He looked at Norm. 'Thanks for letting me know.'

'Um, right.' He scratched his flaky scalp. 'I'll proceed with getting it into trial then.'

Tony nodded. 'Please do. And if you have any problems with TransTel Technology, let me know.' He smiled grimly. 'It appears we have some politics to contend with.'

Talking with the engineers

TONY PULLED UP outside the drab, grey building, listening to the monotonous squeak of the windscreen wipers as he pondered Gerry Clark's words. The Head of R&D had confirmed Tony's suspicions about Harvey Grainger. He was an ambitious young man who would stop at nothing to achieve his goal – his goal generally being promotion.

In other circumstances, Tony would have known exactly what to do. He would have simply curtailed TransTel Technology's association with the smart home project – swiftly and unequivocally. He would have talked to Gable or Draper or Walker-Jones and asked them to settle the matter once and for all. He didn't need hangers-on trying to claim the project as their own. But the situation wasn't that simple. The focus group insight had cast a dark, ugly shadow over the initiative, throwing the whole smart home project into jeopardy. Before he went crying to members of the board, he had to make a decision: continue despite the apparent lack of customer demand, or abort the mission. With every day that passed, the weight of the decision hung a little heavier on his shoulders.

Silencing the engine, he reached for his notes and stepped out of the car, holding the paperwork over his head as he darted across the wet tarmac. He stood in the doorway, shaking off the worst of the rain and looking out at the neat rows of TransTel vans that lined the car park. They reminded him of his early days in Network Direct. As a young graduate, Tony had spent many a happy afternoon shadowing engineers in their rusty old vans, learning work avoidance tricks from men three times his age – men whose sons were probably touring the area in newer, shinier vans today, employing those same tricks to keep their productivity levels down.

'Tony, is it?' said a voice, as the metal door banged shut.

A long-haired, well-tattooed man with multiple piercings was walking towards him, extending a hand. Dave Crouch was a Synapse service engineer. Tony vaguely remembered his Neanderthal looks from the introductions when he'd first taken over.

'Don't see many suits around here,' he explained, looking down at his overalls as they shook hands. 'Fancy a cuppa?'

Tony accepted the offer and perched on the back of a grubby chair as Dave expertly worked the vending machine.

''Ere y'are.' Dave handed Tony a small, plastic cup containing something brown and frothy. 'Take a pew.'

Tony eased himself onto one of the seats and opened his sodden notebook. Tucked inside was the final version of the business plan, folded back to reveal the Operations section that he'd sent over in advance.

'So,' he said, trying to sound bold and assertive. Inside, he was wondering whether there was any point in being here today. 'You looked through the document I sent?'

Dave nodded. 'Be a bit of a waste of time if I ain't done me homework, innit.'

'Right. Yes.' Tony felt embarrassed at having patronised the man.

'Even made a few notes,' Dave said proudly, pulling out a small square of folded-up paper from his pocket. With nimble fingers, he unfurled the sheets and flattened them on the small, pock-marked table between them. Tony could see that whole paragraphs had been circled with a felt-tip pen, some of them marked with exclamation marks and illegible scribbles. 'I got the guys to 'ave a look too. So it ain't just me makin' this stuff up.'

'Great,' he said, managing a smile. 'Thanks. So… Shall we go through it?'

Dave shrugged. 'Probably don't need to, to be honest with you. I can tell you right now what you got wrong.'

'Er, right.' Tony was taken aback by Dave's bluntness. 'Go on, then.'

'Well, for starters, you got your timing estimates all wrong.'

'Oh?'

'Yeah. I mean, that's assuming you ain't got a team of ninjas on speed doin' ya call-outs.' He laughed. Tony tried to laugh too but his throat was dry. 'Basically, what you've got 'ere is the ultimate best-case scenario. It assumes you got all the tools for the job on every job, no traffic, no engineers off sick, no installation hassles... It ain't realistic.'

'Right,' Tony nodded anxiously. He was beginning to wish Amit had joined him today. Amit had written this part of the plan. Or rather, Amit had filled in the preposterously large gaps in the section to which Roy had half-heartedly put his name. Ultimately, it was Roy's fault if these estimates were over-optimistic. The Operations Manager was supposed to know how long a call-out would take.

'So... Do you have an idea of what sort of estimates we should be looking at instead?'

Dave nodded. 'Double your timings and I reckon you'll be just about there.'

'*Double?*' Tony nearly choked. He knew that the estimates would need tweaking; that was why they were writing the operational plan. But to be out by a factor of *two*... He was already thinking about what this would do to the bottom line. Doubling the resource estimates for the engineers would shave off a hefty slab of their profit.

'Yep.' Dave nodded smugly and turned over the wrinkled page. 'And then the one-hour call-out thingumy.' He looked up.

'Wh-what about it?' stammered Tony, already dreading Dave's response.

'Well, it ain't gonna happen, is it? Not with the volumes you're lookin' at. If you're doublin' the call-out time, you're gonna have to up the slot time, aintcha? I'd say you're lookin' at three, maybe four-hour windows.'

Tony gulped. *Four-hour windows?* The one-hour installation window was supposed to be a key selling factor for the offering. He couldn't help thinking back to the skinny girl in the focus group and her comment about the 'tiresome engineer call-out job'. She wouldn't buy into a service that could only offer a three-hour installation window.

'What else?' he asked wearily.

'Well,' said Dave, rustling his papers self-importantly. 'You ain't factored in the network coverage in the different regions…'

Tony listened as the engineer proceeded to list all the other ways in which Roy and Amit had underestimated the investment required for a fully operational roll-out. It was impossible not to apportion blame. If Roy had done a decent job of his part of the business plan then Tony wouldn't have needed to enlist his friend to plug the gaps. Amit had done the best he could, but he was no expert in call-out schedules or engineer networks. Roy *was* an expert in those things but he hadn't bothered to put his expertise to use in the plan.

'Think that's about it,' Dave finished.

'Thanks,' replied Tony, warily eyeing the defaced sheets that lay between them.

Dave noticed his gaze. 'D'you wanna take these away with you?' He collected together the rumpled pages and held them out.

Tony nodded, grasping the pages and rising to his feet. The froth on his tea, he noticed, had been replaced by a dark, oily film. 'That's been extremely helpful.'

Dave saw him out, at pains to express his eagerness for further involvement. Tony couldn't wait to get away. The repercussions of the engineer's thoughts on the business model were depressing. He raised a hand as he stepped out into the rain, no longer caring about getting wet. There were bigger things to worry about.

Tony switched on the engine, the windscreen wipers picking up where they left off in their repetitive squeal. The enormous decision hanging over him seemed more urgent than ever. It was like being lost in a forest, having resolutely pursued a particular direction because of some plausible hunch that was quickly losing its appeal. His conviction had gone but he wasn't sure where else to go.

Crawling along in thick traffic, Tony scrolled through his

emails, his reactions blunted by the growing doubt in his mind. The smart home market was looking dubious, the operational plan unrealistic. It was impossible not to feel glum as he inched along the dual carriageway towards the towering monstrosity that housed the TransTel call centre unit.

Rebecca Palmer, Head of TransTel Communications and one of the youngest business managers in the company, was wearing one of her trademark short skirts. Usually, this would have brightened Tony's mood, but not today. Today, he followed in solemn silence as she led him, high heels clattering, down the dreary corridors to her office on the edge of the call centre floor.

'So!' she said brightly, settling behind her desk and glancing over Tony's shoulder at the rows of operators. 'Forgive me; I'm on edge. We've just implemented a new script for the support team.'

'Ahha.' Tony nodded. 'Issues?'

She waved a hand. 'Teething problems, as ever. You know how it is! Anyway, hopefully we won't have any interruptions.' She batted her long eyelashes and smiled. 'Shall we talk about the plans for this new initiative of yours?'

Tony nodded, sliding out his thumbed copy of the business plan and turning to the relevant page.

'I had a look through,' said Rebecca, glancing across at the digital version on her screen. 'A couple of things sprang to mind.'

'Go on.' Tony nodded. His optimism was starting to trickle back; the Head of Comms was always such a joy to work with.

'Firstly,' she said, still beaming, 'I think your timings estimates are a little way off.'

Tony frowned, his optimism faltering. 'How far off?'

Rebecca's head danced from side to side. 'A few minutes per call. I'd say you need to add fifty percent to your averages.'

'Right,' he replied weakly. He didn't want to think about the combined impact of increasing both the average call duration and the average installation time. It would wreak havoc with the financials.

'And I'm afraid the customer journey doesn't seem to make

a lot of sense,' she added, firmly but kindly, like a nurse administering unpleasant medication.

'What d'you mean?' asked Tony. His appreciation for Rebecca's company was beginning to dwindle.

She went on to explain where the errors lay in Amit's or Roy's plan – Tony couldn't remember who had taken ownership of this particular section. Tony listened, jotting down her suggestions and forcing a smile that matched hers as he swallowed the bad news. After twenty minutes, there was a knock on the glass door and one of the call centre managers burst in, breathlessly explaining some problem they were having on the floor. Tony took the opportunity to slip away, signalling to Rebecca that he'd call her later on.

He sat in the car for some time, staring unseeing at the breezeblock wall of the hideous call centre building. For the last few days, since the unveiling of the focus group insight, Tony had been unclear as to which way to go. Now, suddenly, the decision seemed like less of a dilemma. There was only one sensible alternative. He had to abandon his foolish dreams of building a business around the smart home proposition and he had to do it *soon*, before he wasted too much time and money – before he lost any credibility he might have once had within TransTel. He pulled out his BlackBerry, already mentally composing the email he'd send to Gable.

Tony frowned at the handset, clicking on the latest message and bringing it closer to his face in case he had misread something. It was a meeting request for nine o'clock the following Tuesday. Tony's heart was thumping. The request was from Charles Gable, cc'ing most of the TransTel exec. In the subject line were two ominous words, *Company restructure.* Tony scrolled down in case there was a part of the message he hadn't seen, but the body of the request simply said, *Attendance compulsory.* Tony re-read the words several times, his hands trembling, his mind racing through all the unpleasant possibilities. Then he turned off the device, pushed it deep into his pocket and started the engine. Whatever he ended up telling the board about the smart home project, he decided, it would have to wait until after next Tuesday.

Shock announcement

TONY SWIPED HIS PASS and pushed through the glass doors, removing gloves, scarf and jacket as he went. It was March, but a damp blanket of cold seemed to have draped itself over the country, determinedly prolonging the grip of an already drawn-out winter. He cast an eye over the rows of empty desks and realised, on second glance, that some of the desks weren't empty after all. Louise and a couple of the marketing girls were tapping away on their keyboards and Norm was pressed up against his monitor, frowning, deep in thought.

Tony had lost track of the overtime averages within his team. Ever since the shock of the focus group insight, the marketing girls had been doing their utmost to disprove their own findings. Carrying out quantitative surveys, depth interviews, more focus groups, they were doing everything they could to persuade themselves that there was a market for the damned proposition – so far, to no avail. Likewise, Norm and his technical wizards had been up against it, trying to get the product to a stage where it could be used in people's homes. On more than one occasion, Tony had had to stand over members of his team late at night, forcing them to leave the office. In normal circumstances, he would have felt proud of their motivation. But he couldn't feel proud when he knew that the meeting at nine o'clock would in all likelihood spell out the end of everything they were working towards.

Logging onto his workstation, Tony watched as his inbox slowly filled, too preoccupied to start the morning trawl. He had thought a lot in the last few days about the meeting's likely agenda and had concluded that there were three possibilities. One, they were shutting down Synapse. Two, they were merging Synapse with another part of the firm. Three, they were restructuring in a way that didn't affect Synapse but they wanted to let all heads of business know before the news got out. In his more positive moments, Tony had convinced himself that number three was most likely, but now, with only minutes to go before the moment of truth, he couldn't help feeling nervous.

His employees were in the office, typing, reading, calculating, oblivious to the possible demise of everything they were gunning for. Tony felt terrible. He had plucked these people from their day jobs, convinced them to follow a more risky path, despite the protests, promising them great rewards. And now, potentially, he was going to have to go back on all of those promises. Worse, he was going to have to tell them that because they had trusted him, they would now lose their jobs.

Tony clicked on his emails at random, not even reading their contents. His thoughts moved away from his employees and onto his family. Several times in the last few days, he had tried telling Suze about the meeting, warning her in case the worst happened. But every time he came close, Suze would slip in some remark about the baby or Poppy that made it impossible to talk about the possibility of him not having a job in three months' time.

Perhaps it was just as well, he thought. There was no point in worrying her unnecessarily. If the worst *did* happen, then there were always other jobs. Synapse wasn't the only career path he could take – although it was the one he wanted to take. He wanted to conquer the challenge he'd taken on. Tony looked at the clock. It was five to nine. He grabbed a notebook and pen, pushed himself up on shaky knees and headed for the sixth floor.

Janine Cook's flaming red hair was the first thing he saw when he pushed open the boardroom door. A tentative wave of relief rushed into his bloodstream. Surely they wouldn't make him redundant in front of the Head of BusinessReach, his business equivalent? The relief was soon replaced with alarm as Tony realised that there was another, more unpleasant

197

possibility: they were axing *both* broadband departments. He and Janine were in the same boat.

'Come on in,' bellowed Gable from the head of the table. All the directors were there: Nicholas Draper, Graham Walker-Jones, Anita Reynolds, Carl Spragg and Josh Green. The only non-board members, Tony noted suspiciously, were Janine and himself.

There was a period of awkward silence while the last few directors took their seats. Brows were furrowed, lips pursed. Tony glanced across at Janine, trying to gauge whether she knew any more than he did. Her eyes were firmly set on the blank page in front of her, giving nothing away.

Gable cleared his throat as if trying to cut through the hubbub, despite the complete lack of hubbub. Tony surreptitiously wiped his sweating palms against his thighs.

'Thank you, first of all, for your punctuality. I realise that some of you have been called at relatively short notice, without much information about the subject up for discussion.'

Tony glanced around at the faces, trying to ascertain who knew what. Walker-Jones was nodding slowly as though the chief exec were imparting great pearls of wisdom. Draper was staring straight ahead, eyes narrowed. Spragg was scratching his beard.

'…that this is a difficult time to be in telecoms,' Gable was saying in a dull monotone. Tony continued to search the faces for a clue. He'd heard the CEO's 'troubled times' speech before. It was usually a precursor to bad news. Janine's head was bowed low now, her vibrant locks falling in front of her eyes so that it was impossible to read her expression.

'Deregulation, consumer empowerment and now a deluge of young upstarts trying to compete with our business means that we've had to make some big changes to our business…'

The drone of Gable's voice merged with the alarm bells ringing in Tony's head. There was something different about the American this morning. The bolshy ex-consultant didn't usually hide herself away behind her hair.

'…particularly in the broadband arena. Which is why I'm saddened to say that by mutual agreement, Janine Cook will step down from her position as Head of BusinessReach, with immediate effect.'

Tony's head shot up. He stared at Gable then quickly turned to Janine, along with everyone else in the room.

Janine managed a twitchy smile and then dipped her head once again. Two things occurred to Tony at once. *Mutual agreement*, he realised, was a euphemism. Janine was being pushed. And if Janine had been pre-warned of the news, which she obviously had – her hair was usually scraped back into a knot on the back of her head – then perhaps he wouldn't find himself in the same situation after all.

'Janine has performed a sterling job of heading up the BusinessReach team since she took over eighteen months ago, taking the unit from strength to strength...'

They were being kind, thought Tony. BusinessReach had been loss-making ever since Graham Walker-Jones had effectively priced it out of the market, causing a mass defection of business customers to alternative, cheaper providers. To be fair to Janine, the division had been in a bad way when she'd taken over, but the mysterious 'five-year roadmap' to which she had devoted most of her tenancy had done nothing to help push the unit back into the black.

As the CEO talked of tremendous achievements and stalwart leadership, Tony's mind drifted back to the big question: Why was he here? With Janine gone, the obvious answer was that he would be brought in as her replacement. But surely there would be some consultation, if that were the case? They couldn't just redefine his role with no prior warning. He didn't want to take over the floundering B2B division. If the role had appealed to him, he would have applied eighteen months ago when Graham Walker-Jones had stepped down.

'...decision has been taken to roll BusinessReach into its sister unit, Synapse, and to run the entire broadband business as one.'

It took a couple of seconds for the words to sink in. Tony looked up at Gable, who was smiling expectantly in his direction. BusinessReach was to become part of Synapse. He was to accept the loss-making business as part of his own. Nodding vaguely,

Tony thought about what this would mean for his team. Already, their remit included both the consumer broadband business and his fledgling smart home proposition – if indeed he was to continue with that initiative in light of recent developments – but now it would extend to B2B broadband, a market he knew very little about, other than the disastrous losses achieved by TransTel in recent years.

'It is envisaged that the function heads will remain as they are within Synapse,' Gable went on, addressing Tony specifically, 'with key personnel moving across from BusinessReach as appropriate. This will enable some considerable cost savings through pooled resources and – regrettably – some headcount reductions.'

Tony half-listened, still contemplating the implications of this news. A small part of him was buzzing; he hadn't lost his job and his department was not on the brink of collapse. Suze would never have to know how close he had come to unemployment. He wouldn't need to stand up in front of Matt and Louise and the others and tell them that they'd all been made redundant. But the rest of his brain was wracked with concern. The BusinessReach arm was in a mess. If he absorbed it into Synapse then it would threaten the viability of the whole division. He didn't want the upheaval of a departmental merger on his hands. And what would happen to the smart home project? Would it be canned, by default, with a view to focusing on the core, albeit unprofitable, broadband business?

The room had gone quiet. Tony looked up and realised that everyone was looking at him. He rewound his short-term memory. Gable had asked him a question. *How do you feel about that?*

Tony drew a breath, still not sure what to say. Graham Walker-Jones was staring across the table at him, beady-eyed, clearly eager to hear what would become of his darling BusinessReach and, more importantly, his unvested bonus. The pressure was on to reply positively. But Tony wasn't concerned by the pressure, or the diabolical balance sheet he was being asked to inherit. Nor was he thinking about the pay rise or promotion that would inevitably ensue, should he take on the role. He was thinking about the challenge.

Despite the unknowns, despite the fact that BusinessReach hadn't turned a profit in nearly two years, Tony could feel its potential. His gut instinct was telling him to take it on. There would be hurdles, integrating the two halves of the business, and the demands on his time would no doubt double. But there was life left in this business yet. And if the board felt he was up to the job of resuscitating it, then he was willing to give it a go.

'I think it's a very sensible idea,' he said. 'I look forward to taking it on.'

CREATING THE OPERATIONAL PLAN

CREATING THE OPERATIONAL PLAN

 MarketGravity

In this chapter Tony starts to dig into the detail of the business plan to try and get a better understanding of the delivery challenges and key operational assumptions. This is when the neatness of a well constructed business plan meets the messiness of the real world.

Challenges you're likely to experience at this stage of the journey include:

- Getting push-back from operational teams on key business assumptions
- Uncovering unexpected issues and risks that lie in the detail
- Getting a much clearer understanding of delivery costs and trying to reconcile them back to the investment case
- Realising that most operational staff don't care about your vision and strategy
- Having to re-sell the business plan to new people who are often sceptical, but critical to delivery
- Identifying new capability requirements and not knowing how you are going to fulfil them

Business plans are essentially a series of best guesses to gauge whether an opportunity is worth pursuing. If it is, then the objective of the operational plan is to inject a heavy dose of reality into the equation by validating assumptions and exposing unrealistic elements.

"TO REALLY EARN PEOPLE'S TRUST, AND KNOW YOUR WAY AROUND THE BUSINESS, YOU NEED TO WORK AT ALL LEVELS. I WORKED 'UNDER COVER' AS A DELIVERY DRIVER, DEPOT MANAGER ETC. BEFORE I MADE RECOMMENDATIONS FOR A TAKEOVER TO THE BOARD."

David Wilson, British Gas, City Link, npower

The operational plan is where the business starts to feel real. The full set of capability requirements are identified, the detailed operating model designed and the implementation plan mapped out.

Some tips for developing a strong and executable operating plan are as follows:

1. Understand the difference between a business plan and operational plan. A business plan's job is primarily to bring in investment whereas an operational plan is your blue-print for building the new business.

2. Talk to the people on the ground. The best insight is often locked away in people's heads, whether they're on the front-line with customers, providing internal services, or carrying out day-to-day operations.

3. Use operational knowledge to your advantage. Get a deep understanding of how your business will work in order to protect the business case from would-be assassins.

4. Don't be put off by "we can't do this". It's highly unlikely that the complete set of capability requirements to deliver the new venture already exists in the business. So long as a the numbers stack up, gaps can be filled either by making, buying or partnering.

Capability gaps can be filled through three options: make, buy or partner. Conditions for each decision include:

Make
- Underlying capabilities exist
- Resource and time available
- Ownership provides strategic advantage
- Risk and quality management is key

Buy
- Limited / no capability exists internally
- Rapid growth required
- Scarce capacity in the market
- Value chain capture is important
- Cultural and competence fit

Partner
- Partner availability
- Independence key to value
- Benefit of separate culture
- Flexibility required
- Non-core activity

7

Beware the assassin: avoiding venture death

'There are many ways to kill a new venture in a large company.'

Sleepless night; Matt moaning

TONY BURIED HIS HEAD in the pillow and clamped his eyes shut against the grey light that was streaming through the gap in the curtains. Somewhere outside, a bird was imitating an alarm clock.

It was no good. His brain was awake, flitting through all the problems and questions that were due to confront him that day, taking him further away from the promise of sleep. Poppy had been sick in the night – sick in the sense that she needed attention, her endless whimpering not attributable to any discernable ailment – and Suze had slept through it all. He didn't mind. Tending to their daughter was the least he could do for his wife at the moment. He just wished that the six hours of dozing hadn't been entirely preoccupied with thoughts of revenue streams and internal reshuffles.

He slipped out of bed, taking care not to dislodge the covers around his wife's bump. Dressing quickly and quietly, he planted a kiss on Suze's forehead, scribbled a note on her bedside pad and crept out.

The clock on the dashboard said five-thirty. It was his earliest start yet, not counting the time he had worked through the night for Amit during the launch of TransTel CBN. He rolled the car silently down the drive, starting the engine as he got to the road. Already, he was prioritising, delegating, trying not to panic.

The absorption of BusinessReach into the Synapse division was proving more disruptive than he had anticipated. Quite apart from the obvious issues – the redundancies, the personality clashes, the operational integration – there was the challenge of ploughing through the legacy left by Janine: mounds upon mounds of PowerPoint slides filled with references to strategic alignment and competitive vulnerability. It was a full-time job, making sense of the words.

The roads were eerily quiet and Tony reached the office in record time. As the revolving doors sucked him in, he watched with distracted amusement as the security guard jumped, then waved, trying to pretend he hadn't been napping.

It was safe to say that the honeymoon period in Tony's new role was over. The pride and excitement that accompanied his thirty percent pay rise and promotion – he now held the title of Group Head of Broadband – had lasted about a day. Having looked at the books and realised just how deeply the B2B division was in the red, Tony couldn't muster anything more than a feeling of nervous agitation. And that was just for business-as-usual.

What *really* worried him, more than the dwindling revenue streams or the ambitious targets the board had set for the newly combined enterprise, was the fact that his smart home proposition lay in tatters. Even before the merger, Tony had been having doubts about its viability. In writing the operational plan, he had reluctantly recognised that the market for smart homes was not as large as the team had hoped; that their sales and cost estimates had been way off the mark. He had been on the verge of scrapping the whole idea – and now, with the additional pressure on resources and a whole new set of people to bring on board, it was looking increasingly likely that scrappage was the only option. The pilot was due to start in just over a month; if he was going to pull the plug, he had to pull it soon.

Passing through the empty office, Tony wondered what his team's reaction would be, if he were to can the whole project. Perhaps it was the lack of sleep making him feel emotional, but it felt almost as though his managers had gelled into something akin to a family in recent months. Working late, helping one another out, plotting their future together... It was about more than just the business case now. It was their project. Their brainchild. They *had* to make it happen.

'Hello.'

Tony opened his eyes, mid-yawn, stopping dead in his tracks. He stared as Matt swivelled slowly to meet him, letting his feet swing down off the desk.

'What're you doing in here so early?'

Matt shrugged. 'I'm usually in the gym, but I've sprained something.'

Letting his jacket slither off his shoulder, Tony reached out and switched on his PC. Matt had explained why he was here *early*, but he hadn't explained why he was *here*, re-applying the stickers on his boss' Rubik's Cube.

'You want the good news or the bad news?' he asked sullenly.

Tony sank into his chair, eyeing his Sales Manager warily. The Rubik's Cube had been 'solved', he noticed. 'Um... Good?'

'Okay. I got that Natasha bint on-side with the bonus proposal for the sales team.'

'For the smart home thing?'

Matt rolled his eyes. 'What else?'

'Right. Great.' Tony nodded as encouragingly as he dared. The news *was* great, assuming the smart home project went ahead. 'How the hell did you do that?'

For the first time, Matt showed a glimmer of a smile. 'Best you don't ask.'

Tony looked at the young man's face, half intrigued, half apprehensive about what was to come. Matt certainly had a way with the ladies.

'Bad news is, I'm pissed off.'

'Right.' Tony frowned anxiousy. 'About what?'

'What d'you fuckin' think?' Matt looked at him as if he was stupid. 'I'm supposed to be Head of Sales at Synapse, I've been workin' overtime on this *smart home* shit and now I get staffed with a whole new sales team and another product to sell... All at no extra cost. I want a pay rise.'

Tony nodded, once. Keeping his head bowed, he thought about how to respond. He felt mildly relieved that his Sales Manager hadn't actually mentioned the 'r' word, but he knew that the threat wasn't far away. He also knew how hard it was to elicit a pay rise from HR in the current climate. His own rise consisted largely of share options and had been funded by the redundancy of his B2B counterpart. For managers, the situation was different.

'Okay,' he said, after some contemplation. 'It's... not a good time to be asking for salary increases.' He looked up and took in the manager's expression. One eyebrow was raised, chin jutting out menacingly before him. 'But I'm sure there's scope for improvement, given the situation.'

'Good.'

'Yes. Um... Leave it with me. I'll get onto it now.'

'Cool. Thanks boss.'

Tony felt bad, watching his Sales Manager leave the room, his swagger restored. He had been wrong, he realised, in assuming that his team would be disappointed to see an end to the smart home project. They weren't all here for the love of it. Matt certainly wasn't. He was doing it for the money. It was hardly surprising he'd managed to persuade the HR Manager to authorise the sales team's performance-related pay; he would be the main beneficiary, should the venture become a success. It was all about the incentives.

Tony sat, staring blindly at his computer screen as the options whirled through his tired brain. He could bin the whole project now, leaving Matt and everyone else to get on with their day jobs and the integration programme. That would solve a lot of problems. He could silence the trouble-makers with a small pay rise and that would be that. But it wouldn't solve the biggest problem of all: the fact that his business was in decline.

He wanted to solve that problem. Launching a whole new offering wasn't exactly part of his job description, but for Tony it had never been about sticking to the job description. He was a doer, a grafter. He wanted to make things right. But the harsh reality, he knew, was that his plans for making things right looked highly unlikely to succeed.

His phone buzzed against the desk, jerking him out of his thoughts.

From: Amit Chaudhuri
Mate, if ur up, turn

on Radio 4 - might b
worth thinking about
4 yr venture?
A

Tony opened up a browser and navigated to the Radio 4 homepage.

'...massive impact on enterprises, not necessarily positive,' barked the interviewer. 'Is that fair to say?'

'Absolutely,' replied a man with a deep, languid voice. It sounded as though his response had been pre-recorded and played back at half-speed. 'These regulations go a long way to improve our businesses' green credentials, but the fact remains, these changes cost money. I'll give you an example. For a medium-sized business with a turnover of twenty million, complying with the new codes of practice will cost between fifty and a hundred thousand pounds, in the first two years. That's a lot of money.'

Tony reached over and pushed shut his office door while the interviewer addressed someone else in the studio.

'The importance of reducing our carbon footprint cannot be underestimated,' stressed an earnest-sounding woman – probably an ambassador for Greenpeace or similar. 'We've been burning our planet's resources for long enough; it's high time the government did something to put things right.'

'Agreed, but I think the point is that this is a costly way of going about that...'

Tony tuned out as the debate meandered onto the subject of 'proportional alignment', whatever that was. He could feel something bubbling up inside him. Amit was right. This *was* worth thinking about. The government was evidently about to lay down some new rules that forced businesses to reduce their impact on the environment. Which meant... which meant, surely, that companies up and down the country would want to reduce their energy consumption. And in order to do that, they needed to *monitor* their energy consumption.

Two hours later, having trawled the internet, downloading and digesting the full set of new regulations, Tony felt more excited than ever. The smart home project was dead in the water; it was too soon for consumers to adopt new practices in the home. But in the *workplace,* with these new rules... it made sense, all of a sudden. They had been focusing on the wrong market.

Tony flung open his door as his Head of Marketing walked through the office.

'Louise,' he said, looking her in the eye. 'How much do we know about our BusinessReach customers?'

Business wants consistency;
Roy making trouble

'TO BACK UP these findings, we also carried out some quantitative research,' explained Louise, handing over to her co-presenter, Martin, a skinny young man who had come over from the B2B team.

'Oh, um, yes.' Martin blinked nervously at Tony, who smiled back encouragingly. It was good to see that the merger hadn't been entirely destructive. While most of his direct reports were wrangling over redefined roles and grappling with petty personnel issues, Louise seemed to have blended the two halves of her team effortlessly. The Marketing team was a picture of harmony.

The anxious young graduate fumbled with the remote control for a second, then looked up and waved a hand at the bar chart on the screen.

'So, er, this shows the current level of satisfaction among heads of small- and medium-sized businesses with regards to their energy services.'

Tony continued to nod, letting the young man's monologue wash over him. He didn't need the voiceover. The figures spoke for themselves. Eighty-four percent of business leaders were dissatisfied with their energy services provision. Fifty-two percent had had one or more dispute over billing during the last six months. Twenty-seven percent didn't even know what their average monthly outgoings were.

'...our key conclusion: that businesses would prefer consistent, manageable monthly outgoings to the uncertainty that they experience at the moment. Which is why an energy monitoring service might meet their needs.'

Martin stood for a second, holding Tony's gaze and then looking down at the floor. Tony could feel himself nodding. He was keeping his expression neutral, trying not to get too worked up. They had, after all, been here before, with the B2C concept. It was at exactly this stage in the research that he had started seeing opportunities, started jumping around with glee at the thought of all the consumers who would subscribe – started trying to run before he could walk.

'Thanks, Martin.' He acknowledged the young man's presentation with a final dip of his head. Then he turned to his Head of Marketing.

'This is a very thorough piece of research,' he remarked. 'The findings you highlighted earlier seem to spell out quite clearly that there's a decent market for the proposition.' He ran a hand through his hair, trying to clarify in his own mind what he really thought. 'Is this *enough?* Does this really validate the market, or are we just kidding ourselves?'

Louise leaned forward with the air of someone who was cautiously optimistic.

'I think it is,' she said earnestly. 'I know what you're thinking; that we've been through this once before and been proved wrong, but this time we've been far more rigorous. We went into much more detail and drilled down further with the questions. I really do think there's a market in the B2B space.'

Martin was nodding, too. Tony wondered whether the kid had drawn his own conclusions, or simply bowed to the authority of his new boss. It certainly *seemed* to make sense. The research did appear more robust than the small-sample survey they had used to convince themselves to proceed with the B2C business plan.

'Okay,' he said finally. 'If you send me the raw data to look at, I'll have a think about revising the plan.'

Louise was beaming as she left Tony's office, guiding the lanky young graduate from the room with a maternal arm.

Tony sat, for a second, hearing the ping of emails dropping into his inbox but too preoccupied with his thoughts to register.

It would be awkward, explaining to the board that the target market for the proposition was no longer household bill payers but small- and medium-sized enterprises, but he knew that the real issue wasn't how best to please the board; it was how to turn around his ailing business unit. If the smart home idea wouldn't help him to do that, then he had to find another that would. And from everything he had seen so far, it looked very much as though smart *sites* might be the answer.

A knock on the door interrupted Tony's thoughts. He looked up to find Roy shuffling towards the visitor's chair, shoulders slumped in an expression of self-pity. He was ten minutes late, Tony noted, waiting to catch his Operations Manager's eye.

The bald man sighed heavily, leaning back in the chair. 'Well, y'know...'

Tony raised an eyebrow. He thought he probably did know, but he wanted to hear it in full. The integration of Roy's operations department with the B2B equivalent was not going well. Tony knew this because he had heard it from Roy, but also because he had heard it on the grapevine from engineers, call centre operators and systems architects around the business. He had even caught wind of the friction through Amit, whose team now had very little to do with Synapse. Tony knew all this, but he hadn't had the time or opportunity to confront his manager directly – which was why they were meeting today.

'Go on,' he prompted, when no further explanation was forthcoming.

Roy shrugged. 'Well, it's a bloody nightmare, isn't it?'

'What is?'

'This bleedin' merger!' He rolled his eyes heavenwards. 'I got engineers fightin' like cats an' dogs, I got operators runnin' around like headless chickens...'

Tony looked at him, waiting for the animal analogies to end. 'Can you be more specific?'

Roy was back to his old ways. Perhaps because the promise of inheriting his boss' title seemed all the more distant now that the department had doubled in size and the smart home project was in jeopardy, or perhaps because he was suffering more than others with the organisational reshuffle, but he had gone back to

213

stomping around, making unhelpful comments and generally relishing the prospect of Tony's failure.

'Where d'you want me to start?' barked Roy. 'Look, I'm not being funny, but I can't work miracles.'

Tony wished he had set aside time to prepare for this encounter. Roy was confrontational at the best of times, but now, worn down by corporate politics and in-fighting – he was intolerable.

'What can I do to make things more manageable?' he asked calmly.

Roy snarled at his boss in disgust. It was exactly the response Tony had expected. The Operations Manager had plenty to say by way of complaints, but when it came to solutions, he was markedly quiet.

'Well, have a think,' Tony suggested gently, taking care not to come across as patronising. 'In the meantime, how are you getting on with ring-fencing a pilot team for the smart home proposition?'

Roy stared at him as though he'd just asked an outrageously personal question. 'Are you 'avin' a laugh?'

'No,' replied Tony, feeling the anger bubbling up inside him. 'Two weeks ago, I asked you to establish and brief a team of engineers in the pilot region, ready for the launch in four weeks. I'm asking for an update on your progress.'

Roy leaned forward in his chair, looking Tony squarely in the eye. 'You seriously expect me to be goin' round cherry-picking engineers for some friggin' pilot launch, at a time like this?'

Tony waited a moment, maintaining eye contact, and then nodded. 'Yes, I do.'

'Look, I'm flat out on–'

'We're all flat out, Roy.'

'I don't think you know the half of–'

'Believe me, I do. I know how hard you've been working. I understand that it's not easy, fitting this project around everything else, but believe me, I wouldn't ask you to do it unless it was important.'

Roy said nothing, his face set in a sullen scowl like a child being denied a second helping.

'We *have* to get this thing operational, or the whole department goes under,' Tony prompted.

Still, Roy said nothing.

Tony tried a different tack.

'I need your help on this. I'm relying on you.'

Roy shrugged and pushed back his chair.

'Well,' he said, turning as he reached the door. 'If you really want me to ditch the job I'm being paid to do, to see to this pilot malarkey, then fine.'

'I don't want you to–'

Roy had already left the room. Tony sat, head in hands, thinking about his Operations Manager and wondering whether there was anything he could be doing to rectify the situation. The problem was, Roy didn't *want* the situation rectified. He would like nothing better than to see Tony's brainchild become a high-profile flop. He was a stubborn, pig-headed antagonist – an assassin, determined to kill off the venture.

The only solution, as far as Tony could see, was to cut him out. To remove the Ops Manager from the equation. He was good at his day job, so for the gestation period of the smart site project, or whatever it turned out to be, Tony would have to get by without him.

His phone rang, jolting him out of his melancholy.

'Oh, hi, sorry for calling you at work.' Suze sounded breathless and flustered. 'I'm out with Emmie, trying to get Poppy's – ooh, no Bradley! Em, watch it, he's trying to pee in the toy bathroom.'

Tony smiled, trying to shelve his anxieties for a moment.

'Bradley! Em? Oh God, he's run off with the bedspread... Sorry. Just trying to get Poppy's birthday present, but they don't seem to have the Daisy Princess bike in stock anywhere. Could you – Bradley, come back!'

There was a huffing sound down the line. Tony pictured his wife rushing through the department store after the unruly child, wielding her bump before her like a weapon.

'Can you... stop off... at Halfords... on your way home?'

'Of course,' he said, jiggling his mouse to reveal a depressing number of emails on the screen. 'The one on the high street?'

'Ah.' There was more panting, although this time Tony suspected this time she might be stalling for time. 'Heathrow.'

'Heathrow? That's miles away! Can't we go at the weekend? Her birthday's not for ten days.'

'They're selling out,' Suze explained.

'Can't we get a different bike, then? Doesn't have to be the Rosie Princess, does it?'

'Daisy Princess,' Suze corrected. 'And yes, it does. It's the one all her friends have got.'

'Oh.' Tony wasn't going to argue with playground logic. 'Right. Okay. I'll go tonight.'

'They shut at five.'

'*Five?*'

'She really wants it, Tony.'

He sighed. 'Okay. Don't worry, I'll get it.'

Tony checked the time as he came off the phone. It was ten past three. He hadn't checked his emails since the morning, and if he was going to get to Heathrow by five then he'd have to leave in under an hour. Quickly, he set to work.

It transpired that a good number of emails had come from Amit and Brian. Tony picked the most recent message and read up from the bottom.

From: Charles Gable – CEO, TransTel
Dear Heads of Business,

You will be aware that for some time now, TransTel has been involved in a structural reorganisation with the objective of streamlining operations and reducing costs.

The second phase of our transformational programme is now due to commence. To this end, each department within TransTel will be required to identify the ten percent of its workforce that adds least value to the organisation.

Details will be sent out by HR representatives early next week, so please make every effort to comply with the proposed timescales.

Yours,
Charles

From: Amit Chaudhuri – TransTel Cordless Enterprises
Thoughts?

From: Brian O'Keefe - TransTel Network Direct
Is it April 1st?

From: Amit Chaudhuri – TransTel Cordless Enterprises
I wonder how one is supposed to determine who falls in the
bottom 10%...?

From: Brian O'Keefe - TransTel Network Direct
Russian Roulette?

From: Amit Chaudhuri – TransTel Cordless Enterprises
Ah, and here I was, thinking lengthy, time-consuming
assessments for the entire team.

From: Brian O'Keefe - TransTel Network Direct
That would certainly help with 'streamlining'.

Tony checked his inbox to see whether he had received the same message from Gable. With a sinking heart, he saw that he had.

The CEO was asking him to identify the bottom ten percent of his workforce with a view to making them redundant. How was he supposed to go about this? And how, if he did miraculously find the time to assess and rank every member of his team, was he supposed to manage on an even lower headcount? Tony clicked on the CEO's message and pressed Reply.

From: Tony Sharp – Synapse
Charles,

Unfortunately, due to the pressing matter of getting Synapse
back on track, as well as integration of the two business units,
I will not have sufficient resources to partake in this headcount
reduction programme.
With best wishes,
Tony

Pulse racing, he scan-read his words and pressed Send before there was time for contemplation. Some hurdles, he thought, were just too absurd to jump.

CEO suggests fanfare; supplier issues

THERE WAS A KNOCK on the door and Maureen's plump face came into view.

'Just had the CEO on the line,' she said, pulling an expression that could have meant anything.

'And?'

'He wants to see you.'

'What, now?'

The PA nodded.

Tony could feel the adrenaline kicking in. An impromptu meeting request from Charles Gable was rarely a sign of good news.

'Did he say what it was about?'

It was a painful process, extracting information from Maureen, but Tony was beginning to get the hang of it. You just had to ask a lot of questions. Tony tried not to think back to the golden days, when Marianne's solutions would present themselves before the problems or queries had even arisen.

Maureen shook her head blankly.

Tony decided that there was no more information to extort. 'Thanks. Can you tell Louise to get on with the brainstorm without me? I'll join them when I get back.'

With shaky hands, Tony gathered a notepad and pen, smoothed down his crumpled suit and headed for the sixth floor. He had a feeling he knew what this was about. Not many managers, he guessed, had replied to Charles' email about the headcount reduction programme with a point-blank refusal to take part. He had thought it a little strange that he'd had no reply to the hastily-typed rejoinder he had sent out four days ago.

'Enter!' came the muffled bark from inside. Tony tugged at his shirt sleeves, drew a deep breath and stepped into the oak-panelled suite.

He had no reason to feel nervous, he told himself. He hadn't done anything wrong. The email had been perfectly representative of his views – still was. Perhaps his views could have been more tactfully put, but frankly, he thought, there was no point in beating around the bush.

'Charles.' He gave a brief nod of deference to the large man. 'I know why I'm here. I understand that we're going through hard times and we have to cut back, and in principle I'm all for efficiency drives. But I really can't afford to lose ten percent of my team. And the idea of assessing and ranking each one of them...' Tony lifted his shoulders. 'Again, I'm sorry. I just don't have the time, with the smart site project and the merger and everything else.'

The CEO's brow was deeply furrowed. Tony thought about strengthening his case but decided it would probably come across as waffle and forced himself to wait for the man's reply.

Eventually, with his forehead still creased, the CEO leaned forward and cocked his head at Tony.

'You are referring, I presume, to the streamlining operation that is to be rolled out imminently?'

Tony nodded.

'Ah.' Charles nodded, lips pursed. 'Okay, well, I have to say, I'm not having much to do with that on a day-to-day basis, so perhaps you should address any concerns you have to HR.

'R-right,' Tony stammered. It was suddenly obvious to him that he had misinterpreted the purpose of today's meeting. Charles probably hadn't even received his email; it had no doubt been dealt with by one of his many personal assistants, or simply deleted. He sat up, trying to ignore the burning sensation that was spreading up from his neck, wishing he could re-do the last two minutes of his life. 'So...'

'How is the smart site project progressing?' asked Charles. 'Are we on track for the pilot?'

Tony straightened up, encouraged by the faint, optimistic smile on the CEO's lips. 'We are indeed,' he said. 'One month and counting.'

It had come as a huge relief to Tony when the board had signed off on the revised proposal to serve the business market instead of consumers. The change had slipped through surprisingly easily – or perhaps it wasn't so surprising, given that the revenue estimates were now a long way north of the fifty million originally forecast. With almost no change to the fundamentals of the proposition, the business services market represented a large, well-defined target that the BusinessReach sales team was well-positioned to address. The new direction was seen as a no-brainer for all involved.

'Excellent,' replied the CEO, emphatically. 'So.' The smile spread, slowly, across his ruddy face. 'What are you doing next Friday?'

Tony mentally flipped through his diary. There was definitely something happening on Friday; he just couldn't remember what it was.

'I'll tell you what you're doing,' the CEO went on, before he could form a response. 'You're announcing this project of yours to the investors at our annual results presentation.'

Charles interlocked his sausage-like fingers and sat back in his chair, beaming like an emperor.

'I'm... sorry?' was all Tony could say. Next Friday was the most important day of the corporate calendar. It was the day when Gable and selected board members stood up in front of shareholders and City analysts, outlining their achievements and aspirations for the company. Tony had sat through enough annual results presentations to know exactly what it entailed – and to know that he didn't want to be a part of the ordeal.

'I want to get this thing *out there*,' Charles growled through a grill of yellow teeth. 'Show people what we're all about. Tell them we're not just some stuffy telco that can't keep up. Let's impress our investors – and let's intimidate our competitors! I want to be *proud* of our pipeline. This smart site project of yours could transform our product line, not to mention our top line! Let's get people *talking* about it!'

Tony stared, nodding mutely at the CEO while he took it all in. Two months ago, it had seemed like an impossible task, getting the board to sign off on the business plan. To get their approval, he had jumped through countless hoops, cosying up to the COO and laying out barely-achievable KPIs for a staged financing plan that only just kept the venture afloat. Suddenly, the board wanted to tout it as TransTel's Next Big Thing.

'We were thinking we could pre-record a video of you speaking from the Innovation Labs,' the Chief Exec went on. 'It doesn't have to be long; just an idea of what we're up to, when it's happening and a little something on revenue forecasts.' He winked.

It was all Tony could do to stop his mouth from hanging open in disbelief. The hypocrisy of the board was incredible. Having spent months scratching their heads and frowning at Tony's ideas, when it came to disproving their 'stuffy telco' image, they wanted to haul him up on a pedestal to brag about something that hadn't even gone into pilot.

Charles was still talking. Tony could hear words like 'dynamic' and 'forward-thinking', but he was only part-listening. It was difficult to know what to do. Of course, it was flattering that the board saw his new venture as such an asset. *Proud of our pipeline... Transform our business... Impress our investors...* A few weeks ago, Tony could only have dreamed of hearing such phrases. It boded well for future support. If the board was willing to promote it publicly at such an early stage, then they'd be obliged, from a reputation perspective, to see it through. But that was the problem. It *was* early stage. It was too early to start boasting. Investors would lap up the news of the pilot next week, probably bolstering TransTel's share price by a couple of pence, but then the eyes of the world would be upon them: business journalists, research analysts, competitors... They would all be watching, waiting for it to fail.

'...so, what do you say?'

Tony still didn't know. It was stressful enough, trying to deliver a business and keep internal investors happy, but with fund managers and city institutions keeping tabs on him too... On the other hand, could he really turn down the opportunity to set his venture at the heart of TransTel's strategy for the coming year?

'I think it's a great idea,' he said, eventually. 'I'd be happy to present.'

Charles unclasped his hands and banged them against his desk with panache. 'Splendid,' he said, fixing Tony with a hearty smile. 'I'll get someone to talk you through the details.'

It was only as he padded down the carpeted corridor towards the lifts that Tony remembered what had been in his diary for the following Friday. DAY OFF. It was Poppy's fourth birthday and he had promised to throw her a party.

Distractedly, Tony slipped into the back of the meeting room, where Louise was running a workshop to determine the name and brand of the new proposition. 'Running', it turned out, was something of an exaggeration. Tony stared at the riotous scene, trying to ascertain what was supposed to be happening. The Marketing Manager was cowering at the front, half-hidden by a flip-chart, looking at the floor, while a cacophony of shouts and jeers erupted around her.

'Easy Energy!'

'Probably trademarked. What about Bill Cutter?'

'Sounds like a porn name!'

'Utilit-ease! Get it? Sounds like utilities, but with...?'

'What's wrong with Smart Site?'

People were beginning to notice Tony's presence at the back of the room, and the noise level started to drop. Louise looked up, blinked at the sight of her boss, and started scribbling random words on the flip chart as though she'd just remembered why she was there.

Tony tried to catch her eye. Louise had never been the most organised member of his staff, but she could usually control a roomful of subordinates. Today, she looked flustered and anxious.

'Okay!' she cried eventually, prompting a brief respite from the shouts. 'Thanks, everyone!' Her wobbly voice was still competing with a good deal of chatter. 'We'll need to go away and look at URL availability and so on, but if you have any more ideas in the meantime, please send me an email! We're hoping to get this wrapped up in the next week...'

The door was already open, rowdy Synapse employees spilling through it and trampling their way back to their desks. Tony loitered, waiting for the room to empty before joining Louise at the front.

'How did it go?' he asked, unnecessarily. 'Sorry I missed it. Last minute meeting with Charles.'

Louise shrugged, forcing a smile. 'Not bad.'

Tony nodded solemnly, watching as Louise tore the pages from the flip chart pad. Her hands were shaking, he noticed.

'Did you... Did you get some ideas?'

It wasn't the question he wanted to ask. He wanted to know what was wrong – whether the shaky hands and the wobbly voice were symptoms of something more serious.

In the event, he got the answers without needing to ask. Louise looked at him, opened her mouth to speak, and then suddenly burst into tears. Tony wasn't sure what to do. He considered laying a comforting hand on her shoulder, but then wondered whether there were company rules against that sort of thing.

'What's up?' he asked, guiding her away from the flip-chart towards the table, pulling out a chair that faced away from the open-plan office.

'I'm sorry...' Louise sniffed miserably, rummaging in her bag for a tissue. Tony felt utterly useless.

It wasn't clear why the Marketing Manager was apologising, but Tony didn't feel it was the time to ask.

'It's okay,' he said, softly. 'I know everything's become a bit stressful of late. We're all feeling it. Just let me know what's troubling you and we can try and sort it out. I'm sure–'

'No!' blurted Louise, with a fresh bout of tears. 'No, we can't sort it out, because it's already been done! I've messed up, Tony. I'm sorry. I'm so sorry.'

'What d'you mean?'

'The marketing budget for the pilot. I've over-spent. I forgot to cancel the provisional campaigns!'

'What provisional campaigns?'

'The *consumer* ones! So now we're paying for both consumer *and* business. I've wasted nearly half a million pounds!'

Tony looked at her, lost for words. Tears were streaming down her reddened cheeks, but he was no longer focussed on her face. All he could see was this huge, ugly revelation: Louise had just thrown away half a million pounds.

He heard himself mutter more consoling words: *it's not your fault, don't worry, we can rectify this,* but he didn't know where they were coming from. He felt sick. Louise started muttering about resigning, which didn't seem like such a bad idea to Tony, although he doled out more words of consolation nonetheless. He couldn't believe that such incompetence continued to lurk within his team. He had seen it before, in the very same manager, but a long time ago. Over the course of the last nine months, he had started to believe in his management – to *trust* them. Now, he didn't know what to think. The only thing he knew with absolute certainty was that if he wanted this venture to survive, he had to keep this news from the board. He would come clean on Louise's blunder at some point, but it wouldn't be before next Friday.

Big fanfare ahead of launch; Poppy's birthday

GABLE'S VOICE rose and fell soporifically, the glow of the PowerPoint slide dimly illuminating the front rows of the darkened auditorium. Surreptitiously, Tony drew out his phone and checked the time. It was five past twelve. He'd promised Suze he'd be back shortly after midday to help with the party. He had also promised to stick around for the Q&A to field any questions about the smart site proposition – which had yet to feature. By his calculations, they were still five minutes away from the *Looking Ahead* section and nearly fifteen minutes from the end.

Tony scanned the row of seats that were occupied by members of his team. Roy was picking at a scab on the top of his head. Chek-Han was frantically scribbling numbers on his copy of the presentation. Matt was scrolling through emails and Louise was sitting next to him, her eyes either closed or looking down at her lap.

No more had been said about the five hundred grand overspend. Tony had impressed upon his Marketing Manager the importance of keeping quiet until after today's presentation, and Louise had unquestioningly obliged. Tony sighed. He still hadn't decided how to handle the situation: how to apportion the blame, how to explain it to the board, how to reprimand Louise... They were all issues he needed to address, but this week he'd been unable to focus on anything other than today's presentation. Next week, he knew, he had to tackle them all head-on.

He looked up. A tacky, xylophone jingle was being played

through the speakers and a giant, pixelated image of his face stared back at him, framed in the TransTel Innovation Lab doorway.

'I'm Tony Sharp,' he heard himself say – somewhat woodenly, he thought. 'I head up the team that's responsible for bringing the smart site proposition to life...'

He watched, cringing, as the familiar words boomed out across the auditorium. His hand gestures looked awkward, his smile fake. There was something horribly crass about watching yourself on TV. The timelines and forecasts came out too quickly, he noted, and what was going on with his hair? It looked as though someone had switched on a fan just behind his left ear.

The two-minute clip seemed to go on for hours. Tony glanced around the auditorium, avoiding sight of the screen. The suited clones at the front looked marginally less bored than they had done during Charles' presentation, but that wasn't saying much. Tony wondered what they thought of his forecasts. One or two were nodding. Some were writing things down. Another was falling asleep.

Tony flinched at the sound of his cheesy parting line: '...We're hoping that this proposition will pave the way for a whole range of innovative TransTel products and services, and indeed, a new era for telecoms.'

It wasn't that he didn't believe in his words; he really did feel that if they could make the smart site venture work, they could build a truly sustainable, diversified portfolio of revenue streams for TransTel. He just felt nervous at the idea of putting their plans out there, for all to see, when they were barely out of the starting gates. As an ex-military friend had always said: *no plan survives contact with the enemy.*

Gable took back the mantle and started droning on about the need for transformative change and positive growth. Tony couldn't help thinking about the scale of the task that lay ahead. It was his default train of thought. Whenever his mind wandered, it wandered here. The pilot launch was now only weeks away. There remained some fundamental issues that still had to be resolved – not least of which was the brand. They had literally days left before vans had to be sprayed, uniforms ordered and equipment stamped, yet Louise was clearly spending all her time wallowing in self-loathing and not getting on with the job. Aside from Marketing, things were pretty-much on track. The web interface was in its final phase of development, the monitoring software was tested and ready to go, the engineers, after some heated discussions with Roy, were trained and qualified, and the sales guys were chomping at the bit, thanks to the incentive package that Matt had slipped past HR. It felt as though, with the odd half-million-pound exception, they were almost there.

As Sod's Law would have it, there were no questions on the smart site proposition during the Q&A. Tony slipped out, relieved to have got away without a grilling but frustrated that he was now nearly an hour late for his daughter's party. He could picture Suze's expression already: a sad, disappointed face that said, *Don't worry, I expected nothing more.* He pressed his phone into the hands-free kit and accelerated onto the main road.

'You have two unplayed messages,' the fembot intoned. 'First message...'

'Hi Tony, it's Ian here from Procurement. I don't know whether you picked up the messages I left with your PA...? Anyway. I need to speak to you quite urgently. It's about one of your suppliers for the... *smart... shite...* um, *site,* project? I understand you're using Borwood Electronics for your sensors. We've, er, just been informed by someone in TransTel Technology that we have an existing contract with another supplier – iPlug? Could you drop me a line as soon as you can? Thanks.'

Tony thumped the steering wheel as the traffic lights turned red up ahead. Harvey bloody Grainger. Again. He must have systematically gone through the supplier contracts Synapse had put in place, looking for a way he could intervene. Didn't the man have anything better to do with his time than stick spokes in other people's wheels?

'Second message...'

'Hi, Tony!' It was the irritating, singsong voice of Natasha from HR. 'Me again. Look, I really need to speak to you about this streamlining thing. Can you call me back when you get a chance?'

The lights turned green and Tony slammed his foot down. The driver of the car in front gestured in the rear view mirror. Tony didn't care. He needed to feel the acceleration – to feel that he was getting somewhere. That was all. Everybody and everything he encountered seemed to be standing in his way. The board had set him ludicrous targets and piled on such pressure that the venture was at risk of imploding, his Operations Manager was determined to see him fail, some random department manager he'd never even met kept trying to stir things up and now Human Resources seemed determined to rid him of his resources as part of some personnel tidying-up exercise.

Tony pressed the button for Call Back and pulled out to overtake.

'Natasha speaking.'

'Natasha, it's Tony.'

'Oh, hi! Thanks for calling–'

'Look, I don't have much time. I just wanted to explain the situation, once and for all.'

'Right. Okay... Go ahead.'

'I can't afford to lose ten percent of my workforce.'

'Well, be that as it may, we're still asking all heads of department to *identify* the ten percent that's–'

'What, even though they'll keep their jobs at the end of it?'

'Yes.'

'Doesn't that sound like a bit of a waste of time?' Tony's wheels span as he darted through a gap in the traffic. '*My* time?'

'Look, I understand you're busy, but–'

'*Busy?*' Tony accelerated off the speed bump, hearing a nasty crunch as he pulled away. 'Busy doesn't come *close!*' He was aware that he was sounding like a prick, but he was too angry to care. It was Natasha's job to deal with managers' wrath – just as it was his job to see that things got *done.*

'Perhaps we could work out an extension of the deadline,' she suggested.

'Or perhaps,' he said, pulling into his road and noting that it was five minutes to one, 'we could agree to let me hold onto all my hard-working, valuable staff without having to go through an entirely pointless evaluation process?'

'We're just looking for areas to cut–'

'I'll give you an area to cut,' he interrupted, pulling into the driveway and killing the engine. 'My role. If you think anyone's underperforming, try me. I'm sure the department will function just fine without me. Seriously, Natasha, if anyone's gonna go, I'll be top of the list. Okay?'

Tony pressed the red button and sat, steaming, for a couple of seconds, the echoes of his futile conversation still ringing in his ears. There was, in fact, something he'd intended to discuss with Natasha – the small matter of Matt's pay rise – but evidently, it would have to wait.

The sound of excitable screams hit him as soon as his key turned in the lock. Dropping his bag in the hallway, Tony arranged his face into some sort of smile and stepped into the lounge.

'Daddy!' yelled Poppy, clambering over the sofa. Her movements were restricted by the shimmering swathes of fabric that were wrapped tightly around her legs. Inexplicably, her face was painted green.

Tony picked her up and swung her around a few times, taking care to avoid contact with his suit.

'Happy birthday, my little...' He trailed off, not sure what Poppy was supposed to be. *Frog?*

'Mermaid!' yelled Poppy, with a roll of the eyes that she must have picked up from Suze. She bustled back to her friends, who were all circling a ring of chairs in the lounge, wiping various coloured face paints all over the furniture.

Suze was looking at him from behind the stereo, wearing exactly the look of resigned disappointment he had come to expect. He mouthed 'sorry' in her direction, then blew her a kiss just as Bradley picked his moment to launch himself off a chair.

The three year-old ricocheted off the wall and onto the floor, provoking a sudden, eerie silence. Then the usual wailing ensued, followed by half-hearted whimper, then a shriek of excitement as one of the kids worked out how to open the glass cabinet containing the monstrous bone china dishes that Suze's parents had given them as a wedding gift. Tony watched, hopeful for an accident, until Suze saw what was happening and intervened. Once it was abundantly clear to Tony that he was serving no useful purpose, he slipped upstairs to change.

Emptying his pockets, he caught sight of the flashing red light on his BlackBerry. With great restraint, he laid the device down on the bedside table and walked away. Then he turned back. Anja, Suze and Emmie had it covered downstairs. He retraced his steps and picked up the handset.

There were fifty-three unread emails, including a long, rambling update from Norm on the progress of the web interface, a couple of 'high importance' messages from Natasha, which he deleted without even reading, a string of one-liners from the delivery team about call-out schedule amendments, a note from Facilities about the office move next week (next week?!) and a follow-up from Ian in Procurement about the supposed supplier conflict. Tony sighed. There were times when it felt as though they were *that close* to making this thing happen, and then there were times when it felt as though he was standing at the bottom of Everest, looking up as an army of people hurled rocks in his face.

Only one message required immediate attention. Quickly, he clicked on Compose and started to type.

Dear Harvey,
I understand you have an existing contract with a supplier of sensors, which is interfering with our plans to pilot the smart site project. Please send me a copy of this contract along with any grounds for conflict, as soon as poss.
Tony

Suze was in the kitchen when he re-emerged, preparing the party food while Anja tried in vain to establish a game of Sleeping Lions.

'Still at work?' she asked, quietly.

Briefly, Tony considered making up some excuse about spilling something on his suit, or having a dodgy stomach, but he knew it was futile. Suze knew he'd been checking his emails. She knew he was prioritising his work over his family life.

'Sorry,' he said, stepping out of the way as she swung round, nearly knocking him out with her bump. 'I...'

He wanted to explain, but he couldn't – not just because Suze kept disappearing with platefuls of jammy dodgers and fairy cakes, but because he couldn't think of anything to say that hadn't already been said. Suze knew that his pilot was due to go live in three weeks. She knew about the deadline, the workload and the office politics. She knew, and she was most likely going through exactly the same things herself – yet somehow, she still made time for lollies and balloons.

That was the key difference between them, he thought, stepping towards the pile of crumbs on the floor as a broom was thrust into his hand. He drew a line between the different parts of his life. Work was work; mates were mates; family was family. Suze, though, could draw up shopping lists whilst delivering a presentation on the legalities of a corporate acquisition. Even now, rushing around among the shrieking kids, Suze was probably thinking about some loophole in a client case, but she didn't let it show.

Tony felt envious and guilty. Until recently, the line-drawing skill had been an asset. It meant that he stayed sharp and attentive, whether he was in the boardroom or in the park. But recently, the line had started to shift. His TransTel worries were encroaching on his family life, eating into the precious time he set aside for Poppy and Suze, and he knew that if he wasn't careful, he'd go the same way as some of his older friends and colleagues, losing touch with his family and becoming nothing more than a bread-winner.

'Suze?' He caught her as she picked up the last bowl of treats from the sideboard.

She looked at his face, frowning as he pawed at her wrist.

Suddenly, Tony lost his nerve. Now wasn't the time for profound statements or promises. Perhaps there was never a time, in fact. Perhaps it was all about actions, rather than words.

'What can I do to help?'

Suze smiled, shaking her head in bemusement. 'Well, I suppose you can try and find a way of gift-wrapping a Daisy Princess bicycle...?'

Marketing overspend; financing problems

'GREY CABINET!' yelled Matt, wheeling the furniture into the gangway and returning for the next item. 'Posh swivel chair with leather headrest! Too late, I'm having that. Black desk!'

Roy muscled in, trying to wrestle the chair – which Tony vaguely recognised as his own – from the salesman, who tripped over a stack of in-trays and sent them skidding across the floor, contents flying.

The Facilities team, in their wisdom, had issued each member of the Synapse team with a unique identification number (UIN) with which to mark their possessions, ahead of the office move. It was a plan that might have succeeded, had someone from Facilities been present on arrival at the new location with a key that matched numbers to names. As it was, they were drowning in filing cabinets, desks, phones and printers, all neatly marked with five-digit UINs, with no idea who owned what.

'Tony!' yelled Maureen, from her deskless position in the corner of the room. She was perched on a chair that had been pumped to maximum height and was swivelling, slowly, her rotation stemmed only by the phone cord that spiralled from the floor to her ear. 'I've got Nicholas Draper on the line!'

Tony abandoned the search for his computer and trod a path through the clutter, feeling his stomach tighten.

The brief conversation with Draper confirmed Tony's fears: the email containing details of the five hundred grand overspend had been circulated, and an explanation was required. Tony passed the phone back to Maureen and headed up to the sixth floor, frantically refining his excuse.

It had only been a matter of time. He had made no attempt to disguise the grotesque outgoing; in fact, he had even highlighted the cost so as to bring it to the FD's attention. Even so, he felt anxious. There was no telling how Draper might react to Louise's blunder.

'So?'

The FD's spindly fingers were pressed up against one another like the spikes of a sea anemone.

Quickly, Tony got to the point. It was a simple mistake, he explained, but one that anybody could have made. Well, perhaps not *anybody*, but anybody who had been working eighteen-hour days for weeks on end. Tiredness seemed like as good culprit as any on which to pin the blame.

The idea of sacking Louise on grounds of gross negligence had crossed Tony's mind, but then he had immediately ruled it out. The fact was, at this stage in the development of the venture, Louise was good at her job – most of the time. She was certainly a better option than an unknown. Following a brief but harsh disciplinary meeting and the laying down of some tedious but essential layers of red tape, Tony felt reasonably confident that another balls-up on that scale was not on the cards.

'I see,' said Draper, when he'd finished.

Tony held his breath, waiting to hear the man's verdict. He knew that ultimately, the buck stopped at him; *he* was responsible for the over-spend. His Marketing Manager had signed off on the erroneous contract, but effectively, *he* had thrown away five hundred grand by entrusting the company chequebook to Louise.

They sat in silence for several seconds. Eventually, the FD lowered his hands to the desk and looked up at Tony. 'I suppose that's all there is to it, then.'

Tony didn't quite have the nerve to reply. He sat, waiting for a signal, wondering whether he really could have got away so lightly. A few months ago, this conversation would have been long, heated and uncomfortable. The FD would have conducted a full interrogation. But today, it seemed as though all was forgiven. *Five hundred grand* was forgiven, just like that.

The FD raised an eyebrow, as if to ask why he was still

sitting there. Tentatively, Tony rose to his feet. Perhaps it was something to do with his input to the company presentation the previous week, or perhaps, thought Tony, there was something different about Draper's attitude towards *him*.

The converse was certainly true. Whereas once, Nicholas Draper had come across as a spindly, towering figure of authority known only for his acerbic words and aversion to risk, Tony now saw him in a different light. The FD was no longer intimidating; he was just a gangly, middle-aged accountant who lived a dull existence with his dull wife.

Tony glanced back as he reached the door, feeling a twinge of pity. Suddenly, he realised that Draper was talking.

'I'm sorry?'

The FD looked down at his desk, embarrassed.

'I said, we should set a date in the diary for you to come to dinner,' he mumbled.

'Um, yes,' Tony replied awkwardly. Now didn't feel like the time to be discussing social occasions.

'With your wife,' Draper clarified.

'Yes, that would be nice,' Tony lied. 'I'll check our diary.' He raised a hand and disappeared through the door before anything more could be said.

The image of Nicholas Draper's self-conscious smile continued to haunt him as he returned to the mayhem of the third floor. A small cluster of desks had been erected in the far corner of the office, one of which sat beneath a mountain of paperwork that he recognised as his own. He sank into the plastic chair and started to scroll through messages on his BlackBerry.

'Tony?'

It was Louise. She was wearing a tight-fitting green dress that reminded Tony of his daughter's mermaid costume.

'Can I have a word?'

Tony nodded, reaching out for a stray chair.

She nodded towards the row of glass-walled meeting rooms. 'In private?'

Tony tried to maintain his smile. 'Of course.'

This was bad. There were very few reasons for staff wanting

to 'have a word in private'. Tony guided Louise into the empty corner office, trying to maintain an aura of calm, despite his concerns. He wondered whether he should wheel some chairs into the room. Or a desk. Or something. His hands were making him feel self-conscious; they kept finding their way in and out of his pockets, getting in the way.

'So...' Louise lifted her slender shoulders. 'Well, we've come up with a brand that everyone's happy with.'

'Excellent,' replied Tony with as much gusto as was possible, given that this was clearly not the news that Louise had come to deliver. 'Which one are we going with?'

'EnGauge,' she said. 'It took a while to agree, but...'

Tony nodded earnestly, as though he were contemplating the choice of brand name. In fact, he was trying to work out whether Louise was about to resign.

'We felt it really captured the essence of the scheme. The logo's very smart and the comms guys have come up with some great slogans. I can send you the designs–'

'Great,' he said, interrupting before she got carried away. 'Looking forward to seeing it in action.'

After a moment of hand-wringing, Louise turned to face the window.

'I'm sorry,' she said quietly. 'I let you down.'

He looked over and realised that there were tears welling up in her eyes. His immediate reaction was to panic. How was one supposed to react when one's Marketing Manager burst into tears? This was clearly the start of Louise's resignation speech and he wanted to nip it in the bud, but it felt wrong to butt in so soon. Tony wished he'd had the foresight to suggest that they head out to Starbucks.

'Hey,' he said, pointlessly. This was a fucking disaster. His Marketing Manager was bawling her eyes out in the middle of a glass-walled room and he couldn't even offer her a seat. 'Don't be silly,' he tried, hearing the futility of his words as soon as they came out. Louise wasn't being silly; she was telling the truth. She *had* let him down.

'I want to hand in my notice,' she sniffled.

'No!' Tony finally braved physical contact. He laid an arm

around her shoulders and looked into her eyes, which were swollen and red. 'Please. We need you here. It doesn't matter about the five hundred grand–'

'See?' She pulled away, wiping her bare arm across her face. 'You can't even say it without baulking!'

'I didn't baulk...'

She shook her head, sniffed loudly and blinked a few times. 'No. No, I've made up my mind. I'm sorry, but it's best if I leave.'

Before Tony could think up another lame response, his Marketing Manager was gone, flying through the glass door, head down, through the new office and into the lobby.

Tony stood, his arms hanging uselessly at his sides, looking down at the spot on the floor where Louise had been standing. He had been half-expecting this, but he hadn't prepared for it. Tony tried to remember what notice period Louise was on. To be left with no Head of Marketing just weeks before the launch of EnGauge was worse than careless – it was suicide.

He had to get her back. That was the only conclusion Tony could draw. Hiring would take weeks, maybe months, and even then there would be no guarantee of quality. Louise was scatty and inexperienced, but she knew where the goal was, and she did everything in her power to reach it.

Tony rushed into the main office, ducking to avoid a flying printer cartridge. He tapped the burly Sales Manager on the shoulder and beckoned him inside. It was cowardly, but it seemed like the best option.

'Well,' said Matt, when Tony had spelled out his request. 'I'll see what I can do.'

'Thanks Matt. I appreciate it.'

Matt paused on his way out, cocking his head. 'Any news on my pay rise?'

Tony managed a half-smile. 'It's top of my list, Matt. I'll chase it up today.'

Fifteen minutes passed and there was no sign of either Matt or Louise. Tony adopted one of the glass offices, hauling a desk and a couple of chairs inside and plugging in a laptop that looked vaguely like his. Maureen appeared with a bunch of illegible notes and a couple of TransTel engineers started rummaging around on the floor in an attempt to set up his phone line.

Finally making it through the deluge of emails, Tony looked up to find Chek-Han teetering over the threshold of his new office, holding a bundle of papers to his chest. Tony waved him in.

The young financier smiled timidly and laid the sheets on the desk between them.

'This is the supplier contract between TransTel Tech and iPlug,' he said.

Tony flicked through it, not sure whether he was supposed to be noticing anything in particular, or whether he should be gauging anything from Chek-Han's tentative smile. He had outsourced the problem of getting Harvey Grainger off his back.

'It's expired,' Chek-Han explained, eventually.

Tony rummaged through the pages, in search of some kind of date.

Chek-Han leaned forward and pointed. 'The contract lasted two years from the point of signature, which means we're free as of last Tuesday.'

'So we can go ahead and sign with Borwood?'

Chek-Han nodded, grinning as he left the room. Tony was about to flick through the contract, just to be sure, when he caught sight of Matt, swaggering back into the office. As he watched, Matt turned, looked through the glass and winked. Simultaneously, Tony's BlackBerry buzzed.

Hi Tony,

I'm sorry for getting in a state earlier. I felt awful for letting people down and it seemed as though the only option was to resign. But I've realised now that I'd be more of a let-down if I jumped ship now, so, if you'll have me back, I'll do my best to make amends.

Louise

Tony leaned back in his chair, letting out a long sigh of relief. Then he sat forward again and started to type an email to HR about Matt's pay rise.

AVOIDING "VENTURE DEATH"

AVOIDING
"VENTURE DEATH"

 MarketGravity

Tony's venture could easily have been killed off in this chapter – a victim of a core business integration programme, or the realisation that the consumer proposition was still several years from mass adoption. These are just two examples from the many causes of venture death and the Corporate Entrepreneur must be on their guard against every one of them.

Frequent causes of venture death include:

- Misadventure – enthusiastic amateurs, poor decisions and a part-time approach means that the venture fails to achieve momentum and scale
- Natural selection – in the time it takes to make decisions and build capability, the market has moved on and the venture is no longer relevant
- Suffocation – the venture is stifled by the demands of an overly attentive parent company
- Assassination – rival internal initiatives kill the venture in the early stages
- Death by a thousand cuts – the constant barriers and requests from the core business sap the life blood from the team
- Suicide – worn down by in-fighting and constant demands, the team implodes and breaks up

Despite these challenges and risks, Tony and the team demonstrate that venture death can be cheated, or at least postponed.

"BAU IS ALWAYS TRYING TO KILL YOU: THE BUSINESS UNITS SEE YOU AS A THREAT TO THEIR BUSINESS, THEIR TIME, THEIR RESOURCE, SO YOU HAVE TO PLAY IT CAREFULLY."

José Davila, E.ON, British Gas

Given that the chances of success are heavily stacked against you, how can you ensure that you avoid venture death and create a successful business?

Here are some tips for staying alive:

1. Recognise the threats. Half the battle is in identifying the risks of venture death before it is too late to address them.

2. Keep your enemies close. It is far better to engage sceptical colleagues in your venture than to allow them to snipe from the sidelines.

3. Act fast. Some cause of venture death (e.g. Natural selection or Suicide) can be neutralised by rapid decision making and speedy actions.

4. Value experience. A colleague who has previous new initiatives under his or her belt will have fantastic experience to help the team avoid venture death.

5. Call in Air Support when you need it. Make sure your sponsoring Director will back your venture when you really need help.

Use the checklist below to gauge how well protected you are from the spectre of venture death.

	YES	NO	?
Our initiative is considered important to the future success of the company	☐	☐	☐
We address a tangible threat to our existing business	☐	☐	☐
We have the independence to make the right decisions	☐	☐	☐
Our team has succeeded in a similar field in the past	☐	☐	☐
We have engaged managers from the core business and they support the venture	☐	☐	☐
We have Director-level sponsorship	☐	☐	☐

If you said "Yes" to the majority of these factors, your venture has every chance of success.

8

A child is born: creating a new venture

'The pilot is an opportunity to get things right on a small scale.'

Pilot launch day

TONY STARED at the monitor, chewing nervously on the end of his pen.

'Why aren't we seeing any activity yet? I thought this was a live feed.'

Matt leaned sideways, beckoning the IT geek over as he squinted at Tony's screen. 'Oh, you're looking at completed jobs. You want the middle tab – leads and scheduled site inspections.'

Tony nodded, too full of anxiety to feel embarrassed at having been staring at completely the wrong feed for the last two minutes. Quickly, he took in the figures. Just under two hundred calls had been made so far in the pilot region, of which three had resulted in scheduled site inspections, five were 'in progress', eighteen were 'hot leads' and twelve were 'callbacks'.

'Can we listen in on a call?' he asked.

An IT guy found him a headset, plugged it in and guided his mouse to the relevant link. With a shaky hand, Tony clicked on the call. He hadn't felt this apprehensive since the day Suze had gone into labour with Poppy.

'...new service we're offering to help your company save money on its energy bills?' asked the sales woman in a sing-song, Scottish accent.

'Are you trying to get us to change supplier?' came the somewhat aggressive reply.

'Noo, noooo,' cooed the woman, apparently unruffled. 'This is a service that allows you to monitor *all* the devices in your place of work, then see what you're wasting by means of a very simple online interface. It costs you nothing to install, and–'

'We're perfectly happy with our supplier, thank you.'

There was a click, then the line went quiet.

Tony suddenly realised he'd been holding his breath and let out his lungful, feeling distinctly uncomfortable.

'We'll get a lot of that, to begin with,' said someone behind him.

Tony turned to see Matt, pulling a headset off his ears.

'Even with the standard TransTel products you get a fair few misunderstandings, but with something outside our range...'

Tony nodded uncertainly. He looked across the meeting room, which had become the EnGauge Command Centre, and sought out Louise's mousy curls. He knew that the take-up forecasts had been painstakingly calculated by the combined Sales and Marketing teams and he was reasonably confident about their predictions, but he couldn't help feeling perturbed by what he'd just heard. This was such a new thing for TransTel, it was so far away from their core product range... It had been hard enough getting buy-in from the board of directors; convincing potential customers would be a hundred times harder.

He slipped the headset back on and picked up another call.

'...from TransTel to let you know about a new service...'

The biro that Tony had been chewing suddenly snapped, sending shards of splintered, inky plastic across the desk. He swept them away, placing the pen out of reach and pressing the thin layer of foam against his ear. He hadn't realised until now how much it meant to him, making this pilot a success. Last night, he had barely slept and he hadn't been able to eat since lunchtime yesterday.

'Yes, quite,' the salesman was saying. 'TransTel actually has a range of offerings that aren't *directly* telecom-related...'

Perhaps, he considered, he hadn't realised how much of a leap he was making for the company with the launch of EnGauge. Every other 'new' product that came out of TransTel tended to be an incremental improvement on the last one, or an add-on to an existing offering. EnGauge was totally new. It was a new piece of technology being used to address a new market via a new business model, delivered using a whole new set of capabilities both in and outside of TransTel. There were new partners involved, it was a new customer journey and the idea had come about from new customer insight. The whole proposition was underpinned by a new set of Government regulations in a field that was alien to most of TransTel, and it took the company into untrodden territory. It was only now, sitting in front of this screen full of figures and charts, listening to the salesman doggedly explaining the concept to this facilities manager somewhere just outside Aylesbury, that he saw the enormity of the transition.

'Excellent. So, shall we pencil in next Thursday at noon for a free-of-charge assessment of your premises?'

Tony waited in anxious silence.

'Yes,' the voice said eventually. 'Yes, that should be fine.'

Tony sighed heavily and pulled off his headset.

'That line there,' said one of the tech guys, pointing over his shoulder at a chart on his screen, 'is the cumulative figure for scheduled inspections.'

Tony peered at the graph. 'So, eleven, altogether?' He did some quick mental arithmetic. If the pilot region represented two percent of the nation by volume, then this equated to fifty-five site visits, which, assuming a steady rate of success throughout the day, was around a thousand per day across the country, or five thousand per week... and that was from direct sales alone. When the marketing campaign took effect... Tony flicked to the spreadsheet of daily sales forecasts and realised that if their conversion rates were correct then they were on track to exceed their week one targets.

The next few hours zipped by in a frenzy of nervous excitement. Tony did laps of the room, checking, questioning and advising, while IT guys scurried between desks and department managers sat, frowning at screens, biting their lips and making hurried phone calls. The atmosphere was tense, but there was a sense of camaraderie in the stuffy glass office that Tony hadn't witnessed in a long time.

By two o'clock, Tony's nerves were beginning to subside and he felt his first pang of hunger. He handed Maureen some ten-pound notes, reminded her (again) that he didn't like cucumber, and sent her to get a round of sandwiches for the team.

The figures on the screen continued to rise and Tony began to wonder whether they might have under-priced the offering. They were exceeding their hourly targets by nearly twenty-five percent, even after the lunchtime lull. It was a good problem to have, of course. If they could make the same margin on these increased volumes, then perhaps it didn't matter if subscription rates weren't as high as they might be. It would serve as a barrier to entry for competitors.

'Sandwiches!' squawked Maureen, lumbering into the room and depositing four plastic bags on top of the sign that said DO NOT OBSTRUCT on the server.

Tony waited for flock to disperse, then delved into the one remaining bag and pulled out the contents: a flattened sandwich that appeared to contain nothing but cucumber.

'A HUNDRED!' yelled Matt, thumping the desk with his fist.

The room erupted into a cacophony of whoops and cheers. Tony abandoned his dissection of the cucumber sandwich and headed over to the new Operations Manager in the corner.

'Are we going to manage?' he asked, crouching down beside the young man. 'Do we have enough engineers for all these site visits?'

Billy looked at him. He was young, with thin, sandy hair and an eager smile. Roy had promoted him to Head of EnGauge Operations the previous month and although Tony hadn't said it to his face, it had been the best move the old man had made in his entire career. Billy had a dynamism about him that Roy could never have dreamed of.

'It'll be tight,' replied Billy. 'I was about to flag it with you. If the week carries on like this, we'll need to pull in some more resources. And if they're to hit the ground running, we'll need to start training more engineers.'

Tony nodded and pushed up off his haunches. 'Right. Let's catch up at the end of today and see what we think.'

He was about to ask Maureen to source him some cucumber-free lunch when one of the marketing girls let out a loud, eardrum-splitting shriek.

'Oh my God!' she yelled, waving Louise over to her desk and pointing at her screen.

Several members of the team, Tony included, rushed over to the source of the disturbance.

'Don't panic,' said Louise, sounding slightly panicked. 'I'm sure there's an explanation.'

'For what?' asked several people at once.

'It's um... bad press. We're getting a few complaints.'

Tony stepped forward. This wasn't good; the publicity campaign had cost them hundreds of thousands – on top of the hundreds of thousands that had been thrown away on the erroneous campaign. 'Which ad?'

'Um...' Louise looked white, all of a sudden.

Tony waited. The last thing they wanted at this stage was a fine from Ofcom over their advertising.

'It's not the campaign,' she said, quietly. 'It's something to do with the sales calls.'

'Shit. There's *loads* of complaints,' said the first girl, now speaking in a desperate stage-whisper.

'What are they complaining about?' Tony watched over the girl's shoulder as she clicked on the search results, landing on blogs, consumer websites and forums.

'Something to do with the call-backs...'

'I think people are getting called back when they didn't ask to be,' Louise muttered weakly.

Tony stepped back to his desk, his mouth suddenly dry. The number of call-back requests did seem high, come to think of it. He clicked on the call-back tab, only to see his whole screen freeze over. Despite repeated clicking, there seemed to be no way of bringing it back to life.

'My system's crashed,' he said, in the direction of the nearest IT guy.

'Mine too.'

'And mine.'

Tony sighed. 'Great. The whole thing's gone down.'

'There's a glitch in the call-routing algorithm,' said someone from Norm's team. 'It's setting up call-backs for everyone except those who scheduled a site inspection.'

'Everyone?' echoed Tony, horrified. No wonder they were getting complaints if they were spamming businesses with unwanted phone calls. This was worse than no publicity at all; they'd been live for about six hours and already they had alienated half their potential market. This was why they ran trials, surely? Why hadn't this come out in the tests?

Norm, who was frantically tapping at keys on the giant computer at the back of the room, mumbled something about patching the code. Tony tried again to resuscitate his own machine, to no avail.

'Sales wanna know whether they should carry on,' yelled someone, waving a phone in the air.

'Tell them to hold all calls,' barked Matt, who looked uncharacteristically ruffled.

'No,' said Tony. 'Tell them to continue with outbound calls but halt the call-backs.'

Matt opened his mouth to reply, then shut it again. He sat back down in his chair, frowning hard. Tony was reminded that he still hadn't sorted out the salesman's pay rise; if he didn't do it soon, Matt would probably walk out.

'The complaints line is jammed!' cried one of the Comms girls.

Tony groaned. 'Can we up its capacity? Or get people using the website?'

The website, it transpired, was also jammed, due to the unprecedented volume of traffic. A team was quickly established to take charge of complaints handling, while Tony tried to establish from Norm how long the 'patch' would take.

'System's up and running again!' yelled somebody.

'Oh, Jesus!' Louise wailed despondently. 'They've picked up on it on EnergyWatch. "TransTel EnGauge Off To A Rocky Start..."'

Tony closed his eyes, trying to decide which problem to tackle next. When he opened them, he realised that his phone was ringing.

'Tony speaking.'

'Tony, it's Charles. Just calling for an update. How's it all going?'

'Um...' In the split-second he had before answering, Tony looked around the glass-walled inferno, taking in the desperate expressions on his colleagues' faces, the EnergyWatch bulletin on his screen and the print-off of sales so far. 'Not bad,' he said, tentatively. There was a chance, he thought, that the CEO hadn't yet caught wind of the complaints or bad press.

'Excellent,' said Charles, emphatically. Tony's heart leapt. He knew he couldn't pull the wool over Gable's eyes forever, but for the next few hours, at least, he could tell the chief exec what he wanted to hear.

'Sales are exceeding forecasts by twenty percent.'

'Splendid!' The CEO let out a short, sharp bark of glee. 'You know, I always said this would be a winner. I *always said*. Well done, Tony. I look forward to my end-of-day report.'

Fighting for resources; too much red tape

'BACKS NICE AND STRAIGHT, that's right... And breathe.'

Tony shifted his weight onto the other butt cheek, rearranging his limbs on the hard gym floor and looking up at Suze, who was perched on a shiny, silver Swiss ball beside him, her fingers entwined in his.

'Now, clear your mind...'

Tony looked out of the leisure centre window, where two kids were trying to jump down a flight of steps on skateboards. He wasn't sure whether the instructions applied to the fathers-to-be in the room or just their expectant partners, but either way, he had no intention of clearing his mind. The last week had been spent frantically trying to accumulate and assimilate information following the launch of the EnGauge pilot; he wasn't about to let it all out now for some hippy in Lycra.

'Now tense your core muscles...'

Tony squeezed Suze's hand, feeling a little redundant. It had been her idea to attend these hypno-birth antenatal classes, fearing another gruelling, forty-eight-hour labour like the one she'd been through with Poppy. He wasn't entirely sure how sitting on an inflatable silver ball and clearing your mind was supposed to assist in the birthing process, but he didn't feel it was his place to ask. It would be Suze, not him, screaming in agony and covered in blood in four weeks' time.

The skateboarders wandered off, leaving Tony's attention to drift back to the EnGauge pilot. So much had happened in the last few days – both good and bad. The early teething problems had long since been forgotten amidst a raft of new problems and new revelations. It seemed incredible that a few weeks ago, Tony had been looking forward to pressing Go, as if somehow he'd then be home and dry.

'Gently lean back, keeping your muscles taut...'

The main problem, which manifested itself as a series of smaller problems, was lack of resources. The inbound call centre operators were working flat out, now that news of the offering was spreading, the engineers were putting in twelve-hour days in an attempt to meet demand and the glass-walled command centre where Tony spent most of his time was in constant use. The previous morning, having slept badly, Tony had got in at six o'clock and found Norm at his desk, still grappling with an algorithm from the previous day. Attempts to increase numbers had been met by flat refusal from HR, and Tony knew that if they couldn't recruit more personnel, then those at the coal-face would walk out. The current policy on recruitment would make it impossible to replace them, and Tony was beginning to worry that the headcount freeze might actually bring down the business.

'And roll upright again, that's right. Close your eyes...'

Tony felt his BlackBerry vibrate in his back pocket. He waited for Suze to shut her eyes, then with his free hand, reached round and pulled it out, placing it in his lap where the instructor couldn't see.

There were three missed calls, all from Billy. There was also a voicemail, a text message and an email, all from Billy. Tony didn't need to open the messages to know what it was about. Billy needed his signature on a purchase order – a signature that wouldn't have been required two months previously. The Marketing team's overspend had resulted in several new regulations, none of which had proved popular with the team.

Suze dug her nails into the flesh of his palm. He looked up and saw her looking at him, one eyebrow raised. Tony grinned back sheepishly, slipping the BlackBerry into his pocket.

'Now, slowly, open your eyes and stand up.'

The class appeared to be over. Tony struggled to his feet, dusting off his trousers and reaching out to help Suze up. She was already up. While most of the women in the room looked slightly dazed, his wife was marching towards the exit, rummaging in her bag and cursing the fact that they'd finished six minutes late.

'The whole point of an early morning class is that you can get to work afterwards,' she muttered, pulling out her sunglasses as she waddled as quickly as her stature would allow towards the car. 'Now we'll hit rush-hour traffic and be an hour late for work...'

Tony looked at her. 'Nice and relaxed?'

Reluctantly, Suze smiled.

Reversing at speed out of the space, Tony glanced across at his wife, who was slapping on makeup in the visor mirror. 'Did you actually *try* and do all that mind-clearing thing, just then?' he asked.

'Well... Sort of.'

Tony caught her eye and they both laughed. Clearly, Suze had also spent the hour thinking about what she needed to do when she got to the office.

'I'm not sure we're right for this psycho-birth thing,' he said.

'Hypno-birth,' Suze corrected. Then she screwed up her nose. 'Maybe you're right.'

She leaned over and kissed him as they pulled up outside her office. 'I'll see you later. Don't forget to ask the big man about what we talked about, will you?'

Tony forced a smile. ''Course not.' He watched her march into the vast, marble atrium, then drove off, with a cloud of dread looming over him. He wasn't looking forward to his conversation with the CEO.

Having listened to Billy's voicemail on the way in, Tony arrived at the office in a state of nervous irritation, which wasn't helped by the fact that Maureen had rearranged his ten o'clock meeting with Gable for nine o'clock. It was now nine fifteen.

Rushing up to the sixth floor – marginally more accessible now that they were on the third floor, although still too many stairs to climb in his current state of fitness – he burst into the chief exec's office.

'Sorry... I'm late,' he heaved. 'Antenatal... class.'

'Sit yourself down, Tony. Take a few deep breaths. Anyone

would think *you* were going into labour.' He laughed at his joke. 'How is the wife?'

Tony nodded mutely. 'Good.'

Gable summoned some water from one of his PAs, then waved her away and looked across the desk, his hairy eyebrows arched.

'You wanted to talk through some suggestions?' he prompted.

Tony nodded again. The meeting had been his idea. After countless futile encounters with HR over the resourcing situation, he had decided to go straight to the top. If the board saw EnGauge as a priority for their growth strategy – and they had declared as much in their annual presentation – then as far as Tony was concerned, they had a duty to make the venture a success.

'I've drawn up a recruitment plan,' he said, producing a print-off he'd hastily swiped from his desk, minutes earlier. 'We built the business on a shoestring, and our initial resource estimates were based on a pessimistic scenario. As you know, we're currently exceeding our targets and the workforce is over-stretched.' He handed the sheet to the CEO. 'This is the bare minimum we require to take the business forward.'

Gable frowned at the page for some time. Eventually, he let it flutter onto the desk and looked Tony in the eye.

'You're a week in, and already you need more resource?'

Tony dipped his head. He'd been expecting this reaction. 'With respect, Charles, many of my staff have been doing two jobs, following the merger, and there's been no recognition or compensation for their efforts. If we don't recruit to take off some of the pressure, we'll see a mass walk-out. We also need to offer some pay rises, as I've highlighted here.'

Gable flinched as Tony made his point, saying nothing for several seconds.

'If we invest at this stage, we can really ramp up year-one sales and use our first-mover advantage,' Tony pressed.

Gable nodded, slowly.

'My reluctance,' he said, after a pause that seemed unnecessarily drawn-out, 'is due to the fact that EnGauge has already burned through several hundred thousand pounds, in some cases with nothing to show for it.' He stared at Tony, eyebrows raised. Tony tried to maintain a neutral expression, his cheeks burning. The CEO was referring, of course, to the five hundred grand overspend. 'How am I to know that any further investment will recoup?'

'The sales figures speak for themselves,' Tony replied firmly, determined not to get dragged into another grovelling conversation about Louise's mistake. 'We need more resources to keep up with demand.'

It felt as though Gable knew, deep down, that the new hires were necessary, but he was testing Tony's resolve. Tony leaned forward in his seat and pushed the piece of paper back towards the CEO.

'We both know how important it is for this venture to succeed,' he said. 'We can't make it happen without more resources.'

Gable looked back at him through half-closed eyes.

'Hmm,' he said, after another pregnant pause. 'I'll think about it.'

Tony rose to his feet.

'One more thing,' he said, standing awkwardly between the desk and the door.

'Mmm?'

'I'd like to work a four-day week.'

Gable's head shot up. 'I'm sorry?'

'Just over summer,' he explained, 'once the baby's born, until my eldest starts school. To help my wife out.'

The bewilderment in the older man's eyes was palpable. He blinked a few times, then looked around the room, as if trying to make sense of the request.

'TransTel has a policy whereby new mothers can return to work on a four-day week,' Tony reminded him, 'so I'd like to request a similar package for myself.'

'I...' Gable no longer looked confused, but instead slightly condescending, as though he was wondering how to break it to Tony that his suggestion was absurd.

'I've run the idea past HR,' Tony added. 'They say it's just a question of getting sign-off from you.'

'Well... I suppose...'

Tony waited, watching the ruddy cheeks puff out as Gable exhaled. He knew it was asking a lot, cutting down his hours when it was patently clear that he could barely get everything done in a standard five-day week. He was also aware that despite the large number of women on flexible hours at TransTel, there were very few men in senior positions who had done the same.

'I suppose, if you can fit it all in...'

Tony smiled at the CEO's dubious expression. 'Thanks, Charles. It'll only be for a few months. I'll get HR to put it in writing.'

Business as usual

TONY GLANCED at his Sales Manager as they stood outside the office door. *Ready?* he mouthed, receiving the customary lift of the shoulders and non-committal grunt. He knocked anyway.

It was rare, these days, to extract more than a couple of syllables from the salesman. Tony was getting the distinct impression that he was considering jumping ship. It wasn't surprising, really. Matt had thrown himself into this venture, working overtime, taking on extra responsibilities and pulling out all the stops to make things work. In return, he had received a pat on the back. If the pay rise didn't come through in the next few days, they'd find themselves without a Head of Sales.

'Come in,' came the clipped instruction.

Tony led the way into the Finance Director's office, hoping that Matt would be more forthcoming inside. He had brought him along to the monthly catch-up for two reasons: firstly, because Matt could explain better than anyone why the profit was as low as it was, given the impressive turnover, but also because Tony knew that the FD wouldn't dare come out with another invitation to dinner – something his wife had categorically outlawed – in the presence of another colleague.

'Anthony, hello. Er, Matthew...' Draper might have been surprised to see the salesman; it was difficult to tell.

'I thought Matt could take us quickly through the numbers,' Tony explained.

Locating a third chair, Matt sat down and silently handed out copies of the sales report.

'As you can see,' he began, somewhat morosely, 'our first month exceeded expectations...'

Tony focused on Draper's reaction as they sat, listening to Matt's uncharacteristically dour assessment of the previous month's trading. It was hard to believe they'd been going for a full month. Time had flown by, the daily setbacks and hurried solutions blurring in his mind.

From an outsider's perspective, things were looking rosy. EnGauge was beginning to look like a slick operation, with the ever-evolving marketing campaign starting to penetrate, installation volumes rising and recognition of the brand starting to ramp up.

Behind the scenes, it was a different story. Just as installations had begun to pick up pace, one of their key component suppliers had gone bust, prompting a frantic search for an alternative. Engineers had found themselves visiting sites outside the pilot region, thanks to an error in the database used by the call centre. The online interface had repeatedly collapsed on new customers and Norm's team, which was by far the most stretched, had lost two key personnel in the last five days, sending morale plummeting.

On average, volumes were twenty percent up on expectations, which should have been cause for celebration, but due to the clamp-down on recruitment, the only way Tony had been able to meet demand was to pull in contractors, which had bumped up the costs.

'Your margins look low,' said Draper, when Matt had finished.

Tony stepped in. 'Overall, yes,' he said. 'We had to bring in expensive short-term resources to plug the gaps. This is why we urgently need to boost our headcount, as I've been saying.'

'Hmm.' Draper nodded, still frowning at the summary sheet. 'How does this compare to the Stage Two KPIs?'

Tony took a deep breath. He'd been trying not to think about the key performance indicators. The wretched KPIs were the measures that determined whether the venture was a success or a failure. If he hit them, EnGauge would be rolled out across the nation. If he didn't, the whole project would go under. In two weeks' time, he would have to stand up in front of the board and explain why he believed that the pilot should be scaled up by a factor of fifty. But that was next month. Keeping the business afloat from one day to the next was enough to think about for now.

'We're in line to hit the top-line KPIs,' he replied.

'But these costs...? We've told investors that this venture will pay back within eighteen months...'

Tony shrugged helplessly. He wasn't going to point out that he had had nothing to do with setting the ludicrous targets or announcing to the City that EnGauge would be the saviour of TransTel.

'As I said, costs are higher than they should be because of the contractors. If we were properly resourced, we'd be in line to hit the KPIs.'

The FD let out a long breath through his nose, saying nothing. It was getting tedious, this repeated request for resourcing that never materialised. Tony was beyond frustration now; he had reached a state of resignation. He desperately wanted to haul this venture into profitability, but the very people who were pushing him to make it happen were standing in his way.

'I'll have a word with HR,' said Nicholas Draper, in exactly the same tone that Charles Gable had used three weeks earlier when he'd delivered the same words.

Tony nodded his thanks and stood up, waiting for Matt to lumber out first.

Together, they took the lift down, watching in awkward silence as the numbers flashed up above their heads: six, five, four, three. As the metal jaws slid open, Tony thought about taking his salesman aside, telling him that it wouldn't be for much longer, that the pay rise was just around the corner – but he couldn't. He couldn't, because Matt knew as well as he did how difficult it was to break the rules in this place. He had just sat through a perfect illustration of the stifling corporate culture by which they were constrained. There was a pay freeze across the firm, and that meant that Matt's pay was frozen. End of story.

'Mate.'

As the lift doors opened, Tony found his path blocked by Matt's body. A wave of mild nausea came over him. This was it. This was where he lost his Sales Manager.

'I'm sorry...'

Tony shook his head, in denial. He couldn't do without Matt. Not at this stage in the project.

'I've been offered a job at Netcomm,' said Matt. 'I can't turn it down. The pay's ten percent higher and there's none of this new venture shit.'

Tony looked at him. Matt averted his eyes. *New venture shit.* Was that what he really thought? Did he resent the new initiative? Would he prefer to stay cocooned in his bog-standard nine-to-five, peddling the same tired products to the same uninterested customers?

'Sorry.' Matt grimaced. 'I'm handing in my notice.' He pushed his way into the office, heading for Louise's desk.

With a heavy heart, Tony returned to his office, where he slammed the door shut and drew the blinds, sinking into his chair and staring, unseeing, at the lifeless screen in front of him.

It was the money, Tony suspected. It wasn't the 'new venture shit'. Matt had shown no sign of resentment for the initiative – not since the Christmas do, at least. The problems had only started when it had become apparent that the pay rise would never materialise. The situation was absurd. For the sake of saving a few thousand pounds and sticking to the rules, the company had lost a good salesmen and promising manager to the competition.

Tony considered the idea of calling Louise in, then decided against it. There was no point. Matt's mind was made up; he wouldn't be swayed by any amount of pleading from his girlfriend or whatever she was to him. Tony picked up the phone and dialled Natasha's number. Ordinarily, it would have given him some satisfaction to tell the officious HR Manager that he had been proved right all along, but not today. Today, he only felt frustration.

'Natasha, it's Tony.'

'Oh, hi Tony!'

Her irritating, chirpy tone annoyed him at the best of times, but now it made him want to hit something.

'I've got some bad news,' he said.

'Oh dear.' She let out a short bark of laughter. 'That doesn't sound good.'

The urge to hit something intensified. 'My Head of Sales has just resigned.'

'Oh.' There seemed to be no change in her tone. 'Well, that's a bit of a coincidence, actually, because I have some news for *you*. I was about to call you. Those pay rises you requested have finally been approved.'

'What... Including the one for Matt?'

There was a rustling noise at the other end. 'Norman Crump... Matthew Ward...'

'That's him!' Tony was on his feet, trying to open the door without yanking the office phone off the desk. 'Can you confirm that Matt's rise is more than ten percent?'

'Well...' The sense of urgency didn't seem to have transmitted down the line. 'He was on forty-two thousand before, and he'll be on forty-eight after–'

'Great!' Tony's mental arithmetic was quicker than hers. 'I'll let him know.'

'Oh, and there are a couple more, too, and a change of title for... Roy Smith... And I understand you want to work a four-day week?'

'Yes,' Tony said hurriedly, spotting Matt crouching down beside Louise's desk. He was only half-listening now, determined to catch the salesman before he accepted the offer at Netcomm – if he hadn't already.

'Well, that's been approved to start next week, with a review scheduled for September.'

'Thanks. Look, I've gotta–' Tony stopped. 'Next week?'

'Yes. Is there a problem?'

Tony faltered. He had requested for his reduced hours to begin in July, once his wife had given birth. Perhaps it was an administrative error. Either way, the idea of three-day weekends for their remaining month of relative freedom seemed rather appealing. Suze was due to start her maternity leave next week.

They hadn't been on holiday in over a year. Perhaps they could book a mini-break somewhere. Maybe a Devon farmhouse, or a cottage in the Lake District...

'No,' he said. 'No problem. Thanks for letting me know. I should go. I'll let you know how it goes with Matt.'

Tony put down the phone and raced into the office with a new sense of purpose.

Matt didn't react, initially. He sat, head down, in the visitor chair, nodding slowly as Tony broke the good news.

'I know it's been a bumpy ride, and I know this pay rise is long overdue. But... Don't walk out just as things are starting to come together.'

'Bumpy?' Matt repeated, derisively. 'That's one way of putting it.'

Tony sighed. 'Seriously, Matt. I'll be honest. You've done great things, pulling the Sales team into shape at EnGauge, and I don't want to see you go.'

Matt was frowning at the floor, either considering his options or trying to think of a polite way of telling Tony to go and stuff his offer.

'Please...' Tony could hear the desperation in his voice but he didn't care. This wasn't just a case of maintaining sales volumes or establishing continuity of staff or avoiding the cost of training a replacement. This was personal. Matt was a part of the EnGauge team. He had been there from the start, and Tony wanted him there until the end. 'We need you.'

Eventually, Matt looked up. He was smiling with one half of his mouth.

'Yeah,' he said. 'You do.'

Tony wasn't sure what this meant. 'So...'

Matt rolled his eyes. 'Go on, then. You've convinced me.'

The door clicked shut and Tony couldn't help giving the desk a little thump of triumph. He bashed out an email to Norm, then did the same for Roy, informing him of his new, elevated title: *Managing Director, Synapse Broadband*. After a few minutes spent staring blindly at the stack of emails in his inbox, he opened a browser and Googled 'mini-breaks UK'. Next Friday, he decided, they were going away.

Holiday in the New Forest

TONY HOISTED POPPY onto the pony and watched with trepidation as a young, dreadlocked student led the animal across the waterlogged grass.

'Shouldn't they have harnesses or something, for the kids?' asked Suze.

Tony lifted his shoulders uncertainly. 'I'm sure they know what they're doing.'

In fact, he didn't feel very sure at all. Health and safety didn't seem to be particularly high up on the agenda for New Forest Adventure Treks.

They followed their daughter's progress, sticking to the track while Poppy bounced along happily beside them, whooping in delight every time the bridle was jerked tight by the young Rastafarian.

The sky was a pure, untainted blue – the type of blue that was usually only seen on a weekday during a busy period when there was no opportunity to leave the office. For once, the weather was fitting in with Tony's plans.

He was about to suggest stopping off at the ice cream van when he felt something buzzing against his backside. He assumed that they had hit a rare pocket of mobile phone reception and that it was his emails trickling in, but after the fifth or sixth ring, he realised that it was another call.

'Go on then,' said Suze, rolling her eyes. Just as horses could smell fear, Suze could smell her husband's discomfort for work-life dilemmas. Guiltily, Tony extracted the BlackBerry.

'Hi Chek-Han.'

'Tony... ...call you... ...the email... ...finance section... ...today?'

Tony looked at the screen, turning on the spot to try and find an angle that had some reception.

'Sorry, Chek-Han,' he said. 'You're breaking up. Can you say that again?'

'It's this... ...Draper... ...end-of-play... ...press send?'

Tony sighed. 'Sorry mate. Can you try emailing me?'

Dropping the device back into his pocket, he looked up to find Suze waddling at full-pelt across the moor behind the student, who in turn was pursuing the animal, which had slipped free of its charge and was trotting rather quickly towards a cluster of wild ponies. Poppy's giggling had turned into a high-pitched whimper and she was, Tony noticed with relief as he sprinted across the grass, now clutching the animal's mane quite tightly.

The student got there first, taking the reins and jerking the pony's nose out of the stream. Poppy was beside herself, wailing and burying her face in the matted, unhygienic-looking mane. With Tony's help, Suze lifted her out of the saddle and into her arms. Casting a dirty look in the direction of the student, she stormed off, muttering furiously into Poppy's hair.

'Shall we get an ice cream?' Tony suggested, catching up with them as they returned to the sandy path.

Suze stared at him. 'Oh, you're there!' she cried sardonically.

Tony grimaced, turning to Poppy. 'Ice cream?' he offered again. 'Shall we see if they've got any strawberry?'

'Don't want an ice cream,' she whimpered, burying her face in Suze's cleavage and sniffing some more.

'Right.' Tony nodded. He could feel his BlackBerry vibrating in his pocket again, but didn't dare pull it out. 'I know. Let's walk back to the village and we can look at the animals at the fair!'

Poppy pulled her head up for just long enough to scowl at him. 'Don't like animals.'

'Right.'

It was a no-win situation. Suze was angry that he hadn't been there to chase after the rampant horse (and possibly because he'd suggested the ride in the first place) and Poppy was siding with Suze because that was what she always did when she was upset. The best thing to do in these situations, he had learned, was to keep quiet and to do as he was told.

'Let's walk back to the village and find something else to do,' Suze said authoritatively, easing Poppy off her bump and taking her hand.

Tony nodded and reached for Poppy's other hand, which was quickly snatched away.

The BlackBerry continued to buzz at intervals throughout the next half-hour, but with immense willpower, Tony ignored it. Eventually, Poppy decided she needed to wee and while Suze led her to a nearby bush, Tony surreptitiously retrieved the device and was appalled to see that he'd missed four calls, two voicemails, one text message and forty-six emails.

The voicemails – one from Maureen, one from Louise – sounded as though they'd been left by Daleks. Tony gave up on trying to decipher them and looked at the message from Brian, which read, somewhat cryptically, 'Have u heard?'. Norm had sent a long, rambling email about his section in the Stage Two presentation for next Thursday and Billy, the young Operations Manager, was also panicking about his part of the deck and requesting sign-off on some urgent purchase orders. Chek-Han had followed up on his earlier phone call, explaining in a rather frantic tone that Nicholas Draper had requested an early version of the financials that would be exhibited in Thursday's presentation and that he didn't feel confident sending it over without Tony's approval.

'Strawberry ice cream!' yelled Poppy, trotting back to the path, skirt tucked haphazardly into her pants. Tony just had time to send a single-character reply to Brian – '?' – before pocketing his BlackBerry and running to meet her. He swung her round by the waist and then hoisted her onto his shoulders. All was forgiven and ice cream was back on the agenda.

They waited as Poppy deliberated in front of the daunting array of flavours, Tony feeling unpleasantly agitated. It wasn't that he regretted coming away, or dropping to a four-day week. He loved spending time with Poppy and Suze – when he actually got the chance. It was more that he resented the realisation that the business still relied so heavily upon him. He'd been out of the office for less than four working hours, and already panic was setting in. He wondered how the team would cope if he went away for a fortnight. Would he return to find the pilot in tatters?

Perhaps, thought Tony as his daughter finally picked out a lurid pink lolly, it had been a mistake to step out of the office during such a critical period for EnGauge. Next Thursday was decision day. At this point, not only did the team have to keep the new business afloat, but on top, they had to work on a document that would secure their survival. The likes of Norm and Billy thrived on the day-to-day challenges, but they struggled when it came to high-level presentations. Tony shouldn't have left them alone like this.

Taking her change from the man in the van, Suze looked at him. She had a suspicious look in her eye that implied she already knew what was coming.

'I'm sorry,' he said. 'I'm going to have to make a few calls.'

She rolled her eyes.

'It's...' He was about to explain, but Suze put a finger to his lips.

'Don't worry,' she said, nodding for them to catch up with Poppy, who was dancing along the path, slurping noisily on her ice lolly. 'I understand.'

With a sense of relief, Tony drew out his BlackBerry and checked the reception. He dialled his voicemail whilst walking and listened to Maureen's rambling, pointless message about phone-forwarding and pay slips, then brightened as Louise's bubbly voice informed him that the early customer feedback from EnGauge was 'glowing'. He returned Chek-Han's call, then phoned Billy and Norm in turn, and replied to some of the more pressing emails in his inbox.

When he eventually looked up, he realised that they had arrived at the village. Suze was standing with her back to him, holding Poppy's hand as they waited to cross the road. She turned as he caught up with them.

'Done?' she asked.

He nodded, slipping a hand around her waist.

'Sheeps!' cried Poppy, bolting towards the lamb-filled pens as they reached the curb.

Tony grinned sideways at his wife. 'I thought she didn't like animals.'

'I think she changed her mind.'

They watched as Poppy pressed her nose up against the chicken-wire fence, calling out to the oblivious, grazing sheep. Then Tony felt his BlackBerry buzz.

'Sorry,' he muttered, pulling it out. 'Oh my God.'

'What?'

Tony stared at the message. For a moment, he wondered whether Brian might have been having a laugh.

Gable just stepped down.
With immediate effect.
No replacement been
announced. Big board
reshuffle on the cards.
Might impact your
Stage Two pres...?

'Everything alright?'

Tony looked up, blinking. 'Our CEO just resigned.'

Approval for scale-up; new arrival

ONE BY ONE, the suits filed into the room. Tony settled at the end of the long, polished table, wiping the sweat off his palms and mentally reciting his opening line.

It wasn't a new experience, presenting to the board. He'd been here before – proposing new ideas, giving updates, requesting more budget – but never in his five years at TransTel had Tony felt this much pressure on himself.

This time, his every word mattered. His delivery made the difference between leading TransTel into a whole new market, potentially changing the future of the company, and seeing his venture implode, sending him back to the day job in the declining business unit. This time, he really cared.

It seemed wrong, seeing Nicholas Draper's spindly figure at the head of the table. As Acting Chief Executive, he held the same set of powers as Charles Gable had done until his departure a week before. Somehow, though, he didn't come across like a CEO. He lacked gravitas.

'Okay,' Draper called, to little effect. He cleared his throat awkwardly. 'Okay!' he said again, louder.

There was a brief lull in the noise and Draper seized it.

'Okay, let's begin!'

Taking a deep breath, Tony rose to his feet and conducted a brief scan of the room. Most of the board members looked either bored or combative – nothing in between. A couple were already nodding off.

'We're now two months into the pilot of our smart site business, EnGauge.'

As soon as the words started to flow, the adrenaline dissipated. It was always like this: the anticipation was worse than the event – and besides, Tony wasn't worried about the presentation. The directors weren't here to look at his fancy slides; they were here to discuss the numbers. For the likes of Nicholas Draper and Carl Spragg, no amount of PowerPoint wizardry could convince them to invest if the numbers didn't add up. In Tony's opinion, the numbers spoke for themselves.

EnGauge had exceeded its turnover targets by eighteen percent. The subscription model had proved itself, and operationally, they were running a tight – if sometimes unpredictable – ship. Over the course of two months, the pilot had generated sales of two hundred thousand pounds, across just one county. There was, however, a catch. Tony had no way of disguising the excessive, unforeseen costs that had trodden the profit margins to a fraction of what had been forecast.

'It's a simple resource issue,' he explained, keeping his tone light despite the furrowed brows confronting him around the table. 'We under-estimated our requirements so our costs are unexpectedly high, due to contractor costs.'

Draper had heard this before. On his insistence, he had seen the numbers in advance of the presentation, but his feedback had remained infuriatingly vague. The decision as to whether or not TransTel would authorise a full scaling up of EnGauge, Tony suspected, would be made on the basis of today's discussion.

A hand was already in the air as he made his final point in favour of the national roll-out.

'So your costs will rise in proportion to your sales?' barked Carl Spragg. As usual, he hadn't been listening.

'As I explained in the–'

'Because if so,' Spragg went on, scratching at his beard as though highly sceptical of the whole idea, 'I would be bloody reluctant to invest, I'll tell ya. If it's already costin'–'

'As I explained,' Tony replied loudly, trying to mask his irritation with a smile, 'this is a scalable business. That's the beauty of it; the unit costs fall with volume. By using centralised call centres and shared regional hubs we can reduce our cost of acquisition and ultimately, retention.'

Anita Reynolds coughed meaningfully. 'And when you talk of acquisition and retention,' she said haughtily, 'are you assuming a similar conversion rate across the country? I can't see any mention of it here.'

'Yes. I mean no,' Tony faltered. His phone was vibrating in his pocket. 'We're not assuming a flat-rate conversion, we're allowing for–'

'You do realise that there are likely to be significant regional variations?'

'Yes,' he said, pulling together his thoughts and trying to turn his phone off. He knew what he wanted to say; he just didn't respond well to aggressive questioning. 'We're allowing for variations driven by location, business density and so on.'

This was harder than Tony had imagined. Half of the directors in the room were nodding gently, their minds no doubt elsewhere, and the other half were teaming up to play Devil's Advocate. Could nobody see the massive potential of EnGauge? Had they all been asleep for the last half-hour? This was an opportunity, not a threat.

'I have to say,' Josh Green said quietly, 'I can't see why we're all sitting around discussing this.'

For a moment, Tony just stared at him. Of all people, the Head of Sustainability should have been with him on this.

'We're going over the same old ground, answering the same questions... We should be doing this already!' Josh looked around at the other board members, eyes wide. Tony's hackles went down again, pleased to see that he had one ally. 'Don't you see? This is our chance to push TransTel to the forefront of the industry! If we don't jump on this, then someone else will and we'll be left–'

'Steady on!' Sir Anthony Knowles was holding up a wrinkly hand. 'Whatever we do, we mustn't rush into anything.'

Tony wondered when the old man was going to retire. He knew nothing about today's telecom industry, or any other industry for that matter. He didn't use email and he refused to own a mobile phone. *Mustn't rush into anything*. That was the unofficial mantra of TransTel. It was no wonder they were sinking while all their competitors raced on past.

His phone started buzzing again while a polite row ensued between Josh and Sir Anthony.

'With all due respect...'

'More haste, less speed. That's the way.'

'We *do* need to act.'

'Always *now, now, now*. That's the trouble, these days...'

Tony fumbled in his pocket to find the Off button. It was probably a problem with the new sales script that they were trialling as a precursor to rolling out nationally. That would teach him for pre-empting the board's decision.

'I think we're all saying the same thing,' declared Draper, taking care not to speak over anyone. 'We see the value in this business, but we want to make sure it's executed properly.'

Tony looked up, eventually locating the button and silencing the humming phone. It sounded very much as though Draper was endorsing the execution of a national roll-out. Heads were nodding, too, including that of Graham Walker-Jones, who was mumbling buzzwords like 'primary innovators' and 'future-proof positioning'.

Suddenly, the door of the boardroom flew open to reveal Maureen, red-faced and gasping for air, performing what looked like some grotesque sexual act on the door. Tony tried to interpret, aware that Maureen was looking directly at him as she thrust this way and that.

'Your wife...'

Tony leapt backwards, sending his chair toppling to the floor. *Suze was in labour.* He grabbed his suit jacket from the upturned chair, righted it and gabbled a hurried explanation to the board. Had he stopped to think, he might have apologised for his lack of courtesy, or given some indication as to when he'd be back, but his mind was already on overnight bags and damp flannels and all the things he was supposed to remember from the classes.

He ran down the three flights of stairs, crossed the car park and sped through a series of amber lights. He had no idea what stage Suze had reached; the message he'd taken from Maureen referred to centimetres dilated and minutes between contractions, but all the carefully-learned facts and figures seemed to have fled his mind. All he knew was that he had to reach Ward Two of the Maternity Bay as soon as quickly as possible.

Suze was propped up in bed when he arrived. She was dressed in an NHS maternity smock and her forehead was moist with sweat.

'Hey.' He approached the hospital bed, just as her face twisted into a desperate grimace. 'Oh, shit.'

Suze winced, grabbing his hand and digging her nails into the flesh of his fingers. It hurt quite a lot, although he was determined not to let on. When the ordeal was over, he switched hands in preparation for the next one.

'So you're quite far gone?' he asked.

Suze nodded. 'My waters broke all over Emmie's new carpet. Seems to be happening a bit quicker than the last time.'

He reached round and plumped the cushions around her back, the way he remembered from one of the antenatal videos. 'How far apart are they now?'

'About four minutes.'

'Okay.' Tony tried to remember what this meant.

'So he could arrive any minute,' Suze prompted.

'How are you feeling?'

'Scared shitless.'

'Right.' Tony nodded. He had a feeling that Suze was supposed to be feeling calm and relaxed at this stage, not scared shitless. 'Have you been doing your psychic breathing exercises?'

She screwed up her face in agony. 'It's... oh... ow! It's hypnosis! Not psychosis! Oh...'

Tony shut his eyes as the fingernails dug deeper. When he opened them again, he realised that he was surrounded by activity. Suze was shouting at the midwife, who was shouting back at her to push, then a doctor came on the scene, gas was administered, Suze became very red and sweaty, a nurse started poking beneath the curtain around Suze's legs and all the while, Tony's fingers were being slowly crushed by her razor-sharp talons.

The screaming and yelling continued, with authoritative words that Tony didn't understand being barked by the anaesthetist and frantic, unfamiliar noises coming out of his wife's mouth. Then out of it all came a shrill, high-pitched scream. The other noises subsided and he realised, with a rush of joy, that he was listening to the sound of his baby son.

The feeling stayed with him as he sat, perched on the edge of the bed, cuddled up to his wife and looking at the tiny, red child in her arms. Everything about him was perfect.

'He's beautiful.'

She nodded. 'He's not a Cedric, is he?'

Tony laughed at the reference to his mother-in-law's suggestion and found himself, rather embarrassingly, wiping away a tear.

'No,' he said, softly brushing the baby's button nose. 'I think he's... a Jamie.'

Suze smiled. 'Jamie.' The baby gurgled happily against her chest. 'Yes. I think you're right.'

'We should tell Poppy,' said Tony, before remembering that he didn't actually know where Poppy was. 'Who's...'

'She's with Emmie.'

Tony reached for his phone. As he unlocked the keypad, he noticed a text message from an unknown number.

GOOD LUCK WITH THE
BIRTH & CONGRATULATIONS
ON A SUCCESSFUL PILOT.
FULL ROLLOUT SCHEDULED
TO START 1 JULY.
NICK DRAPER

'Who's that?' asked Suze.

'Oh...' Tony tried to exit from the message but Suze had already grabbed the handset.

'Wow.' She looked at him and smiled. 'That's great news, isn't it?'

'It's nothing compared to–'

Suze reached out and touched his shoulder.

'I know how much this all means to you. It's like... It's like a child, too, isn't it?'

Tony looked at his wife and realised that in fact, as usual, Suze was right. The launch of EnGauge was nothing in comparison to what had just happened, but it was, in a way, like a child.

CREATING
THE NEW VENTURE

CREATING THE NEW VENTURE

 MarketGravity

In this chapter Tony gets the go-ahead to launch the pilot business, and despite encountering some early hiccups gets it up and running. An over zealous governance process, a focus on sales targets over operational learning and a battle for resources threaten to derail things, and all on top of the day-to-day pressures of business as usual.

Similar challenges you're likely to experience include:

- Being saddled with an imbalanced scorecard where sales or earnings are the only measures of success
- Compromising your ability to be agile and experimental due to an overbearing governance process
- Dealing with poor management information due to unsophisticated data collection systems
- Not having enough staff to run new pilots and existing business functions
- Increasing interference from senior stakeholders and reporting functions
- Pressure to scale up before the pilot has run its course and proven the ability to deliver

Despite these and other pressures, piloting is essential for ironing out all the operational bugbears that would jeopardise the venture when it scales, and for validating the key cost and revenue assumptions behind the business case.

"THINK LIKE A COMPETITOR: ONCE YOU'VE DEALT WITH THE INTERNAL POLITICS, GOT THE BOARD ONSIDE ETC., THINK LIKE A START-UP

—

BECAUSE THAT'S WHO YOU'LL BE COMPETING WITH."

Rachel Sheridan, Cocosa (Bauer)

Designing a good pilot is more art than science. The key is to use the pilot to help the business achieve scale as quickly and as profitability as possible, and not as an early sales drive. Here are some things to consider when piloting your venture:

1. Create a balanced scorecard for success. Don't just measure sales; include performance measures around operations as inefficiencies will magnify and costs will soar as the business grows.

2. Get the customer view. Take time to find out what customers really think about the offering and to understand where improvements can be made.

3. Test the extremes. The beauty of a pilot is its ability to really test the edges of what the business can do. Don't simply replicate the mature business model, but experiment to find out where the limits lie.

4. Look for the cracks. Sometimes it is hard to spot what might fall over when you only have a handful of customers. Don't just rely on the data feed, get in there and see what's happening on the ground.

5. Get the customer experience right. Ultimately it's the way you do things, not what you do, that sets you apart form others. Use the pilot to fine-tune the customer experience and ensure that you can deliver time and time again with confidence.

6. Celebrate your successes. A pilot can be a long and testing slog. Learn from your mistakes, but also make sure you celebrate your successes with the whole team.

To answer the questions "should we scale?", "can we scale?" ensure your pilot success factors measure a broad range of sales, cost and organisational dimensions. An example Key Performance Indicator (KPI) tree is illustrated below.

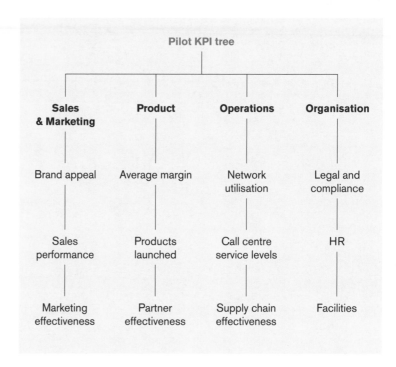

Pilot KPI tree

Sales & Marketing	**Product**	**Operations**	**Organisation**
Brand appeal	Average margin	Network utilisation	Legal and compliance
Sales performance	Products launched	Call centre service levels	HR
Marketing effectiveness	Partner effectiveness	Supply chain effectiveness	Facilities

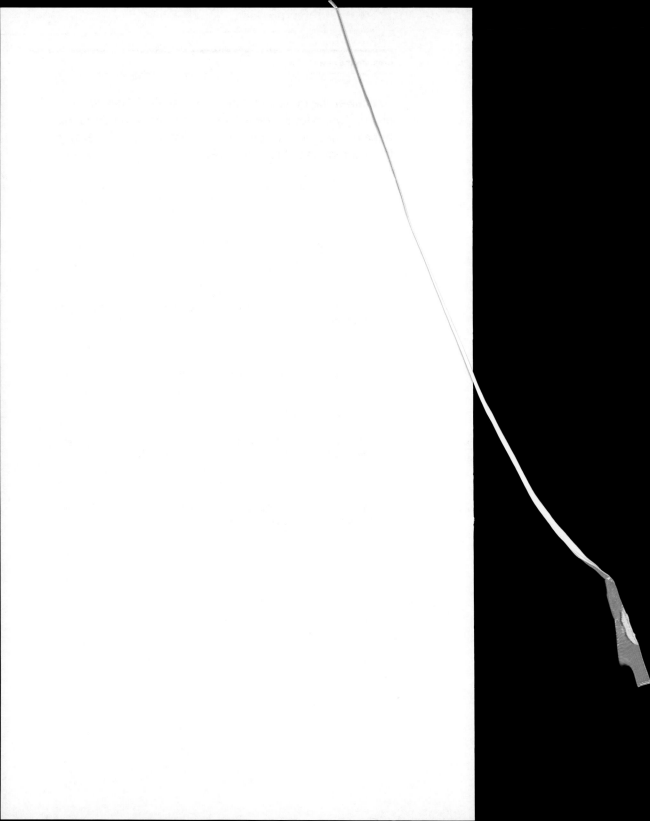

9

Defying gravity:
keeping afloat and achieving scale

'Small is beautiful, the real challenge is in scaling up'

Meeting regional sales heads

TONY FOUND HIMSELF nodding, his eyes staying shut for longer and longer with every blink. He jolted upright, took a sip of water and looked sideways at his Head of Sales. He had failed to take in a single word of what had been said in the last ten minutes.

It wasn't that Matt's presentation lacked energy; quite the opposite. From the moment his pay rise had come into effect, the young man had transformed himself into a dynamic, enthusiastic workhorse – a proud advocate of the growing business. Matt was doing a great job of convincing this roomful of staid nine-to-fivers that their roles were about to change for the better. Tony's lack of attention was simply that he was *tired.*

He had forgotten, over the last three years, how it felt to be truly tired. The initial euphoria that had consumed him after the birth had transformed into a state of constant, endless weariness. Not that he resented the eardrum-splitting screams that broke through his shallow sleep every hour, every night. Jamie was still perfect, still a little miracle. He was just... needy. Tony had taken for granted the six hours of uninterrupted sleep he'd been getting until a few weeks ago. Now, like a weight around his shoulders, the tiredness hung, always there and impossible to shrug off. He was living a zombie-like existence: one foot in front of the other, eyes glazed, brain permanently in neutral. It took all his energy to focus on a single problem or question, and even when he focussed, he found himself losing grip on his thoughts within seconds.

There were eight sales people around the table: seven men

and one woman. Tamsin Wright was TransTel's only female Regional Sales Head and she liked people to remember this fact. Tony glanced across at the low-cut, translucent blouse and the power-dressing suit, then averted his eyes as they wandered to the micro-skirt that wouldn't have looked out of place in a lap-dancing club. Ms Wright headed up the South East sales team and although their paths hadn't crossed until now, Tony knew her by reputation. Among the lads, she was known as Ramsin Tight, or, in another context, The Iron Lady. She was not a woman to be messed with.

'Any questions?' Matt casually shoved a hand in his pocket and looked around the table.

Immediately, Tamsin leaned forwards, her breasts pressing distractingly against the blouse.

'I don't see how the incentives are aligned with the value driven to the business,' she said tartly. 'If I want my sales teams to sell this new service, they have to be *incentivised*. It's not clear to me why we wouldn't just continue to sell the standard product lines.'

Matt was already nodding, clearly preparing to tackle the question himself. Tony mentally congratulated himself for getting the pay rise arranged in time. The regional sales heads were always going to be the hardest nuts to crack. Most of them had worked their way into their positions over a number of years, selling their way through a series of TransTel products and services. They didn't take kindly to change. Unfortunately though, change was exactly what was required if EnGauge was to succeed at a national level.

'Our men are stretched as it is,' barked one of the guys, whose name Tony had already forgotten. Bob? Rob? He was from the North East if the accent was anything to go by. Jesus, this was embarrassing. Tony prided himself on being good with names.

'We know they're stretched,' Matt replied. 'But if we can prove the business case, we can hire more of them.'

It was odd, seeing Matt get behind the EnGauge proposition. A few months ago, it had been him asking the awkward questions. He'd been the one with the loud voice and the claims that there was no mileage in the smart site idea. Now, the tables were turned. It was people like Bob, or Rob, who stood in the way.

They'd all come round soon enough, once they realised that the board had sanctioned the expansion and that there was nothing they could do to fight it. Soon, they'd be selling it to their sales teams, who in turn would resist for a while until they realised that the commission worked out better for EnGauge than it did for their existing lines, and then it would just be a case of convincing the customers. Selling, Tony was beginning to realise, was a never-ending chain.

He looked down as his BlackBerry vibrated in his lap, and noticed a smear of dried baby-sick streaked across his left thigh. He scratched at it with a fingernail. The more he rubbed, the whiter it became. After a minute or so of futile rubbing, he gave up and surreptitiously, while Matt was fielding another accusation from Bob or Rob, unlocked the key pad of his BlackBerry.

Six messages had arrived in quick succession, alternately from Brian and Amit. Tony opened the latest and read up from the bottom.

From: Brian O'Keefe - TransTel Network Direct
News from the grapevine: New CEO likely to be Alistair Marchant. Maybe a good thing you got your expansion signed off when you did, Tony...

From: Amit Chaudhuri – TransTel Cordless Enterprises
What, Alistair Marchant of National Energy?

From: Brian O'Keefe - TransTel Network Direct
The very same.

From: Amit Chaudhuri – TransTel Cordless Enterprises
As in, the man responsible for the steady decline in revenues of the once-largest UK utilities provider?

From: Brian O'Keefe - TransTel Network Direct
That's the one.

From: Amit Chaudhuri – TransTel Cordless Enterprises
Well, that settles it then. I am officially looking around.

Tony stared at the words, feeling his focus start to slip and his morale slump. If the rumours turned out to be true then it was indeed a blessing for him that the national rollout of EnGauge was already underway. Alistair Marchant had featured in enough in-flight magazines for Tony to know how he operated. He was hard-nosed, opinionated and utterly, religiously, conservative. Ten years ago, to great fanfare, he had turned some of National Energy's loss-making divisions profitable by cutting out the dead wood and improving efficiency. Since then, the company had stagnated and lost most of its customers to the competition. Entire business units had been sold off at a loss or shut down.

The effect Alistair Marchant would have on TransTel would be disastrous. Already, the business was suffering from a lack of investment in the future. There existed an unfounded belief that last decade's cash cows would continue to produce the goods and that innovation pipelines were akin to stargazing. Now, perversely, the board was bringing in a leader that would only serve to amplify its outdated beliefs.

'So what the hell are we supposed to do about that, like?' demanded Rob or Bob, loudly enough to bring Tony back from his depressing daydreams.

Matt looked sideways at Tony. 'D'you wanna take this one?'

Tony straightened up and looked at the North East Sales Head, if indeed that was his title. He had no idea what the question had been.

'I think there's always going to be a feeling that *new is bad*, and that we should stick with what we've been doing for...'

He trailed off, aware that the northerner and several other regional sales heads were all looking at him quizzically.

'Sorry...' He looked at Matt for a clue.

Matt also appeared perplexed.

'Sorry, I think I went off on a tangent there...'

He floundered for what seemed like minutes, trying desperately to summon the echo of the question. Eventually, Matt helped him out.

'I think we'd probably need to know more about their offering before we can answer that one,' he said, glancing at Tony, who dutifully nodded. 'Do we know much about them? Are they big?'

Tony waited for the man's response, hoping it might shed some light on what was being discussed.

'Big enough to be a fair competitor.'

Competitor? Tony scribbled something down on his notebook. How had he missed this? Were they saying there was some sort of EnGauge equivalent in the North East? It was too late to ask.

'Okay,' said Matt, taking control. 'Thanks George. Sounds as though this might warrant a separate conversation.'

Matt lifted an eyebrow in Tony's direction. Tony nodded again. *George?* It wasn't even close to Bob or Rob.

'Check 'em out.' George shrugged. 'Automaton dot com. You might get a few ideas from them, if nothing else.'

Tony scribbled *Automaton* in his notebook, then circled it several times, mainly to avoid meeting anyone's eye. The fact that his North East Sales Head was implying they needed to take some tips from the competition had not gone unnoticed.

Tamsin was bashing her papers noisily against the table – a rather blatant indication that she'd had enough. Matt took the hint and dismissed the group, fielding a couple of outstanding questions from individuals on their way out.

Tony waited until the last person had left the room and then turned to his Head of Sales.

'Thanks.'

'What for?'

'Well.' Tony grimaced. 'For taking the lead.'

'Well, with all due respect mate, it's *my* job to scale up the sales teams, isn't it?'

Tony looked at him for a second, then down at the floor. Matt was right. It hadn't occurred to him until now, but the EnGauge proposition was no longer *his* baby; it was a venture in its own right. It was getting too big for one person to own and control – especially a sleep-deprived person such as himself. He had to trust his team members to carry it forward.

'Yes,' he said. 'It is. And you're doing a great job.'

Growing up

'I HEAR WHAT YOU'RE SAYING, but if they can't meet demand...'

Tony pulled the handset away from his ear and pressed the speakerphone button, leaning forward and scrolling through the stack of emails that had popped into his inbox.

'It's not that they can't meet demand,' Billy explained, with an admirable mix of confidence and tact. 'It's the fact that they take longer for high-volume orders because they use a different manufacturing plant.'

'Why can't they just use the same plant?' asked someone.

'It's a capacity thing.'

Tony tuned out for a second as he read the email from HR declaring that all new hires had to go through an extra screening process until a personnel department was put in place within EnGauge.

'Can't we go with another supplier?' someone piped up.

They were discussing, or rather, they were supposed to be discussing, ways to improve supply chain efficiency within EnGauge now that the proposition was to be rolled out across the whole of the South East. In reality, in the absence of anyone more senior than Billy, they were getting hung up over the minutiae of various contracts and procedures that had been put in place during the pilot.

'Perhaps we should move onto the next item on the agenda,' Tony suggested. 'We can come back to the Optics contract.'

He felt slightly more alert than he had done a fortnight ago. On Suze's insistence, he was sleeping in the spare room on weeknights, having concluded, eventually, that there was no point in taking turns to see to Jamie during the night, given that (a) by the time they worked out whose turn it was, they were both awake and (b) Suze was on maternity leave so in theory she could make up for lost sleep during the day – although Tony suspected she never did.

'Right. Last item then, CSR.'

There was a collective groan from the various participants on the call. Billy did his best to shout over them about the importance of corporate social responsibility in today's society, but it was clear that people's attention had been lost.

Tony started deleting messages in an attempt to bring his inbox down to a manageable size, wondering whether he should intervene. He worried about the young Operations Manager. It wasn't that Billy wasn't up to the job; he was one of those switched-on, quick-thinking university graduates who got things done. He was an organiser, a problem-solver and a good manager of people, too. The problem was with the people he had to manage.

Three months ago, Billy had been in charge of a small part of a start-up operation in a division of TransTel that nobody had ever heard of. Now, he was on the cusp of managing the operational side of a multi-million pound business. There were more moving parts and more personalities to deal with. Quite apart from his lack of experience, Billy looked about eighteen. His eyes were bright blue, like a baby's, and his chin was devoid of stubble. Tony knew how the rest of TransTel would see him: another keen, young whippersnapper who had leapfrogged the traditional career path because of his A-Level grades. They would see him as cannon fodder.

'Okay!' shouted Billy, above the cacophony. Nobody cared about CSR. 'That's enough! Let's call it a day. Any questions?'

There was more general noise.

'Okay, great. I'll circulate the minutes in an email. Thanks all. 'Bye!'

Tony pressed the red button and opened an email from Natasha that was marked HIGH PRIORITY. It was referring to the back-filling of certain positions in Synapse and the imminent transfer of EnGauge personnel to the new offices. Tony failed to see what it was that rendered the communication high priority, but he clicked on Reply all the same. Keeping Human Resources on-side was worth doing at any cost.

Dear Natasha,
I am confident that the remaining Synapse team can handle the day-to-day issues under Roy's command. Please find attached a list of current personnel who will be moving across to the new offices.
Tony

He delved into the labyrinth of the EnGauge electronic filing system in search of the relevant document.

It felt like only yesterday that they'd moved from the second floor to their almost identical third floor location, but soon they'd be moving again – this time to a whole new building, and this time for a reason. The new office was only a few hundred metres away from the TransTel premises, in the same business park, but the move felt like progress.

They had out-grown their current premises. In line with their operational plan, EnGauge was expanding at central, regional and local levels. Marketing, which was to be run by a single team headed up by Louise, had seen the biggest uplift in numbers, now standing at six, with a new recruit starting on Monday. Sales were being handled by Matt, through the Regional Sales Heads, starting with Tamsin Wright's team in the South East. The installation teams were being boosted across Surrey, Kent and Sussex, with local fleets being acquired and branded over the coming weeks. Even walking through the cramped, over-filled offices, Tony found that he no longer recognised all the faces.

In a strange way, it felt as though EnGauge was growing up. It was still reliant on its parent company, financially and in other ways, but every day it was taking on a little more responsibility, starting to fend for itself. TransTel was still very much a presence, bearing down on EnGauge in the form of HR correspondence, procurement headaches, pressure from the board and countless other departments and individuals who liked to think they had a say in how things were run, but *they* were now holding the reins.

Tony's phone rang just as he located the spreadsheet and clicked on Attach.

'You coming down, or what?'

It was Brian. Tony checked the time. He was ten minutes late for lunch with Amit and Brian. Clicking Send, he locked the computer, pushed back his chair and rushed out.

'You shouldn't have waited!' cried Tony, sarcastically. Brian was just polishing off a chocolate dessert and Amit was nibbling on the remains of an apple core.

Brian rolled his eyes and shuffled up. 'Got the impression we weren't top of your priority list.'

'Well, no,' Tony conceded. 'You're not.'

'How's it all going?' Amit discarded the small, neat core on his plate. 'Any growing pains?'

Tony nodded as he tried to spear a piece of watery pasta with his fork. 'Plenty.'

'Better or worse than the pilot?' asked Brian.

Chewing the tasteless penne, Tony made a wavering gesture.

'It's weird,' he said eventually. 'I keep thinking that things will get easier – that we've done the hard work, launching the business. But there's always a new set of problems. This week, it's looking as though we won't have a fleet ready for the Sussex roll-out, the outdoor ad campaign in Kent will be two weeks delayed and the South East Sales Manager seems to have issues reporting to Matt.'

Amit nodded, smiling faintly. 'Always the sales guys.'

Tony looked at him. 'She's not a guy.'

Brian started to laugh. 'Oh... Oh, dear. You haven't started your roll-out with Ramsin Tight, have you? Whose idea was that?'

Tony shrugged. Personalities hadn't come into the operational plan. The South East had seemed like the natural place to start, given its proximity to the pilot region and offices.

'She's a bit of a ball-breaker,' he admitted.

'A bit?' Brian banged the table and let out a loud, hearty

chuckle. 'Jesus, mate. They don't call her Titanium Tamsin for nothing...'

Tony fished around in his pasta for something with a bit of flavour. He hadn't heard that particular nickname before.

'Actually,' Brian mused, 'I think they call her that because of her tits. I dunno.'

'Tony,' said Amit, leaning forward, eyes narrowed. 'If there's one thing I learned about sales people, it's this. You can't afford to not have them on your side. These... these ones with the loud voices, you need to take them aside, bring them round – however you can. If they're blocking your way, you'll never move forward.'

Brian was nodding too, with mock sagacity. 'Wise words,' he said. 'Wise words.'

Tony smiled. Amit had been here before, with the launch of TransTel CBN. 'You're right. There's only a few of them who don't back the idea, but they're loud, and they're infecting the way the others think. And besides, I *need* Tamsin for the South East roll-out. It starts in two weeks.'

'Well,' Brian laughed darkly. 'A man's gotta do what a man's gotta do...'

Tony grimaced as he swallowed his mouthful. Whatever it was Brian was insinuating, he wouldn't be going there.

'How's the recruitment drive?' asked Amit.

Tony sighed. 'Busy,' he said, thinking of the number of times he'd typed 'TBA' on the spreadsheet he'd just sent HR. 'Fancy joining us?'

Amit looked at him, slowly raising one eyebrow.

Tony stopped chewing.

For some reason, he had assumed that Amit's dissatisfaction with Cordless Enterprises extended to the whole of TransTel. He was beginning to doubt his assumption.

Suddenly, his mind jumped back to the conference call earlier and his worries about Billy's lack of experience. Amit was an operational expert. He had even helped write that part of the plan for EnGauge. He was the obvious recruit.

'Are you free for an interview later this week?'

Amit's expression morphed into a calm, broad smile.

'Thought you'd never ask.'

Tony was about to tell Amit about the issues he'd been having with his young Ops Manager when his phone rang.

With a brief apology to his friends, Tony picked up the call.

'Mate, it's me.'

Tony braced himself. The 'me' in question was Matt, and he was using that tight, stressed tone that Tony had only heard a couple of times before. 'Bad news.'

'Go on.'

'It's this company up in the North East,' Matt explained. 'Automaton. I've checked 'em out. They're big. They're gonna cause us problems.'

'How big?' Tony pushed away his cold pasta and lifted a hand as Brian got up to leave.

'In terms of coverage and contracts, the equivalent to us in year four.

'Shit.' Tony closed his eyes and rubbed them. 'And what do they do? Is it exactly the same service that we're offering?'

'Almost to the letter.'

Tony groaned. 'Right. Okay, leave it with me. Send me anything you've got on them and I'll decide what to do. In the meantime, tell Bob – Rob –'

'George?'

'Yeah. Tell George we're still going for full roll-out as planned.'

'Will do.'

Amit was looking at him when he came off the call.

'Competition already?' he asked.

Tony nodded wearily.

'Whereabouts?'

'The North East. All over. They're the size that we wanna get to in year four.'

'Ouch. Well, only one thing you can do...'

'Crush them?' Tony offered lamely. It was as specific a tactic as he could muster.

'No,' said Amit. '*Acquire* them.'

Tamsin comes round; Basingstoke billing issues

TAMSIN WRIGHT LEANED BACK in her chair and sighed.

'I don't think you're listening,' she said, thrusting her chest forward again and fixing Tony with a hard stare. 'I can see why this plan might be good for *your* department, given the state of your B2B sales, but you're asking me to put *my* neck on the line and have *my* men promote a new, untested product in place of a number of perfectly successful ones. I'm sorry, Tony. I just won't do it.'

Tony closed his eyes for a second. He had already used up every conceivable argument, to no effect. He had reasoned, he had explained, he had even tried throwing his weight around and reminding her that the decision wasn't actually hers to make. The South East Regional Sales Head wouldn't budge. She knew, and Tony knew that she knew, that he wasn't about to complain to the upper echelons about her refusal to play ball. This was something they had to work out for themselves, preferably in the next twenty-four hours, given that the roll-out was set to take place in eight days' time.

Tony leaned backwards and opened a window. The new office was not dissimilar to the old one in design, but they were now on the fifth floor, overlooking the man-made lake with its plastic heron, and the sign on the door said *EnGauge*, not *Synapse*. The air-conditioning was equally ineffective, the meeting rooms were still designed like greenhouses and the heating still switched itself on randomly throughout summer. Still, he couldn't complain. At least it was theirs.

'Okay,' he said, thinking of another way of saying what he'd already said a dozen times before. 'I understand that you don't want to be the first full region to take on EnGauge. But national roll-out has been sanctioned by the board and it *will* happen, given the success of the pilot, so even if we start with say... the South West, it'll come to you eventually.'

Tamsin narrowed her well-painted lips. It was absurd, thought Tony, that he had to justify the new proposition to such an extent. It wasn't as though this was an encumbrance they were talking about. It was an *opportunity*. An opportunity to make money. Tamsin herself would do well, if she only let it happen. The commission structure had been carefully calculated to incentivise the relevant sales forces to take on the new proposition.

What *was* her objection? That was what Tony didn't understand. She was making claims about the upheaval and uncertainty of taking on new product lines, but it didn't stack up. Tamsin Wright wasn't stupid. She knew about the success of the pilot. She understood that in order to move the business forward, it had to evolve. She had launched new products before – ones with less favourable commission structures for her men.

A warm breeze swirled into the room and lifted the corner of Tony's blank page. He pressed it down, lingering on his latest thought. Perhaps her men were at the bottom of this, he mused. Perhaps for Tamsin, it was more about making a point than making money. Given that she had originally opposed the national roll-out of EnGauge, she wasn't going to cave in now and endorse it, or she might lose face.

'You've led your sales team for a number of years, haven't you?' he asked, testing the water.

'I have,' she replied, with a mixture of pride and wariness.

'Your team has a great deal of respect for you,' Tony went on, more as a statement than a question.

Tamsin pushed back her padded shoulders. 'I'm not sure what this has to do with anything, but yes, they do.'

Tony hesitated. He had to tread carefully. His theory wasn't water-tight, but if it did hold, then it stood to reason that Tamsin's ego was actually as fragile as that of an alpha-male. Deep down, she wasn't the Titanium Lady. At any rate, it was the best hypothesis Tony could come up with and he was going to run with it.

'If this business is going to take off as I hope, the sales team will need strong leadership.'

Tamsin arched one eyebrow.

'So...' Tony wasn't quite sure where this was going, but it felt as though he was getting warmer. 'So, I need your help. To bring round the doubters.'

Tamsin said nothing, which Tony took to be a positive sign.

'Will you do that? Will you convince them for me? You'd obviously explain to them the concessions I'm making in accordance with what you've requested...'

'Concessions?'

Tony raised an eyebrow. What he was trying to say was that if any of Tamsin's salesmen questioned her sudden U-turn, she could explain that it was only on the basis of certain provisos stipulated by her. He was trying to save her face. '*Are* there any concessions you'd like me to think about? Anything that might change people's minds?'

Tamsin drew back her head and looked at him for a moment. It was a risky tactic, thought Tony, opening up to negotiations at this late hour, but if it won him the backing he needed...

'I'll have a think.'

'Great.'

Tamsin rose up in her six-inch heels and thrust a hand in his face.

'I'll be in touch,' she said curtly.

He followed her into the open-plan office and asked Maureen to show her out.

Even before he had turned to go back to his desk, Tony knew that something was wrong. People were looking at him, glancing anxiously around the office, making eye contact with one another and pulling desperate faces. Even Maureen looked as though she wanted to tell him something as she rose, sloth-like, from her chair.

'Tony?'

Louise was the only one brave enough to step forward. In fact, on the bravery front, Louise had developed remarkably in the last few weeks. She had stepped up to the extra responsibility, managing her ever-growing team and coordinating the national ad campaigns with relative ease. That said, her current expression made her look like a shadow of her usual, bubbly self.

'Did Billy get hold of you?'

'I've been in a meeting all afternoon,' he explained, looking around for the young Ops Manager. 'What's wrong?'

'Well...' Louise grimaced and took a deep breath. 'Apparently–'

'Tony!' Billy burst into the room, red-faced and sweating. 'Been looking for you,' he panted.

Tony considered pointing out to Maureen, who had just reappeared from chaperoning the Titanium Lady down to reception, that it was in fact part of her job to inform people of his whereabouts and not to leave employees running about in search of their boss. But Billy's body language indicated that there were more pressing matters to discuss.

'It's Basingstoke,' he said breathlessly.

Tony looked at him. Basingstoke was, as of the previous Tuesday, home to the EnGauge billing centre – the hub through which every invoice and every payment for every subscription passed on its way to and from the customer. The relocation from TransTel Head Office to Basingstoke had not been without bumps, but over the last few days the noises seemed to have become quieter and less frequent. Tony had assumed – perhaps prematurely – that the worst of the teething problems were over.

'We're gonna have to get everyone in at the weekend,' gabbled Billy. 'Most of the last two days' invoices haven't been processed, and even now half the orders aren't going through right...' Billy ran a hand through his hair. 'I dunno how it went unnoticed for so long.'

'Calm down.' Tony laid a hand on the young manager's shoulder. It was clammy and hot. 'What exactly is the problem here?'

'Um, basically, when the engineers pick up the equipment for an installation, the warehouse sends a notification to generate the invoice at our end. But the notifications having been coming through, so the invoices aren't being generated.'

'Why not?'

'Well, I don't know. It's a manual process.' Billy's breathing was returning to normal, but his face was blotchy with heat or embarrassment.

Tony frowned. He knew that there had been manual elements to the process during the pilot. During the pilot there had been plenty of quick-fixes and stop-gaps to tide them over. It hadn't been worth the investment in long-term, automated solutions. Now though, there was no room for error.

'I'll have to look into it,' said Billy. 'I know that when Margaret moved to Basingstoke she handed over to a guy called Gary, and he had a different way of doing things...'

Tony nodded solemnly. The details of Margaret's handover to Gary were not of primary importance, but the implications were. Things were falling between the cracks. Processes that had worked for ten or twenty invoices per day were no good when the volumes were ramped up. Resources were being stretched and errors were creeping in. The operating model had been built for pilot and it needed to be rebuilt for scale.

'I'm sorry,' Billy said, wringing his hands limply. 'I should've spotted it.'

Tony looked at him. Billy was right; he should have spotted it, but then, looking up the chain, *Tony* should have spotted that Billy didn't have the experience to single-handedly scale up the operational side of the business.

'It's okay,' he said eventually. 'I know someone who might be able to help.'

Two weeks ago, Amit had sat across the desk from Tony for a full half-hour in an admirable yet farcical attempt at a job interview. They both knew that the older man was ideally suited to the role – a role that would sit alongside Billy's to support the operational expansion of EnGauge – but it was HR policy that the interview, and countless others, should go ahead. Unsurprisingly, after a suitable length of time had elapsed, Amit had been offered the job, and now it was a case of sitting through weeks, if not months, of apparently essential hoop-jumping on the part of Natasha's team in order that Amit could make the transfer.

Tony motioned for Billy to follow him back to his office and picked up the phone. He knew Amit's extension by heart.

'Hello?'

'Hey, it's me. Are you busy?'

He laughed wryly. 'This is Cordless Enterprises, remember. The land of the retirement home payphone.'

'Right.' Tony smiled at Billy, who was hovering nervously by the empty chair. 'Fancy starting your new job a few weeks early?'

'I'll be right there.'

'Thanks, mate.'

'By the way, did you manage to secure some investment cash for your acquisition?'

Tony jiggled his mouse and watched as the screensaver dissolved to reveal his part-written proposal for Draper on the rationale for acquiring Automaton. 'I'm working on it.'

'Errrr, right.'

'What does "errrr, right" mean?'

'Have you checked your email recently?'

Tony flicked to his inbox and scanned the messages, wondering what Amit was referring to. Then he saw it, nestled among a batch of sales updates.

From: Nicholas Draper, Finance Director /Acting CEO
To: TransTel – all
Subject: New Chief Executive

Dear all,
It is with great excitement that I share with you the news that Alistair Marchant, formerly of National Energy and a key figure in the company's formidable turnaround, will be joining TransTel with immediate effect as Chief Executive Officer.
You will no doubt be hearing from Alistair once he settles into the new role, but in the meantime, please make every effort to welcome him to the organisation.
Yours,
Nicholas Draper

Tony let out a long, low groan. 'Well, there goes that idea.'

Too much process; ignored by new CEO

'OKAY, LET'S SEE what the recipe – oh. Um, shall we try and keep the ingredients in the bowl? That's right. We need to make sure there's enough for six of us, don't we...'

Tony leaned over and scooped a stray raspberry from the side of the toaster, dropping it back in the lumpy concoction. It was a Friday, his day off, and in a bold attempt at chivalry, he had suggested that Suze treat herself to an afternoon of solitude in the sunshine while he and the children 'knocked something up for dinner'. Truth be told, the gallant gesture had been proposed before Suze's reminder that Emmie and Luke were coming over with Bradley that night, but it was hardly an offer that could be retracted.

Tony peered at the cream-spattered recipe book. Suddenly, a piercing scream rose up in stereo around him. He turned to find Poppy slithering down from the work surface, having lost her footing on the stool, and Jamie, in the cot by the door, his fists screwed into tight little balls of rage and his face an alarming shade of purple. Tony deposited his daughter next to the bawling child and tried to remember where he'd left the milk.

Jamie, it turned out, didn't want milk. The screams continued unabated as the teat was repeatedly rejected from his mouth, now accompanied by a hiccupping whimper from Poppy, who was unharmed but evidently put out by the fact that her baby brother was taking all the attention. Tony picked up his son and tried jiggling him. He tried rocking him, winding him, tickling him, fanning him... Then he peered inside the nappy and found the source of the problem.

Part-way through the nappy change, Tony was beginning to feel quietly proud of the contented gurgling sound coming from his baby, when the oven alarm went off, prompting more screams. Balancing Jamie in the fold of the sofa, Tony silenced the bleeps, rescued the duck and realised he had left half of the toxic nappy contents inside the oven glove. Throwing it into the yard as a temporary measure, Tony returned to soothe his son, at which point Mrs Lambert from next door popped her head through the open window to check that things were alright.

Children and neighbour appeased, Tony looked around, wondering where the last fifteen minutes had gone and wondering how Suze did this every day. She even managed to check her emails – he had seen her do it.

Emails. Tony looked at the table where his BlackBerry lay. Right on cue, it bleeped. He leaned over, unable to walk due to Poppy's arms being wrapped around his shins, and remembered that he had promised to join the Operations conference call at half past five. It was a quarter to six.

'Please say your name after the tone,' directed the automated woman in a sing-song voice.

Tony said nothing, hoping that an expanse of silence would be recorded so that the other delegates wouldn't realise he'd missed the first fifteen minutes of the call.

'I'm sorry. I didn't catch that. Please say your name after the tone,' the woman said again. Tony cursed, preparing to mumble something incomprehensible, when Jamie got in first with a high-pitched yelp as he threw up a globule of baby sick.

'Thank you,' said the voice.

'...just sayin' that things take forever now. My team ain't paid to fill out forms. They're stretched - '

'Er, hello?' said someone. 'Is that Tony?'

'Hi, guys. Sorry I'm late.'

'We wondered what you were doing to that poor kid.'

Tony forced a chuckle, putting the BlackBerry on speakerphone and pressing 'mute' as he returned to the Raspberry Mess, which was looking exactly as one might expect a Raspberry Mess to look.

'Yeah. Ethan here. I was just sayin', we ain't got time for all these new rules on the who, what, where an' when. It worked fine when we just *talked* to each other.'

Amit's voice came on the line, explaining calmly that the rules had been implemented because it *didn't* work fine when they talked to each other, as the billing blunder the previous month had illustrated.

Tony started breaking up the meringue, wondering what he would have done without Amit in the last few weeks. Billy was diligent and sharp, but he lacked experience and he garnered no respect from the likes of Ethan Scott. If it had been Billy chairing today's update call, then Ethan probably would have bullied his way into getting the carefully devised protocols lifted, and they would have gone back to the old ways, when everyone guessed which jobs to install and used their own judgement to decide whether to send an invoice. Billy was still Operations Manager, but Amit's title was Operations Director, which officially put him above the younger man – not that Billy seemed to mind. To Tony's relief, the men got on well.

EnGauge was now a growing presence across the Southern Counties, with the Midlands due to follow the next month. Tamsin Wright had eventually come round, as Tony had hoped she might, with only a few minor demands that involved minor changes to the commission rates – mainly, Tony suspected, so that she could tell her men that she'd been the one in control. Tony didn't mind. The South East region was pulling in more subscriptions than the financial forecasts had predicted, due to the concentration of medium-sized businesses and the new Government legislation that had come into force.

Tony thought back to his Eureka moment six months before – a Eureka moment prompted by Amit, in fact – when he'd heard the radio debate and realised that they should be targeting the business market. The new Environmental Enterprise Code of Practice had been a key part of their rationale for taking the business forward and featured heavily in the business plan, yet as the first few weeks of trading illustrated, the proposition could have taken off without it. They might not have experienced the surge in sales that they were seeing now, but they wouldn't have gone under. Although, of course, hindsight was a wonderful thing. The truth was that the board would never have signed off on the business plan without the promise of the new legislation, because they didn't like taking risks. *That* was the hurdle to overcome.

'Sorry, but Ethan's got a point,' someone droned, predictably. Installation managers all had the same tone, Tony noticed. They all sounded bored and pissed off. He wondered whether it was an attribute they picked up during the course of their careers or whether the role attracted a certain type of person.

'It's extra work that we ain't gettin' paid for...'

Tony spooned a dollop into the glass bowl, then leaned over and unmuted his phone with his least sticky finger.

'Actually,' he said, keeping an eye on Poppy as she unfurled herself from his leg and tottered over to the sofa where Jamie was lying, whimpering. 'It's *not* extra work, and you *are* getting paid for it. An example of extra work would be what happened at Basingstoke the other week. Every member of that team spent most of their weekend sorting out a mess that could have been avoided with some simple procedures that have now been implemented. If anyone else has complaints about the new processes Amit has put in place, please address them to me.'

For a moment, there was silence. Then the Operations Director asked whether anyone had any other issues to discuss. After more silence, the call was brought to an end. Tony smiled as he pressed the red button. He probably wasn't the most popular managing director out there, but at least he was efficient.

He revelled in this thought for just long enough to realise that it was nearly half-past six and he hadn't prepared the starter and hadn't done anything with the hunk of duck on the sideboard. Nor had he hung out the washing as Suze had asked.

He wiped the cream from his keypad. It vibrated in his hand. Guiltily, he unlocked the device and navigated to his unread messages. It was definitely a form of addiction. Either his phone or EnGauge, he wasn't sure which, was turning him into a workaholic.

Most of the emails were daily updates from various regional heads. He'd have to make time to plough through them later. The four-day week wasn't quite turning out as he'd hoped; it was more of a five-day week that involved spending four days at the office, but still, at least he was getting to spend some time with the kids. He brought the device closer to his face. One email stood out from the rest. Its subject line was filled with just one word, *Announcement*, and the sender was none other than the recently appointed CEO, Alistair Marchant.

Tony felt his spirits lift and then promptly fall again as he realised that the To box was filled with the names of all the departmental heads within TransTel, which meant that still, after four weeks and countless emails, voicemails and messages left with various PAs and assistants, he hadn't been acknowledged by the new Chief Exec.

There were always going to be problems, thought Tony, scrolling fractiously through the long list of recipients in search of the message text. Given Marchant's conservative views and his unimaginative approach to business, it was clear that he wouldn't endorse his predecessor's plan to put EnGauge at the heart of the company strategy. The man's career had been built upon boosting traditional businesses using traditional means – investing heavily in sales, cutting out dead wood and signing off giant marketing budgets to stamp out the competition. He was never going to understand the true benefit of an enterprise like EnGauge. But this... this *silent* treatment, it was worse than being at loggerheads. At least if Marchant had voiced his disapproval, Tony would have grounds for a fight.

From: Alistair Marchant, Chief Executive
Subject: Announcement

Dear heads of business,
It is with sadness that I announce the departure of Chief Operating Officer, Graham Walker-Jones, who steps down from his post to take a well-deserved early retirement. We are immensely grateful for everything he has done for the firm and wish him all the best for the future.
I am pleased to announce that in Graham's place, Harvey Grainger, previously Head of Technology for TransTel Retail, will be taking on the role of COO. Harvey has served TransTel

for seven years and brings a wealth of experience from his current position and previous posts. I have no doubt that he will make a valuable and impactful contribution to the organisation.

Yours,

Alistair

Tony read the email twice, taking in the subtleties of wording while he let the implications sink in. *Well-deserved early retirement.* Yeah, right. Clearly Walker-Jones' share options had finally vested and he had decided to officially spend his days on the golf course, rather than doing it on TransTel time. *Immensely grateful.* For what? Sitting at the boardroom table, contributing the occasional word of incomprehensible business jargon? Tony stared at the words. It wasn't the first paragraph that held his attention. By far the more interesting – and potentially damaging – was the news that Harvey Grainger now sat on the board of directors.

Valuable and impactful contribution. What did that mean? Tony couldn't help thinking back to his previous encounters with the Head of Technology and feeling a dark cloud descend upon him. Until now, Tony had navigated the boardroom quagmire by nudging, cajoling and sweet-talking. EnGauge was only where it was today because of Tony's well-honed relationships with certain high-level personnel. Now, the two most important players in the game were new, and they seemed to be playing for the opposition. How was he going to get sign-off on the capital investment required to buy out Automaton?

He was still staring at the text on the screen, still wondering how to plug the giant hole in his forecasts for the North East, when the door burst open to reveal a tsunami of shopping bags and somewhere deep within it, his wife.

'Mummy!' Poppy rushed towards her, tripping headfirst over the barrage.

Suze reached down and swung Poppy into her arms, masterfully distracting her from the imminent wave of tears.

'Have you had a lovely afternoon with Daddy?'

Tony quickly slid the BlackBerry into his back pocket.

'I'm hungry,' declared Poppy, wriggling to be released.

'Have you had your tea?' Suze deposited her outside the ring of shopping bags. 'Tony? Has she had her tea?'

Tony frowned. 'I thought we were eating later, with Emmie and Luke?'

'That's hours away!' Suze strode into the kitchen, pulling a face at the sight of the Raspberry Mess and setting about feeding their daughter. Then she carved the duck into perfect slivers, hung out the washing and swept up a surprising volume of meringue crumbs from the floor.

'Has Jamie had his bottle?' she asked, wiping a stray blob of raspberry juice from the kitchen window.

Tony pulled a face. 'He, um, he had a bit.'

Suze was already holding the bottle up to the light. It looked strangely full.

Tony sighed, feeling inadequate. 'I'm sorry, Suze. It was...' He shrugged. It had felt like a very long, hard afternoon, but he knew it was probably no different to any other that Suze endured on a daily basis. 'I'm useless, I know.'

Suze threw the cloth into the sink and turned to face him. She was smiling.

He leaned back on the kitchen unit as Suze came towards him, wrapping her slender arms round his waist and looking into his eyes.

'No, you're not,' she said. 'You've just got other things on your mind.'

Tony nodded. It was true, but it was no excuse. The national roll-out of EnGauge was taking up too much of his head space. It was important, but it wasn't *that* important. He had failed to feed his children, for God's sake.

'Just one question,' said Suze, glancing over his shoulder and smiling quizzically. 'Why is our oven glove in Mrs Lambert's tree?'

National roll-out

THE CHIEF EXECUTIVE leaned back in his chair and sighed.

'I'm sorry,' he said, pushing the heavy-framed glasses up his nose. 'I can't see that I'm able to help you.'

Tony maintained eye contact, trying not to let his exasperation show. Alistair Marchant looked exactly the same in the flesh as he did in the press photographs: bald, angular and somewhat unattractive, with asymmetrical features that appeared to have been thrown together in a hurry. Despite the heat of the day, he was wearing a pinstriped suit jacket and was sweating profusely.

'It's not really a question of helping *me*,' Tony explained. 'This is about making an investment for TransTel that will generate a return of millions over the next few years.'

'Hmm.' Marchant wiped a handkerchief across his beaded brow. His adam's apple was disconcertingly large, and seemed to travel great distances every time he spoke. 'And therein lies the problem.'

Tony frowned. He couldn't see a problem with the prospect of a multi-million pound return.

'Yes. You see, I'm struggling to see where your little enterprise fits into the TransTel portfolio.'

Tony said nothing for a moment, ignoring the patronising reference to the size of his enterprise – an enterprise that would soon dwarf many TransTel business units if forecasts proved correct. He had two options: Either he could make the point, again, that EnGauge was providing a sizeable and growing new revenue stream in a new market that sat outside the core area in which TransTel played but that was *growing*, or he could give up, return to his office and try to think of another way to raise the capital for the acquisition.

After a moment's indecision, Tony cleared his throat and thanked the Chief Executive for his time. He shook Marchant's clammy hand and walked out, not sure whether he felt more frustrated or less, having finally met the man.

It was a miracle that the meeting had even taken place. After six weeks of silence, the CEO had finally deigned to accept the half-hour meeting with the head of what had, until recently, been one of TransTel's Level 1 priorities for the next five years. There had been no mention of the unreturned phone calls, emails, voicemails or messages.

On autopilot, Tony trod his way down the carpeted corridor to the lift, emerging six floors down and heading into the blinding sunshine. At least they were located away from the main TransTel premises, he thought; that was something.

Impulsively, Tony cut left at the base of the building and perched on the bench overlooking the fake pond. With head in hands, he let out a quiet groan. Marchant was never going to hand over the cap-ex for the acquisition of Automaton – or anything else, for that matter. It was extremely fortunate for Tony that permission – and most importantly, *funding* – to scale up the business had already been granted by the time Marchant had appeared on the scene. EnGauge had sufficient investment to keep going for the next eighteen months, which, at a pinch, would tide them over until break-even, if current sales volumes were indicative. He wasn't so concerned about the long-term; if they could make it through the next two years, their future would be their own. They just needed to get round this singular, burning issue.

Tony pulled out his phone and called the North East Regional Sales Head.

'George speak'n.'

'Hi George, it's Tony.'

'Orrr, right. Hi. What's the story?'

Tony ran a hand through his hair. 'Not good, I'm afraid.'

'So, we're stuck wi'the competition, then?'

'I'm afraid it's looking that way,' Tony admitted. This wasn't the phone call he had been hoping to make to the North East Regional Sales Manager. George had already laid out in no uncertain terms what it would mean for EnGauge if they continued to try and operate in the same area as Automaton.

'Well, like I said, I can't promise you sales – not at these rates. They're all over Tyneside like a rash, and they're cheaper than us.'

Tony sighed. He knew this already. 'Just do your best, eh?'

'And they've got a good name in the area,' George pointed out.

'*We've* got a good name,' Tony countered. 'TransTel's a respected national brand.'

George snorted. 'Hmm. Well, that depends on y'point of view, like.'

'Okay, well...' Tony had had enough. 'I'll catch up with you after the sales call. Speak soon.'

Feeling hot and frustrated, Tony rose from the bench and made his way into the EnGauge atrium, which wasn't noticeably cooler than the air outside, due to its all-glass construction and heating foibles. The Automaton thing was taking up too much of his time. He had to do something: either find a way of competing with the local outfit – which seemed to offer the same service at an extraordinarily low rate, implying that perhaps their quality wasn't as high – or find a way of extinguishing them.

As soon as he reached his desk, there was a knock and Louise's mousy curls appeared at the door.

'Got a mo?'

Tony looked down at his to-do list. He had a dozen regional sales updates to look through, a Q1 report to file, an organisational structure to file for the new COO, the quarterly budget, not to mention rustling up either a killer solution for the North East or a way of generating twelve million pounds. He nodded all the same.

'Did you get my email?' asked Louise, sitting herself down in the spare chair.

Tony half-heartedly glanced at his screen, where

approximately one hundred and twenty emails languished, unread.

'Don't worry,' she said, smiling and producing two identical sheets from the pile on her lap. 'Here.'

Tony nodded his thanks and looked down at the piece of paper. The title read 'Fleet Branding' and the central image on the page was one of green van that looked strangely fuzzy around the edges. He peered closer, then turned to Louise.

'Is that *grass*?'

'It's Astroturf.' She smiled. 'Eye-catching, isn't it?'

Tony held the page up to the light and looked again. It certainly was eye-catching. The vehicle looked like some kind of giant, furry caterpillar that had escaped from captivity.

'We just couldn't *not* go for it,' Louise explained zealously. 'It captures the whole energy-saving, insulating idea perfectly... and it's *green!*'

'It is.'

Tony began to nod, slowly. He didn't want to give the wrong impression; he loved the concept and there was no doubt that it ticked all the boxes. Up until now, EnGauge engineers had been driving up and down the country in plain white vans, identifiable only by the small, green logo below the passenger side door. There was an urgent need to transform the fleet into an advertisement for the service and with marketing like this, Tony could see how effectively it might work. He could even imagine them winning the hearts and minds of consumers – being seen as 'the guys in the grass eco vans'. He just had one small, niggling question. 'How much does it cost?'

Louise looked down at the floor for a second. 'Well, it's a *bit* more expensive than the usual wrapping...'

'How much?' he prompted, wary of her lack of eye contact.

'Six hundred pounds a van.'

Tony fell silent. Some quick mental arithmetic told him they were looking at a half-million pound expenditure – on coating their vans in fake grass. 'How much does a normal wrap cost?'

Louise sucked on her teeth. Until this moment, she'd been a picture of confidence, brimming with pride at her team's creation. Now, Tony caught a glimpse of the old, timid Marketing

Manager who had joined the team eighteen months ago. 'A hundred.'

'Right.' He nodded, letting the silence speak for itself.

After a few seconds, Louise raised her head.

'Please, Tony,' she said, quietly but determinedly. 'It'll pay for itself. Think about it. It's free, mobile advertising – better than TV and outdoor campaigns.'

He raised an eyebrow. 'So we're spending our TV budget on this, are we?'

Louise looked sheepish again. 'Um, well, no... I was hoping we could get some extra...'

Tony managed a wry laugh. 'From TransTel?'

They exchanged a look. There was no need for Tony to spell it out. From now on, they had to survive on the funding they'd been allocated by the Stage Two investment committee. There would be no extra hand-outs from the board.

'Right.' Louise started to nod, looking forlornly at the illustration on her lap. 'I guess not.'

Tony suspected that Louise wasn't altogether surprised by the news; she had just been pushing her luck, carried away by the brilliance of the grass van concept. Everyone within EnGauge understood how things had changed. The rules were different under Alistair Marchant's reign. Feelings were rarely voiced out loud – or at least, not within Tony's earshot – but they all knew. As Managing Director, Tony had done his best to shield his employees from the cold shoulder he was experiencing from the Chief Exec, but they weren't stupid. They knew they had fallen to the bottom of TransTel's priority list.

It wasn't all bad. In a strange way, having a common enemy was a positive thing for the team. It brought them together, made them stronger. In the last few weeks, Tony had noticed a sense of solidarity within EnGauge that he hadn't seen since the early days, when it had been eight people huddled around a meeting room table surrounded by pizza boxes.

'Look,' he said, smiling. 'I can see how much you want this.' He looked again at the turfed van. 'But there's no way the budget can stretch. Can you find a way of doing it for... say, four hundred per van?'

Louise's face remained crumpled. 'Not like this, no.'

Tony sighed. 'I'm sorry, Louise. It's not –'

'I know, it's okay.' Louise was already nodding. 'It's beyond your control, I know.'

The door fell shut behind the Marketing Manager and for a moment, Tony just sat, listening to the hum of the air conditioning and watching the silhouettes of his team through the frosted glass. They had come so far, he thought. *He* had taken them this far, and yet he couldn't take them any further. Louise's request had brought home to him the extent to which his hands were tied. It wasn't as though he expected a green light on an unlimited budget; they could do without turfed vans, he knew that. He just wanted some executive freedom.

The thought of Automaton entered his head once again, along with a familiar sense of frustration. EnGauge was a national business now; it was no longer a fledgling startup within a flailing business unit. It was generating revenues; it deserved some respect. They needed capital in order to progress and if Marchant wasn't going to provide it then he'd have to find some other way.

He made a decision. Suze would hate him for it, he knew, but Tony had reached the end of his tether. He picked up the phone.

'Nicholas speaking.'

'Hi, Nicholas. Tony here. How's it going?'

'Well...' The Finance Director cleared his throat awkwardly. 'So-so.'

Tony made a sympathetic noise. For a man who had until six weeks ago been Acting CEO, it was, he imagined, a bit of a come-down to revert to the role of Finance Director, particularly when it meant reporting to the authoritarian Alistair Marchant. Draper still held the purse-strings, but it was Marchant who called the shots.

'I was wondering...' Tony banished all thoughts of Suze from his mind. 'Whether you fancied dinner again sometime soon?'

'Oh... Well...'

'At ours again, if you like – it's easier, with the children.'

'Oh, yes... of course.' Draper sounded flustered. Tony suspected that he didn't receive many invitations to dinner. 'Well, I'll have to check with Edith, but I'm sure... yes, that would be lovely!'

They bounced various dates back and forth, finally arriving at a couple of options that were suitably distant to give Tony time to break it to his wife, at which point he brought up the real reason for his call.

'Oh – I almost forgot! I wanted to talk to you about a couple of things. Work-related.'

'Fire away.'

'Well, it's a... an opportunity that's come up. I think we'd need to sit down for an hour or so.'

'Ah. Right. Well, this week is fairly chocca...' More tapping noises came down the line. 'How about now?'

Tony looked around at the half-finished due diligence that littered his desk: market share estimates for Automaton, back-of-envelope valuations and marketing collateral collected on the sly. He wasn't ready to discuss the details of the proposed takeover bid – but then, if he didn't take this chance, it might not come again for weeks. He *had* to finance this acquisition.

'I'll be over in five.'

KEEPING AFLOAT
AND
ACHIEVING SCALE

KEEPING AFLOAT AND ACHIEVING SCALE

 MarketGravity

In this chapter EnGauge becomes a real business and no longer a 'trial'.

Many new challenges appear at this stage to test the mettle of a team that is already stretched and battle-weary:

- Infrastructure – systems and processes that were built for a pilot scale are no longer adequate for a full-scale business
- People – team members who have limited experience in managing large scale business issues are unable to make the transition from small-scale trials and pilots
- Processes, structure and procedures – you are a big company now, so structure and efficiency become important, at a risk of stifling the entrepreneurialism
- Integration – you want to exploit the strengths of the parent company, but without squashing the venture by integrating too soon
- Commercialisation routes – there is uncertainty about how to grow and which path to take, either internal or external

This is the time when the business plan is really tested and the company faces a big decision – how to commercialise and scale the venture.

"BEYOND 30 PEOPLE, YOU LOSE THAT SENSE OF 'SMALL BUSINESS'. YOU HAVE TO START DIVIDING, GIVING EACH GROUP 'TEAM GOALS' TO KEEP THEM OPERATING AS A UNIT. THIS MEANS YOU HAVE TO HAVE PEOPLE RESPONSIBLE FOR THE 'JOIN' BETWEEN SILOS."

Veera Johnson, ProcServe

The choice of commercialisation route is influenced by financial and strategic factors. This is illustrated on the framework opposite.

In general:

- If a venture has high strategic relevance and creates a new growth platform, a new business unit should be set up to exploit the opportunity.

- If growth is more linear, but the venture still has strong relevance, then it should be integrated into an existing line of business.

- Initiatives should be exited if they have low growth potential. Companies often take too long to kill off underperforming initiatives, instead undertaking perpetual pilots and trials.

- If a moderate growth venture is not relevant to the future core business, it should be sold to an organisation that will invest.

- A high-growth venture with limited strategic alignment to the core business should be spun out, potentially in partnership with others to create the right conditions for success.

Try applying the framework to a venture that you've worked on and see if the company made the right decision.

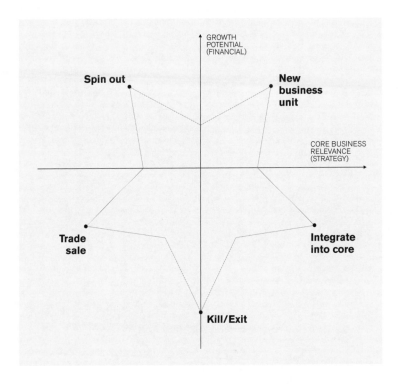

10

Coming down: what to do now that the world's stopped spinning

'Letting go is the hardest part - a corporate entrepreneur never stops innovating.'

Competitive offering emerges

TONY PULLED UP another browser and typed the company name into the search box again. Dozens of results filled the screen, all of them less than a day old. A-LISTERS DEMAND ANSWERS, screamed the latest headline. TransTel SHARES PLUMMET ON THE BACK OF DATA ERROR, read another. PRIVACY ROW RE-IGNITED. Tony scanned the words with mounting despair, clicking on an article at random, entitled CELEBRITY DATABASE LEAK: HOW IT HAPPENED. He closed his eyes, leaned back in his chair and let out a long, exasperated sigh.

The previous week, a junior analyst from somewhere deep within TransTel Data Processing had sent a data file to a colleague, by email. This file had contained the names, addresses and bank card details of every celebrity who had donated or contributed to TransTel's most recent fundraising effort, the Charity Singathon. Unfortunately for the junior analyst – who had not been named, although Tony suspected it was only a matter of time – the email address of the recipient had contained a small typing error, which meant that the data had arrived, unencrypted, in the hands of a young man at Transtel.org. who had sold the file to a tabloid newspaper, which had printed the contents of the file, as well as the story behind its leak, across yesterday's pages. TransTel's name, thanks to one small error of the letter 'e', was mud.

The repercussions were deep and far-flung. Celebrities were voicing their rage in every gossip column and trashy magazine on the shelves, corporate clients were threatening to withdraw their business on grounds of inadequate security, phone lines were jammed with concerned customers and TransTel shares were down six percent on the previous week. Every business unit that had some association with TransTel, however small, was affected, and EnGauge was no different.

There was a knock on the door. Tony hauled his eyes open and looked up.

'Hey, Matt.' He wearily beckoned the Sales Manager in. 'Don't tell me, you're not hitting targets because nobody wants to buy from TransTel and all your resources have been sent to field the complaints calls.'

'Well,' Matt fell heavily into the visitors' chair. 'No, actually. I assumed you'd already know that.'

Tony raised an eyebrow. 'Go on, then.'

'Measure.'

'I'm sorry?'

'Mare shore.'

'What?'

'Me sure.'

Tony leaned forward and frowned at Matt. 'I'm sorry, but what are you trying to say?'

Matt shrugged. 'We dunno how it's supposed to be pronounced, but it's National Electric's energy monitoring service. Spelt Me-Sure, like En-Gauge. It launched today. Bloody identical to ours. Check it out.' He nodded toward Tony's computer screen, which was filled with depressing words about TransTel's plummeting reputation.

Tony typed MeSure into the search box and was alarmed to see nearly fifty million hits, until he realised that the word was also French for 'measure', and that only the paid-for results actually related to National Electric's offering.

'Hmm,' he said quietly, browsing the website and assessing the various subscription packages available. From what he could tell, the service was indeed identical to that of EnGauge, right down to the promise of *fitting without the fuss* – or, in this case, *installation without the aggravation.*

Tony eventually pulled himself away from the website, which was remarkably similar to that of EnGauge but in blue instead of green.

'They couldn't have struck luckier on the timing front,' he said, his mind wandering back to the raft of negative press that reflected the current sentiment for all things TransTel. 'We should find out where they're operating. They can't be national, yet. Maybe–'

'South East,' said Matt. 'I checked. Looks like they're following the same roll-out plan as us.'

Tony nodded unhappily. 'I wonder whether we could put a call in, do a bit of a mystery shop thing, to find out their–'

'Already did. Their pricing's the same as ours. To the penny, pretty-much.'

Tony nodded again, relieved to hear that they weren't being undercut, but also ashamed that his every suggestion had been pre-empted. It wasn't that he didn't approve of Matt's initiative; it was a blessing, and a vast improvement on the resentful apathy that had come before. It was just... Well, he was supposed to be in charge. Increasingly these days, Tony found himself serving as more of a mute onlooker than a chief.

'I suggest we keep a close eye on them,' Tony replied, desperately trying to think of something more useful to add. We can look to step up our sales efforts in the areas we know they're targeting.'

Matt nodded, heaving himself to his feet.

Tony watched as the salesman lumbered towards the door. 'Oh, and Matt?' He *was* going to add value. 'Don't worry. We knew this would happen. We were the first-movers, but there were always going to be fast-followers. We just have to make sure we use our advantage.'

Alone in his office, Tony sat, thinking about this new rival and what it meant for EnGauge. They'd been live across the nation for months now, they had proven the business case, so it was natural to expect copycat entrants. As the incumbent, EnGauge had to expect some erosion of its customer base. It wasn't just the customers who were at risk of jumping across to the opposition, either. More of a threat, in Tony's mind, was the risk of losing key personnel.

He knew what he had to do. To ward off both threats, he had to keep moving, keep changing. If the business stood still, competitors would overtake and EnGauge would cease to be seen as an interesting, dynamic place to work. In short, he had to bring some variety into 'business as usual'.

Clicking around on the blue-tinted website, Tony found his thoughts wandering to the other, more established competitor on the scene: Automaton. His meeting with Draper had been nearly a week ago; by now the FD must have met with the Chief Executive.

A quick scan of his emails revealed nothing from Draper, only a rather ominous message from Harvey Grainger, announcing to all Heads of Department that he would shortly be implementing a company-wide 'streamlining initiative'. Tony groaned out loud as he picked up the phone. He knew from experience what streamlining initiatives usually entailed.

'Nicholas, it's Tony.'

'Ah. Anthony.' Draper's tone implied that he rather regretted picking up the phone.

'Just wondered whether there's any movement on the Automaton front.'

'Right. Yes. Um... Well, I have certainly broached the subject with Alistair.'

'Oh yes?'

'Y-yes,' Draper stammered. 'Yes. He wasn't... *entirely* convinced, shall we say.'

Tony said nothing.

'Not yet,' Draper clarified awkwardly. 'It's not dead in the water, you understand. I'm sure I can work on him.'

Tony felt a flicker of hope rise up inside him, then fade again as he remembered his sole encounter with the domineering CEO. 'Thanks,' he said. 'Please do, if you can.'

Dropping the phone into its cradle, Tony turned to his computer and made a half-hearted attempt to get on with his work. The browsers were still open behind his emails, reminding him simultaneously of the mounting competitive pressure and the crashing reputation of the parent company. He felt angry, all of a sudden: angry that TransTel still wielded so much power over EnGauge despite its total lack of ongoing commitment, and angry that EnGauge was suffering so badly as a result of TransTel's failings.

TransTel was acting like an over-protective parent, trying to maintain control over a child who had flown the nest. True, the parent had invested a great deal during the early years, but that was what happened when you brought something into the world. Now, the child had grown up; it was independent. If TransTel couldn't stump up the cash for the Automaton bid, they would find it elsewhere. EnGauge could stand on its own two feet.

'Louise?' he called, sticking his head round the door and nodding for her to follow him inside. 'Where do we stand on the fleet branding? Have we pressed go yet?'

'Not quite,' she replied, apologetically. 'We're just waiting for the high-res image from the–'

'Good,' he said.

'We should have it any minute,' she explained. 'I can hurry–'

'No, I mean, good that we *haven't* pressed go yet.'

'Sorry?'

'I want to change something.'

'On the... the designs?' Louise looked at him anxiously.

'Yes, on the designs.' Tony bent over his desk and pulled up the most recent email from Louise, containing the final graphics for the green, partially-turfed vans. 'Here,' he said, pointing to the text underneath the logo. 'I want you to delete this line.'

Louise frowned. 'What... You want to remove *A TransTel company*?'

Tony nodded. 'That's right. And the same on every element of our branding.'

'Um...' Louise clearly thought he had lost it, but didn't voice her concerns. 'Okay.'

Tony smiled as she left the room.

Until recently, the TransTel brand had opened doors. Now, it was slamming them shut. EnGauge was growing up. It was no longer defined by its parents; it was an entity in its own right. It was time they cut themselves loose.

Picnic with Emmie and Luke; no longer needed?

'BADDY NEEDS a wee! Baddy needs a wee!'

Poppy galloped up to the picnic rug, Bradley limping along with his head in the crook of her arm.

Emmie was already on her feet, foraging for her flip-flops in the long grass and turning down her husband's belated offers of assistance – which, even by Tony's standards, seemed lame. By the time Luke had hauled himself into an upright position, his wife and son had already disappeared behind a nearby bush.

It was a hot, sunny Friday in August. The picnic had been Emmie's idea, although Tony and Luke – Luke having sacked off a community radio convention in Coventry and Tony making use of his day off – had played a key part in the organisation. Tony's day away from the office was becoming a rather enjoyable feature in his week. He was finding that his workload no longer dictated which day he took off, but rather the other way round. He had taken to checking the long-range weather forecast and picking the day with the sunniest outlook to spend with the kids.

'What are you doing?'

Tony looked up. Suze was using her stern, warning tone.

The perpetrator, this time, was Poppy, who had discovered the bag in which Suze had hidden the chocolate brownies and was trying to crawl inside it.

'Just checking.'

Poppy emerged, looking wide-eyed and innocent, then proceeded to poke at the multiple layers of plastic behind her back.

'Do you want a carrot stick?' offered Suze.

Poppy screwed up her nose. 'No.'

Nice try, mouthed Tony, catching his wife's eye.

'An apple?' she suggested, one-handedly doing up the clasp on her bra whilst manoeuvring Jamie into a sleeping position.

Poppy shook her head, feeling her way further into the bag. 'I want a *brownie!*'

After a confusing exchange of facial expressions, Tony realised that his wife was implying that he ought to intervene, which he did, by reaching for the bag of brownies and distributing the contents between Poppy and Bradley, who had just reappeared on the scene.

Suze flashed him her customary despairing look as the children skipped off to build a den in the nearby sandpit, full of energy. Tony didn't mind. He liked to spoil his little girl.

It wasn't just the sight of Poppy, skipping about, or the feel of the warm sunshine on his bare flesh that was lifting his spirits today. There was something else, too. Something he couldn't disclose to anyone else yet, but something that would, he hoped, change the course of history – well, in the North East, at least.

At one o'clock the previous day, TransTel had presented Automaton with a takeover bid worth twelve million pounds. It wasn't yet public, and it was too soon to have an answer from the target, but Tony had a good feeling about it. According to his calculations, the figure was an over-valuation to start with, and he knew that the board never went into these negotiations without some contingency up their sleeve. The fact that Marchant had eventually endorsed the bid was an indication that he was planning to see it through. It wasn't a done deal, as Tony kept reminding himself, but it had the best possible chances.

'What're you smirking for?' slurred Luke.

Tony quickly wiped the moronic grin from his face and realised that Luke had probably been squinting at him for some time. 'Just... thinking.'

'About work?' Luke raised an eyebrow. It was more of a statement than a question.

As if on command, Tony's BlackBerry buzzed. He glanced

sideways at Suze, who was studiously ignoring him, then down at the handset. It was Amit.

Tony watched the device as it vibrated on his lap. He was considering not picking up. Amit was more than capable of making decisions in his absence. But then... Tony thought for a second and decided that Amit probably wouldn't be calling unless it was urgent.

He picked up the phone just as the line went dead. Pressing redial, Tony went straight through to voicemail, so he hung up. A minute later, there was still no message, so he tried again.

Amit wasn't picking up. Tony rose to his feet and wandered across the grass so that he was out of earshot. He knew how Suze hated his business calls.

'Hi Maureen, it's Tony. Is Amit there?'

There was a long pause during which, presumably, Maureen eased herself into a position from which she could see Amit's desk. In the distance, Poppy was conducting a military-style squad selection for the construction of her den.

'No,' Maureen replied, eventually.

'Right. Well, I missed a call from him. D'you know what that would've been about?'

The question turned out to be too complex for Maureen, who started mumbling incoherently in a way that Tony had learned to ignore.

'Is Billy there?' he asked, speaking over her.

There was more laboured breathing while Maureen sought out the Operations Manager in the open-plan office.

'No,' came the long-awaited reply.

'Do you know if either Amit or Billy has been having problems with anything today?'

'Mmm... No...'

Tony considered trying to break down Maureen's response, but then realised that there was a quicker and easier option. He would send an email.

'Okay, thanks Maureen. I'll see you on Monday.'

Tony sighed as he put down the phone, frustrated and mildly concerned. Across the park, Poppy was shrieking instructions at her young recruits as the beginnings of a somewhat ambitious, igloo-like structure began to rise up out of sand.

Scanning his inbox, Tony could find no clues as to why his Operations Director might have called. He did, however, spot a follow-up email from the new COO, regarding the imminent 'streamlining initiative' that was to be rolled out across the firm. With a feeling of trepidation, Tony clicked on the message. Three words immediately jumped out at him: *essential headcount reductions.* He knew what this meant. He knew, even before he had read the remainder of the email, what he would have to do – and he wasn't looking forward to it.

'Problem solved?' asked Luke, as he returned to the picnic rug, having fired off an email to Amit and Billy.

'Sort of.' Tony shrugged, trying to let go of his anxieties. The headcount reductions could wait until the following week.

'What're you up to now, anyway? You haven't moaned to me in a while; surely you haven't got everything running smoothly, have you?'

Tony gave a hollow laugh, watching as his daughter, in the distance, laid the final spadeful of sand on the precarious canopy and whooped in delight before running round and perching just inside, like a queen on a throne.

He thought about Luke's question. *Had* he got everything running smoothly? Every day, there were niggles, like regional managers not playing ball, salesmen receiving the wrong commission and installations getting double-booked, but they were small, local issues that could be resolved with a phone call or a site visit. On the whole, through a combination of his own tenacity and the combined efforts of the team, things were ship-shape. The truth was, he *had* got everything running smoothly at EnGauge.

Luke rolled onto his stomach and looking at Tony. 'Spill the beans. What's new?'

Tony looked over to the sand igloo, where Poppy, Bradley and a handful of helpers were playing. What was new? Nothing. The landscape was changing, gradually, with the influx of new competitors and a few changes to the regulations, but in terms of what was happening inside EnGauge, it was business as usual. The only thing 'going on' was the acquisition of Automaton, which was confidential for the time being, and that, if or when it happened, was essentially the final piece in the jigsaw. After that, Tony's job was to keep things moving – not to *make* things move.

A shudder ran through Tony, despite the heat of the day. The jigsaw was nearly complete. Some people, he suspected, might feel some kind of thrill, to know that their work was virtually done – that they were so close to achieving their goal. For Tony, though, it was a sensation that felt more like... dread. His working life was developing a rhythm. There were ups and downs, but they were small. He came in at nine every day and rarely stayed beyond six. He was becoming... *settled*.

The sandpit, he noticed, was now empty, the igloo abandoned. Mission complete, the kids had wandered off in search of a fresh challenge. As he contemplated his response to Luke's question, he felt his BlackBerry buzz.

It was Amit.

'Hey, I'm sorry I missed your call,' gabbled Tony. 'I couldn't get hold of you when I tried to call back. Is everything okay?'

Amit laughed softly. 'Calm down, mate. We just had a bit of an issue with the Edinburgh call centre, but–'

'An issue?'

'Yeah, just a resourcing thing. But look, it's fine now. I'd forgotten it was your day off.'

'Oh.' Tony nodded into the handset, half inclined to enquire further about the resourcing issue but not wanting to doubt Amit's abilities.

'I'm just calling to put your mind at rest. There's nothing for you to worry about.'

'Right. So you don't need...'

'Everything's fine, Tony. Enjoy your day off.'

Luke was smiling when he came off the phone.

'Sounds as though everything's running a bit *too* smoothly.' He chuckled. 'You've done yourself out of a job.'

Tony smiled wryly. He wasn't going to voice his opinions out loud, but the truth was, for a while now he had been thinking exactly that.

Tony makes some redundancies

TONY STARED at the email, trying to feel some of the excitement he knew he ought to be feeling. The final piece of the jigsaw had been laid. Late last night, after lengthy negotiations, Automaton had accepted an offer of £12.3m, which meant that EnGauge would shortly become the largest and most prolific energy monitoring service in the country. It was a momentous day for the business – but it was also a sad one.

Harvey Grainger's streamlining initiative had kicked off in earnest and TransTel was a blood bath. Heads were rolling from every division and from every level. There were employees who had joined the apprenticeship scheme more than twenty years ago being turned out onto the street alongside new graduates.

Earlier in the day, Tony had ventured over to the main TransTel offices and seen the effects for himself. People were avoiding eye contact, as though fearful of drawing attention to themselves. Corridors and stairwells were eerily quiet. You could smell the fear in the air.

Despite his best efforts, Tony had failed to secure any form of exemption for EnGauge. He'd tried reasoning, he'd tried hard-talking and he'd even attempted to tug on Harvey Grainger's heart strings, telling stories from the early days of EnGauge when his team had pulled together, working late, abandoning their families... to no avail. Harvey Grainger had no heart.

On reflection, thought Tony, it was hardly surprising that Grainger wouldn't budge. Their altercations during the early days of EnGauge had involved the then Head of Technology attempting and failing to claim the initiative as his own. The two men had been at loggerheads ever since they had met. And besides, it was becoming increasingly obvious to Tony that this streamlining exercise did not actually come from Grainger at all.

Alistair Marchant was behind the cuts. He had delegated the task to his new COO, perhaps as a test, or perhaps because he wanted a scapegoat, but ultimately, the instructions had come from the top. It shouldn't have come as a surprise; efficiency drives were Marchant's mode d'emploi. This was his operational signature.

It was five minutes to ten. Tony tried to read through some emails, but he couldn't concentrate. All he could think about was the person who would soon be walking through his office door for the very last time. He thought back to the early days, when the EnGauge concept hadn't even been conceived. In workshops, when everyone else had been throwing sweets and coming up with ludicrous ideas, one person had remained focused. Then, when the pilot had gone live, this person had nurtured it to success – always the last to leave at night, often still there in the morning, having fallen asleep in the makeshift HQ, grappling with algorithms and codes.

There was a knock at the door. With a heavy heart, Tony rose to his feet. It had been Norm, he suddenly realised, who had mentioned the eFlow widget in the first place – the device that underpinned the whole EnGauge business.

'How's things?' asked Tony, motioning for him to take a seat. The sense of guilt was overwhelming.

Norm shrugged. His posture seemed different. He was stooping, like an older man.

Every fibre in Tony's body was willing him to abort the mission, to open up a discussion about the technical challenges that Norm's team faced. But he couldn't. He had made his decision and it was only fair to get straight to the point. 'I suppose you know about the streamlining operation that's being rolled out across TransTel?'

Norm nodded without making eye contact. *He knew*, thought Tony. He was just waiting to be told.

'I've been asked to make some cost savings, despite the fact that EnGauge is only a few months old and we're trying to expand.'

Another nod. Jesus, this was hard. It wasn't the first time Tony had given this speech, but this was definitely the worst.

'As you know, Technology is one of the areas in which we're no longer expanding so rapidly, and after some careful consideration, I've decided that some of the positions within the division can be merged with others. Unfortunately, yours is one of those positions.'

Norm's facial expression barely changed. He just sat, staring into space as though nothing had happened.

After a few seconds, Tony found it too much to bear.

'I'm sorry, mate,' he said. 'You've done incredible things here at EnGauge. Please don't see this as a reflection of your work. It's just a numbers game... I had to make cuts, and technology was the obvious place.'

Slowly, Norm nodded again. Tony forced himself not to dwell on the questions that had started to mushroom in his mind: What would he do now? Did he have savings? Had he ever worked anywhere other than TransTel? Did he have a family to support, or did he really live with his mum, as the rumours suggested?

'There's no need to work your notice period,' Tony explained, watching as Norm rose to his feet, still nodding. It was as though he had gone into a state of shock. 'I've told HR you'll be over to see them later today. If that's... okay?'

'Fine,' Norm said quietly. A shaky hand rose up to straighten the knot in his worn, brown tie. 'Do I go over at a particular time?'

'Probably best you call them before you head over,' Tony replied. It was as though they were acting out a bad screenplay. Nothing sounded natural. The words were just being read from the script.

With a final nod, Norm turned and shuffled out, leaving Tony feeling utterly cold. It was true, in a way, what he'd said about the merger of roles; Norm's position had become less and less important as the business had grown, but what he hadn't explained was the fact that Norm's skill set was no longer of use to the business. He had been invaluable in the early days, but now the codes were written. The circuits worked. The online interface was a networked solution. There was no need for Norm's expertise.

Tony sighed, forced the guilt from his mind and looked down at his list. One down, five to go.

Almost immediately, there was another knock on the door. Tony checked the time and frowned. His next victim was only due at eleven.

'Come in,' he said wearily.

Louise poked her head round the door.

'I've got some news,' she said, skipping over to the chair that Norm had just vacated and perching daintily on its edge.

Ordinarily, the promise of news would have made Tony's heart sink, but today, he suspected it couldn't sink much lower, and besides, Louise's expression implied that the news might actually be positive.

'I don't know if you've heard,' she said with a toothy grin. 'But Matt and I are getting married.'

For a moment, Tony couldn't speak. The news was so far removed from everything else on his mind, it took a few seconds for him to shift gear and work out what Louise actually meant.

'That's... fantastic!' he managed, eventually. Louise wasn't to know that minutes earlier, he had been doling out equally life-changing news that was as bad as this was good. And it really was fantastic. This was a genuine EnGauge romance – an EnGauge *engagement!* If it hadn't been for the Christmas party he'd laid on last year, this relationship might never have happened.

'Congratulations!' he cried, jumping up and embracing his Marketing Manager.

'Thanks,' she replied, looking away bashfully, the grin still engulfing her face.

Louise didn't leave the room. She stood, shifting her weight from foot to foot, looking at him. Tony sensed there was more news to come.

'We... figured that with all this restructuring and streamlining, and given that we didn't want to be working *and* living together when we were married...'

Tony waited anxiously for the punch line. He had already guessed what it was.

'I applied for another job – an internal move – and today I found out I got it. So as of September, I'll be Head of Marketing for TransTel Retail, reporting to Anita Reynolds.'

'Oh.'

Tony was struggling to take it all in. Louise really was leaving him.

'I think Julie will grow into the role,' Louise said quickly. 'She's very assertive and she's been under my wing for a while now.'

Tony nodded, not doubting her words. He was still coming to terms with all the changes. Less than a year ago, Louise had tried to resign as a result of her inexperience and lack of self-confidence. Now, she was going off to work for the frumpy, suited bulldog that was Anita Reynolds. Louise had changed. She had grown with the business, and Matt, well, he had changed too.

'Sorry if it comes as a shock,' said Louise. She was still smiling as she rose to her feet and headed for the door. 'We were trying to keep things under wraps, you know...'

'No, yes, of course.' Tony nodded. 'Congratulations, again – on both fronts.'

'Thanks.'

Louise was halfway through the door when she stopped and turned.

'Did you hear about Roy, by the way?'

'What about him?' Tony thought for a second. Since EnGauge had split off from Synapse, he had barely crossed paths with the man.

'He, um, well...'

Tony closed his eyes. He knew exactly what she was trying to say. Roy had been made redundant from Synapse. Since the separation of EnGauge from the main part of TransTel, Tony had all but lost touch with the colleagues he'd left behind.

'I think he was offered another position, in TransTel Cordless Enterprises or somewhere, but he decided to call it a day. He's taking early retirement.'

Tony nodded, managing a thin smile as she left the room. After forty-odd years, Roy Smith was leaving TransTel. His head was swimming. Images from the last two years flashed across his mind: Roy arguing, Louise apologising, Matt moaning, and Norm, hunched over his keyboard late at night, rubbing his eyes and talking in unintelligible code.

It was the end of an era. It was, he realised, time to move on.

Coffee with Amit and Brian

'NOW, TONY. Hear me out. This is a great opportunity, and from what I can tell, the role is a perfect fit with your *extensive* skill set. Let me just tell you a little more about the initiative...'

Tony nodded his head, pretending to listen, not quite bold enough to stop the Chief Executive in his tracks. *Extensive skill set* indeed. He thought back to their first encounter and the number of phone calls and emails it had taken to make it happen. It was amazing what a few million pounds of revenue did for your reputation.

One hour and forty-five minutes was the precise length of time that had elapsed between Tony walking out of Natasha's office that morning and a window miraculously appearing in Alistair Marchant's diary. Tony had known that HR would do their best to persuade him to stay, trying to tempt him with vacant positions, suggesting that he went away and reconsidered his decision, but the call from Marchant's PA had come as something of a surprise. It was flattering, he thought, half-tuning in to the stream of bullshit and noticing for the first time that the Chief Executive was sporting the beginnings of a comb-over.

'...exciting, ground-breaking initiative... ...someone with creativity and *tenacity*... ...bottom up approach...'

He tuned out again. It felt good to have resigned. The previous night, Tony had started to doubt his intentions. As his wife had rightfully pointed out, her maternity pay was barely enough to keep Jamie in nappies, let alone feed a family of four, and as yet, Tony hadn't started to think about alternative roles.

But now, hearing the CEO's lame and somewhat hypocritical attempt to keep him at the firm, his decision made more sense than ever.

'Isn't that the sort of role you'd be good at? Aren't you the type of man who likes a challenge?'

Tony looked at the man.

'Sorry,' he said. 'But you don't seem to have explained what the challenge actually *is*.'

'Well...' Marchant looked nonplussed. 'It's a strategic initiative aimed at bringing TransTel closer to the regulatory bodies–'

'But what *is* it?' Tony demanded. 'What does it do?'

Marchant cleared his throat, maintaining his false smile. 'The initiative consists of a core team of people,' he said, slowly, 'that develops key strategic relationships between regulatory bodies and core elements of the TransTel network.'

'So...' He had one last go at clarifying. 'It's not actually a business unit at all? It doesn't generate any money for the firm?'

'Oh, it does!' Marchant leaned forward and slammed his hand down on the table. 'Indirectly. These relationships will be *critical* to generating and sustaining revenues across the firm!'

Tony looked Marchant in the eye. The man was so far off the mark, it was almost laughable.

'I'm sorry, but I just don't think it's for me.'

Predictably, Marchant started waffling on about boundless development potential and once-in-a-lifetime opportunities. Tony looked at the clock and realised that he was five minutes late for his coffee with Amit and Brian.

'I'm sorry,' he said again, more firmly this time. 'I've made up my mind. I wouldn't be right for the role – or for any other role at TransTel, in fact.' Tony looked him in the eye. 'I'm after a fresh challenge.'

Eventually, Marchant accepted defeat and held out a sweaty palm. There were a few mumbled, parting words as they shook hands, then, with a sense of mounting excitement, Tony walked out of the oak-panelled room for the very last time.

It was true, what he'd told the CEO. He *was* after a fresh challenge. He wasn't right for the regulatory relationships role and actually, he was no longer right for TransTel. The catalyst for change had been the realisation that EnGauge no longer needed him; his skills lay in turning business units around and EnGauge was now sailing straight. But there was more to it than that. TransTel had changed. The incoming management was steering the firm in a new direction that didn't entirely make sense in his mind, and although he wasn't going to admit it to Marchant, Tony wasn't sure he could continue to operate in such a constrained environment.

Brian and Amit were sitting at their usual table in the canteen, nearest the exit and furthest from the giant screen that was blaring out uninspiring revelations from the TransTel Initiatives Centre.

'Sorry I'm late.'

Tony pulled out a chair and set down the plate of chocolate cookies between them.

'Special occasion?' asked Brian, glancing sideways at Amit and reaching for one of the cookies.

Tony gave a mysterious smile as he sat down.

'As it happens,' he said, watching Brian fish around in the dregs of his coffee for a lump of congealed cookie, 'I do have some news.'

Brian reached for Tony's teaspoon. Amit was watching him with a bemused smile on his face.

'I've resigned,' said Tony.

Brian made a half-hearted 'mmm' noise, although it wasn't clear whether this was in response to Tony's announcement or the fact that he'd just retrieved the bulk of the cookie from his cup. Amit said nothing.

'Er, did anyone hear me?' Tony looked from Brian to Amit and then back again. 'I said, I've resigned.'

Brian tipped back his cup, swallowed the contents and set it back down on the table, looking at Tony and letting out a quiet belch.

'Yeah, we heard. We were waiting for some *news*, Tony.'

'What?'

'Jesus Christ, mate. Did you expect us to be surprised? You've been on your way out for months!'

Tony frowned, looking at Amit for an explanation.

Amit shrugged. 'It was rather obvious,' he said, quietly. 'We assumed this was why you'd suggested the coffee.'

'We were thinking of running a sweepstake on how long it'd take,' added Brian.

Tony wasn't sure how to react. *He* had had no idea that he'd been on his way out for months.

'Is it a done deal, then?' asked Amit. 'Or are they in the process of trying to claw you back?'

'They tried,' he replied, smiling. 'But I broke off negotiations to come and have coffee.'

'I'm honoured,' said Brian.

'Who was chief negotiator?' asked Amit. 'The lovely Natasha?'

Tony smiled. 'Mr Marchant himself.'

'I *am* honoured,' said Brian, eyes wide.

'Don't be. I walked out because I couldn't stand any more of his bullshit. And because the carrot they seem to be dangling in front of me consists of some regulatory relationships bollocks that would mean reporting to Harvey Grainger.'

Amit let out a slow, hollow laugh. 'Oh dear. They really haven't understood you very well, have they?' He took a long sip of his coffee and looked at Tony. 'Have you got something else lined up?'

Tony shook his head. 'Not yet. I'll start looking around while I'm working my notice.'

Brian nudged Amit. 'Go on,' he said, in a quiet, urgent tone.

Amit glanced sideways at Brian and smiled.

'What?' Tony asked again.

'Well, I had a call from Charles the other day.'

Tony frowned. 'Charles Gable? The old Chief Exec?'

'Indeed. He's a non-executive director for a firm called EcoElectric, one of the new green energy firms. They're looking for someone to expand the business.'

Tony felt something flicker inside him. 'Really?'

'I told him you'd soon be available.'

'Wh... You what?'

Amit just shrugged.

Slowly, Tony began to smile. 'Well,' he said. 'Nice to know I'm that transparent.'

Brian and Amit both nodded.

'I'll send you his contact details,' Amit promised.

By mutual agreement, they pushed aside their empty cups and stood up.

'So,' said Brian, as he prepared to head off. 'I guess this means your role needs filling...?' He turned and looked pointedly at Amit.

It was Tony's turn to smile. 'Oh, don't you worry, Amit. I've already put in a good word.'

Amit turned to him. 'What?'

Tony nodded. 'Looks as though I'm not the only transparent one around here.'

Letting go

'DADDY, WHERE'S my bottle?'

Tony opened the cupboard under the sink and realised, to his astonishment, that he had subconsciously remembered the whereabouts of his daughter's special bottle without having to ask his wife. This was unprecedented. It was incredible the difference it made, not having your mind filled with thoughts of product extensions and competitive threats and regulatory change.

A week ago, he had said his goodbyes and driven out of the TransTel business park for the very last time. He still thought about the world he had left behind, of course, but it was no longer his job to do so. Amit now held that responsibility, and Tony had no doubt he would take on the role with ease.

Bottle filled, lunch box packed, shoes on, they were finally ready to go.

'Do you want to go and say 'bye to mummy?'

Poppy rushed upstairs and barged noisily into the bedroom, where Suze, Tony realised too late, was trying to pacify her son after a fitful night's sleep. Eventually, they closed the front door on the screams and set off into the September sunshine.

Conveniently, St Gregory's Primary School was located less than half a mile down the road. It was known for its state-of-the-art building design and its imaginative take on the national curriculum – something that seemed well-suited to Poppy's personality. Over the course of the last few weeks, Suze had taken great care to cultivate an enticing image of the establishment, making detours on sunny afternoons and pointing out all the exciting activities on offer at break time and all the fun the 'big girls' were having. Predictably, Poppy now couldn't wait to enrol.

'Will I be able to play on the roof?' asked Poppy, skipping along beside him, explorer rucksack strapped to her back.

Tony reached for her hand as they crossed a side road. The roof of St Gregory's was something of a local feature. In keeping with the modern design of the school, it was fitted with solar panels and, between the panels, an array of plants that changed colour throughout the year. It was currently a vivid shade of pink. 'I'm not sure the roof is for playing on,' he explained, 'but I think there's an adventure playground.'

Poppy frowned, contemplating what would no doubt be the first of many anticlimaxes that day.

'Will I meet the Elephant Woman?' she asked.

Tony quickly switched to his stern voice, hoping to prevent an awkward playground situation. 'If you do, then you shouldn't call her that.'

As part of the preparation for Poppy's big day, Suze had insisted they look at the website for St Gregory's, which displayed, among other things, images of every teacher, as drawn by pupils of the school. Unfortunately, one such teacher had been drawn with enormous ears, grey complexion and trunk-like legs. It had been Tony who had referred to her as the Elephant Woman, not thinking at the time that the phrase might stick.

'Why not?' asked Poppy.

'Because it's rude. Elephants are ugly, so by calling her Elephant Woman, you're implying that *she* is ugly.'

'Elephants aren't ugly.'

'Well, some people think they are.'

'But *I* don't, so if I call her Elephant Woman then I'm not calling her ugly.'

Tony silently cursed his four-year-old's impeccable logic. 'It's probably best you don't call her Elephant Woman, just in case.'

Poppy fell silent again.

They turned the corner and headed towards the giant, floral

roof up ahead. Tony's thoughts lingered momentarily on the Elephant Woman, but soon drifted. He wondered what would happen when Louise vacated her post. Would Julie step into her shoes, or would they find an interim replacement? Tony knew what he'd do in that situation. Given his experiences with Billy, he wouldn't entrust such a junior executive to such an important role.

'Daddy?'

Tony blinked. He *had* to stop worrying about these things.

'Yes?'

'Why isn't Baddy coming to school?'

'Because he's a little bit younger than you,' he replied. 'He starts in January.'

Poppy seemed satisfied with this response, then a few seconds later, she looked up again.

'I wish Baddy was starting now.'

Tony looked down at his daughter and smiled. She had put on an admirable display of bravado up until now, but she was clearly apprehensive about her first day.

'Listen,' he said, crouching beside her as they waited to cross the main road. 'The reason you're starting school today is that you're a *big girl*. You're ready to go and have fun on the adventure playground and make new friends. You're lucky that your birthday is in April. Poor Bradley has to wait another four months!'

Poppy eyed him warily, reaching for his hand as he rose to his feet again and the traffic – the only thing separating them from their destination – whooshed past. Tony wondered what effect his words had had – if any. Poppy was only four, but she was old enough to feel fear. And for all her parents' heartening words, there was, Tony knew, something terrifying about starting something new and unknown. He understood this as well as anyone, not least because he was feeling the same thing himself.

Two weeks ago, following multiple rounds of interviews, Tony had been offered a job at EcoElectricity. His challenge, which started the following Monday, was to take on the company's Residential Business Unit – a unit that had been teetering on the brink of collapse since its inception half a decade ago – and to turn it profitable within five years. Even before he had stepped into his first interview, Tony had known that it was the right job for him. When the task had been deemed 'near impossible' by none other than Charles Gable, the man who had set him his last challenge, Tony's suspicions had been confirmed. He had found his next project.

'Daddy, look!'

Tony felt a sharp tug on his arm and realised the lights had changed. Then he saw what his daughter was looking at. It wasn't the traffic lights; it was the vehicle pulling up at the crossing. Tufts of fake grass stuck up from its roof and sides, and a large, familiar logo adorned the driver's door.

'En-gay!' she cried excitedly, pulling him in front of the van as a brightly coloured crossing attendant ushered them across.

Tony felt a rush of unexpected emotion. He smiled and raised a hand to the driver, who nodded back, oblivious to the significance of the encounter. As they reached the other side, Tony couldn't help glancing over his shoulder and watching the van pull away, feeling an overwhelming sense of pride. *He* was responsible for that van. He was the one who had made it all happen.

'Can I take your name, please?'

'Poppy Sharp,' his daughter replied, before Tony had registered the question.

The woman on the gate looked down at her clipboard, muttering the name under her breath until she found it on the list.

'Right! So, Poppy, you're in Reception Class One, which means you need to head to the corner of the playground and then go through the red door at the end, with the other children, okay?'

Poppy nodded and started to walk off in the direction indicated.

'Er, Mr Sharp?' The woman looked at him.

Tony stopped in the middle of the playground.

'No parents beyond the school gates, I'm afraid.'

He faltered, watching as his daughter headed boldly for the door in the corner of the yard. He thought about calling out to wish her good luck, or to remind her about her packed lunch, or her drink. Then he realised. His little girl was growing up. It was time to let go.

LETTING GO

LETTING GO

 MarketGravity

Tony has reached the end of his journey and EnGauge is a commercial success.

This is the time to take stock and reflect on the experience you have gained, the skills you have acquired and most importantly the wealth of relationships you have established.

For those who catch the venturing bug, corporate life will never be the same again. The challenges are numerous and the sacrifice high, but there can be no greater satisfaction or sense of achievement than looking back on the early days of a successful venture and seeing what it has become.

So the inevitable question becomes… Are you ready for the next challenge?

If so, good luck!

"ONCE YOU'VE DONE IT – EITHER WITHIN THE CORPORATE STRUCTURE OR WELL OUTSIDE OF IT – THERE'S NO LOOKING BACK!"

Stelios Haji-Ioannou, easyGroup

Keep in touch with Tony and find out more about
corporate entrepreneurship at

www.tonydefyinggravity.com